THE
LODGER

HELEN SCARLETT

QUERCUS

First published in Great Britain in 2023 by

QUERCUS

Quercus Editions Ltd
Carmelite House
50 Victoria Embankment
London EC4Y 0DZ

An Hachette UK company

A CIP catalogue record for this book is available
from the British Library

HB ISBN 978 1 52940 759 4
TPB ISBN 978 1 52940 760 0
EBOOK 978 1 52940 761 7

10 9 8 7 6 5 4 3 2 1

Typeset by Jouve (UK), Milton Keynes

Printed and bound in Great Britain by Clays Ltd, Elcograf S.p.A.

Papers used by Quercus are from well-managed forests and other responsible sources.

THE LODGER

To Maddie, Izzy, Mark, and Mary,
with love always.

PROLOGUE

The dawn spread itself slowly across the sky, the horizon merging with the dull waters of the Thames. It had been oppressively hot for weeks, and the river had shrunk, revealing the mudflats by the water's edge, which were strewn with empty bottles, sandwich papers and cigarette ends — souvenirs of the cheering crowds that had thronged London's streets on Peace Day. They had long gone now, in a haze of alcohol and good humour, taking the lonely journey homewards to the far shores of the Metropolitan line.

At first the body had been indistinct, a bundle of rags that the currents nudged rhythmically back and forth against the brick supports of London Bridge. But as the sun climbed slowly into the sky, it resolved into an outstretched arm, a crumpled blue coat and finally a face. An early morning commuter, pausing to light a cigarette by the side of the bridge, had been shocked to find that he was gazing down into a woman's blank stare, and his shout of horror brought a crowd of curious onlookers.

Of an indeterminate age, with bluntly cut brown hair and drab clothes, still there was a kind of defiant beauty about her. A livid bruise of purple and yellow bloomed across the left side of her face and her lips were slightly parted, as if there were something final she wished to say. Although she was long past saving, the police ambulance arrived from St Barts and she was taken away, wrapped in a white sheet.

CHAPTER ONE

It was strange that it was Elizabeth of all people who suggested they play the memory game, because she so rarely talked about her life before Ryedale Villa. In hindsight, Grace believed that she simply wanted to break the silence that hung so heavily over the three of them that diminished Christmas, when it was impossible not to remember earlier times. Edward's friends dropping in unexpectedly, laughing, their faces red with the cold; her mother playing sentimental songs on the piano; and the tables that were laden with stuffed goose, mince pies and figs.

Even in wartime, Christmas had still felt sacred. The guns had gone silent all along the Western Front, bringing a brief respite from the horror of news from the trenches. Now there was only Grace, her father and Elizabeth, who all pretended to celebrate in a house that was too large for them. In past years, her mother had transformed the sitting room into an extravaganza of brightly coloured paper chains and ribbons. There was always a huge fir tree, shimmering with silver angels and the clumsy decorations she and Edward had made as children. They hadn't had the heart to buy a tree. Instead, Elizabeth had collected holly branches from the garden, intertwining them about the room so their red berries brought small dashes of colour amid the December gloom.

They had shared a bottle of wine by the log fire and that was when Elizabeth had suggested that each of them should retell their happiest childhood memory. Grace's father was the first to speak. Mr Armstrong described coming home from boarding school at the end of term and meeting his baby sister Alexandra. 'She was like a china doll, she looked so perfect and small, and then she hiccupped loudly,' he said, 'and I jumped with surprise because she was alive. Mother and Father laughed, but Alex smiled up at me and that was the first time she had acknowledged anyone at all.'

For Grace, it was difficult to choose, because so many of her memories had been clouded by the recent past. In the end, she settled upon the time Mother had taken her and Edward to Regent's Park and promised that they could travel home on the Underground train from Great Portland Street. Edward had pretended that the rumbling sound coming from the tunnel was the roar of a giant tiger. Terrified that she would be eaten alive, she had refused to get on the train. 'Mother was furious with Edward for teasing me,' she said.

'It doesn't sound a very good memory,' Elizabeth interrupted, laughing. 'Is that really your happiest?'

'No, no, not that part, but Edward was so sorry for upsetting me that Mother relented and forgave him. She took us both for tea at the Langham Hotel. All that afternoon, Edward and I pretended we were tigers and growled at each other across the table, as we ate scones with jam and clotted cream.'

Then it was Elizabeth's turn.

She looked thoughtful and, after a while, said, 'In the early 1890s, when I was twelve – before you were even born, Grace – we used to go to the Woodford Cycle Meet every June. Even now, I can remember the sense of excitement. We would walk three or so miles to the Castle Inn to see the parade of cyclists before they set off for Buckhurst Hill and Chingford. Arcadia Farm was nearer to George Lane, you see, and the roads would have been too crowded for the carriage. Well, there were hundreds of them, or at least that's how it seemed to me as a child. All of the riders were in fancy dress. Dozens of harlequins, milkmaids and Prince Charmings and they had all decorated their bicycles with peonies and roses, bunches of hay and ribbons. It was like being in a fairy tale.'

'How magical!' Grace exclaimed, watching her friend's face glow in the orange flickers of the flames, her usual anxious frown softened by memory.

'Yes, it was. One year we stayed until midnight. When it got dark, the cyclists travelled through the country lanes with Chinese lanterns on the handlebars to light their way. I remember saying that the stars had come down from the sky and were floating all around us.' She smiled. 'Of course, Mother told me not to be fanciful, but Father quietly squeezed my hand, and I knew he agreed.'

Elizabeth was a very private person. In the eight years she had lodged with the Armstrongs, she had almost never talked about Arcadia Farm, even though she visited her family home every Sunday afternoon. But emboldened by the semi-darkness, Grace dared to ask, 'What is Essex like? You speak of it so rarely.'

There was a pause.

'Essex?' Elizabeth finally said, 'There are proper seasons in the countryside, not like here in London. In the summer the sky is an endless, cloudless blue. When I was younger, I used to climb the oak tree at the back of our house and see the shimmering haze of heat across the fields. But it gets so cold in December and January, we always have snow, even when it's quite mild here in Tufnell Park. Then there's nothing but white for miles and miles around, apart from deer foraging for tree bark in the distance.'

'Would you ever live in Essex again? Go back to Arcadia Farm and your family?' Grace asked.

'No, I've made my life here now.' Her voice had lost its animation. 'There's nothing but big skies and turnips in Essex. It could be very lonely sometimes when I was a child.'

'I quite agree,' Grace's father said. 'Life on a farm doesn't appeal to me at all. I like the busyness of a city. I wouldn't want to be miles from anywhere.'

'But it must be pleasant to escape the grime of London when you visit your parents,' Grace said.

'Yes, it's different.' Elizabeth smiled ruefully. 'But Mr Armstrong, Grace, it's late now and I must turn in for bed. Thank you for inviting me to supper and for a lovely evening. It's very kind of you.'

'It's not kind at all, you've become part of our family. We

couldn't celebrate Christmas without you,' Grace protested. 'You're like the older sister I never had and always longed for.'

'Didn't want to think of you sitting all alone in your lodgings,' Mr Armstrong added.

For a moment Elizabeth was silent, and her eyes filled with tears. 'You can never know how much your words mean to me. Merry Christmas to you both.'

When Elizabeth Smith vanished seven months later, that was almost all anyone knew of her past. A pinprick of remembrance in the winter darkness. She had gone in the last week of July, when Grace was in Worthing visiting her mother. According to their general maid, Bridget, as soon as she had received the letter from Payne & Partners, she turned as white as paper and handed in her notice, with three months' rent in lieu. She had left the basement lodgings that very same night. She would be in touch, she said, once things were more settled. But there had been no letter or telephone call since then and that was nearly two weeks ago.

Grace was devastated. They had been close and now she was gone quite suddenly and without a word. The previous day, Grace had found herself halfway down the steps to the basement, planning to tell Elizabeth about the latest intrigues at *Nursing World*. Then she had remembered with a jolt that her friend was not there, and the lodgings were locked up and empty. This new loss opened old wounds, because it had been Elizabeth she had turned to when death seeped through every part of her life. She had comforted her as first Robert and then Edward were swallowed up by the horrors of the Great War. And now Elizabeth too was gone.

CHAPTER TWO

The summer of 1919 was unusually hot and the newspapers were filled with dire predictions of water shortages and failed harvests. It was not yet eight o'clock in the morning, but already the mercury on the thermometer in the hall had reached the high seventies. Almost every window in the house was open but there was no breeze and the air was heavy and still. Grace had slept fitfully, waking in the early hours from a vivid nightmare and unable to get back to sleep. She felt exhausted before the day had properly begun. If she could only get one night's good rest, she thought, then she could start to get things straight in her mind.

After failing to eat a slice of burned toast, she went into the kitchen to discuss the evening meal with Mrs Watson. The pantry door was wide open and Bridget Sullivan was kneeling inside it, cleaning. Seeing Grace, she said, 'This has needed doing for months now, for it's in a terrible state but it's only today that I've had the time to get round to it.'

'And it's the coolest room in the house,' the cook replied sourly, getting up from her seat, 'which I'm sure isn't coincidental.'

Bridget shrugged and returned to washing down the surfaces with a paste of bicarbonate of soda. The two servants rarely had a good word to say for each other, despite being in each other's company all day.

'Mary, did you remember about our guests tonight? Arthur will be coming and he's bringing a friend of Edward's, a fellow officer from the Middlesex, a Mr Monaghan. Apparently, he knew my brother well and Arthur thought it might be nice for us to meet him.' She tried to say the words lightly, but she had been dreading this evening for over a week now.

'I've not forgotten, don't worry. I thought we'd have the glazed roast duck. It usually goes down well with young Mr Broadbent.'

'Thank you, Mary. We can always rely on you.' Grace smiled, putting on her ivory cotton gloves.

Bridget emerged from the cool sanctuary of the pantry to wring out her cloth. 'Mind, Miss Armstrong, I don't envy you at all going into London today. The Underground will be little better than a furnace. Mrs Lowick, who cleans two doors down, said you could fry an egg on the railway tracks!'

'No, I don't envy me either,' Grace replied grimly, thinking of her cubicle at Nursing World, which was stuffy and airless even in the middle of winter.

Still, this was what she most wanted. The chance to be a writer. When she nursed for the Voluntary Aid Detachment during the war, she had taken a correspondence course in shorthand, snatching moments between the shifts at the First Camberwell General Hospital to study its symbols and abbreviations and then to diligently make notes on news stories from the broadsheets. Through a family friend, she found a position at *Nursing World*, which proudly declared it had been supporting this most honourable of callings for young ladies since 1899. She was little more than a glorified dogsbody, only working a few days a week, and the pittance she received just covered her Tube fare and lunch, but it was a start.

Their offices were a few doors along from the British Medical Association on Tavistock Square, but while that building was resplendent with a doorman and its own flag, *Nursing World* was tucked away in a corner on the second floor of a slightly ramshackle building, which was subdivided into rented offices for an ever-changing array of businesses: the marriage bureau for colonial wives was soon replaced by a wholesaler of exotic animals, which made way in its turn for a purveyor of genuine ancient Greek artefacts.

The stairs were covered in linoleum and Grace became adept at predicting who was about to come through the door from their distinctive tread. That Tuesday morning in August, pushing open the glass partition door, she was struck again by the smell of cabbage soup and lavender polish which permeated the building.

'Good morning, Miss Armstrong,' said Vera Boddy, the office manager, a famously intimidating figure in the world of monthly periodicals. 'I'm pleased to see that you are timely this morning and trust that you will curtail your lunch break by two minutes to repay the additional time you took on Monday.'

'There was a very long queue at the Lyons' Corner House, Miss Boddy, that was why I was late yesterday.'

'A queue at the Lyons' Corner House is neither here nor there. *Nursing World* expects you to be at your desk on the chime of one o'clock, ready and prepared for work.' She tapped her fountain pen on the desk to emphasize her words.

'Yes, Miss Boddy,' she said, rolling her eyes as she removed her hat. Fergus Cooper, the other junior, caught her eye and grinned.

'Good, now you'll find a set of proofs for the October edition on the desk in your office. Vigilance must be your watchword. The reading public does not expect *Nursing World* to err in either grammar or spelling, any more than it would err in its moral judgements.'

Proofreading the copy was a thankless job. Grace assumed there was an element of punishment for her lateness the previous day.

'The morning meeting will take place at nine o'clock as always,' Miss Boddy sniffed in their general direction.

Grace sat down in her partitioned cubbyhole, which contained a desk, typewriter and chair and nothing else. She was never quite sure whether Miss Boddy was being ironic when she referred to it as an 'office'. Most of her days were spent in this cramped box deciphering pages of the rambling shorthand she had taken from Mr Wagstaff.

The publication was run on a shoestring and there were five members of staff in total. The editor was Timothy Wagstaff, who claimed to know the family of Florence Nightingale socially and lived in fading grandeur in Bayswater. Very much a gentleman of the old school, he was determined to protect the journal from the encroachment of the modern world. The chief reporter, Roger Dale, had survived the war by the skin of his teeth and now lived life to the full, often turning up at work bleary-eyed and with tales of all-night parties and moonlit drives out to Chessington. Grace and Fergus frequently lied to cover for him when he failed to turn up at the morning staff meetings, which were held in Mr Wagstaff's office, the only room large enough to hold all five of them.

That morning was no exception. 'Is Mr Dale present?' Vera Boddy asked, as they settled themselves around the table. As there were only four of them in the room, this was a rhetorical question; however, she continued, 'This is the fifth time in a fortnight that he has not been at the morning meeting, Mr Wagstaff. Are either of you two aware of any reason as to why he has not graced us with his presence?'

She turned to them accusingly. Fergus was young, only eighteen and fighting a losing battle against pimples. However, he had a writer's imagination when it came to inventing excuses for his colleague. 'I believe Roger got wind that the renowned Ethel Fenwick was to speak about the campaign for nurses' registration. He most probably wanted to be the first to report her latest thoughts on the matter. You can't miss an opportunity like that.'

'Absolutely not,' Mr Wagstaff agreed. 'Dale has the instincts of a bloodhound when it comes to a good news story.'

With unfortunate timing, the chief reporter chose that exact moment to appear at the door of Mr Wagstaff's office, slightly out of breath and with oil stains on his knees.

Miss Boddy commented drily it was clearly a very short speech from Miss Fenwick but apart from that the meeting proceeded as usual, and she allocated the tasks for the day.

When she had gone, Roger confided to them both, 'Bad scrape with the motor. Bit of a prang. Hopefully, not too much damage is done but I need to find out whether Merville can get it fixed. Cover for me with the old dragon. Might be back after a spot of lunch.' With that he was out of the door and gone for the rest of the day.

Grace, in contrast, spent her time typing up Mr Wagstaff's October editorial letter and checking and rechecking the proofs. His observations on the chill of autumn evenings and the fast approach of Christmas seemed out of place in the wilting August heat. The print danced in front of her eyes and she nearly dozed off several times but it was a relief to have something to concentrate on apart from her own misery.

She resolutely tried not to think about Elizabeth's sudden departure. It didn't make sense that there had been no letter or telephone call. She pushed aside the idea that something dreadful might have happened to her friend. There had already been too much loss at Ryedale Villa. Biting hard on her pencil, she forced herself back to a page four article on the virtues of a newly patented disinfectant and concentrated her mind on the present.

Even though she knew guests were coming for dinner that evening, Grace worked late, partly to placate Miss Boddy but mostly because she didn't want to go home. She didn't want to talk about the war with Arthur and Mr Monaghan. Forgetting was better.

CHAPTER THREE

It was still busy when she got to Tottenham Court Road station and the Underground train was packed with tired commuters, travelling out to the green of the suburbs. Although the windows were pushed out as far as possible, it was stuffy inside the carriage, drawing in the soot of the black tunnels and recirculating stale air. The young woman opposite Grace fanned herself listlessly with a newspaper. Gazing into the distance, she ignored the small child on her knee, who whined for his mother's attention. The woman was dressed in black. 'But everyone is now,' Grace thought.

Exhausted, she leaned back in the seat and longed to ease off her too tight shoes. When the mother and son got off the train at Warren Street, Grace closed her eyes and tried to sleep but she was too tense and on edge. Eventually, the rocking motion of the railway carriage lulled her into an uneasy doze, punctuated by the rustle of newspapers and the screech of metal against the tracks.

The train braked sharply as they came into Camden Town, and she jolted awake. It was then Grace saw him. A flash of khaki uniform out of place among the stockbrokers and shoppers on the Hampstead line. He was at the other end of the crowded carriage and turned slightly away, just about to exit. It was impossible to be certain, but he was so like Robert. The familiar shape of his shoulders, the way his head jutted slightly forward when he was in a hurry, and the dark gold hair.

Hardly daring to believe what she was seeing, Grace leaped from her seat, apologizing as she tried to force her way through the press of weary commuters in the carriage. She reached the doors just before they closed and jumped onto the platform. 'Robert!' she shouted, but her voice was drowned out by the clamour of the rush hour and now the man was nowhere to be seen. Grace looked around desperately and spotted him striding up the passageway to the station's lifts. Dodging her way along the edge of the platform, she tried to catch him. 'Robert! Please, please stop. It's me. It's Grace.' She willed him to glance round and see her.

A sharp-faced woman stepped slightly in front of her, blocking her path, 'Where d'you think you're going? Mind yourself and wait like everyone else.'

'I'm terribly sorry, I must get through. I have to catch someone.'

'We've all got things to do,' the woman grumbled, 'and how would we get on if people thought they could just push theirselves to the front?'

Grace didn't bother to respond, but when she looked ahead again, the black metal doors of the lift were closed. Desperate to know if it was Robert, she turned and ran up the emergency stairs, a stitch stinging at her side. She emerged into the sweltering August evening and stood by the exit, panting and out of breath.

The crowd of commuters flooded from the Tube station. An anonymous mass, intent only on returning home, eyes cast downwards and collar buttons now loosened in the heat. As Grace looked around, he was suddenly there again. On the other side of the road. He walked quickly past the Old Mother Red Cap public house and then turned decisively into a tobacconist just off Camden High Street. Her despair of a moment ago was replaced by joy and she raced across the road and into the shop. 'Robert, you've come back! They tried to tell me you were dead.'

It was empty, except for the startled owner, a sandy-haired man, with a slight stoop. They stared at each other.

'Have you seen a man? He came in here a moment ago. A young man, about . . . ,' she paused. How old? In her mind, Robert was forever twenty-two – golden and invincible. He had already frozen into a memory, as his train pulled away from Waterloo Station and his waving figure diminished into the distance. But time hadn't stopped, and he must be older now. 'A man of twenty-five, in an officer's uniform. Tall, with golden-brown hair.'

He shook his head, looking at her strangely. 'Ain't nobody come in here. Not for the last quarter of an hour or so.'

'No, he did. I followed him.'

'I can see everything that's here, miss, and there isn't no man.' He gestured at the empty shop to prove his point.

'Could you have gone into the back for a minute?' she suggested. 'He might have come in then.'

The man was shaking his head more firmly now. 'No one's come in here. That I can swear to.'

'I'm sorry, I thought . . .' There was a sick feeling in her stomach. The terror that her own eyes had betrayed her.

'Are you quite all right, miss? You do look awful pale. I can fetch you a glass of water if you'd like.' His eyes were creased with concern.

'No, no, thank you. I was mistaken. I'm sorry to disturb you. I must go.' She started towards the door. She needed to be in the fresh air. After the vivid excitement of believing she had seen Robert, she felt deflated and foolish. He couldn't come back from the grave. His body was lost in the mud of the Somme. And that's why her nights were haunted by the thought of him buried in a field in France, his flesh dissolved away and only scraps of metal and fabric and bone remaining.

Three years ago, the black-edged telegram had come to say that he was missing in action. Called to the sitting room by her mother that July morning, she was surprised to find Robert's father there, standing red-eyed by the mantlepiece. He had handed Grace the crumpled piece of paper. 'He's dead,' he said.

'They haven't found a body. We must be optimistic,' Isobel Armstrong said, thinking perhaps of her own son, who was also on the Western Front.

'Missing always means dead.' Eric Hammond's voice broke. 'There is no hope. The second post brought a letter from his commanding officer, who wrote that Robert was reckless for his own safety when he led his men over the top.

He was our only child but now we must all be brave, just as he was.'

Grace couldn't be brave. Nineteen, and her life felt as if it were over. They had been engaged for four brief weeks. The whirlwind of the proposal in Whitby. That idyllic week in June when Robert and Arthur had joined the family on holiday. They had all stayed at Brambles Cottage, which had been owned by Grace's great-grandfather. Squat and built of sandstone, it perched at the very edge of the cliff and was encircled by the plaintive cries of curlews. On the last day, Robert had set off alone along the cliffs towards Loftus. He was gone for hours and it was getting dark. They had just started to worry about him, and the men were planning to send out a search party, when he had returned, red-faced and out of breath, having run the last few miles. He had declared his love for Grace and taken her in his arms, begging that they might be engaged before he returned to France.

This was one of the memories she tried to shut out.

It was Elizabeth who had closed all the curtains at Ryedale Villa, one by one, in a silent acknowledgement of his death. The ritual enacted in so many homes during the sad months of 1916, when summer turned sour and the newspapers carried pages, not columns, of the missing and the dead. Even then, Grace must have sensed that her mother was too fragile to be burdened with so much grief and so she turned to their lodger.

That night, she had crept down to the basement lodgings and cried silently for hours on end, while Elizabeth comforted her and promised that one day the pain wouldn't be so sharp.

'He was able to declare his love for you before he left. That must bring you some small consolation,' she said, trying to smile.

Grace could only nod bleakly.

Elizabeth added. 'You are young. You must carry on living.'

Looking back, Grace didn't know how she had survived the first brutal months. Only two days later, she'd reported back for duty at the First Camberwell General. Her parents thought her insane, but Elizabeth understood that she would rather be doing something. The back-breaking drudgery of cleaning hospital floors, of running between the groans of injured men, or cleaning the dead before they were laid out. Anything was better than thinking.

One day the brisk matron had caught her standing above a vat of boiling water, trance-like, her hands raised as if to plunge them in. 'What on earth do you think you're doing, Nurse Armstrong?'

She shook her head. 'I don't know.' Although part of her had wondered whether there might be a physical pain strong enough to block out her sorrow. She became frightened of her own thoughts, in case they whispered to her again and lured her into doing something reckless and irreversible.

All through the bleak autumn and the frost of winter, she kept going by holding on to the fact they hadn't found a body.

Life fed her just enough optimism, during the cold months that followed, to tempt her into climbing out of bed, when all she wanted was to turn her face to the wall and refuse to live. She created stories about what had happened to Robert after he had disappeared. She imagined him stumbling as he ran into the enemy fire, caught by a bullet and now lying in a field hospital, suffering from amnesia. Or captured by the Germans, a prisoner of war, forbidden to contact anyone. But the cruel spring came, and she faced the truth.

He was dead and she had gone on living. When Armistice was eventually declared, she ignored the newspaper stories about dead husbands, sweethearts, fathers and sons miraculously returning home and erasing forever the misery of those black-lined telegrams. She knew Robert wouldn't be among them. It was part of the unspoken knowledge that hovered over the sad Christmas of 1918, when they had toasted each other in the quiet house in Tufnell Park and thought silently of all that had been lost.

CHAPTER FOUR

Too shaken to face the forced intimacy of the Underground, she decided to walk the mile or so home. On the corner of Kentish Town Road, Grace passed a former soldier who was propped awkwardly against the doorway of the post office, a row of campaign medals across his chest and grey trousers pinned neatly at the knee. He was there every day except Sunday, selling bags of lavender at a penny a time. Beside him was a battered cap with its scattering of coins and a piece of cardboard, on which he had written in block capitals, 'BILLY DAVIES. FOUGHT BRAVELY FOR KING AND COUNTRY. LOST LEGS AT ARRAS. WIFE AND CHILDREN TO SUPPORT.'

She thought of Mary Watson, who prided herself on not suffering fools gladly and declared that he might as well be begging. He was brought there every morning by his two sons in a motor van, she claimed, who deposited him on the pavement before driving off. 'I don't know why they don't take care of him themselves – two big, strapping lads like that. Look after your own, is what I say.'

But Grace always stopped. She thought of Robert and Edward, and guilt made her buy the lavender or books of matches or whatever was being sold by ex-servicemen who had come back from the fighting. They had returned to a world that was embarrassed to acknowledge what they had sacrificed, knowing that the debt was impossible to repay. The shell-shocked veteran screaming out at night, the young boy whose lungs were poisoned by gas, the blind hero hidden behind closed curtains – they were part of the new scarred landscape. A place of absences as much as presences. The legions of missing young men who should have filled trams, played football and cricket in parks, and laughed together in the public houses. The air was thick with the souls of the dead.

'Robert is one of those lost boys,' she thought, as she came reluctantly to Ryedale Villa, an imposing Victorian house on Lady Eleanor Road. Opening the front door, her eyes adjusted to the interior gloom. Superstitiously, she followed her ritual of not looking at the silver framed photographs arranged on the occasional table in the hallway. She didn't need to see the images; they were always in her mind. An innocent family group, smiling hopefully up at the photographer, optimistically facing their future. James and Isobel Armstrong, and Edward and Grace, their children. In the photograph, they were frozen in the golden innocence of a pre-war world before everything was irrevocably changed. The happy group in the picture could have no knowledge of the destruction that lay just ahead. There was another photograph, its frame now covered in black crepe, of her handsome brother dressed in khaki, already on the slow march to his death.

Her nerves were paper thin and she tried to enter quietly,

hoping to get straight to the kitchen and see how preparations for the evening meal were going, but her father had been awaiting her arrival, primed for the sound of the key in the lock.

'Grace, is that you? Was there a problem on the Underground?' On the face of it, a simple question, but she knew how her father dreaded social occasions. He had relied on his wife to keep the conversation going and make sure that everyone felt looked after. James Armstrong was a little lost without her.

'I had to work late, Father, and then the Tube was crowded. I got out at Camden Town and walked.' As she said this, she came into the sitting room and found him in the armchair by an empty fireplace. *The Times* newspaper lay open next to him and the warm fug of pipe smoke filled the room. He was a tall, angular man, in his mid-fifties, whose somewhat gruff manner hid a natural shyness.

'I'm sorry, it took longer than I expected.' She hesitated a moment. 'Is there something the matter?'

He nodded and drew a breath. 'When I got home from the ministry this afternoon, I was ambushed by crying women the second I was through the door.' Her father was hopeless in the face of female emotion.

Surprised, she asked, 'Mary and Bridget? Whatever has happened?'

'You must ask them yourself. I couldn't get any sense out of them.' He shuddered. 'Bridget was on the stairs sobbing. Why on earth did you allow her to have her position back? She has a very volatile nature.'

Grace shrugged. She liked Bridget. 'She was the only person who applied for the post. No one wants to be a servant any more.'

'How is a household to be run, then?' Her father observed, before returning to the comforting opinions of *The Times*.

The kitchen itself was in a state of chaos. The air was thick with steam from boiling pans and the pervasive smell of roasting duck. Bridget was sitting at the kitchen table, sobbing loudly, her pretty freckled face was blotched from crying and strands of long dark hair had come loose from her white cap. Her fiancé Patrick Hannon had been killed at the Front and any distressing news was likely to remind her of that loss. She had a damp copy of the *Evening Standard* in front of her, alongside an unpolished set of knives and forks. The cook was nearby, torn between consoling the younger woman and keeping an eye on the pans hissing on the kitchen range.

'Bridget, whatever is wrong? Father said you were upset.'

'Oh Miss Armstrong, 'tis her, look.' She thrust the newspaper into Grace's hands. 'It's Elizabeth. See the headline. "BODY FOUND BY LONDON BRIDGE".'

Grace felt cold with fear. 'What do you mean, it's Elizabeth?' She glanced at the front page.

'Didn't I say there would be a death, Mrs Watson?' Bridget turned towards her fellow servant.

The cook nodded, her mind on the food that was at risk of spoiling.

'A bird flew into the scullery the other day and couldn't get free. A sure sign of a soul struggling to stay in this world.'

Ignoring Bridget, Grace began to read the article and

prayed inwardly that she was wrong. 'The description is very vague. It could be almost anyone.'

Bridget shook her head, 'No, look further down. At the description of the clothes. Now was she ever out of that blue coat in the spring and summer? And there, they say in the paper, "wearing a blue coat". Even Mrs Watson agrees with me.'

'I'm not one for hysterics,' the cook responded, briefly glancing across at Bridget, 'but it seems strange. Elizabeth's been gone two weeks and not a word from her. She'd lived here, what, seven years?'

'Eight,' Grace corrected her mechanically, her mind filled with dread.

'Eight years and just gone without a backward glance.'

'I'm surprised she hasn't written or telephoned,' Grace agreed. 'But this?' she gestured helplessly, 'A body in the river. It can't be Elizabeth.'

'I have an awful bad feeling about it,' Bridget countered. 'And the police don't know if the death was foul play or suicide, not that either wouldn't be bad enough. I shudder to think of her dying at the hands of a murderer!'

Having given up on any help from the maid, Mrs Watson was busy checking the seasoning. She said darkly, 'It will be connected to that man, the one you spoke of, Bridget.'

'What man?' asked Grace.

'The one who came calling at the house, with a Rolls-Royce motor car and chauffeur.'

'You didn't mention this before, Bridget,' Grace said, surprised.

'It was while you were away seeing your mother.' There

was a moment's silence, and Grace saw the two women glance at each other, but she ignored it.

Mrs Watson said, 'After that, Elizabeth was a changed woman. She was frightened. Just like a scared rabbit, jumping at the slightest noise.'

Bridget took up the story, 'A man came to the door, asking to see Miss Smith. He was dressed like a gentleman, but I knew at once that he was as rough as the road beneath his cashmere suit and silk cravat. And when he smiled – well that put the shiver of death through me – for his teeth were all crooked and broken. I said to Mrs Watson,' she nodded towards the cook, 'if I had his wealth, the first thing I'd do is get myself a nice new set of dentures.'

'And he came to see Elizabeth,' Grace prompted.

'Well, yes. I went and fetched her – I left him on the door-step, I didn't want a stranger like that in the house.'

'And she knew this man?'

'When she saw him, her face crumpled and she insisted on speaking to him out on the street, away from everyone, but before they were out of hearing, he called her by another name. I didn't quite catch it, but it wasn't Elizabeth.'

The cook was bustling around the room and looked pointedly at the clock, but Bridget continued, 'A terrible state she was in after he'd gone, so I made her a cup of tea and asked who on earth he was. She wouldn't say much, just that he was a face from her past.'

'Her past? But Elizabeth lived such a quiet life. How would she know someone like that?' Grace asked. 'With a Rolls-Royce and chauffeur.'

'Oh, she knew him all right. She called him "a wicked

man". She wouldn't tell me why either – said it was best not to know – just that he was someone it was dangerous to cross. I asked her if she'd crossed him and she wouldn't reply but just put her face in her hands.'

'Poor Elizabeth,' Grace gasped. 'Bridget, why didn't you tell me this before? Perhaps I could have done something to help.'

'She'd already gone by the time you returned and there didn't seem much point in raking over old news. You've troubles enough of your own,' she finished.

'Well, there'll be trouble for all of us tonight if you don't start polishing the knives and forks,' Mrs Watson chimed in. 'You know how particular Mr Armstrong can be about the silverware. And about punctuality.'

Bridget picked up a lint cloth and made a half-hearted attempt at polishing a soup spoon.

'And you think that's why she's left?' Grace wanted to know.

'I don't think so, well not directly anyway. She was shaken afterwards, that can't be denied, but it wasn't until she got that letter from Payne & Partners a few days later. That's when she upped and went.'

'It was strange that she received a letter from them in July,' Grace said.

It was the only correspondence Elizabeth Smith had ever received in all the years she had lodged with them. Annually, on the Monday following the first of January, a thick package in a heavy vellum envelope arrived, its return address of Payne & Partners, Gracechurch Street, EC1 written in elaborate flourishes on the back of the envelope.

'It was only thin, mind,' Bridget added. 'Not like the usual ones.'

'Bridget Sullivan, did you go feeling the envelope?' the cook exclaimed.

'There's no denying you were as curious as me about the contents of those letters,' she retorted.

Mrs Watson now came and sat alongside them at the table. 'Elizabeth was a bit of a dark horse, mind. There was never a visitor for her at the door, which I always thought was strange because she could talk to anyone about anything.'

'She might have friends at the church bookshop, for all we know.' Bridget stirred her tea pensively. 'It's a sad state of affairs not to have a single friend.'

'We are her friends,' Grace said, surprised at how upset she felt. After a moment, she asked, 'Do you know what was in the letter?'

Bridget shook her head, 'But when she read it, it was like she'd been struck in the face. She just stood there, looking at the letter over and over again.'

'I did ask her what was wrong,' Mrs Watson added, 'and if I could help, but she didn't say a word.'

'And what's strange,' Bridget said, 'is that she insisted that she'd be the one to clean her rooms before she left – spent all morning scrubbing them out with bleach and her with such soft, lily-white hands.'

The maid's words reminded Grace of the stench of bleach that had hung about the house in the days after she had returned home from Worthing.

'Elizabeth made a bonfire at the bottom of the garden.

She was in and out of the basement, carting armfuls of books, letters, paintings and whatever she could lay a hand to and set fire to them all – threw paraffin on it to make it burn brighter.'

'I asked if I could have one of her pretty watercolours,' Bridget added. When the cook looked surprised and went to remonstrate with her, she shrugged, 'Well, she was just going to burn them anyway and she did have a rare talent with her painting. But she refused, said she must leave no trace. I thought it was a strange thing to say.'

'She went from the house with the smallest of travelling bags. If the lady in the newspaper is her, then truly she's left no trace that she ever lived here. God rest her soul.' Mary closed her eyes briefly.

'We must hope it isn't Elizabeth and please can we stop speculating.' It felt as if it were tempting fate to talk about her as if she were dead.

'You're quite right, Miss Armstrong,' Mrs Watson said, shaking her head. 'Now, Bridget, this won't get the food cooked or the guests served. Those knives are crying out to be polished and I can't be doing it all on my own.'

Bridget stood up reluctantly. 'It says here, if anyone has an idea of the identity of the woman, or the circumstances of her death, they should contact Cloak Lane police station.'

Grace rose too. 'Bridget, I promise to go there tomorrow. But Cook is right, we must be practical, there are people coming for dinner.'

Being practical. That's what she had learned as a volunteer on the wards of the First Camberwell during the war.

When she was overwhelmed with pity at the shattered bodies of the young men she nursed, or fear at the thought of Edward, Robert and Arthur away at the Front, then she would stop herself from thinking too deeply. Instead, she would concentrate on whatever the job was to hand, whether it was changing dressings, washing floors or checking dosages. She sometimes thought that was how they had all got through the war, by ignoring the devastating reality that was in front of them and doing what was practical.

Bridget interrupted her thoughts. 'We should look through her lodgings, to see whether she has left any clues behind.'

'Yes, you and I can do that first thing tomorrow morning, but, Bridget, this is not a detective novel.' Grace suspected she was relishing the drama rather more than she should be.

Ever sensible, Mrs Watson changed the subject. 'What time will the guests be arriving?'

'Arthur said they should be here at half past seven.'

'Now, Mr Broadbent. He's a good young man,' Mary Watson said, turning back to her pans. 'You'd best be getting yourself ready, miss.'

Grace smiled in semi-acknowledgement. Mr Broadbent. Arthur was the only one of the three best friends to outlive the war. A bullet in his thigh in the closing weeks of the Battle of the Somme had kept him away from the front line for several months and probably saved his life. Honourable, kind, reliable. A link to the old, safe, pre-war world and the life she should have had. He was always the most tolerant of Edward's friends when his younger sister had insisted on tagging along. He was interested in what she had done and her ambition to be a writer. But she had fallen in love with Robert, even though she worried she was too dull and naïve for him. Brilliant, dazzling Robert, who held the easy confidence of someone destined to succeed.

CHAPTER FIVE

Back in her bedroom, she brushed out her glossy brown hair, which was cut fashionably short and came down to her shoulders. She remembered Father's shocked face when he had first seen it, but she liked the feeling of freedom. No more wasted night-time hours spent carefully pinning her hair into curls. The change had been so radical that even she had been unsure at first, but Elizabeth had said it drew attention to her eyes, which were the blue of June skies and her best feature. Grace knew she wasn't conventionally pretty. But when Robert had kissed her, that first time in Whitby, he had told her that when she was animated, her whole face lit up and then she was beautiful.

As she sat in front of the dressing-table mirror, it was impossible not to take stock of her life. Almost twenty-three years old and already she had known too much death. The war had broken out when she was seventeen, and dominated the years when she should have been dancing, falling in love, widening her circle of friends. She thought of the tennis club she had played at in Hampstead and all the gallant young men who had partnered her there. How many of them were still alive, she wondered. She hadn't dared to go back after the war to find out.

Love had proved dangerous for her generation. Both she and Bridget had lost their fiancés in France. Then she thought of Miss Limon, the beautiful young French teacher at her girls' school in Highgate. She lived in and so the telegram had been delivered to St Ursula's with the news that her fiancé, an officer in the professional army, had been killed in September 1914. Grace remembered being in her biology class and hearing a terrible scream – a howl of absolute desolation and then the words, 'No, no!' Her teacher, always so perfect and precise, had to be helped along the corridor, crying. Gwendolen Abbot, whom she'd never liked, muttered, 'How can she behave like that? She's English and it's an honour for a soldier to die for his country.' It was early in the war then, and people still believed in the glory of sacrifice. There was less talk of honour by 1918.

Miss Limon returned in the spring term, but she was a different person. No longer smiling or gazing with dreaming eyes out of the window. Instead, she had become hard and brittle, as if embracing the role of a spinster schoolteacher.

Grace came out of her thoughts when Bridget poked her head around the door. 'The two young men are here and your father's asking where you are, Miss Armstrong. You know how he hates to be left alone with guests.'

'Tell him I'll be down in a minute.'

If only Mother was here, Grace thought. She would set everyone at ease and even chivvy Father into being more sociable. Now he was likely to drink too much whisky and talk about politics.

Standing up reluctantly, she walked over to the wardrobe. The simple dresses hanging there were unlike the clothes she had worn in 1914, when frocks were nearly down to her ankles and always worn with layers of underskirts, corsets and long stockings. That had been one good thing to come out of the war at least. Hastily, she pulled out a crêpe de chine dress in olive green. Entertaining guests was the last thing in the world she wanted to do at the moment. She would have to talk about the past and Edward and all those things that were much better buried.

When she came into the sitting room, her father was leaning against the fireplace, a glass in his hand and holding forth. Her heart sank. 'Thank goodness for the Police Act, is all I can say. Not a moment too soon. We can't have policemen striking on the streets, as if they were coal miners or railway workers.'

Arthur made some noise that might or might not be agreement and jumped up with relief when he saw her, kissing her glancingly on the cheek. 'Hello, Grace, you look lovely. Your father has just been setting the world to rights.' They half smiled at each other, sharing the joke. Much too respectful to criticize her father openly, she suspected she knew what Arthur was thinking. He was blue-eyed and fair, with a lick of hair that fell across his eyes and which he had to move so frequently that she wondered whether he was conscious of doing it. She always thought he looked out of place in his formal suit. He was much more suited to life on a farm in Durham – living on the land owned by his family for generations. She couldn't imagine him in the dusty offices of an insurance syndicate, any more than she could imagine him in the desolation and mud of the trenches.

He then turned towards a tall, dark-haired man, who was standing in the corner of the room, partly in shadow. He had his hands in his pockets and looked ill at ease. 'This is Tom Monaghan. He was an officer in the Middlesex and knew Edward well. He was with him at Ypres. Just before . . .' He faltered.

Tom looked directly at her. His eyes were a deep, jade green. 'You must be Grace, Edward's sister. You're not alike.'

Whatever did he mean by that, she wondered.

'He spoke of you all often, and of your mother especially,' he continued. His vowels were flat and northern and out of place in the middle-class setting of Ryedale Villa. She couldn't help noticing that the collar of his shirt was frayed and the suit he wore was too big.

There was something about the frankness of his stare that unnerved her. 'Edward and Mother were very close.' She took a breath. She rarely spoke of her mother unless she could help it but now the words were out.

'How is Mrs Armstrong?' Arthur asked. 'Your father said you'd been to see her at the nursing home the other week.'

All the eyes in the room were on her and it was impossible not to answer. She hesitated, unsure of what to say. 'She's just, just – unchanged,' she responded flatly. Picking at the hem of her sleeve, the room suddenly felt too hot. She couldn't bear to think about the last time she'd seen her once beautiful, vivacious mother. Isobel Armstrong had slept most of the time she'd been there, finding the waking world frightening. Hunched in a chair, her eyes dead, she had hardly acknowledged Grace as she said goodbye. It broke her heart that when Edward died, she had lost her mother too.

A week later, a letter had arrived from the proprietor of the nursing home stating that the recent visit had been detrimental to her mother's health and had set back her recovery. Therefore, their firm medical advice was that any communication should be by letter and telephone, until Mrs Armstrong was sufficiently robust to face the outside world. 'She is still not prepared to accept the reality of what has happened,' the letter had finished, 'and family visits are upsetting because they remind her of it.'

Perhaps her father guessed something of what she felt because he quickly asked, 'Do you know what time dinner will be served? We don't want to keep our guests waiting.'

She jumped up, glad to have a purpose. 'I should think it will be ready soon. I'm sorry it's been delayed, but there's been trouble in the kitchen.' She looked at Tom. 'Our maid, Bridget, has been getting herself upset,' she explained. As she spoke, she was aware of how trivial and ridiculous her words were, but she didn't want to talk about Elizabeth. He glanced at her and a look of mild contempt flashed across his eyes.

'Bridget is Irish,' Mr Armstrong said, as if that somehow explained the whole matter of the late meal.

Arthur tactfully changed the subject. 'I bumped into Tom in King William Street a few weeks ago, as I was on my way home. It's an incredible coincidence. We hadn't seen each other in over a year.'

'You work in the City, then?' her father asked.

Tom looked firmly at the floor, 'Aye, sir, you could say that.' But he would be drawn no further.

Grace thought his awkwardness must be catching. 'I'll just see what's happening in the kitchen.' She jumped up and was about to leave the room when the maid appeared at the door. 'Oh, should we move into the dining room?'

Bridget shook her head and muttered darkly, 'There's been more trouble,' but would offer no further explanation. 'It'll only be a few minutes now, mind.'

'Grace should have been overseeing the kitchen, but she's rarely at home these days,' Mr Armstrong complained. 'She does some typing at *Nursing Times* a few days a week. Doesn't even get paid for it. Well, a pittance.'

'It's *Nursing World*, Father,' she interrupted, 'and I know it's not much, but I want to be a reporter. Working there is a way into the world of newspapers.'

'It is good to have a job, though,' Tom said. 'There are men who risked their lives at the Front, who are now unemployed.'

Something in his tone made her stop. 'Yes, of course,' she agreed. 'But it wasn't only men . . .'

Unthinkingly, her father added. 'Frankly, Grace, if I'd known how much of your time *Nursing World* would take up, I'd never have asked Neville to pull some strings.'

Grace reddened slightly. 'I didn't get the position just because of Uncle Neville.'

'Uncle Neville?' Tom asked.

'Yes, Mr Monaghan. He is the proprietor, but I have to prove myself like everybody else.'

He shook his head slightly.

'I work jolly hard,' she went on. 'At least as hard as the men there.' An image of Roger Dale in his wine-stained dinner jacket flashed into her head. 'Harder, in fact.'

Arthur placed his hand warningly on his friend's arm. 'Grace is very well qualified for the position. During the war she nursed with the Voluntary Aid Detachment. She was a VAD at the First Camberwell General.'

'I'm sorry, Miss Armstrong, I had assumed . . .' He had the grace to look embarrassed.

'I didn't just sit at home, Mr Monaghan. I volunteered from November 1914 until the worst of the Spanish influenza had subsided and I was needed at home.'

'Apologies, I shouldn't have made that assumption,' he said and looked as if he were about to continue speaking but she interrupted.

'In any case, why should men hold a monopoly on jobs? Women are equally capable.' She could feel her face go slightly red, which annoyingly always happened when she was passionate about a topic.

Her father and Arthur were looking at her, a little surprised at her outburst, but there was an arrogance about Tom Monaghan and she felt the need to defend herself.

Finally, the bell called them for supper. The meal was going to last an eternity at this rate, she thought.

CHAPTER SIX

The dining room was at the back of the house and its windows were shaded by the overhanging branches of an oak tree. They had meant to have the gardener cut it back but, after Edward's death, no one had the heart to get round to very much at all. Indeed, as Mr Armstrong had an aversion to the overhead electric light, meals were illuminated by candles alone and conducted in a gloomy half-darkness.

A large walnut table stood at the centre of the room and the walls were covered with paintings of small woodland animals. Crowding the armoire were silver-framed photographs. Tom stopped in front of one – wrapped with black crepe ribbon, lovingly arranged by Mother before she had left. He picked it up.

'It's Edward. Was this from 1916?' he asked.

She suspected he was trying to make peace after their earlier exchange, yet she was strangely annoyed at him for touching her brother's photograph and took it from him. 'No, August 1914. Just after he'd joined up.' She turned to Arthur. 'He said that the queues to enlist snaked all the way around the Old Scotland Yard.'

Arthur looked down embarrassed. 'There were hundreds of men there. The recruiting sergeant told us to come back the next day because they were too busy. But we stayed. Everybody thought it would all be over by Christmas, and nobody wanted to miss out on getting to France.'

'My wife begged Edward not to go. She wanted him to finish his studies at Cambridge, but he was determined to be with all the other chaps. I told her it would be wrong to stop him. American, you know. They weren't in the war then and had a different view of the world.'

Tom looked confused and Grace felt compelled to provide an explanation. 'Mother is originally from New York. She visited London in 1893, with her friend Bunty, and that's when she met Father.'

'The friend was Bunty Schuman, from Schuman Biscuits,' her father added. 'She married into the Jaggers family. You know, a big estate up near Barnard Castle and one of the best town houses in London.'

'Really?' Tom raised an eyebrow.

Grace suspected that he was unimpressed by this piece of information.

'The war was very difficult for Isobel. Half her family had stayed in Germany and not gone to America. It was only the paternal grandfather who'd emigrated from Duisburg,' he added. 'Split loyalties. Her maiden name was Schmidt.'

'Two of my cousins from the Ruhr were killed, as well as Edward,' Grace said quietly. 'Mother found it dreadful that her family had been broken in two. She thought the world had been seized by a kind of hysteria in the summer of 1914 and that Edward had no business being a soldier.'

'What else was he to do?' asked her father.

'But he wasn't a fighter. Edward was happiest when he was reading or playing music.' She paused and looked at Arthur. 'Out of you all, only Robert was really cut out to be a soldier. Despite everything, I think he continued to believe there was something rather glorious about war.'

'The Germans had just invaded poor Belgium,' her father said. 'Why, if I'd been twenty years younger, I'd have been out there myself, not stuck behind some boring desk.'

Tom made an indistinct noise and Arthur was forced to jump in again before the conversation took another unfortunate turn. 'Tom was awarded the Military Cross at Havrincourt for conspicuous bravery. He waded off into no man's land to rescue one of his soldiers, even though he was under machine-gun fire.'

For the first time since Grace had come downstairs, her father actually smiled at their guest. 'Military Cross. I say, now that's something. I bet you're terribly proud.'

Tom looked embarrassed and shrugged slightly. 'Not really. I considered throwing it into the Tees but I gave it to my mam in the end. She's proud of it, all right, but it didn't seem right to be honoured when so many others died.'

Grace saw her father roll his eyes, but the timely entrance of Bridget, complete with a glazed roasted duck, cut short the conversation. Once they had started eating, Grace looked across at her father. What Tom had said touched a nerve.

'Perhaps my generation feels differently about the war. I remember that when the guns were fired to announce the Armistice I was with Sian at Camberwell. We nursed together,' she said, for Tom's benefit. 'Neither of us said we'd won the war, just that the war was over.'

Arthur nodded. 'I knew I should have been exhilarated and, at first, I was delighted. It was what we'd spent the last four and a half years fighting for, but it was only an anticlimax.'

'There were too many pointless deaths,' Tom said. 'And when I returned to England, people complained about the lack of butter and the servant shortage, as if any of that mattered.'

Grace had to agree with him. They were a unique generation, she thought, who had experiences that bound them together, stronger than flesh and blood.

'Young people drink too many cocktails and dance to jazz all night,' her father grumbled. 'All they want to do is forget it ever happened.'

'What's the point in remembering?' Tom said bitterly.

Arthur cut across, quickly. 'I'm afraid I shall be taking Grace out to drink too many cocktails and dance to jazz next week, Mr Armstrong.'

'Really, Grace?' He looked up from his plate.

'Yes Daddy, I forgot to mention it. We're going to Rector's on Tottenham Court Road. It's supposed to be the swankiest place in London.' Arthur smiled across at her.

'The King's English, please Grace. We're in Tufnell Park, not the Bronx.'

'Sorry. Anyway, Sian has a subscription there and managed to get us some tickets. The Original Dixieland Jazz Band are playing. They're meant to be awfully good.'

'The Original Dixieland Jazz Band? No, you want to hear the SSO – the Southern Syncopated Orchestra – now that's real jazz music,' Tom said, suddenly looking animated.

He was handsome in a brooding, Heathcliff kind of way, she had to acknowledge, but overly opinionated about everything.

'I am sure, Mr Monaghan, that you must be right. Anyway, Sian's bringing her new beau. He's a musician.'

'He would be,' Mr Armstrong commented wryly. 'Why can't she find a young man with a proper job?'

Tom looked as if he were about to say something but clearly thought better of it and returned to the roast duck.

Arthur continued valiantly to fill the gaps in the conversation by offering a commentary on the cricket, horse racing and weather. Finally, having exhausted every other topic, he turned to his host and said, 'How are things at the ministry, Mr Armstrong? Is it still terribly busy?'

'Things are quietening down a little. It has been pandemonium. A logistical nightmare ever since the Armistice.' He nodded at the assembled group and then continued, 'It's very difficult coordinating the movement of thousands of men.'

Tom looked up. 'You're in Whitehall, I presume?' His comment hung in the air and Grace wondered where this was leading.

Feeling that she had neglected her duties as hostess, she explained, 'Yes, Daddy is at the War Office. He's responsible for overseeing the transportation of troops back from overseas.'

'How do people in the war ministries of Great Britain and Germany live with what they've done?' Tom asked simply. 'If you had both tried to negotiate with each other at the start of the century, instead of rattling your sabres, there wouldn't be millions of young men lying in premature graves.'

Her father looked up at him, his face pale. 'I lost my only son, Mr Monaghan. There is no greater sacrifice for a father, but I must believe that his death was not in vain, and he gave his life for a noble cause. He died for his King and country.'

Nobody spoke, until Arthur, ever the peacemaker said, 'Tom, old boy, don't you think you've said enough?'

He looked a little ashamed before replying, 'Yes, Arthur. I probably have. Would you excuse me for a moment?'

He got up abruptly and left the room, presumably for the lavatory.

As soon as the door was shut, her father exploded. 'Well! I can't believe that he was a friend of Edward's! How dare he speak to me like that in my own home?'

Arthur looked so downcast that Grace felt sorry for him.

'I thought you'd like to meet him,' he said. 'He was close to Edward and he really is awfully decent – and brave – but can be a bit prickly. He's had a tough time since the war, I believe.'

'I don't understand how my son could have been friends with such a boorish man! How on earth did he get into the Middlesex as an officer?' Mr Armstrong pushed his plate away in disgust.

'He was at the Royal College of Music – a lot of the music

students signed up — and he was damned talented, by all accounts. A scholarship student. His mother was a widow and worked as a housekeeper for the vicar in Yarm, up in Yorkshire. Apparently, he spotted his musical promise.'

'A scholarship student and a mother who was a servant. Well, that would explain things.' Her father was in a foul mood.

At that exact moment, Tom came back into the room. Grace knew he must have heard what had been said and he walked awkwardly to his chair. Even her father looked embarrassed.

Attempting to recover the situation, she said, 'Arthur was just telling us that you were at the Royal College of Music. What instrument do you play?'

He looked at her carefully and pulled his left hand out of his pocket. He placed both hands on the table in front of them. The fingers of his right hand were long and tapered, but his left hand was badly scarred, and she gasped to see that two of his fingers were truncated at the middle joint. 'I used to play the violin. I don't any more, for obvious reasons.'

'I'm so sorry,' Grace said, but Tom brushed her words aside. 'I'm still alive and there are many who are not.'

This created a silence that couldn't be broken, and even Arthur seemed to have given up any pretence that it was possible to redeem the evening.

After the briefest of pauses, Tom said, 'I'd best be off as I've got a bus to catch. I wanted to see you,' he nodded to Grace and her father, 'to pay my respects to Edward. He was a good man. One of the best. I'm sorry about his death.'

They all stood up, but he shook his head. 'Thank you for the evening. I'll see myself out.'

Bridget was hovering near the door, clearly listening to the conversation. 'I can show Mr Monaghan to the door,' she said. Grace had the distinct feeling that she was eyeing him with a certain amount of interest.

CHAPTER SEVEN

After Tom's premature exit, the meal limped on. Grace had no stomach for the rich food but felt she owed it to Arthur to at least try. She wondered whether she should tell him about Elizabeth, but decided it wasn't the right time. It would be good to hear his calm advice on the newspaper story.

She was anticipating some further outburst from her father and he didn't disappoint, although it wasn't until they were back in the sitting room and Bridget had been dismissed for the evening that he said anything.

'Arthur, I don't know what you were thinking, bringing that man here. I'm going to bed. It's given me a dreadful headache. Grace, tell Mary she'll have to lock up.' He left the room, banging the door for good measure.

Arthur shifted from one foot to the other, looking sheepish. 'It didn't go terribly well, did it?'

For the first time on that long, draining day, Grace laughed. A ridiculous laugh that couldn't be contained. 'Oh, Arthur, that's an understatement! Was Tom honestly a friend of Edward's? They seem so different.'

He was grinning too now. 'Tom wasn't always quite so angry in those days. I think the war does that to some chaps.'

'But not to you?'

Momentarily, Grace thought she saw his eyes darken. She remembered the time, when so many were slaughtered during the Battle of the Somme, that his letters had become more brusque, not full of the jovial banter about the dreadful food or descriptions of the French landscape. Instead, they had been brief and bleak – an admission that there was nothing he could think of to say.

'I don't know. Not like Tom, I suppose. I think it's important to keep going.' He shrugged. 'What was the point of fighting, if we can't make everything go back to normal?'

With a jolt, she realized this was the most honest Arthur had ever been with her. 'After the Somme, your letters felt different. As if you'd changed in some way.'

'The Somme was a pretty bad show. There was Robert – just gone – and quite a few of the other chaps. It seemed a bit pointless, really. Leading the men over the top to their deaths. It made me question things.'

'You never really talk about that time.' She looked at him closely.

'Grace, we both know there are some things best not talked about. It was in the past and we just need to get on with things.'

'Yes, I suppose it's better not to think too much.' She stood up awkwardly. 'It's better to throw oneself into a daily routine. I'm afraid I seem to have developed Father's headache. Maybe we should call it a night.'

Ever gallant, Arthur jumped up and lightly grasped

Grace's hands. 'Righto. I'm sorry about this evening. It didn't pan out quite the way I thought it would.'

'It's not your fault, Arthur. You did your best to save the situation.'

'I'll telephone you tomorrow, if that isn't too much of an imposition, and see if you're feeling any better.'

'Yes, of course, thank you,' she responded, as they walked to the front door.

Grace was worn out by the events of the day, but her nightmares had made her dread sleep. Elizabeth's disappearance had brought back all her terrors about loss, about the loved ones who suddenly disappeared and left a void. It didn't help that her bedroom was stiflingly warm, and she lay for hours staring at the ceiling, trying to make her mind perfectly empty. She deliberately focused on trivial household matters – the menus she would prepare with Mrs Watson for the weekend and the breakfast-room curtains that must go to the dry cleaner's. But her mind kept returning to Elizabeth and the body in the Thames, and that glimpse of someone who seemed so like Robert. And even Arthur's friend, Mr Monaghan, who had made the evening so uncomfortable.

She turned onto her side and found herself drifting into unconsciousness. In a state somewhere between dreaming and wakefulness, she imagined that she was walking on Hampstead Heath. It was a perfect summer's day, with beautiful blue skies and a glory of green grass and trees. But Grace couldn't stop to enjoy the scene because she knew she was needed somewhere else, urgently. It was the same anxious feeling she had had when the hospital train arrived and all the nurses rushed out to meet the injured soldiers.

As she tried to go forward, it became harder and harder to move. Looking down, she could see that the ground around her was stirring. Grey earth forced its way to the surface, churning up the fresh green that had existed only moments before and pitting the land with deep grooves like scars. The sky clouded over, so that everything was under a half-light.

In her dreamlike state, she remembered that the Heath was being used by new recruits to practise digging trenches for the front line. That was why the landscape had turned into one of total desolation. There was no sign of nature, no birdsong, nothing but broken grey mud.

Then, a single shot rang out.

'Of course,' she thought. 'This is France.'

The crust of the earth was stirring, as if there were a powerful river beneath that had burst its banks and was trying to push to the surface. And she knew that Robert was there. Fighting to get out. Drowning in the churned mud. She was desperate to see him. Three long years of waiting and hoping for him to return. And he was here now. The water was so powerful that surely it must break through the thin crust. She stepped forward to the heart of the disturbance and knelt on the grey soil.

'Robert,' she cried. 'Robert, you've come home.'

Suddenly the horror hit her of what Robert now was. His mutilated body would be torn by bullets and shrapnel. She must decide whether to allow him back into the living world or leave him with the dead. Time was speeding up. It was so hot and clammy. The choice must be made. The earth parted, seemingly to open.

She jerked awake, her senses heightened, as if she were under some immediate threat and the horror of her dream had insinuated itself into her waking life. Panting, she looked around to see whether Robert was there. Nothing, of course. Gradually, the familiarity of the room reassured her, the safety of the everyday – the framed photographs, the pots of face powder on the dressing table, the clothes strewn across the back of the chair.

She must have slept for longer than she realized because it was no longer dark, and the sky was dappled with bars of golden light. She walked to the open window, desperate to breathe in fresh air and throw off her nightmare. The garden was filled with the scents of buddleia and jasmine and lit with the promise of dawn. She pretended that, if she stood quietly enough, she could still hear the whispers and laughter of the sun-drenched summer of 1914, when events in distant Serbia formed the smallest shadow against clear blue skies. She pictured them all as they must once have appeared: gilded, blessed, enjoying the languid heat of a summer's day. What had they talked of? Their words seemed to dance in the wind – if she could reach out a little further, she would catch them.

She remembered sitting quietly among the group, hoping that Robert would notice her. He came from a far more glamorous world than that of suburban Tufnell Park and his conversations were peppered with casual references to exotic places, people and books that seemed altogether magical to her. His mother Sylvia had been a renowned actress, who had been described as the definitive Ophelia of her generation. His father, Eric Hammond, owned several leading theatres in London's West End and the provinces. Robert himself was a poet, a writer, and had been head boy and the captain of the school rugby team. Edward had confided in Mother that he was incredibly talented, the member of the friendship group most likely to go far.

Hidden at the bottom of the bedside drawers was a crumpled packet of cigarettes. Sian had bought them when they met up in Greenwich at the beginning of July. Giggling, they had tried to smoke in the shelter of a great chestnut tree, just as they sometimes had after a long shift on the wards at Camberwell. The cigarettes had tasted foul and made them both cough, the acrid smell of tobacco getting into their hair and on their fingers. She wasn't quite sure why she'd held on to them. Now she had a desire to feel the raspy smoke fill her lungs. She crept downstairs and found a box of matches in the kitchen, jumping when she saw a sleepy Bridget come into the room to begin preparations for the new day.

'Whatever are you doing up at this time?' Bridget's eyes were barely open and she made no effort to be polite. As she moved around the kitchen, she was clumsy and, it seemed to Grace, deliberately noisy.

'I just came to fetch something.' Grace clutched the stolen matches in her pocket and hoped that they weren't needed.

Bridget looked at her suspiciously. 'Strange time of the morning for it.'

Father said he didn't think Bridget would last much longer as a general maid. During the war she had worked in a munitions factory and had become used to independence, decent wages and the freedom to come and go as she pleased. She had returned reluctantly to Ryedale Villa when the factory closed and there was no other work. Her dreams for a home and family seemed destroyed in the machine-gun fire of the Western Front, when Patrick fell dead. But she chafed against the indignity of service and deference. She belonged to the new world.

'He didn't stay long, did he, that Mr Monaghan?'

'No, thank goodness. I didn't like him at all.'

'Well, he's a good-looking fellow, mind. Like one of those film stars from Hollywood.'

'Goodness, that's quite a claim!' Grace wondered whether Bridget secretly admired the way he had spoken to Father.

Back in her bedroom she lit the cigarette with trembling fingers and inhaled its noxious smoke, leaning as far as she possibly could out of the window and holding her hair back so it wouldn't smell of tobacco. It was a small, futile act of rebellion but satisfying all the same. Looking among the silver shadows and shapes of the garden, she saw a darker circle at the bottom and remembered what Bridget had said about Elizabeth creating a bonfire and setting fire to everything she owned. Why on earth would she do that? Grace stubbed out the cigarette against the wall next to the window and went back to bed. Later today she would try to find out the truth.

CHAPTER EIGHT

When Grace came down a few hours later, Bridget was in a better mood, although she did ask suspiciously if Miss Armstrong had found whatever it was she'd been searching for so early in the morning. The kitchen was quiet because Mary had gone to the greengrocer in Kentish Town to buy vegetables for the evening meal. As they had agreed, the two women went down the outdoor steps to the door of the basement lodgings. Following Elizabeth's departure, her father had had a stronger lock fitted. There had been several burglaries in the area since the end of the war and he had become increasingly anxious about security. Once he had left for the office, Grace went to fetch the heavy ring of keys, which was kept in his study.

Bridget struggled for several minutes with the stiff lock before managing to turn the key. 'I never thought I'd be able to undo the damned thing,' she declared, before throwing the door open with an air of triumph.

As soon as they walked inside, the sharp tang of bleach hit the back of Grace's throat and they both coughed.

'Doesn't it just stink to high heaven in here,' Bridget

complained, putting her apron over her nose. 'It's not as if the rooms were dirty. I don't know what she was thinking of with all that scrubbing.'

'It's oppressive,' Grace agreed, her eyes stinging. 'We must open the windows.' And then she looked around and the bleakness of the rooms hit her.

It was the blank walls – that was it, thought Grace. That's why it felt so completely different even though the same furniture was there. Elizabeth had covered the empty walls with dozens of watercolours in delicate pastels. Now all that was left was a crucifix, painted in bright, raw colours, showing a suffering Christ.

Bridget must have seen her glance at the cross, for she said, 'I never knew anyone more devout than Elizabeth. Every Friday, she volunteered at the Catholic bookshop and every day she went to early mass. She must have worn her knees out with praying.'

'Yes, she was very religious,' Grace agreed, as she walked slowly around the main room of the basement. There was a small table with two chairs and a tobacco-brown leather sofa that had been inherited from her grandfather. Curtained off in a corner was a small stove and washing basin for pots, while the tiny bathroom, with a sink and toilet, was off to the left. The bedroom was at the back of the building, overlooking the garden. That was where Elizabeth painted. She said the light was just perfect in the morning when the sun flooded the garden.

She had made a living from creating life-like images of flowers and birds, which were sold through an agent in Clerkenwell to nature journals and books. Grace thought the watercolours wondrous: birds caught hovering in the perfect balance of flight, sweet peas and larkspur spilling across the page in a froth of pink, cream and purple. But Elizabeth would dismiss any praise. 'I only reproduce what I see. A real artist would be able to show the soul of things. My paintings are just like photographs, really.'

Grace remembered coming into the basement for the first time when she was about fifteen and thinking how magical it was. Now she could see that it was a small, mean set of rooms. She shook her head, 'It's so changed. But I don't understand. Why did she destroy everything on a bonfire?'

'Well, Miss Armstrong, there is the mystery. But to my way of thinking, there was something in that letter that turned her.'

'And you think the letter was connected to the man . . .'

'Oh, yes. It can't just be coincidental.'

They slowly walked towards the back of the house. Bridget went on ahead, climbing the stone steps to the garden but Grace stopped for a few moments, looking around and remembering. Every shelf in the lodgings had been crowded with books. Elizabeth's taste had been eclectic, and she had read all the current writers like H.G. Wells and Joseph Conrad, alongside Shakespeare and the great novelists of the nineteenth century.

Every Saturday, no matter what the weather, she would walk to Hatchards in Piccadilly and then catch the omnibus back, returning with a new book wrapped in brown paper. 'It's my one indulgence, Gracie,' she used to say. 'I'd rather live on nothing but bread and cheese than have no books!' Not that she did. Instead, she would coax delicious meals out of the cheapest ingredients on her temperamental Primus stove. When Grace wanted to escape the formality of meals with her family, she would creep downstairs and then they would talk together for hours on end, about politics, books, music and their hopes for the future.'

She had been generous with her knowledge and introduced Grace to a world that was far beyond the confines of St Ursula's School for Young Ladies. It was she who had encouraged Grace in her ambitions to be a reporter. 'It's important that people of integrity write for newspapers. They can do such a power of good. And, Grace, that is exactly what you are. You would record the news truthfully and give a voice to the powerless.'

It was in this room, too, that Elizabeth had held her silently as she wept for Robert and the knowledge that he would not return. When her heart was broken, only Elizabeth seemed able to find the words to console her.

At the end of the garden, Bridget pointed out the remains of the fire. It was a heap of grey ashes; nothing had escaped the flames. There was no remnant of the woman who had lived at Ryedale Villa for eight years and become a part of the lives of its occupants.

'Bridget, why would she choose to do this?' Grace found herself close to tears. 'Everything's gone.'

Bridget looked at her, concerned. 'It is an awful thing, I know.'

'I must stop myself welling up. There may be a perfectly good reason for moving out in the way she did. And the body from the Thames is unlikely to be Elizabeth's.'

Bridget shook her head and said, 'My Great Auntie Moira

from Dublin had the second sight and my mother always said I'd been cursed with it too. That trapped bird in the scullery was a sign of a death.' Then, more practically, she added, 'In any case, there was something not right in the way she left. It was as if she was running away. I mean, will you take a look at this.' She indicated the scorched earth.

'But what would she be running from? She lived such a quiet life. She didn't seem to know anybody apart from us.'

'That man in the Rolls-Royce knew her all right. It seems to me she had something to hide.'

'Do you know Robert said she was one of the most beautiful women he had ever met?' Grace surprised herself by saying.

If Bridget was taken aback by the abrupt change in the conversation, she didn't show it. 'Did he now? There always was quite a friendship between them,' she commented.

'She wore the dowdiest clothes,' she added, 'but after he'd said it, I looked at her again and he was right. When you observed her properly, she was beautiful. I know Elizabeth didn't care much about appearances, she thought other things were more important, but it was almost as if she was trying to make herself invisible.'

Bridget agreed. 'She was always very close, mind, and not one to talk about herself. But Father Daley spoke highly of her. It was he who gave the letter of recommendation before she took up the rooms, and he's not one to gild the lily.'

'Oh Bridget, I couldn't bear it if it was Elizabeth who was drowned.'

'I've been offering up Hail Marys ever since I read the

newspaper, but we must know for certain whether it was her or not,' Bridget replied.

'Yes, I know that you're right,' Grace agreed miserably. 'Do you still have the *Evening Standard*, so that I can check what needs to be done?'

'Oh yes, it's saved and in the dresser. I'll fetch it for you.'

They walked silently back to the kitchen, where they found Mrs Watson clearly annoyed that Bridget had disappeared from her duties yet again. 'Wherever have you been? The range is a disgrace and coated with burnt duck fat. That should have been the first job on your list this morning.'

Bridget shot her a sideways look, knowing there was a limit to what the cook could say in Grace's presence. 'Miss Armstrong and I have just been down to check on the basement and see whether there's any clue to Elizabeth's departure.'

Mrs Watson contented herself with an exasperated sigh, while Bridget retrieved the *Evening Standard* and gave it to Grace.

She looked again at the sad story of the woman dredged from the river. 'It says to contact Cloak Lane police station, either in person or by telephone. I suppose it's better to go there.' She dreaded the thought of seeing a dead body, but not knowing what had happened to her friend was worse.

'Well, Cloak Lane is easy enough to find. It's just by Cannon Street station,' Bridget informed her. 'You could take the omnibus for most of the way from the stop on Fortess Road.'

Mrs Watson was aghast. 'A corpse? You intend to look at a corpse?'

'Well, she can hardly see who it is over the telephone,' Bridget retorted.

'Rather you than me, Miss Armstrong,' she muttered.

'Why don't you take a photograph with you?' Bridget suggested. 'Then you can show it to the police constables and not have to see the dead body.'

They all agreed that was a much better idea, which then raised the question of whether they had a photograph of Elizabeth.

'I've never known a woman so camera-shy in my life,' Bridget said. 'As soon as someone had a camera, she'd disappear. She said she never took a good picture.'

'*I* know!' Mrs Watson exclaimed after some thought, 'She's on the photograph of the household. The one taken before Edward . . . I mean, young Mr Armstrong, went off to war. He begged her most particularly so he could have everyone together in the picture.'

There was a copy of the photograph in the hall and the cook went and took it down from the wall. The three women looked at it in silence. Edward was at the centre of the picture.

Finally, Bridget said, 'He always was ever so handsome, wasn't he?'

The words hung in the air.

'It's frightening how much younger we all look,' said Grace, changing the subject. 'Look, there's Elizabeth, in the corner.'

''Tis a very good likeness of her,' said Bridget. 'She's looking just as she did in life and, despite what she said, I'd think that was a good picture.'

'Should I take it in the frame? It's very bulky.'

'There's some unframed ones,' Mrs Watson said. 'Remember, your mother had a dozen or so likenesses made. I think there should be copies stored in her bureau. If you could bring it to me, Miss Armstrong, I'll wrap it up for you in brown paper.'

CHAPTER NINE

Cloak Lane ran through the heart of the City. Long and narrow, its high buildings of brick and stucco crowded out the sun and it was in shadow for much of the day. The police station itself was at the corner, with an imposing oak door that was firmly shut. That familiar fear rose in her. Remembrances of places like this, institutions, with their murmured conversations and bad news. Edward. Mother. For a moment, she hesitated. But she had promised she would find out whether the drowned woman was Elizabeth. She owed it to her friend to be braver.

When she pushed open the door, she found herself in a gloomy room, lined with tall cupboards of dark wood and a wide counter at the back. The man behind it looked up expectantly. He could be little more than twenty, Grace thought, with straw-coloured hair and a freckled, open face.

'Hello, miss – Police Constable Fred Alston. Can I be of assistance?'

She took the carefully folded newspaper from her handbag. 'Good morning, Constable, I'm Grace Armstrong. I've come in response to this story in yesterday's *Evening*

Standard. It's possible I know the person whose body was found.' She tried to keep her voice from shaking.

'The lady by London Bridge? Very sad, miss, very sad. It was me who pulled the body from the river.' He looked reflective before asking, 'Who do you believe it might be?'

'Elizabeth Smith. She lodged with my family in Tufnell Park and moved out two weeks ago,' she replied. 'She always wore a blue coat. In the spring and summer, at least, and . . .'

She didn't finish the sentence and Fred Alston nodded sympathetically. 'The lady in the water was wearing a blue coat.'

'Will I need to look at the body to identify whether it is her?' she asked. Suddenly she was gripped with the terror of seeing Elizabeth lying dead on a cold slab.

'Oh, the body's not here, miss. She was taken to St Bart's by police ambulance when we got her out of the Thames. The coroner will need to examine her.'

'The article said to contact Cloak Lane.' She offered up the brown paper parcel. 'I've got a photograph of Miss Smith here, if that would be at all helpful.'

'Let me have a look at it, I might recognize her,' he replied. 'It was the first time I'd ever seen a dead body. Something like that doesn't leave you easily. A month too young to be sent to the Front,' he added apologetically.

She unrolled the photograph. 'It's a portrait of the whole household. Before my brother went away to war.' She pointed to the image. 'This is Elizabeth here, in the right-hand corner.'

He looked at the picture carefully. 'Obviously I couldn't absolutely swear to it, miss, seeing as she isn't right here in front of me, but I'd say that was the woman we took out of the river.'

'I see,' she said carefully.

He nodded, 'Couldn't swear to it, as I said, but it looks very like. I'm sorry. Were you close?'

For a moment, Grace was silent. Then she said, 'She was my friend. She lodged at our house in Tufnell Park for eight years. Would you mind awfully if I sat down for a moment or two?'

'Yes, of course, miss. There are chairs in the back.' He opened the counter. 'I'll just get someone to look after the front desk and then I'll take you through. I'm afraid I need some more details about the dead lady if you don't mind.'

A few minutes later, he reappeared and ushered her to a small, overheated office. The room was dominated by a large desk, which was empty apart from a neat stack of thin manilla cardboard folders.

'It's very tidy,' Grace couldn't help commenting.

'Ah, yes. Sergeant Williams prides himself on it. A tidy desk reflects a tidy mind, he always says. He gets his cases solved quickly. Would you like to sit down?'

Constable Alston pulled out a chair for Grace and placed himself in the sergeant's chair, looking slightly sheepish as though he shouldn't be there. He opened the folder at the top of the pile. 'It would normally be the sergeant who'd speak to you, but he's out at the moment.'

She nodded bleakly in acknowledgement. She felt numb. Elizabeth was dead. She hadn't believed it until now. Too shocked to cry, she clasped her hands together tightly.

'Are you quite well, miss? Would you rather come back tomorrow?' She could see the sympathy in his eyes.

'No, no. I just need a moment or two to compose myself. I'm here and it would be better to have it over and done with.' When she got home, then she could cry. When she was safely in her room, she could lock the door and mourn this new loss. For now, she must be practical. She owed that to Elizabeth.

He picked up his pen. 'Her full name was Elizabeth Smith?'

She looked down at her hands. 'I'm not aware of a middle name.'

'And what was her last address?'

'Our address is 129 Lady Eleanor Road in Tufnell Park. I don't know where she went after she left us. She might have been going to her family in Essex.'

'I'll put down Tufnell Park for the time being,' he said.

Grace had to ask, 'Did she suffer? When she died, I mean. The *Evening Standard* said it might have been murder.' It was dreadful to think of her friend frightened and in pain.

'Doctor Fletcher at Bart's said death was by drowning. She'd been in the river overnight,' he paused, as if wondering whether to say more. 'There was some bruising on her face and body but no more than would be consistent with the currents throwing her against the bridge before she died. Sergeant Williams is in charge of the investigation and he doesn't think it was murder.'

'Did anyone see her go into the water?' Grace asked.

'Not as far as we know. Certainly, no one's come forward to say that they did. The body was spotted by a bank clerk going into the office early. He was shocked, by all accounts. We've taken a statement from him.'

Grace was silent for a moment. 'But the bruising . . . Doesn't that suggest . . . ?'

The constable made a non-committal gesture. 'As I said, that was probably caused by the currents. It will go to the coroner.'

Grace shook her head. 'Do you think it was suicide or murder?' This question mattered very much to her. Could Elizabeth's death be linked to the wicked man or the solicitor's letter?

He looked taken aback by her directness but before he could answer it, the door opened and a large, dark-haired man came into room. He scowled at them both.

With a guilty start, Fred Alston jumped out of the borrowed chair. 'Sergeant Williams, this is Miss Armstrong. She's identified the woman who was found drowned by London Bridge on Monday morning.'

The sergeant looked at him with disdain; she decided he was clearly unhappy about the requisitioning of his office. Sergeant Williams settled himself onto the vacated seat, while the younger man filled him in on the details about Elizabeth.

'Of course, you'll already have asked Miss Armstrong about the deceased's next of kin.' He addressed Fred as if Grace weren't there.

'Sorry, sir. I hadn't got around to that yet.'

Sergeant Williams made a disapproving sound.

What an unpleasant man, Grace thought. She shook her head. 'Elizabeth had relatives out in Essex, whom she visited every week, but I never met them.'

'Any known friends?' Fred Alston asked more sympathetically.

'We were her friends, but no, no one else ever visited her and she didn't speak of any other friends.' It seemed so sad when she said it out loud.

Sergeant Williams leaned back in his chair. 'Interesting. So, tell me a little bit about Elizabeth Smith. Did she have any occupation or financial means?'

'I don't think she had much money. She made a living from illustrating guides to nature. She was a talented artist. She also volunteered in a religious bookshop. She was Roman Catholic, very devout.' Grace felt her words coming out in a rush. 'That's how she came to be living in our house. Our maid saw the advertisement at the back of the church – "A gentlewoman looking for lodgings" – and we had the rooms to let.'

Sergeant Williams nodded and sat back in his chair. 'How would you describe Miss Smith's temperament? Any melancholic thoughts?'

'Elizabeth? No, absolutely not. She was always very self-possessed. I don't think she allowed herself to become unduly upset about anything. Although . . .' She hesitated. 'Although, something had happened recently. A threatening man came to visit her and then she received a letter, from a solicitors' firm. I was away at that time, but our maid said she changed after that.'

'In what way was she changed?' the sergeant asked.

'She was shocked and left her lodgings almost immediately. No one knows where she's been since. She hasn't been in contact with any of us.'

The sergeant nodded at his younger colleague. 'Some recent bad news. A woman of limited means, without family or friends. It merely confirms what I thought from the start.'

The constable opened his mouth to respond but Grace cut across him. 'Suicide? Aren't you even going to entertain the possibility she might have been murdered?'

'I'm sorry to be blunt,' he said, 'but it seems to me that all the evidence suggests your Miss Smith most likely died by her own hand and unless anything else comes to light, that is what I will be advising the coroner.'

'Elizabeth really wasn't the sort of person to commit suicide. And as I told you, a man came to see her just before her departure—'

'There's often a romantic interest in cases such as this,' he interrupted.

'No, he wasn't a romantic interest; in fact, I've never known Elizabeth to have a romantic interest, as you call it. Our maid said he was a very threatening and intimidating man. Surely that must be suspicious?'

Sergeant Williams snorted. 'You want the City of London Police force to launch a murder investigation because your maid takes a dislike to someone?'

Grace could feel herself losing her temper, but tried to speak civilly. 'I'd just like you to consider every possibility. There was bruising on the side of her face!'

The sergeant shot a poisonous glance at his younger colleague, who seemed to be trying to make himself look as inconspicuous as possible. 'Any bruising is likely to have occurred once she was in the water. It's all in the doctor's report.'

'But no one saw her go into the water. The article in the *Evening Standard* suggested it could have been a deliberate killing.'

He sighed and spoke to her slowly as if spelling out the obvious. 'It's a reporter's job to create a story where none exists.'

'I am a reporter too, Sergeant Williams,' she responded furiously.

For a moment he looked perturbed. 'Which newspaper?' he asked suspiciously.

She wished she could have announced *The Times* or the *Manchester Guardian*. When she said *Nursing World*, he smirked and continued, 'There is no doubt in my mind that it's suicide.'

Grace went to protest, but he waved her words away with his hand. 'Look at the evidence. Drowning. No significant injuries. She was unmarried, friendless and poor. I would suggest that gave her ample motivation to do away with herself.'

She looked at him defiantly. 'She was my friend and Elizabeth's life had value. Please don't dismiss her as nothing.'

'Miss Armstrong, of course, the sergeant isn't suggesting . . .' Fred Alston wasn't a hard-hearted man; even in her distressed state, Grace could see that clearly.

'It's for the coroner to give a verdict. Now, if you'd be so kind, Miss Armstrong, I've work to do and I'm sure Constable Alston is capable of completing all the formalities.' He turned to him: 'The end office is free.'

CHAPTER TEN

Constable Alston showed her to a small room, identical to Sergeant Williams's, except that the desk was piled high with folders and piles of paper. He closed the door and looked at Grace apologetically. 'I'm sorry about that. He'll have been annoyed that we were in his office, and he can be a little curt at times.'

'More than curt – I thought he was horrible,' she said. He didn't contradict her.

'He doesn't want people to think that there's a killer on the loose. Sergeant Williams likes to clear things up quickly.' He shook his head, as if this explained everything, and they began the slow process of completing Grace's statement. Finally, it was finished.

'What will happen next?' she asked.

'You might be invited to view the body, but . . .' He heard her sharp intake of breath. 'If we hold on to the photograph, then we could send it over to St Barts to use for identification. The coroner might decide that's sufficient. Would you mind if we kept it for the time being?'

'No, it would be better if you used the photograph. But I meant, what will happen to Elizabeth's body?'

'Well, we'll try to contact her family to arrange the funeral. Do you know the address of any relatives?' he asked, picking up his pen again.

'She talked about an Arcadia Farm, somewhere out in Essex. I'm afraid I don't know anything more specific than that,' she said. Inwardly, Grace berated herself. Why had she never asked Elizabeth more about her life? Perhaps she had been too busy talking about her own.

He put his pen down again.

'I could try to find her family,' she said. 'They need to know about her death as soon as possible and will want to arrange the funeral.'

'It would be helpful if you could, Miss Armstrong. Much better to learn about it from someone who knew her, rather than the police. And to be frank,' he confided, leaning slightly forward in his chair, 'we'd have no idea where to begin. Elizabeth Smith is such a common name.'

She nodded.

'The inquest will have to take place first, of course, but after that, the funeral arrangements can go ahead.'

She smiled weakly and Constable Alston started to put his notes away into the manilla folder. However, at the last moment, she looked directly at him. 'I asked you a question earlier that you didn't answer. Do you think it was suicide or murder?'

Surprised, he hesitated for a few moments. 'If I'm honest, I'm not sure.' He lowered his voice, as if betraying a confidence, 'Maybe the sergeant has been a bit quick to jump the gun. Everything points to suicide, but—'

'What is the "but"?' she asked.

'Well, she didn't leave a note. No farewells, or apologies, not even an explanation. That seemed strange to me. Most people who . . . who kill themselves want to leave some final message.'

'I know Elizabeth would say something if . . .' She shivered. 'Will the police investigate her death further?'

He looked uncomfortable. 'Not unless more information comes to light or the coroner decides otherwise. The station has been stretched over the last few months, what with the number of guns in circulation and the increase in robberies.'

'Why are guns in circulation?' she asked surprised.

'Soldiers brought them back from the war as souvenirs. Though why they'd want a gun to remember it by is beyond me, but they're getting into the wrong hands.' He shrugged his shoulders. 'It's led to an increase in crime right across the country, not just in London.'

Grace was silent for a few moments before saying, 'If Elizabeth was murdered, then her killer is out there somewhere and should be brought to justice.'

'If she was murdered, then you're right, Miss Armstrong, but the sergeant doesn't believe she was, and he won't allow any more police time.' Seeing the look of despair on her face, he added, 'Look, I'll keep an eye out, Miss Armstrong. I promise I won't let it drop.'

CHAPTER ELEVEN

Grace left the police station and came out into the sharp August sunshine. She moved numbly through the early lunchtime crowd, hoping that the physical act of walking would reduce her distress. The rest of the world was going on as normal, but her world was irrevocably changed. By now she ought to be immune to death, she reflected, but this loss was so bitter and unexpected. There was no war being fought in a foreign land, no reason for Elizabeth to die.

She reached Bank Underground station and stopped. When she got home, she would have to explain that Elizabeth was dead and that would make it more real somehow. First she needed some time alone to accept what had happened. There was a Fuller's just round the corner. Safe, reassuring Fuller's, with its swarms of waitresses in smart black dresses, revolving displays of gateaux, and a discreet trio playing waltzes in the background. She had often gone with her family in the pre-war years and now she sometimes met Arthur there for afternoon tea.

The maître d', Mr Bousfield, remembered Grace and

beckoned her over to a small table by the window. She ordered a pot of tea and a slice of walnut cake. Perhaps it was too soon to even try to comprehend that Elizabeth was dead. Instead, she tried to lose herself in watching the crowds of people who were hurrying past. Slowly recovering from the dreadful shock, she felt somewhat revived by the tea and cake. She had to do something. It was only right that the truth was discovered about Elizabeth's death. It didn't matter what the obnoxious Sergeant Williams thought.

At that very moment she spotted Tom Monaghan walking along King William Street, dressed in stained overalls and carrying a large pot of paint. He was the last person she wanted to see. Sliding back down in her chair, she tried to look as inconspicuous as possible and cursed her choice of seat. But when he drew alongside the tea room, he stopped and glanced through the window, spotted her and waved in surprise. She was forced to smile in return. Then, to her dismay, he marched towards the doors of Fuller's. She consoled herself that Mr Bousfield was known for being very particular and was unlikely to let in a workman dressed in dirty overalls. Reassured by this thought, she settled back to finishing her cake, leaving the fondant icing until last.

As she had expected, there was a commotion at the door. The imposing maître d' was looking suspiciously at Tom's scruffy appearance and asked in a loud voice, 'Perhaps sir is looking for the tradesmen's entrance?'

A cut-glass accent floated across the room. 'Absolutely not. I've just spotted an old chum – Miss Grace Armstrong – and couldn't possibly walk past without saying hello.' He smiled over at her.

Grace groaned inwardly.

'Would it be possible to bag the seat next to Miss Armstrong?' Tom went on. 'I've just been doing a spot of helping out at the club.' He indicated his paint-stained clothes. 'Not my normal sort of wear at all.'

'Yes, of course, sir. Would you like to leave your paint pot in the cloakroom?'

'Splendid idea! Just check it in, would you? You couldn't bring over another pot of tea for myself and Miss Armstrong while you're at it?'

Grace was astonished at his transformed speech. As soon as he was seated at the table, she demanded, 'Where did that come from? You sounded like the Prince of Wales.'

He laughed. 'D'you think they'd have let me in here, dressed like this and speaking like I do?' Reverting to his normal accent, he said, 'I learned to talk like this at the Royal College of Music and in various officers' messes.'

'How very convenient.'

'Except that the way I speak shouldn't dictate which establishments I'm allowed to enter,' he said, 'but that's how it is in this country.'

'It must be tiring being so angry all the time,' she responded. She had no desire to be polite to him.

He looked at her for a moment, before continuing, 'This is my job in the City. A bit different from the professions of the rich young men of your acquaintance, I expect.'

'Perhaps you shouldn't make assumptions about me.'

He shrugged. 'A friend of mine carries out decorating jobs around Leadenhall and King William Street. I'm not skilled enough to do the painting yet, so I fetch and carry pots of paint between jobs. Anyway, I'd best get myself cleaned up.'

He disappeared. Grace was considering getting up and leaving when he returned. His hands were scrubbed clean. He sat down. 'I thought you worked for *Nursing World*. That's nowhere near here, is it?'

'If you must know, I've spent the morning at Cloak Lane police station,' she replied, and felt a momentary triumph when he looked at her in astonishment. Before he could ask her anything more, the waitress appeared with tea.

When she had gone, he said, 'I'm actually glad I've met you today, Miss Armstrong.'

Now it was her turn to feel surprised. 'Oh? Why ever is that, Mr Monaghan?'

'Tom, you must call me Tom. I hate the whole ridiculous business where you have to know someone a certain amount of time before you can call them by their Christian name. No, I'm glad to have met you because I wanted to apologize for the way I behaved last night. I know I was rude.'

She was forced to agree. 'I felt you'd decided to dislike us before you'd even set foot over the door, and all we'd done was invite you for supper.'

'I know, I know. I'm out of practice with polite company. Although to be fair to me, your dad,' he sighed, 'well, you weren't there at the start, but he wouldn't stop talking about politics. And then, when he started on about noble sacrifices and dying for King and country, that was exactly what we all hated in the trenches. Old men back home telling us we should be glad to die.' He looked at her. 'I'm not doing very well at this. I should probably stop now.'

'Apologizing doesn't seem to be your greatest strength. I suppose Father can go on a bit,' she conceded. 'He's quite uncomfortable in company. Not like Mother, who always made everyone feel at ease. Just like Edward could.'

'That's the main reason I felt bad. Instead of catching the bus, I walked home and all the way I was kicking myself. Me and Edward were good mates and I wanted to let his family know how much I had respected him. I wanted to honour his memory and it all went wrong.'

Until that point, he had been glaring down at the table, but now he looked up at her and smiled. Suddenly, she could see why Bridget thought he was handsome. He was tall and lean with dark hair and green eyes, an angular face, fierce looking, but the smile changed his whole face and lit it up.

'We were in the same company from 1915 onwards. I think the circumstances of war meant that friendships were more intense.'

'I can imagine that would be the case,' she agreed.

'The last time I saw Edward was at Ypres. It was carnage. At the start of the day, there were ten junior officers – we all got on well enough. Two of them, alongside your brother, I'd say were good friends. By the time the smoke and guns and the sound of men's screams had stopped, there were only four of us left and we survived by chance, nothing else.'

His smile had died now and, as he stirred his tea, she could see his thoughts were far from London. 'Perhaps I shouldn't have said that.'

'It's the truth, though.' She shook her head.

He looked at her carefully. 'I always thought Edward would be one of the lucky ones and make it to the end of the war. I know he took a pretty bad shrapnel wound but they got him onto the ambulance train home, didn't they?'

'Yes,' she replied carefully.

'We just didn't hear from him again. Then a few months later, we got word that his death had been announced in *The Times*. It was a shock.'

She hesitated. 'Being back in England was no guarantee of survival. He had suffered a dreadful facial wound and there were complications.' Some things were too painful to talk about, even after the passage of time. 'Mother took it very badly.'

Tom went to say something, but she wanted to turn the conversation away from her family. 'We used to take the soldiers from the hospital trains . . .'

'Of course, Arthur said you were a VAD. At the First Camberwell?'

She nodded. 'In the early months of the war, we spent most of our time polishing floors and washing bedpans but the longer it lasted . . .' She held up her hands, recalling the despair she had often felt. 'I remember the first time I sat at the bedside of a dying man. He was terribly wounded but refused to cry out in pain because he didn't want to distress me. He was only eighteen and I knew he wouldn't last until the morning. We were the same age and I wondered how it must feel to be so close to death.' She paused, feeling exposed that she had spoken so frankly. 'I understand a little of what Edward – and you – must have endured.'

The weak tea in her cup was growing cold. Just as she was wondering how to make an excuse and leave, he asked, 'So why were you at Cloak Lane police station earlier on?'

At first, she couldn't speak. Finally, she said, 'I can't seem to escape death.' Elizabeth's drowning, her nightmares, thinking she had seen Robert when he hadn't been there. Everything was too much. She didn't want to weep but, despite herself, she began to sob.

'Grace, what's happened?' he asked, clearly at a loss. She found a handkerchief and wiped her eyes, aware of the discreet stares from the people around them, who probably thought he was responsible for her tears.

'I'm sorry,' he said. 'Have I said the wrong thing?'

'It's not you or anything you've said. I've just discovered that a good friend has died.' Her feelings under control now, she explained her visit to the police, the shock of Elizabeth's death and the fact it was likely to go uninvestigated. 'Her family don't know she's dead and I've offered to find them, but I'm not sure where to begin. I haven't even got an address.'

'I could help if you wanted me to.'

She looked up at him, knowing her face must be red and tear-stained.

'For Edward's sake, as a way to make up for how I behaved last night. I could hunt around and see if I can find her family.'

She shook her head. 'No, I really can't ask that of you. You didn't know her.'

'But I've got time on my hands, and I'd be happy to help. I usually only work mornings. It'll give me something to do. What do you know about her family?'

'She didn't talk about them very much and they never came to visit. They live at Arcadia Farm. It's somewhere in

Essex.' She smiled ruefully. 'Yes, I understand it's a big county.'

He smiled back in return. 'As I said, I've got time on my hands.'

Grace took a piece of paper out of her handbag and wrote down the details. 'She mentioned George Lane once and the Woodford Cycle Meet. If you could find where Arcadia Farm is, I'll tell them about Elizabeth's death in person. A letter is too cold.'

He nodded and said, 'May I have your telephone number?'

She looked at him. 'Why would you want that?'

He laughed. 'I need a way to contact you about Arcadia Farm. You needn't worry, it's nothing romantic.'

'Good,' she retorted. 'I would hate to see you disappointed.' She wrote down her number and stood up. Tom followed suit, leaving behind money for the teas.

'I'll be in touch as soon as I've found out anything about Arcadia Farm. You take care of yourself – I'm sorry about your friend,' he finished awkwardly.

They said a farewell to each other and set off home in different directions.

CHAPTER TWELVE

As soon as she turned the key in the door at Ryedale Villa, Bridget's voice rang out from somewhere at the back of the house: 'Is that you, Miss Armstrong?'

'Yes. Just let me take off my hat and coat.' She stood a few moments in the hall, reluctant to go into the kitchen and tell them about Elizabeth.

It was baking day and the warm smell of sugar and lemon filled the house. Bridget and Mrs Watson were waiting expectantly for her, a pot of tea on the kitchen table and a third cup set for her. News of death was out of place in such a homely setting.

Even before she had opened her mouth, Bridget put her hand to her face. 'It was her, wasn't it? I can tell by the look on your face.'

Grace nodded wearily and sat down.

'Well, may her soul rest in peace,' Bridget said quietly. 'Drowning. It's a terrible way to go.'

'We've been sitting here for an hour or so, hoping it wasn't her but all we can think of is poor Elizabeth, lying cold and dead. She was a lovely woman,' Mrs Watson said.

'What did the police have to say about it?' Bridget wanted to know. 'Do they think it was murder?'

Grace sipped her tea and drew a breath. 'Death by drowning, with no obvious signs of violence on her. There was a sergeant there, who was very officious, and he was determined that it was suicide.' Bridget went to interrupt but Grace continued, 'I told them about the wicked man. He wasn't interested.'

Bridget asked, 'And what would Elizabeth want to go killing herself for?'

'I don't know. Sergeant Williams made her life sound as if it were hopeless. Once he was out of the room, the younger one, Constable Alston, was more helpful. He was less cynical, anyway.'

'Does that mean they're not looking into her death?' Bridget asked indignantly.

Grace shook her head. 'Not unless some new information comes to light.'

'How can that be the case?' The maid slammed down her teacup. 'If she'd been a wealthy woman, there'd have been a police investigation all right.'

'I agree, Bridget. I promise you that I'll do everything I can to find out about her death. I'm going to contact her family but I'm not sure how.' She was going to say that Tom Monaghan had agreed to help but stopped for some reason. 'I expect they will want to organize the funeral but I dread having to tell them.'

The three women sat silent for a moment, until Mrs Watson exclaimed, 'What about Payne & Partners? They might have a forwarding address. From the first January she was here, she always had letters from them.'

'I could telephone Payne & Partners,' Grace said. 'Good idea, Mary.'

'There's the Catholic bookshop in Victoria,' Bridget pronounced triumphantly. 'She volunteered there for donkey's years. Surely someone will have an address. In fact, I'll get myself to it right away. If Cook doesn't need my help, that is.'

Mrs Watson opened her mouth, most likely to announce that she definitely did need help, but Bridget was already on her feet and putting a pin into her hat. 'I can catch the Underground train. It will be an act of charity. I shall pop into the church and say a prayer for Patrick – and for Elizabeth too – and then go across to the bookshop. It's run by Father Daley. He's English. A bit stuck up but then, he's a convert,' she added conspiratorially and was practically out of the door before anyone could raise an objection.

'She's workshy, that one,' Mrs Watson declared, as she opened her mouth and took a huge bite of lemon cake. 'We'll not see her for the rest of the afternoon.'

Grace was aware that the cook liked things the way they used to be, where everybody knew their place and there were no 'new-fangled inventions', as she called them, such as suction cleaners, motor cars or washing machines. She didn't altogether approve of Grace having a job and she definitely didn't approve of Bridget's conception of what life below stairs should be like. But it was impossible to find anyone to work in service since the war, especially not for a respectable middle-class household like theirs, where the money and social opportunities weren't as good as in the grander houses.

Fearing an afternoon spent listening to Mrs Watson's complaints about her fellow servant, Grace took herself off to her father's study to telephone the solicitors.

The operator put her through, and she heard a woman say politely, 'Good afternoon, Payne & Partners. May I be of assistance?'

Grace explained that she was trying to trace the next of kin for an Elizabeth Smith who had recently died and whom she believed had a connection with the firm.

'Mr Payne is the only partner in today. I'll speak to him but he's a very busy man. I think it unlikely he'll be able to help you.'

However, several minutes later, she returned to the telephone. There was a note of surprise in her voice. 'I'll just take some details and then I shall put you through.'

Mr Payne was brisk and curt. 'Pauline believes that I might be of assistance to you in some way. She said you were looking for information about a woman who is deceased?' His question hung in the air.

'Yes, Elizabeth Smith. She lodged with my family in Tufnell Park for several years. Her body was found in the Thames on Monday morning.'

There was a pause before he said, 'How very distressing for you, Miss Armstrong. However, I do not quite understand why you have contacted Payne & Partners. We deal almost exclusively with the financial affairs of companies and a small number of very wealthy individuals. I think we are unlikely to have had dealings with a lodger from a north London suburb.'

She explained the annual letters from Payne & Partners and the final one just before her death. 'I'm trying to find Elizabeth's family to inform them of her death, but I don't have an address. Perhaps your firm might hold one.'

'The name Elizabeth Smith means nothing to me. It is possible that one of the other partners might have dealt with her in some capacity. Have you this correspondence to hand?'

Grace hesitated. 'No, Elizabeth burned all her documents before she left our house.'

There was a note of surprise in his voice. 'What? Absolutely everything? Every letter supposedly from Payne & Partners?'

'Yes,' she was forced to admit.

'I see. Well, I'll speak to Pauline and ask her to locate any records for a Miss Elizabeth Smith. Although I would be surprised if there were a connection.'

Grace was sure there was a note of relief in his voice.

A few minutes later, he returned to the telephone. 'Miss Armstrong, we have reviewed our files and can assure you that there is absolutely no link between Elizabeth Smith and ourselves.'

'But that's not possible. There was a letter each year, with the address of your firm written on the back.'

'I'm afraid you must have been mistaken. We have no record of her. However, if I should learn anything further, we have your details and I will ask Pauline to contact you. I wish you well in your search. Good day, Miss Armstrong.'

The telephone clicked dead before Grace could protest.

He was lying. The letter that had arrived every year had

been her proof. But that was gone. Destroyed by paraffin and flame.

The grandfather clock in the hall was edging to half past five before Bridget made her entrance. Mrs Watson was already grumbling about being left to run the house single-handed and Grace was in the kitchen slicing runner beans to placate her.

'Look at the time,' the cook said pointedly, as Bridget sauntered into the kitchen. 'And what's that you've got? You've not been out shopping again?'

Bridget unwrapped a small china bowl. 'It's my only vice and the Army & Navy Store is practically next door to the church bookshop, as well you know, Mary. Now, isn't this a lovely thing?'

'An expensive thing,' Mrs Watson observed sourly. 'Why would you waste your money on something you don't need and can't afford?'

'Who's to say I won't need it in the future? Now, my throat is drier than this paper bag in my hand. Would there be any chance of a cup of tea? Then I'll tell you how I got on.'

Bridget had spirit, Grace had to give her that. Mrs Watson's face set in a grim line of disapproval.

Grudgingly, she set the kettle to boil. 'So, did you speak to anyone?' she asked.

'Well, first I lit two candles in the church, as I said I would, and then I went to the shop down the road, the one where she volunteered. A poky little place it is, with hardly any natural light, and rows of statues and bottles of holy water. I bought some of the water though, as it's good to have it to hand in such turbulent times.'

'Did they know anything about Elizabeth?' Grace asked.

'There was a lady behind the counter — Mrs Hewitt, it was. Wearing navy and pearls — although only paste, from the look of it. She said that nobody had heard from Elizabeth for two weeks and when I said she was dead, Mrs Hewitt sank into a chair and burst into tears.'

'Death is always a shocking thing,' Mrs Watson commented.

'Well, once she had composed herself a little, she said she must go fetch Father Daley because he had always been especially close to Miss Smith. When they returned, I had to announce the death all over again. And the strangest thing is that he said, "She was a good woman, when all was said and done."'

'What did he mean by that? Had anyone said she wasn't a good woman?' Grace asked.

Bridget shook her head. 'No, that's what was so strange.'

'Did you ask him whether he could help to find her family?' the cook wanted to know.

'Father Daley said Elizabeth Smith had no family, which is nonsense for everyone has one.'

'I always thought she was mysterious,' Mrs Watson declared, as she looked into her teacup.

'When I spoke to the senior partner at Payne & Partners, he claimed there was no record of Elizabeth,' Grace added.

'Really? Well, I've not finished my story,' Bridget said, 'for then it gets even more puzzling. The lady was sobbing, and Father Daley was definite that Elizabeth had no next of kin, and I needed to be away quickly, for I wished to stop at the Army & Navy store, knowing that there was no need to rush.'

The cook went to protest but Bridget carried on, 'Well, there I was, on my way out of the shop when Mrs Hewitt said, "She has a right to know." '

'A right to know what?' Mrs Watson asked.

'That must remain a mystery, for Father Daley said, "No. It's finished now." And that was that.'

'There's a story there,' she declared, 'and the wicked man will—'

'Please, can we stop speculating!' Grace exclaimed. 'Elizabeth is dead. We must show her some respect.'

'Yes, Miss Armstrong, I'm sorry,' Mrs Watson muttered.

Her father insisted on maintaining pre-war standards, and dinner was always taken at seven-thirty in the gloomy dining room, even though there were only two of them and the table felt too large. Her father was very subdued and barely looked up when Grace came into the room. When she asked him what the matter was, he replied bleakly that he had telephoned the nursing home and the proprietor had told him that his wife's condition had worsened.

'I tried to speak to Isobel,' he continued, 'but she was asleep. She does seem to sleep an awful lot these days.'

He stared distractedly into space and it was only once the soup had been served that Grace felt able to say, 'I'm afraid I've some more bad news.'

He looked up at her resignedly.

'There was a report of a body near London Bridge in the newspaper yesterday. Mary and Bridget believed it could be Elizabeth, so I went to the police station, taking a photograph, and I'm afraid it was.' She found that she was too choked up to continue.

He put down his spoon and reached his hand across the table. 'Oh, Gracie. That's terribly sad. I know you two were very close.'

She nodded in response.

'How did she die?'

'She drowned. The police believe it was probably by her own hand, but no one saw her go into the water.'

'Terrible, terrible,' he murmured.

'I hope to find her family.' She paused. 'If I can't find them in time, could we take responsibility for the funeral?'

Although neither said it, they both knew Grace was thinking of Robert's unfound body and the absence of a grave.

'Of course, Grace, it's only right. She was part of the household.' He paused for a moment and then said, 'I do know how difficult things have been for you since Robert was declared missing, but you and I are the stoics, aren't we? Just get on with whatever life throws at us.'

She wanted to say that life had thrown too much at her, but instead asked, 'Do you know anything about Elizabeth before she came here?'

'No. She was always a bit of a closed book. In any case, your mother dealt with all the household matters.' He shook his head. 'Poor, poor Elizabeth.'

CHAPTER THIRTEEN

Even though the trip to Rector's nightclub had been planned for several weeks, Grace tried to cry off at the last moment. She couldn't face the thought of going out and enjoying herself. It seemed disrespectful when Elizabeth was so recently dead.

However, Sian refused to contemplate it. In a late-night telephone call she told her, 'I'm so sorry, Gracie, about losing her but we were surrounded by death at the First Camberwell. Young men who should have lived for another fifty or more years were buried by their parents. Their grandparents, even. And what did we do? We went out dancing and drank cheap wine whenever we could escape the wards, even if we were desperate to sleep. That's exactly what you need to do now. The best way to pay tribute to the dead is to live life to the full.'

Her friend was something of a force of nature and it was difficult to disagree, which was why Grace and Arthur found themselves settled at a table in the nightclub, waiting for Sian and Maurice, her new boyfriend. Grace had spent the last hour or so explaining the circumstances of Elizabeth's death to a sympathetic Arthur.

'Her death is tragic. Absolutely dreadful, but it's strange, isn't it,' he said, 'that we never met her family.'

Grace agreed. 'I was so close to Elizabeth, but I'm shocked at how little I actually know about her.'

He looked at her. 'I did like her very much, but Robert was closer to her than me.'

'Yes,' she agreed. 'They always got on well together. But Arthur, there's something that doesn't feel quite right about her death. I just have all these nagging doubts that it wasn't suicide and I need to find out what actually happened.'

'Grace, shouldn't you leave investigating her death to the police? That's their job, after all. If it is a murder, it's hardly suitable for you to become involved.'

'Yes, but they don't seem interested . . .' She broke off, seeing Sian and Maurice entering the nightclub. Sian was small and blonde, wearing a red slash of lipstick and a silver dress cut daringly to the knee. She exuded self-confidence and knew that most of the men in the nightclub were looking at her. Her hair was still slightly damp from swimming earlier that evening at the municipal baths. Maurice was tall and dark-haired and walked with the air of a man who knew how to handle himself. They made a handsome pair. Sian spotted them and darted across to their table and embraced her friend.

'I'm so glad you've come tonight after all, Gracie. There really is nothing worse than moping at home, don't you agree, Arthur?'

'Definitely, Rector's is a rather splendid place, isn't it?' he replied as he stood up.

'The swankiest in London,' Grace reminded him.

'Don't let your father hear you say that!' Arthur laughed. Sian looked at them both quizzically.

'Father has decided that I speak as if I'm from the Bronx – but as I'm half American, I don't see why I shouldn't! Rector's is supposedly the most fashionable nightclub in London,' she went on, 'so why not call it the swankiest?'

'They all claim that.' Maurice was now standing next to Sian, and she introduced them to each other. He spoke with a clipped Brooklyn accent.

'Maurice is from New York,' she said, 'just like your mother.'

Grace smiled and looked around the newly opened club. She had to agree with Arthur, it really was rather splendid. At the centre was a huge parquet dance floor, overhung with softly lit lanterns and surrounded by oversized golden pots containing graceful palm plants. Off to the side, an energetic band played popular jazz songs, while beautifully dressed couples laughed as they danced together. Around the dance floor were tables covered with pristine white cloths, where those exhausted by their exertions could sit out the next song and drink vibrantly coloured cocktails.

'How are things at St Thomas's, Sian?' Arthur asked. 'I never really had you down as a ministering angel, dressed in pale blue with a white starched apron.'

'Ministering angel, Arthur! I'm more like a charlady. My morning starts at six, with floors to sweep, baths and lavatories to clean, and bedpans. You don't want to know about bedpans. When Matron disapproves of me – which is most of the time – she will put me on bedpan duty. As of August 1919, I have awarded myself the official title of most proficient bedpan cleaner in the world!'

'I must admit I was surprised when you stayed on and decided to qualify as a nurse. You did complain a lot about the conditions at the hospital – not that I didn't too,' Grace added hastily.

'That's because we weren't allowed to do any of the proper nursing as VADs.'

Grace went to interrupt but Sian continued. 'I know, I know. I'm not saying that what we did wasn't worthwhile, but I wanted to understand proper medical procedures. Of course, my parents were horrified. They'd expected me to come home to Penarth after the fighting ended, join the choral society or something similar, attend a few specially organized parties and find myself a suitable match, although quite frankly I'd rather find an unsuitable one!'

She said this looking in the direction of Maurice, who was returning to the table with more champagne. 'Maurice here is an almost penniless musician and highly unsuitable, but I do like him rather a lot.'

'So, is Matron still being dreadful?' Grace asked.

'The worst. Twice this week she has told me that she was appalled at my behaviour.'

'What did you do to make Matron so appalled?' Maurice wanted to know.

She laughed. 'It's a long list. Yesterday morning I'd just finished dispensing medicines on the ward when Matron sent for me. As you can imagine, my head was filled with possible misdeeds. But d'you know why she wanted to see me?'

The others shook their heads, awaiting a dramatic announcement.

'Apparently, I had been spotted leaving the hospital without wearing my hat! Can you believe it? I was relieved that it wasn't much worse, but I had to pretend to be apologetic and promise it wouldn't happen again.'

'Does Matron know where you are tonight?' Grace asked.

'Tonight,' Sian announced, taking a swig of champagne, 'tonight, I'm meeting my maiden aunt Regina, who has unexpectedly arrived in London.'

'Well, let's drink a toast to Aunt Regina,' Maurice said, raising a glass. 'And may she have many more surprise visits to London!'

'And Aunt Regina's train back to Tunbridge Wells will be delayed, so I shall be late back to the hostel. Matron can't argue with a train to Tunbridge Wells.'

They all agreed and the conversation turned to other matters. The two men began discussing the cricket scores and Sian leaned towards Grace and lowered her voice. 'I really am most terribly sorry about Elizabeth. She was someone I admired.'

Grace looked up at her sadly. 'Oh, Sian, I do miss her. To make it worse, the circumstances of her death are so strange but the police don't seem interested.' At that moment, the song came to an end and Grace waited until the music had restarted before telling Sian something of the questions that surrounded the lodger's death and how little she knew about her past life.

Sian listened gravely and then said, 'The strange man who came to your house. Was he really in a chauffeur-driven Rolls-Royce?'

'That's what Bridget said.'

'Bridget does like to embellish a story, though,' Sian laughed. 'Remember when she claimed Ryedale Villa was haunted because she'd heard a strange humming noise?'

'And it turned out to be a bluebottle!' Grace laughed in return. 'Mrs Watson was convinced it was because she didn't want to make up the bedrooms on the second floor. But I don't think she's exaggerating about this man. She seemed very shaken by him.'

'It's mysterious,' Sian said thoughtfully. 'You've had such an awful year – poor Gracie.' They sat in silence for a few moments, until Sian began to talk about mutual friends from nursing and Grace tried to push her anxieties out of her mind.

It was impossible to be miserable for long and, after more champagne, the two couples decided to take to the dance floor. Sian and Maurice were clearly experienced at dancing to the new music imported from America. However, Grace and Arthur were much less expert. They tried to copy the couples around them, laughing as they failed to coordinate their steps.

'Oh Arthur, we're really quite hopeless at this,' Grace exclaimed. 'We shall have to take lessons.'

'It's good fun, though. Look at Sian and Maurice, they're putting us to shame.'

She looked in their direction. To her shock, she caught a glimpse of a man in khaki at the far end of the dance floor. He looked out of place among the young people in their smart evening wear. 'Goodness, Arthur, over there. There's a soldier, in uniform. How odd! It happened all the time in the war, but now nobody comes out dancing in khaki.'

Suddenly, she desperately needed to see the man properly.

Holding Arthur by the hand, she moved through the dancing couples, apologizing as she went. 'Arthur, he's just there. Can you see him?'

'Grace, I really can't see anyone in uniform,' he said, following her as she weaved through the crowds. 'We're getting in everyone's way.'

'No, there, see.' The man was walking away rapidly from the dance floor. His back was turned. 'Can't you see him?' she begged Arthur.

'There's no one in khaki, Grace. It's not the dress code. He wouldn't be allowed in.'

'But I can see him, over there.'

They had reached the edge of the dance floor, which led onto the terrace. 'He must have gone outside,' she said to Arthur breathlessly.

'Grace, there was no one there.' He looked at her with concern etched on his face.

She pushed open the glass door and looked around in the late summer twilight. There were a few couples on the terrace, deep in conversation, but no soldier in uniform. She said quietly, 'I was sure he would be here.'

'Let's sit down and have something to eat, Grace. You've had a horrible time. What with Elizabeth's death and your mother's problems, it must be so difficult for you.'

That's how he sees me, Grace thought. I'm my mother's daughter. We're both touched by the same insanity of loss.

'I was being foolish,' she said weakly, but the spell of the evening was broken. She just wanted to be home now.

CHAPTER FOURTEEN

Monday was grey and overcast, in contrast to the brilliant blue skies of the previous weeks. Grace woke late and had to hurry to Tufnell Park station. There was a delay on the line, and she stood impatiently as the platform filled up with passengers. To pass the time, she read the advertisements that lined the walls. Her attention was caught by a fading poster for that year's Royal Academy Exhibition.

Her mind was suddenly stung with memories. She and Elizabeth had gone there together in May, and she remembered the excitement of the day and their preparations. They had chosen a Tuesday morning because the crowds were likely to be smaller. Having carefully read all the newspaper reviews, they had already planned what they would see and the route to take around the exhibits.

Even in art, it had been impossible to ignore the Great War. They joined the shocked crowd who stood silent in front of John Singer Sargent's *Gassed*. It dominated the upstairs gallery, with its almost life-size depiction of blindfolded soldiers, holding on to each other in a tragic procession, as they stumbled their way to safety, all of them blinded by poison gas.

As they walked away, Elizabeth had squeezed her hand. 'At least neither Robert nor Edward was gassed,' she said, gently leading Grace from the picture.

Grace tried to erase the haunting image from her mind, and they walked towards the South Room, where the watercolours were housed. 'I used to dream of being exhibited here,' Elizabeth said, looking around wistfully at the dozens of pictures displayed on the walls.

'You should enter one of your paintings,' Grace replied. 'They are awfully good. Better than lots of the ones here.'

'No,' Elizabeth insisted. 'I really don't think I could. See,' she said, changing the subject, 'this is how I want to paint.'

She was standing in front of *The Line of the Plough* by Sir Arnesby Brown and exclaimed with delight. 'Gracie, look at it. The composition is almost perfect. The landscape is melting in on itself, as if all of nature is in harmony.' She turned to Grace. 'It's the opposite of the shattered trenches of France and Belgium.'

Grace joined her and peered at the painting of misty blue skies dissolving into the warmth of brown earth.

'It's Norfolk. I stayed there once, just after . . .' Elizabeth shook her head but didn't continue. 'All I can do is reproduce flowers and birds accurately. That isn't art.'

Although Grace had said nothing at the time, she knew that wasn't true. Years ago, not long after Elizabeth had come to lodge with the Armstrongs, she had spent an afternoon in the garden sketching furiously at a small table, while the fifteen-year-old Grace played nearby, hitting a tennis ball back and forth against the wall. It was a stifling day, too hot to be indoors and after an hour or so Elizabeth had disappeared to fetch a jug of iced water, leaving her folder of sketches firmly closed.

A misjudged shot by Grace knocked the table and sent the drawings tumbling to the ground. She went over to retrieve the ball and absentmindedly leafed through the loose sheets of paper.

A cloud crossed in front of the sun and she shivered in spite of the heat of the day.

These were very different images from the elegant water-colours that lined Elizabeth's walls. Although they were of a normal domestic setting, they were threatening and claustro-phobic. The same suburban bedroom had been sketched from several different angles, over and over again. Bleak scratches of black and grey charcoal created the bars of an iron bed-stead, the sinister outline of a washstand and a threadbare armchair that jutted awkwardly out towards the observer.

At the centre of the room was an empty fireplace. Unlike the bare simplicity of the rest of the room, it had a tiled sur-round which had been decorated with an intricate repeated pattern of a small bird trapped inside a cage. There was no one in the room, these were ordinary objects, but they were terrifying. The walls themselves seemed to close in on the observer and create a dreadful sense of imprisonment.

She was so engrossed in the drawings that she didn't hear Elizabeth's light footsteps as she came back up the stone stairs from the basement.

As soon as she realized what Grace was looking at, Eliza-beth stopped as if stung and demanded furiously, 'Why are you prying into my private things?'

She jumped back guiltily. 'I'm so sorry, I didn't mean to

pry. I'd knocked the folder onto the ground and picked it up.'

Elizabeth snatched the pictures back. 'Don't ever do this again.'

Grace tried to explain herself, but Elizabeth walked away and slammed the basement door behind her.

There was a coolness between them over the next few days and Grace avoided the garden at times when she thought the lodger might be there. However, the following Sunday, when she was in the garden deadheading cornflowers, a shadow fell across the lawn. Elizabeth was standing there.

'Grace, I wanted to apologize for the way I reacted the other day.' She twisted her hands together.

'No, it's my fault. I really shouldn't have looked through the pictures. Mother said I act too much as if we were friends and I am to respect your privacy more.'

'I want you to think of me as a friend.' There was a note of anxiety in her voice. 'It's just . . . It's just I was experimenting with different styles.' She half smiled. 'I had been embarrassingly influenced by Walter Sickert, but I've torn those pictures up now.'

Grace smiled, relieved that they were friends again. However, she had no idea who Walter Sickert was and had to ask Edward about him, pretending it was for a school project. He laughed, 'Sickert is part of the Camden School of Artists, Gracie. Known for his dark subject matter and haunting interiors, quite often of music hall performers and ladies of the night. I wouldn't have thought he was the kind of artist Saint Ursula's would be encouraging.'

She mumbled something about a progressive new art

teacher but for weeks afterwards her dreams were haunted by this bleak room. It radiated a horror that was more than the sum of its parts. With hindsight, she believed this was what Elizabeth had meant when she spoke of the difference between reproducing something and interpreting its meaning.

Grace was the last to arrive at Tavistock Square and Miss Boddy made a point of glancing at the clock in an exaggerated way as she walked through the door. Although she wasn't actually late, she felt obliged to mutter an excuse about the train, before taking her place at the table in Mr Wagstaff's room for the morning meeting.

Roger Dale was already there, but he looked grey-faced, with a claret-coloured stain on his jacket pocket. A cup of black coffee and an open notebook sat in front of him. She couldn't help noticing that the page was dominated by a rather accurate caricature of Miss Boddy, sporting devil's horns and a tail. It was general knowledge at *Nursing World* that she was keeping a dossier of all the times he was late or absent and intended to present this to Mr Wagstaff as irrefutable evidence that Roger should be dismissed. He was equally determined to avoid losing one of his main sources of income. Having been at prep school with the editor's son, he hoped this would keep him safe from Miss Boddy's manoeuvres.

'So, ladies and gentlemen,' Mr Wagstaff began, nodding at them and rubbing his spectacles, 'as it is the beginning of the week, what news stories have we identified as being of value to *Nursing World*?'

There were a number of general suggestions, before Roger Dale looked up from his notebook as if he had something important to announce. 'I think it's essential that we have a presence at the peace conference taking place in Paris. The nurses of Great Britain have a right to know exactly what is being negotiated on their behalf. Given my knowledge of the French language, I would be happy to offer—'

'You just want a jolly overseas,' the office manager cut across him.

'Not at all, Miss Boddy. It could be an invaluable scoop for our periodical.'

'The travel budget stretches no further than Colchester,' she stated firmly. 'In any case, the great daily newspapers of our time are already represented at the conference. Our nurses can learn about it by reading them.'

He was about to answer when a motor car backfired in the street below and he suddenly flung himself under the table. 'Get down, everyone! Quick!' he shouted.

'Mr Dale . . . Roger, are you quite all right?' Mr Wagstaff asked, peering at him.

He emerged shaking and refusing any offer of help. 'I thought for a moment it was . . .' He looked at their concerned faces. 'My pencil. I must have dropped it. I was just retrieving my pencil.'

Later that morning he walked out of the office and didn't return for the rest of the day. Vera Boddy's brother had been mown down by machine-gun fire on the Western Front. She had no sympathy. 'If you've survived the war and your body's still in one piece, then you're one of the lucky ones,' she muttered.

The other three members of staff were not so callous.

As Grace and Fergus had to cover Roger's tasks as well as their own, it was well after six before Grace returned from work. Exhausted, she wanted nothing more than to go up to her bedroom for half an hour and rest, but Bridget was waiting in the hallway.

'Hello, Bridget. Is there anything the matter?' she asked, surprised.

'There was a telephone call for you, Miss Armstrong, so I thought I'd better tell you straight away.'

'Is it something important?' Her heart skipped a beat. Could it be connected to Elizabeth?

'I'm not sure. Only you will know that.'

'Who telephoned?' Grace replied, wondering why Bridget hadn't just left a note.

'That young man, Mr Monaghan, who was here the other week.'

Grace had almost forgotten about Tom and his promise to look for Elizabeth's family.

'He said he had something to tell you and to meet him tomorrow at King's Cross station, underneath the clock in the ticket hall. At 6 p.m.'

Grace felt herself colour slightly.

Bridget scrutinized her suspiciously. 'He's a handsome fella and no mistake.'

'Really, Bridget!' She could go too far at times. 'Mr Monaghan has offered to find information about Elizabeth.'

'That's very kind of him, I'm sure.'

Grace let this go. For a moment she considered asking Bridget not to say anything to Father, but that would only make her more curious. 'He's trying to be helpful because of his friendship with Edward.'

'So, he won't be calling at the house again?' There was a definite note of disappointment in Bridget's voice.

'I doubt it. I must get changed, it's been a long day. Thank you for letting me know about the message.'

She reflected that it was typical of Tom Monaghan to assume she had no other plans for the next day. But once she had calmed down, she thought more charitably that he probably didn't have a telephone.

That evening, Grace went to bed early. She didn't want to have to make conversation. It had been a grim day and she was still mourning Elizabeth's death. But sleep brought no peace. It was almost four in the morning before she finally dozed off.

She was walking on Hampstead Heath again, but it was a bleak winter's day and the ground was covered in snow that crunched under her boots. In the distance, she could hear children playing, somewhere over by the ponds. Suddenly, a scream pierced their laughter and she ran towards them through the mist, seized by a dreadful sense of foreboding. Her feet were heavy on the icy ground and all her movements were clumsy and slow. She sensed the presence of a man alongside her, but at first she was too frightened to look at him directly. It was late afternoon and the light was grey and indistinct. The lower part of his face was covered by a scarf, but she knew it was Robert. When they reached the water, the children had disappeared, and she turned to him.

'Where have the children gone?'

He shook his head.

'Why are you here?' she asked.

Instead of answering, he lowered the covering from his

face. She saw that his lips had been sewn shut with black stitches, like those used to seal a wound. His eyes were blank and her terrified face was reflected back in them.

She cried out in horror, 'What does this mean? You must tell me, please.'

But Robert shook his head and pointed at the grotesque scar where his mouth should have been. He began to move away. She wanted to follow him, but he raised an arm to stop her and then he was gone, swallowed up by the murky fog.

CHAPTER FIFTEEN

The next morning, she told Mary that she wouldn't be home in time for supper, as she had a meeting. She wondered what it was that Tom had discovered and why he needed to see her so urgently. When she left work that afternoon, the streets were alive with the bustle of people intent on going somewhere and there was a sense that something exciting was just around the corner. And even in dusty London, plants and flowers were in bloom and the air full of promise. She was still only twenty-two. It was the war that made her feel so ancient, she thought.

There were delays at Euston station, and it was nearly a quarter past six by the time she got to King's Cross. She ran up the escalator, but when she reached the top there was no one standing underneath the clock. Looking around, she glimpsed him disappearing into the crowd, his hands thrust into his pockets. 'Tom!' she shouted.

He turned around and she felt a flutter as she saw his green eyes widen and his mouth settle into a grin. 'I thought you weren't coming.'

'I nearly didn't,' she said. 'I can't believe you expected me to drop everything to meet you.' She regretted the words as soon as she had spoken them. Something about Tom Monaghan made her argumentative.

'I'm sure Uncle Neville wouldn't mind you leaving work a little early.'

That was the reason, she thought. He was so annoying!

'It's not my fault that a family friend owns *Nursing World*!' she retorted. 'I want to be a writer, so the experience is useful. Anyway, it's none of your business. You had something to tell me, I believe.'

'Yes, look, let's find a café.'

They walked out onto King's Cross Road. The air felt heavy with dust thrown out by the motor lorries, trams and horse-drawn vans that crowded the streets. The area around the railway station was rundown, the buildings squalid and dilapidated with piles of rubbish littering the pavements. The narrow alleyways that ran off the main road looked dark and threatening, even on a summer evening.

Finally, they found a café that was open, and Tom bought them both a cup of tea. She thanked him and looked up expectantly.

He shuffled awkwardly in his seat. 'I thought it would be better to meet face to face because I'm not quite sure how to tell you this.'

'Tell me what?' she asked. 'Did you find Arcadia Farm?'

He shook his head. 'Not exactly. The day after I saw you, I caught the train from Liverpool Street out to George Lane in Woodford. You mentioned it?'

'Yes, Elizabeth spoke of it last Christmas.'

'As the train approached Woodford, I expected to see trees and fields, but instead, it was the heart of suburbia.

There were rows of red-brick houses which must have gone up since the turn of the century, and plots marked out for new properties to be built, but no sign of any farmland.'

'Perhaps it was further away from the station, being a farm.'

'I thought that too and walked all around Woodford,' he continued. 'Then over the next few days, I travelled up and down the Loughton branch line to see if I could find Arcadia Farm . . .'

'It must exist somewhere.'

He looked uncomfortable. 'I started asking around. There was a rank for motorized taxis outside Woodford station. One of the drivers said he'd lived there all his life, so I asked if he knew Arcadia Farm.'

'And?' she looked at him expectantly.

'He said there was a road called Arcadia Farm Avenue. Apparently, there was a farm there twenty years or so ago, but the owner was declared bankrupt and had to sell off all his land. The name's all that is left.'

Grace sipped her tea, stunned at this piece of information. 'Every Sunday without fail, Elizabeth walked towards Tufnell Park Underground to travel to Essex. I don't understand where she could have gone.'

'I'm sorry, Grace, I don't know.' He looked genuinely upset at having to deliver this news. 'If there's any way I can help you, for Edward's sake, then please let me know.'

'Thank you,' she said, 'but I don't even know how to begin to look for Elizabeth's family now.' A feeling of hopelessness came over her. 'I'll go back to Cloak Lane. Perhaps they have found something.'

'You mean about her drowning?' he asked.

'Yes, and her family too.' She stirred the dregs at the bottom of her cup. 'If you'd known Elizabeth,' she said, looking up at him steadfastly now, 'you'd know that she would never have killed herself. She was always so resilient.'

'Grace, you can't always know how someone else is feeling inside.'

'I suppose not.' She put the spoon down. 'But I do want to find out the truth.'

'Will you tell me if there's any new information? I can telephone. I meant what I said about wanting to help.'

'Of course.' She hoped that it would not be Bridget – or Father – who answered his call.

They left the café and both walked in silence for a few moments. Finally, she said, 'Arthur thinks I should leave investigating Elizabeth's death to the police.'

'He'll be concerned about you,' Tom said. 'Are you two courting?'

'Courting?' she laughed. 'No, we're just friends.' But she realized the words sounded inadequate. She paused. How could she explain her relationship with Arthur? 'We're more than that, I suppose. He's one of the few people who's known both parts of my life. My life before the war and how things used to be then. And now after the war when everything is so different.' As she spoke, she looked down at the ground, but when she glanced up, he was staring at her intently.

'Life changes, it has to move on,' he said.

'So people say, and I know they're right.' She hesitated. 'Have you moved on?'

'My life now is totally different in every way from the life

I lived before the war, so yes, you could say I've moved on.' His voice was bitter. 'Just before the war broke out, I had an audition for the London Symphony Orchestra. I missed it so I could sign up. I was in love and wanted to impress my fiancée by going off to fight.'

'What happened?'

'Well, this.' He took his maimed hand from his pocket. 'I was hit by shrapnel at Amiens – not too badly, though. I ended up in the military hospital at Étaples, dumped there sometime in the middle of the night. The doctor couldn't have cared less, he stank of whisky and clearly just wanted to get off duty. I was his last patient of the day.'

Grace shuddered. This story wouldn't end well.

'I had some pain in my hand,' he went on, 'and told the nurse. I thought they'd give me an injection of morphine to help me sleep. When the doctor came over, he told me it was just fluid and they'd tap it off under an anaesthetic. When I came round, he'd amputated two of my fingers.'

'That's terrible! I'm so sorry.'

'Two days later the same doctor was doing his rounds. The first thing he said to me was, "I didn't realize you were an officer. I do surgery for the officers in the morning." Meaning, I suppose, that if he'd known I wasn't just an ordinary soldier, he'd have taken more care. And he might have been sober and not hacked off half my hand.'

'Surely that can't be the case? It's appalling.'

'Didn't you have different wards for officers and privates at the First Camberwell?'

'Well, yes, but it didn't mean—'

He shook his head. 'When I got back to London, I was

treated by a civilian doctor, who was a good bloke. The wound had become gangrenous, and he had to operate again to make the cut cleaner. Even so, I knew I would never play the violin again.'

'And what about the woman you were in love with?'

'Evelyn? Oh, Evelyn didn't stick around. She wasn't about to sacrifice her life for me. While I was recovering, she sent me a letter saying that she'd met someone else. She was very sorry, of course. He owned a garment factory and they made army uniforms throughout the war. A protected profession, so he never even had to fight. He'd stayed at home and made a fortune.'

She shook her head. 'Life isn't fair.' What else was there to say? She remembered Arthur telling her how much Tom had been changed by the war.

'I was engaged too, you know. In the June of 1916. My fiancé Robert was killed at the Somme a few weeks later. Or was declared missing in action,' she corrected herself.

She thought of the beautiful summer evening three years previously, the night before Robert returned to France, when the daylight stretched on forever, and her skin glowed with the heat of the sun and the joy of being young and in love.

'Along with Edward and Arthur, we took a bottle of red wine up to Parliament Hill Fields to toast the engagement. All of London was before us and our lives were filled with promise.' She paused. 'But Robert was silent, more silent than I had known him. I think he knew what was going to happen. As soon as he arrived in France, he wrote to say that he'd asked Arthur to take care of me if anything should happen. That letter arrived two days after the telegram announcing he was missing in action.'

'I think a lot of soldiers had a premonition of their own deaths.'

They had reached King's Cross station and stopped in the ticket hall.

'I've never been back to Hampstead Heath since,' she said.

'Too many ghosts?'

'London is full of ghosts.' She shook her head.

'Arthur is in love with you, you know,' Tom said simply. 'Your life could begin again.'

'Oh no, Arthur is just honouring his promise to Robert. They were best friends. The three of them, Edward, Robert and Arthur.'

'I only had to spend ten minutes with you and Arthur to see that he's in love.'

Grace tried to protest, but Tom said, 'I'd best be going. Say hello to Arthur for me when you see him. He's a good man.' He looked at her significantly and disappeared into the crowd.

CHAPTER SIXTEEN

The next morning, there was a folded note lying on the doormat of 129 Lady Eleanor Road. Grace picked it up on her way to the breakfast table, reading it as she walked.

To whom it may concern,
Thank you for informing us of dear Elizabeth's death. Please forgive my writing to you, but after much soul searching, I have decided to tell you the truth about her. I looked up your address in Father Daley's correspondence file. He never throws anything away and I know that you had applied to him for a letter of recommendation many years ago.

He is not aware I have done this, and I would be grateful if you would not disclose it, as this is a matter on which the Reverend Father and I disagree.

However, I believe her family has a right to be informed of the death. Elizabeth Smith's true name is Lizzy Burdett-Smith. She once led a very different kind of life and I presume you will be familiar with her previous name. Unfortunately, I cannot furnish an address for any living relative but wish you success in your attempts to locate them.

Yours faithfully,
Mrs M. Hewitt

Astonished, Grace stopped reading and stood in the middle of the hallway. Bridget had just left the kitchen with a full teapot. 'Whatever is the matter, Miss Armstrong? You look as if you've seen a ghost.'

'This note came today from Mrs Hewitt. The lady from the Catholic bookshop.'

'I know who you mean – the one who could only afford the paste pearls. Now, what did she have to say?' Bridget balanced the teapot awkwardly on the hall table.

'She said Elizabeth was really called Lizzy Burdett-Smith and seems to assume we will know that name.'

'A false name. Well, this is a turn up for the books! I told you the wicked man called her by another name and when I come to think of it, that name could well have been Lizzy. Mary, come and hear this,' she shouted in the direction of the kitchen.

'Bridget, please, a little quieter,' Grace pleaded.

When she was informed about the letter, Mrs Watson thought she might have heard the name before but couldn't quite remember where. 'It will come to me, but why would she use a name that wasn't her own?' she wanted to know.

'She'll be running from something,' Bridget declared. 'The wicked man will be mixed up in this. Most likely it is him who's murdered her.'

'Bridget, please don't be so melodramatic. I'll ask Father when he comes down to breakfast. He might know.'

Her father did know, and his response was quite unexpected. His porridge spoon clattered to the table. 'Our Elizabeth was Lizzy Burdett-Smith. No, surely not. Living under our roof!'

'That's what Mrs Hewitt from the church bookshop said.'

'Elizabeth always seemed most respectable, but . . .' He had retrieved his spoon and wiped it on his napkin. He looked aghast.

'Who was Lizzy Burdett-Smith?' Grace wanted to know.

'It was a long time ago, when you were very small. A dreadful murder case. Terrible business. A blackmail gone wrong, I believe.'

'Elizabeth was accused of murder and blackmail?' Now it was Grace's turn to be shocked. 'But whoever—'

'Lizzy Burdett-Smith stood trial at the Old Bailey accused of the murder of Sir Hugh Clifton. He was very prominent in the Liberal Party. She was found not guilty, much to everyone's astonishment.'

'Goodness,' Grace managed weakly.

'There were boos in court when the verdict was announced. The *Daily Mail* described her as the most immoral woman in Britain.'

'Elizabeth!' she exclaimed horrified. 'It doesn't sound like her at all—'

'Absolutely not. Are you sure this woman from the church was correct?' He fortified himself with a sip of tea.

'It's what she put in the note.' She looked at him in

despair. 'And, in any case, how could I find out whether it was her or not?'

He thought for a moment. 'Your mother's friend Bunty knew Lizzy Burdett-Smith. She ran with a fast set at the turn of the century. You could ask her.' He began to eat his breakfast, still shaken. 'Lizzy Burdett-Smith, eh? Yes, it's Lady Bunty Jaggers you need to talk to.'

CHAPTER SEVENTEEN

Lady Bunty was her mother's closest friend, although they inhabited very different social worlds. Isobel had come with Bunty as her companion on the Europe trip, her passage paid for by Bunty's immensely wealthy family. She had wed Grace's father, a civil servant, just starting out in Whitehall, while Bunty had married into the well-connected but imprudent Jaggers family, bringing with her hundreds of thousands of dollars in a bridal settlement.

As a child, Grace had relished their regular visits to the opulent splendour of the Jaggers' town house in Cheyne Walk and accepted without question that Bunty could hardly be expected to find her way out to suburban Tufnell Park. However, there had been a coldness between Bunty and James Armstrong ever since his decision to put his wife into the nursing home the previous December. Bunty had furiously opposed this, leading to an intense argument with her father, held in hushed undertones so Mother wouldn't hear.

'It's grief, not madness. Her reaction is perfectly normal in the circumstances and Isobel will rot away in Worthing. She needs to be here, with her family.'

Her father saw this as an attack on his judgement. 'She is my wife. If anyone knows what is right for her, then it is me. She needs specialist help and I can't give that to her.' Grace was surprised to see that her normally reserved father had tears gathering in his eyes.

Grace telephoned her mother's old friend with some trepidation, but Bunty was delighted to hear from her and insisted that they meet the next evening. No mention was made of the long silence between the Armstrongs and the Jaggers family.

When Grace arrived at Cheyne Walk she was shown to the drawing room by a handsome young man whose Italian accent was so pronounced that it sounded theatrical. He ushered her into a room furnished with exquisite mint greens and soft greys, the walls covered with an eclectic mixture of paintings – imperious-looking members of the Jaggers family jostled for attention alongside some paintings Grace recognized as Impressionist. The most imposing painting in the room was an oversized Stubbs.

Bunty was sitting on a cerise sofa, with a half-finished cocktail on a side table and a cigarette holder in her hand. She stubbed it out decisively in a silver ashtray and jumped up to greet her visitor. 'Thank you, Rodolpho, and, honey, it's good to see you. You look divine.' Twenty-five years of living in England seemed only to have strengthened her New York accent. As she embraced Grace, she exuded waves of violet and jasmine. Grace had been told that Bunty was breathtakingly lovely when younger, blonde and slim, with eyes that were almost violet. Now the slender girl had been replaced by a much more solid middle-aged version. She was swathed in layers of colourful silk and bold costume jewellery, topped with an aquamarine turban. Although her youthful beauty had faded, she had a presence and an exuberance that was very appealing, and Grace admired her. She was still an attractive woman.

'It's good to see you too, Lady Bunty. You look very well.'

'Honey, you must call me Bunty. Lady Bunty makes me sound like I'm a hundred years old! Anyway, why'd you leave it so long between visits?'

Grace started to explain that she had been busy with work but was cut off when Bunty asked, 'And your mother, your poor, dear mother. Grace, I visited her last week.'

'You saw Mother? The home said she mustn't see anyone, and we should only make contact by telephone or letter.'

Bunty made a snorting noise. 'Yes, so the proprietor kept telling me. However, I refused to leave, and was allowed an hour or so with Isobel. She's like a ghost, Gracie. At first she wouldn't speak but by the end she held me and wept.'

'No,' Grace put her hands to her face in horror. 'Please don't say that, Bunty.' It was unbearable to think of her mother so destroyed. She had to believe that she was getting better. Otherwise, there was no reason for her banishment to Seaview Nursing Home.

'They're giving Isobel too much medication.'

'She really hasn't been well. The home said she was getting distressed and they needed to calm her.' Grace paused. She could feel her voice trembling.

'You need to insist on visiting her, Grace. Even if your mother refuses to see you.'

'Yes, I know that you're right. We talk on the telephone every week, but it isn't the same as actually seeing her.'

Those awful conversations, where Grace spoke desperately about the tiniest details of her life and her mother stayed silent at the other end of the line. Fading away from them all.

'It will be good for her and you too,' Bunty said decisively. 'Make sure you see the proprietor and tell her to go easy on the pills. You'll know the woman I mean. With a heart made of steel.'

Grace tried to smile. 'Yes, Mrs Pickford. I remember her from my last visit.'

Seeing her shut-down face, Bunty stopped. 'I've told Cook to make some of those little cakes you adored when you were a child. And this . . .' She held her glass up to the light, as if inspecting it. 'You must try this. Rodolpho makes the meanest Manhattan this side of Paris. I've employed him as my chauffeur, but I find him terribly versatile.' There was something in the way she said 'chauffeur' that made the position sound positively indecent.

Bunty had a long-held belief that London air was damaging to the skin and so refused to allow windows to be open when she was in residence at Cheyne Walk. As a result, the room was hot and still, but Grace knew this would be the case and had come prepared in a light dress. She settled herself into a deep sofa and awaited her cocktail.

'How is Lord Jaggers?' she asked, out of politeness more than anything else.

'Rupert? He's at Romaldkirk Towers, with his blessed hyacinths and amaryllises, which is quite frankly the best place for him. Now why is Rodolpho taking so long with the cakes and cocktails?' She looked at her gold wristwatch and declared with horror, 'It's way past six and we haven't fed you or given you anything to drink! I feel dreadful.'

'I've just got here, Bunty,' Grace protested.

'I shall go and find Rodolpho. He never answers when I ring the bell.'

She disappeared from the room, which gave Grace the chance to think about what she knew of the Jaggers. From overheard conversations and confidences from her mother, Grace had a good idea of the state of their marriage.

According to Isobel Armstrong, the young Rupert Jaggers had been considered a great catch in the nineties and the romance between him and Bunty had been the talk of the season. Dashingly handsome and with beautiful manners, she had mistaken his silence for great depth, not realizing it reflected his total lack of interest in anything much beyond hunting and the vast gardens of his estate in the North Riding of Yorkshire. In turn, he had foolishly believed that his young American bride couldn't fail to be entranced by the charms of Romaldkirk Towers.

'That would have been my life, Isobel,' Grace had heard Bunty confide to her mother, over coffee and cake, 'living miles from a city and ending up covered in mildew from the interminable damp there. In any case, I knew it was over when Rupert acquired the habit of shouting, "God save the King!" whenever we had conjugal relations.'

'No! But why didn't you just leave him if you were so unhappy?' her mother had asked.

'Isobel, I could not face the thought of returning home as a nineteen-year-old divorcee. Imagine how that would have been received by the Four Hundred of New York society and how people would have gloated. No, I'm made of sterner stuff. Daddy signed a huge cheque to restore that albatross, Romaldkirk Towers, and bought me this town house. Lord Jaggers visits once a year, so that we can keep up the pretence of being happily married and that suits us both very well.'

From the society diaries in newspapers, Grace had always known that Bunty's wealth and good nature had placed her at the heart of London society. There were even rumours she had been the mistress of the King.

Grace remembered her father grumbling, 'She'll have started those stories herself,' as he read the Sunday newspapers at the breakfast table.

Bunty finally returned with a reluctant Rodolpho, who was carrying a tray laden with the German *Kuchen* that reminded Grace of her childhood. They both selected a slice of plum cake and Bunty leaned forward, her breath a fog of sweet alcohol and stale cigarettes, 'So, how is it that I can help you, Gracie? You must have wanted to see me for a reason, and you sounded real mysterious on the telephone.'

Grace paused for a moment. 'Father thinks you might know a woman named Lizzy Burdett-Smith and I'm trying to find out about her.'

'Lizzy Burdett-Smith?' Bunty repeated, amazed. 'Wow, now she is a piece of ancient history!'

'You knew her personally?'

'Sweetheart, there was a time when I knew everyone who was anyone. But in the spring and summer of 1901, there wasn't a single person in the whole of Great Britain who didn't know Mrs Burdett-Smith!'

'Father told me she stood trial for murder. At the Old Bailey.'

Bunty snorted, 'She certainly did. I'm not easily shocked but . . . ! What was it the prosecution called her? Something about being an adventuress who . . . Let me see if I can remember. Who used her immoral charms to destroy a good man. Or words to that effect, anyway.'

Grace felt an increasing certainty that the woman she was describing could not have been Elizabeth. Mrs Hewitt must have been mistaken.

After a substantial sip from her glass, Bunty continued, 'Now, I was never intimate with her, but we attended the same parties and soirées. People said she was dreadfully ambitious. She came from absolutely nowhere – well, Essex – but got herself accepted into society. But being ambitious myself, I quite admired her. Although, obviously, I didn't approve of what came out later.' She paused, 'But why ever do you want to know about Lizzy Burdett-Smith?'

'This might sound strange, but I think she lodged in our basement, although she called herself by a different name.'

'I can imagine she would. But she lodged in your house? Well, she had to live somewhere, and she just totally disap-peared after the court case. I guess living in a basement in Tufnell Park might count as suitable punishment. No offence, honey,' she corrected herself quickly. 'You do know the details of the murder of Sir Hugh, don't you?'

'Not really. Was it very dreadful?'

Bunty nodded emphatically. 'Are you absolutely certain that this lodger of yours was Lizzy?'

'I'm not sure at all, so I've brought a photograph of her.' She handed over the framed picture of the Ryedale Villa household.

Bunty took a few moments looking at it. 'Oh honey, it's so sad.' Then, in a quieter voice, she said, 'How many of the people in this photograph are still living in Lady Eleanor Road?'

Grace tilted the photograph towards herself, although she knew the answer without looking. 'Edward, as you know, is dead.'

Bunty opened her mouth as if to say something, but Grace pointed at a tall man. 'Paul was our gardener, and he was killed quite early on. At the Battle of Mons.' She was aware of a stilted formality in her voice. It was difficult to list so many blighted lives.

Bunty nodded.

'And this is Henry Holscroft. He lied about his age to get into the First Middlesex and lost an arm from shrapnel damage. Mary Watson is still at Ryedale Villa and both Annie and Bridget worked at the munitions factories. Annie's married now and Bridget returned to us, but she didn't really want to.'

'I don't blame her. I've never understood the British belief that being *servile* is somehow a desirable thing. I don't think anyone under twenty-five returned to service in Romald-kirk Towers. I guess they're a different generation and don't want to be servants any more.' She lit a cigarette and coughed. 'So, thank God that Rodolpho is twenty-six.' At this very moment, he returned to replenish their cocktails, and she smiled at him gratefully. 'Anyway, you say that Lizzy is somewhere on this photograph.'

'Yes, just there. She's looking straight at the camera. It's a good likeness.'

Bunty scrutinized the picture carefully. 'I'm not sure whether it's her or not. It would have been what, eighteen or so years since I last saw her. Couldn't show her face, you understand.'

Grace watched her anxiously. Perhaps the woman from the bookshop had been wrong. However, after a moment or two more, Bunty exclaimed, 'D'you know, it is her! What misled me was the hair. Lizzy had the most beautiful golden hair – it gave her the look of an angel. But her hair is dark in this photograph. I guess she must have coloured it. Yes, I can see it now. Have you only just found out her true identity?'

'We knew her as Elizabeth Smith.' She paused, took a breath, trying to absorb the news that her friend really was Lizzy Burdett-Smith. 'Her body was found in the Thames.'

Bunty put her hand to her face. 'Oh God, no! Poor Lizzy. Poor, poor Lizzy.' She paused for a moment and then drained her glass. 'I don't think she had a very nice life. Her husband, Reginald, was much older and had a reputation as a drunkard. He was a handsome man but dissolute. In fact, he had the audacity to propose to me in the summer of '93. I turned him down flat, of course.'

'A husband!' Grace said, amazed. 'And you knew him.'

'He was a Captain in the army but left under rather a cloud. Allegations of cheating at gambling, I seem to recall, although nothing was ever proved. The Burdett-Smiths certainly lived beyond their means. There were lots of rumours about where the money came from, but in the months before the murder, they'd fallen on hard times and moved out to lodgings somewhere in Surrey.'

'Lizzy – I mean, Elizabeth – never mentioned that she had been married.'

'No? That's odd.' Lady Bunty shook her head. 'But how did she end up in your house?'

'She attended the same Catholic church as our servant Bridget and she advertised for lodgings. The rooms in our basement were free at the time.'

At this Bunty laughed. 'I'd never have put her down as a churchgoer.'

'She went to mass every morning.' Ignoring Bunty's obvious shock at this, Grace continued, 'Were there grounds to charge Elizabeth with murder?'

Bunty nodded vigorously. 'Now, it was such a long time ago that I can't quite remember the details, but I do remember thinking Reginald Burdett-Smith was lucky not to be in the dock beside her. The prosecution's case was that she had killed Sir Hugh in a fit of jealous passion. After the verdict, the police never investigated anyone else for the killing.'

'Father said she was called the most immoral woman in Britain.'

'Oh, Grace, you should have heard what else she was called! Her own husband made salacious allegations about her relationship with Sir Hugh the previous summer. There was talk of daytime trysts and . . .' Bunty took a large gulp of her cocktail, warming to her theme. 'And even indecent practices after a trip to the British Museum.'

'Elizabeth?' Then indignation kicked in. 'Her husband will have told awful lies about her, just to save himself! She must have refuted his words.'

'Lizzy didn't give evidence. However, she allowed her barrister to confirm that every word was true. That's what was so strange. Her words destroyed her own reputation, as well as that of Sir Hugh.'

Grace exclaimed. 'It seems so, so improbable. Why ever would she do that?'

'Apparently, she couldn't deny it. Captain Burdett-Smith had found her secret diary which detailed the affair, or at least that's what he testified at the Old Bailey. The penny-dreadful newspapers absolutely loved the story. Sir Hugh's poor wife said it was all an invention and denied the relationship could ever have taken place, but no one really listened.'

'The Elizabeth I knew was nothing like the person you're describing.' Now it was Grace's turn to take a large gulp of her cocktail. 'Would I be able to find out more about the murder? I don't understand how she could be involved in such an awful crime. And, at the very least, it might provide information about her family. I need to inform them of the death.'

'D'you know, I think I've got clippings from the case. If I have, they will be in my scrapbooks for 1901. Wait a moment and I'll ask Rodolpho to dig them out from the attic.' She put down her drink decisively.

CHAPTER EIGHTEEN

As they waited for Rodolpho to return, Grace asked, 'What was Sir Hugh like?'

Lady Bunty considered for a moment. 'I met him several times at suppers and parties but I never knew him well. He seemed pleasant. Intelligent and well-read. He was always welcome in the best society drawing rooms.'

'What about his wife?'

'Lady Constance. A bit sanctimonious, although I probably shouldn't say that. Now Rupert – not that he's a good judge – called him the best leader the Liberal Party never had. He was involved in the fight for female suffrage and was on the radical side of the party.'

'I'd never really heard of him till now,' Grace admitted.

'He died before he could achieve anything of substance and the murder cast a shadow over his memory – the circumstances were so seedy. Lady Constance took that very badly. She believed she had no justice for his death. I guess she had a point. It did feel like his reputation was on trial.'

Several minutes later, Rodolpho appeared carrying a scrapbook covered in pink silk and embossed with the Jaggers' family crest. 'I could only find one of your little books. Too many spiders and cobwebs in the attic.' He placed it on the table in front of them and dusted down his jacket in disgust.

'That might be enough,' Bunty replied. 'I can't quite remember when the trial was.' She looked at the scrapbook and then said wistfully, 'I used to have such an exciting life. Things haven't been the same since the Great War. Or maybe it's simply that I'm getting older.' She lingered as she turned the pages. Pulling herself together, she promised, 'I'll find it for you in a moment. Look, everything is still in order.' Bunty then pointed to a newspaper clipping which was incongruously pasted between menus from the Savoy, a winning betting slip for the 1901 Derby and dance cards from a Londonderry House ball.

'I much preferred the coverage in the *Pall Mall Gazette*, it included all the details *The Times* considered too distasteful. Don't you find that those are always the most interesting?' she confided, slightly tipsy now from her cocktails.

Grace took the scrapbook and began to read the first extract. The date 19 April had been scrawled across the top.

Sir Hugh Clifton Brutally Murdered
Terror stalks the streets of south London after the dreadful slaying of Sir Hugh Clifton. Mysterious letter found in victim's pocket.

As reported in final editions of yesterday's *Pall Mall Gazette*, the bullet-riddled corpse of Sir Hugh was discovered in the main letting bedroom at the Golden Hind public house in Portland Road, South Norwood. The publican, Mr Stephen

Ryman, was alerted to its presence when he noticed copious quantities of blood seeping through the ceiling.

Sir Hugh Clifton, of Sloane Street, was the Member for Chelsea West and a leading voice in the Liberal Party. Politicians on both sides of the House have expressed their shock and grave sorrow at the news.

Mr Henry Campbell-Bannerman, leader of the Liberal Party, said, 'His death is a devastating loss to British politics. Sir Hugh was a personal friend and a man often spoken of as a potential leader of our party and, indeed, as a future Prime Minister. He would have had a stellar career ahead of him, had he lived.'

Superintendent Horatio Wright of the Metropolitan Police confirmed that Sir Hugh had been shot several times and a velvet cushion had been used to muffle the sound of gunfire. He went on to say that the Golden Hind is well known for its unruly and raucous character and there had been a loud Irish ceilidh band playing on the night of the murder. A number of the revellers are believed to have heard raised voices and a series of bangs around about 10 p.m.

Mystery surrounds the married Member of Parliament's presence at the public house, which is known to rent out rooms on a nightly basis. These rooms are afforded a high degree of privacy as they are accessed by a separate door and staircase from the rest of the building. Sir Hugh had arrived at the Golden Hind the previous evening and signed the visitors' register as Mr A. Clarke. He was the only paying guest that night.

The Superintendent said that a swift identification of the corpse was possible due to a letter found in the victim's pocket. It was type written and signed 'L'. He refused to reveal the contents of the letter but said that the Metropolitan Police has not ruled out the theory that Sir Hugh was deliberately lured to his death or that he was the victim of an abortive blackmail attempt. He had withdrawn five hundred pounds from his account at Coutts & Co. that day, but his wallet was empty.

The thoughts of the *Pall Mall Gazette* are with Lady Constance Clifton at this distressing time. Sir Hugh and Lady Constance were married only three months ago in the Chapel of Trinity College Cambridge. It was a second marriage for both parties. Sir Hugh's first wife, Lady Emma, died in 1889 in childbirth. Lady Constance was recently widowed when her husband, the Reverend Lincoln, passed away after a long illness.

'The Golden Hind doesn't sound like the kind of place you'd find a Member of Parliament,' Grace said.

Bunty cackled. 'It's exactly the kind of place I would expect to find one! "Unruly and raucous" – that's a euphemism if I ever heard one.' Then she said more soberly, 'The poor man. He was only in his fifties.'

'And how tragic for Lady Constance,' Grace said. 'They'd been married such a short time.'

'Supposedly, Hugh had loved her for many years, but she was married and certainly not the type of woman to indulge in an extramarital affair,' Bunty sniffed slightly. 'He had to wait until her husband was cold and buried four months before they walked down the aisle. And then Sir Hugh was dead himself three months later.'

'What about the allegations of an affair? That must have been very difficult for her,' Grace said.

'She was devastated, absolutely inconsolable,' Bunty said. 'I will be honest and say she wasn't a woman I warmed to – very principled in the worst possible way – but it was dreadful to see how broken she was by what happened. She insisted that every word Captain Burdett-Smith said was untrue and that her husband had never been involved with Lizzy. She devoted her life to proving that the Burdett-Smiths had lied. But I'm getting a little ahead of the story.'

'Did the police ever reveal what was in the letter?'

'They made a big thing about it. It was signed "L", you see. That might be in the next article. Let me find it. It was a few days later and I know it's here somewhere.'

After a few minutes of searching, she pointed to a new page. The second article had a faint chocolate stain on it.

Startling Developments in Norwood Murder Probe
The Metropolitan Police are on the brink of making arrests in the Sir Hugh Clifton Slaying. Metropolitan Police reveal contents of mysterious note. Murder room was booked by a Lady of Quality.

We are now at liberty to disclose startling new developments in the investigation into the brutal murder of Sir Hugh Clifton. Two people, believed to be a husband and wife, are being questioned at an undisclosed police station in south London and arrests are thought to be imminent.

This follows the revelation that the bedroom where the murder was committed had been hired three days previously by someone described as 'a Lady of Quality'. Mrs Hannah Ryman, the landlady of the Golden Hind public house, said the lady had called herself Mrs A. Clarke and paid for the lodgings with a one-pound note, claiming the room was for herself and her husband. She remembered the lady most particularly, on account of her superior demeanour. Furthermore, Mrs Ryman has claimed that she caught a glimpse of this same person on the night of Sir Hugh's murder, ascending the back stairs.

Superintendent Horatio Wright also revealed that an item of interest had been found in the bedchamber but refused to elaborate. He believes it could provide 'the final missing piece in the jigsaw'. The Metropolitan Police have now released details of the note found in Sir Hugh's pocket, which serves only to strengthen the idea that the killing was premeditated, and Sir Hugh was lured to his death. The contents of the note are as follows:

Dearest Hugh,
It would be very much to your advantage that we meet. I do not know what the consequences will be otherwise. The Golden Hind in South Norwood is most discreet – as you well know! A room is booked in the name of Mr A. Clarke for 17 April. Please be there at eight o'clock pm.

With fondest love
L x

The release of the note came after startling revelations about Sir Hugh's personal life were leaked to the press. The *Pall Mall Gazette* has taken the principled decision not to publish the details.

Grace stopped reading for a moment and looked up at Bunty. 'What were the startling revelations?'

'Oh, nothing so shocking, really. An alleged liaison – or liaisons – with Lizzy in the summer of 1900. It gave her a motive. Supposedly, she couldn't forgive him for marrying another woman.'

'Elizabeth was married in the summer of 1900?' Grace confirmed.

Bunty nodded in response and Grace returned to the article.

It is also a matter of public record that Sir Hugh recently had a very public falling out – in the lobby of the House of Commons – with Sir Ernest Whitehouse, the Member of Parliament for Bradford Central and a colleague from the Liberal Party. There is no suggestion that Sir Ernest played any part in the murder.

'Sir Ernest? Why mention him if he played no part?' Grace asked.

'Because everyone assumed he must be involved, and he was a very frightening man,' Bunty replied. 'I'm surprised the *Pall Mall Gazette* dared to name him. He was big in the Liberal Party and then defected to the Unionist faction. Always very much a presence behind the scenes.'

'I think Daddy might have mentioned him,' Grace said, thoughtfully. 'He's quite high up, isn't he? He made a fortune from speculating in property.'

Bunty waved her hand. 'There were a lot of powerful people in the Cliftons' social circle. Ambitious and ruthless people, too, but none more so than Sir Ernest. Even though he'd publicly threatened Sir Hugh, he could never be directly connected to the murder.' She suddenly gave a yelp of disgust. 'The next part and the trial must come in the second scrap album! Rodolpho, are you sure it isn't somewhere in the attic?'

There was no response and then she remembered she had left it at the Jaggers' country estate on one of her rare visits there. 'My parents were over in the summer of 1901, and they wanted to see Romaldkirk Towers. I guess they were interested to see what they were spending all their money on.'

'But what happened next? What was disclosed at the trial?' Grace was desperate to know more.

'I don't quite remember the ins and outs of it now. It was all terribly complicated. The testimony from the landlady was important. She placed Lizzy at the scene. And as for Captain Burdett-Smith! There were queues snaking around the Old Bailey on the days he swore to his wife's infidelities.'

'He must have hated her to say such dreadful things in an open court.' Grace tried to imagine how Elizabeth must have felt, standing in the dock, on trial for her life and listening to her husband destroy her character.

'I think he did, but he was also motivated by the desire to save his own neck. The police originally arrested them both, but only a lady could definitely be placed at the Golden

Hind that night.' Lady Bunty shook her head. 'Not that it did him much good; he died of a heart attack less than two years later.'

'What a sad story. No one seems to come out of it very well.' Grace felt a chill settle upon her, despite the warmth of the evening.

'She's alive, though.'

'Who?'

'His wife. Lady Constance Clifton. She lives just round the corner from here. She's spent most of her fortune and life proving that the Burdett-Smiths were liars.'

'Do you still see her?'

'Only if it's absolutely unavoidable. I find her a bit of a bore, if I'm honest.' Bunty was now on to her third cocktail and the confidences were flowing freely.

'Do you think I could meet her?' Grace too felt emboldened by the strong alcohol.

'Why would you want to do that?'

'I don't know where to begin with tracing Elizabeth's family and Lady Constance is a link between the past and the present.'

'Honey, Constance Clifton hated – I mean, absolutely hated – Lizzy. I can't believe she would be exchanging pleasantries with the wider Burdett-Smith family.'

'Still, would it be possible to meet her? I can't help thinking that what happened in the past is somehow tied up with Elizabeth's death.' She considered her words carefully. 'And I'd like to prove that she isn't the dreadful murderess the world believes she is.'

'I'll give it to you, Grace, you're just like your mother.'

It was true, Isobel Armstrong wasn't a woman to allow a wrong to go unrighted.

Bunty thought for a moment. 'Constance is obsessed with the case. The last time I saw her she thrust a pile of yellowing documents beneath my nose and said she had definite proof Lizzy lied about the relationship with Sir Hugh. I wasn't interested. Nobody's interested. It's a scandal from a different world. But suppose you pretended you *were* interested. You could tell her you're a reporter.'

'I *am* a reporter, or at least I aim to be one,' Grace said indignantly.

'And that you are investigating famous miscarriages of justice, and you think Sir Hugh was treated very badly. Then she might meet you. She's always desperate to salvage his reputation.'

'Wouldn't it be immoral to lie about my reasons for seeing her?' Grace asked, feeling slightly uneasy about Bunty's suggestion.

'I thought you wanted to be a reporter, Gracie! If you want to see her, you can't tell her the truth. And you certainly can't worry about being immoral if you want to work for a newspaper. Back in the summer of '99, I had a terribly close relationship with a renowned journalist and he was the most immoral person I've ever met.' The last confidence was said with a rather satisfied smile.

'Very well. Would you be able to arrange it?' She glanced at the older woman hopefully.

Seeing her look, Bunty responded, 'Grace, I usually go out of my way to avoid her. She's a bit too serious for my liking.' Bunty surveyed the bottom of her cocktail glass and burped quietly. 'She was part of the National Suffrage for Women movement. Not that there's anything wrong with that. I never could understand why men had the vote and women didn't, when men are such numbskulls. No, it was how she went about everything. Always so convinced she was right. Funnily enough, Lizzy was also a member but there was bad blood between Constance and Lizzy's family.'

'Why was that?'

'Oh honey, I don't know. There are so many stories from the past that they all get mixed up in my head. Anyway, I could arrange an introduction. I'll pretend you're my niece. Rupert's brother Augustus and his wife Henrietta breed like rabbits – there are so many of them, I can never remember which is which.'

'Do you think it would work?'

'Why shouldn't it? Lady Constance will take me at my word. This is exciting. It's like one of those crime mysteries they serialize in the newspapers. I'll let you know once everything is arranged.'

CHAPTER NINETEEN

The next morning, Grace's head was heavy and she regretted being quite so enthusiastic in sampling the range of cocktails provided by the talented Rodolpho. As she slunk down to breakfast and poured herself a strong cup of tea, she found herself sympathizing with Roger Dale, the chief reporter, and his legendary hangovers. He had now temporarily exported his mammoth drinking to Paris. Using his family connections with the Wagstaffs, he had somehow contrived to get himself across to France for the peace conference and booked into a cheap set of rooms in Montmartre. Miss Vera Boddy was incandescent with rage and made clear her displeasure on a daily basis.

'How was Bunty?' her father asked, as he tucked into his eggs and bacon.

Revived by porridge and the tea, Grace felt more capable of making conversation. 'She was very well, Father. She sent her best regards.' She hesitated nervously for a second. 'She's been to see Mother and is worried that the nurses at the home are sedating her too heavily.'

There was a silence. 'They'll know what they're doing. Lady Bunty is hardly medically qualified.' He carried on eating.

Grace continued, 'Elizabeth was Lizzy Burdett-Smith, after all. Bunty recognized her from the photograph.'

'Goodness,' was his somewhat muted response. 'I suppose she told you about all that business with Sir Hugh and the murder?'

'She did,' Grace replied. 'What was your opinion of what happened?'

He looked thoughtful. 'I'm not sure. The Lizzy Burdett-Smith who was described in court was nothing like our Elizabeth.'

'Yes,' Grace agreed eagerly. 'That's what I think as well.'

He took a reflective sip of tea. 'On balance, I rather think Mrs Burdett-Smith was guilty of murder, but her barrister created enough reasonable doubt for her to escape conviction. Juries are always more reluctant to convict when it's a capital offence. It's a big responsibility to send someone to the gallows, especially a young woman.'

'What was the reasonable doubt?' Grace wanted to know.

'There was no eyewitness to the killing itself and the murder weapon was never found. It was Sir Benedict Huguenot, you know. The barrister. When he was at the absolute top of his game. Hawley Crippen would still be dispensing homeopathic remedies in Islington if Sir Benedict had been his brief.'

'Yet I can't believe Elizabeth guilty of murder. She just seemed too good. I would like to find the truth of what happened,' Grace said passionately.

'Absolutely,' her father agreed, 'it is completely out of

character. Now I must get myself off to Whitehall. Yet another meeting with the minister.'

Once he'd gone, she went to her father's study and telephoned the nursing home. Bunty was right. She must insist on speaking to her mother and seeing her. When she was finally put through, her mother greeted her with total silence. After a few minutes Grace said, 'I've decided to visit. I thought it would be lovely to come to Worthing this weekend.'

A frail voice cut her off. 'Gracie, please, you shouldn't come. I wouldn't be a very good hostess.'

She tried to protest. 'I don't need to be entertained. I would just like to be with you.'

'Darling, I don't want you to see me like this, when my heart is filled with so much sorrow and I can't think of the words to say.'

'Please, Mummy—'

'When I feel better, then you can come. It really is for the best.'

The line went dead and Grace was left heartbroken, holding the silent receiver. How could it be for the best not to see her mother? If she felt she was protecting Grace, the opposite was true. This rejection left her feeling absolutely bereft. She shut the study door and sobbed quietly, hoping the servants couldn't hear.

Finally, she dried her eyes and checked in her compact mirror that her face wasn't tear-stained. If she were to get through the day at work, she must not think too deeply about her mother's words.

Grace left the house and caught the Underground train to Tottenham Court Road. She arrived at Tavistock Square with minutes to spare and hid herself in the tiny work cubicle. Despite what her mother said, she intended going to Worthing.

At 9 a.m., both Grace and Fergus stood up, ready to go into Mr Wagstaff's office. However, Vera Boddy appeared and said, 'There's no morning meeting today.'

They looked at each other in confusion. The daily meeting was the unfailing foundation on which life was built at *Nursing World*.

'Now, Fergus, as you know, Mr Dale is not with us at the moment, the French capital having the benefit of his presence.' There was something in her tone that strongly suggested she would like this to be a permanent arrangement. 'Therefore, you will be interviewing Sir Anthony West OBE about his fundraising in Orpington. You must catch the overground train out to Kent. I will need to see the questions you intend to ask before you depart.'

'Yes, of course, Miss Boddy. I shall write them out immediately.'

'This is a big opportunity for you, Fergus. Such an interview is likely to appear on page four or five of the Christmas edition, and who knows where that might lead.'

Grace glanced across at him. He was escaping the cramped confines of 24 Tavistock Square, even if it was only for a morning. She sighed. The day held no such prospect for her.

'Grace, you will take shorthand for Mr Wagstaff.' Miss Boddy paused. 'However, you must wait a little while. He is indisposed.'

She swept back into her office and Grace returned reluctantly to her cubicle to arrange and rearrange the paper, ink pot and jotter on her desk. Having exhausted the number of combinations for her writing materials, she surreptitiously took out a copy of P.G. Wodehouse's *My Man Jeeves* and began to read.

By half past ten there was still no sign of Mr Wagstaff and she began to worry that she should be doing something. Perhaps she had misunderstood the instructions. Miss Boddy had told her to wait a little while and it had now been an hour and a half. She put the novel down and left her desk.

She knocked quietly on his office door before entering. Mr Wagstaff was turned away, facing the window. The room was thick with cigarette smoke and an overflowing ashtray sat on his desk. She watched him stub out one cigarette and light another mechanically. He seemed unaware of her presence.

'Good morning, Mr Wagstaff, sir,' she said hesitantly.

He didn't turn around but continued, staring, unseeing, out of the window. She stood awkwardly at the edge of the room, unsure of whether he was deliberately ignoring her or just hadn't heard. When the silence continued, she coughed loudly and walked closer to him. 'Miss Boddy asked me to see if you wanted any shorthand taking.'

She was standing almost immediately behind him, and he looked around slowly. He had been crying. His eyes were red and swollen, and his cheeks were wet with tears he hadn't bothered to brush away. She sensed she was intruding on something wholly private and raw.

He shook his head.

'Mr Wagstaff, are you well? Can I fetch you a glass of water?'

He looked past her. 'Exactly four years ago today that he was killed. At Gallipoli. What a bloody, bloody waste.' Angrily, he stubbed out his still smouldering cigarette.

'Herbert. He was the only boy in the family. The youngest by more than five years. My wife called him our miracle baby. His sisters all made a fuss of him. Four years ago today,' he repeated.

'I'm so sorry,' she faltered. 'Is there anything I can do to help?'

'There's nothing anyone can do, Miss Armstrong.' He took a deep breath. 'I must allow this to pass. What else can be done?' He turned back to the window. 'I will let you know when you are needed.' Grace left the room.

About two hours later, he emerged from his office, as if nothing had happened. 'The newspaper will not get itself written, now will it, Miss Armstrong? Where were we? Let us get started immediately.'

His manner was so brusque, cheerful even, that she found herself questioning whether she had imagined his previous despair. But his smile didn't reach his eyes and the heap of cigarette ends in the ashtray betrayed his true state of mind.

It was a sombre day, made more so because she planned to return to Cloak Lane and explain what she had learned about Elizabeth and see whether there had been any other developments. The clock finally crawled its way to five and she grabbed her coat and set off so quickly that it caused Vera Boddy to remark how everyone seemed quite out of sorts today.

When Grace arrived at the police station she was relieved to see Constable Alston behind the desk. A much more welcome sight than Sergeant Williams. He looked up at her expectantly.

'Good afternoon, Constable,' she said.

He smiled. 'Hello, Miss Armstrong, how can I help you? Have you managed to speak to Miss Smith's family yet?'

She explained that she hadn't been able to find them but intended to keep searching. 'There is something else I need to tell you, but I'd rather not do it here.'

He looked around a little furtively. 'Tell you what, I'll fetch another constable to watch the front desk and then we can chat somewhere a bit more private.'

A few minutes later he opened the counter and she followed him into the depths of the station's back offices. They walked past Sergeant Williams's room, the door of which was very firmly shut, and he ushered her into the same office they had been in last time, with its overflowing desk. He pushed a small gap in the cardboard folders that covered every inch of its surface.

'The coroner was going to rule on Miss Smith's death on Tuesday next, but that's been pushed back. I'm afraid it will delay any funeral.'

He clearly expected her to be concerned but, if anything, she was relieved. It would give her more time to try to locate any relatives.

'What would happen if I can't find her family by the time of the inquest?' Grace asked.

'Then she'll be buried in a pauper's grave. Most likely at St Botolph in Aldgate. It's the nearest churchyard.'

'A communal grave. Oh no. That sounds so bleak.'

'It is,' he said flatly.

Suddenly Grace thought of Robert and how her dreams had been haunted by images of his body lying in the mud of the Somme, just one of a heap of tangled bodies merged into the wet clay, with no loved ones to bid farewell.

'I won't let her lie in an unmarked grave,' she declared. 'If I can find her family, so much the better, but if I don't, at least Elizabeth will have a proper burial.' She paused. 'Has there been any new information about the circumstances of her death?'

'I'm sorry, but no new witnesses have come forward. Sergeant Williams still has it down as a suicide, but Miss Armstrong, what is it that you wanted to tell me?'

First she informed him that Elizabeth had been known as Lizzy Burdett-Smith. He nodded quietly as she spoke and then said, 'It's a long time ago, but it was a notorious murder and I understand there were other allegations made too. Gentlemen who were blackmailed. Which might provide a motive to kill Miss Smith. You know, a resentment that has simmered away over the years.'

She agreed. 'I've decided to find out more about the Sir Hugh case. It could be linked to her death, as you say.'

Constable Alston shook his head, alarmed. 'Miss Armstrong, with all due respect, this is police work, and if there's a killer on the loose who's bitter enough to wait eighteen years . . .' His voice trailed away. 'You really don't want to be getting yourself mixed up in it.'

'But nothing has happened. Nothing new has been discovered,' Grace said despairingly.

'Maybe there is nothing more to be discovered. Knowing Miss Smith's past history – what you've just described – makes me inclined to believe it was suicide. Remorse, perhaps.' He looked at her furious face and quickly added, 'But I'll keep my ears open and let you know anything I find out.'

It all felt hopeless, Grace thought as she walked briskly from the police station. She had no intention of heeding Constable Alston's warning. She was determined to find out what had happened, not only for Elizabeth's sake but also to prove to herself that she was capable of being a real reporter – someone who was not frightened of searching for the truth.

It was after six in the evening and the city workers had already caught the Tube, bus or train out to the suburbs. There was an eerie sense of desolation in the streets around Bank and Monument and she had the strangest sensation that she was being watched. She kept her head down, focusing on Elizabeth and any pieces of information she could remember.

She was exhausted by the time she opened the door of Ryedale Villa. Bridget came straight into the hall and handed her a scribbled note saying, 'Lady Bunty. Lady C, 6 p.m. Friday 12th, 89 Sloane Street. You work for the Ham & High.'

'I'm sure it will mean something to you, miss, for I cannot make head nor tail of it,' she sniffed.

Just after seven, Tom Monaghan telephoned and she told him what she had discovered.

When she had finished, he whistled. 'That's quite a story! So, Elizabeth Smith was involved in a murder?'

'But it doesn't match who she was at all, Tom, it really doesn't. I'm going to meet Lady Constance, the wife of Sir Hugh. If there is a link between Elizabeth's death and the past, hopefully she will reveal it.' She stopped. The only person who seemed prepared to help her was Tom Monaghan.

She knew that Arthur wouldn't approve of what she was about to do, and her father would be appalled.

'Could I ask you a huge favour? I don't know who else to turn to.'

'What?' he asked cautiously.

'I'd like to go to the Golden Hind public house in Norwood where the murder took place and see if I can find out anything more about it. The landlady there was the chief witness for the prosecution. She claimed Lizzy Burdett-Smith booked the room and was there on the night of the murder.'

'Are you sure that's wise? What could you hope to find twenty years later, anyway?'

'Eighteen' she corrected him. 'I don't know, but I feel that I owe it to Elizabeth to try everything. If you'd rather not come, that's fine . . .'

'No, no, Grace, I said I'd help and from what you've told me the Golden Hind doesn't sound the safest of places. Perhaps they'll have closed it down by now.'

'Perhaps,' she agreed.

That night she was exhausted, but it was impossible to sleep. It had been a horrible, horrible day. Finally, she fell into a fitful dream, with a sense of inevitability about what she would see. The landscape was grey and again she was walking on Hampstead Heath. Time had slowed down and her feet were as heavy as lead. She could only make the slowest progress, dragging herself along.

There was a figure ahead of her, but it was indistinct.

Was it Robert?

And then the mist cleared a little and she could see a second shape, which slowly resolved itself into the form of Elizabeth. Somehow, she had known they would both be present.

Grace cried out, 'You're both living. I knew they lied. I never saw a body, cold and dead in the ground.'

Seemingly taking part in some carefully rehearsed dance, the figures turned around in unison and looked directly at her. Their faces were crude and misshapen, as if moulded from clay, and both shook their heads. Elizabeth first and then Robert pointed to their faces, to where a mouth should be. In its place was a slit, crudely sewn up with black stitches. Each then put a finger to their lips. Grace cried out in horror and awoke with a start in the darkness. The same horrible dream, only with Elizabeth this time. Sleep did not come again that night.

CHAPTER TWENTY

Arthur had managed to get two tickets for *The Girl for the Boy*, a popular musical which had just opened at the Duke of York's Theatre and Grace had talked about wanting to see. He'd offered to take her for supper at the Savoy first and she now hurried along the Strand, conscious that she was late and threading her way quickly through the Friday night crowds. She was unsettled and had an increasing sense of foreboding about Elizabeth's death. Hopefully, the meeting with Lady Constance the following Friday would provide some answers.

It was not yet seven o'clock, but it had been overcast all day, with ominous grey clouds threatening a downpour. The lights of the restaurants and theatres of the Strand were a blur. If it rained, her flimsy shoes would be wrecked and she didn't even have an umbrella. It only was when she glanced up briefly that he was suddenly there – Robert, just a few yards ahead of her. He was dressed in his khaki uniform and looked out of place in the smart evening crowds. He was turned away from her and walked with his shoulders slightly hunched, as if carrying some terrible burden.

He seemed frail and his gait was that of a much older man. Yet she knew at once it was him. The people around him were laughing and excited, on their way to meet friends. Part of the normal weekend throng. Robert was separate from them, shrouded in his own misery, and her heart ached for him.

She shouted, 'Robert, Robert, please turn around! It's Grace.'

Those close by stopped and looked at her in surprise. She didn't care. It was Robert. He was so close to her. Yet, he didn't look back and instead continued determinedly through the crowds. She kept losing sight of him as the groups swelled and thinned, but she was certain it was her fiancé.

Hurrying, she had almost caught up with him when he suddenly veered sharply to the right and disappeared down a narrow alleyway off the Strand. She hesitated for a moment before following. Even in the early evening, this was a sinister place of distorted shapes and shadows. There was a smell of stale beer, cigarettes and urine. Although she was so close to the Strand, with its lights and people, this was like entering another world – a dark world of silence. She shivered. It was cold, and she pulled her light coat tightly around her. Nervous, she followed him into the gloom.

'Robert, Robert. Is it you?' Her words echoed and re-echoed around the buildings. What if he were in danger, lost in the heart of the city, not knowing who he was or what he had been?

The far end of the alley led out towards the Thames. It was so dark, darker than it should have been at this time of the evening. She heard panting, a strange scuffling noise but could see no more than his outline. She wouldn't let him disappear. Slipping on the damp cobbles in her high-heeled shoes, she bitterly regretted changing out of her sensible work brogues.

Then he turned around, his face picked out by a shard of light. It was Robert. Her heart stood still, but this wasn't the Robert she had known. Confident and glamorous. This was a very different man. His face was gaunt and haunted. 'Robert,' she said and held out her hand. 'It's Grace, you can come home now.' She knew that her face was covered with tears. He was a broken man, but she would try to put him back together. He moved away from her like a wild animal, terrified of human contact. His face was partly covered in shade. He shook his head. His mouth was in shadow. 'Robert, I can't let you go now.'

He slipped again into the deep darkness. There were no street lamps here, no comforting brightly lit shop windows. She heard a noise and turned around sharply. When she looked back, he was running away towards the Thames. She went to follow and then there was that noise again. Suddenly a man loomed at her out of the darkness, blocking the way to Robert. He stank of cheap alcohol and sweat.

'Hello, miss. Come here, miss. Give a kiss to an old soldier.'

With a half-scream, she was forced to turn and flee back to the civilized safety of the Strand and the reassurance of Arthur. Safe and kind Arthur, who was waiting for her at the entrance to the Savoy.

'Grace, whatever is wrong?' He looked with concern at her pale face and terrified eyes.

She shook her head, unable to speak. What could she say to him? She had already made him chase illusions when they had been at Rectors nightclub together. He wouldn't believe that she had seen Robert and would be horrified that she had tried to follow him into the darkness of the alleyway.

He didn't probe any further, but instead found their table in the restaurant and filled her silences with reassuring talk about a planned visit to his parents in Durham. 'You know you should come up, Grace. You'd love it there and Mother and Father would be delighted to see you.'

She tried to smile but her head was too full of the ghosts of the past.

Arthur had ordered lobster and she toyed with the food on her plate, having no appetite to finish it. 'Are you sure that you are all right, Grace?' he asked finally, all concern and solicitude. 'You've hardly spoken.'

'Yes, I'm sorry. I've just been distracted with everything that's happened.'

'Oh, I know. Elizabeth's death – what a dreadful business.'

'Arthur, I'm convinced that she was murdered,' she said passionately, 'and I have no confidence the police will investigate it properly. I intend going to the Golden Hind public house, the place of Sir Hugh's murder, with Tom, Mr Monaghan. I want to see if I can find out anything more.'

'With Tom?' he interrupted. 'I thought you didn't approve of him.'

'Well,' she took a sip of water, 'he's said he'll help me find out what happened to Elizabeth and he went out to Essex to look for her family.'

She saw that he was looking intently at her. 'Now it's you who's not talking, Arthur.'

He wiped his mouth with the napkin. 'I suppose, Grace, I just feel that perhaps you should avoid getting involved in all of this. It's the police's job to solve murders, not yours. And Elizabeth . . .' His voice trailed off.

'What about Elizabeth?' she demanded.

He went a little pink in the face. 'I'm worried that you're getting too involved in this, Grace, and it's not good for you. You've told me how she was lying about who she was and suddenly there are all those revelations about her past. I do remember something about the Burdett-Smith murder trial. It really was quite scandalous.'

'So I should simply forget that she existed.' She put her fork down, no longer able to pretend she was interested in the food. 'Perhaps we should leave for the theatre, Arthur? We don't want to be late.'

'Yes, of course. Whatever you prefer. I'll just call the waiter over.'

Once in the theatre they sat in silence, aware of the happy couples around them, laughing and talking before the play began. Grace deliberately didn't look at Arthur, staring at the theatre programme as if it held some important information. From the corner of her vision, she was aware of Arthur looking glumly at the closed red velvet curtains of the stage.

'Grace, I didn't mean to upset you.'

'No?'

'No, and what I said came out wrong. I liked Elizabeth. I just feel that you don't know what you're getting yourself into. What dark secrets from the past you might be stirring up. They were all powerful people who were involved in the Clifton case.'

'Except Elizabeth,' she pointed out.

'Yes, except her,' he agreed. He considered for a moment. 'You've heard of Sir Ernest Whitehouse, I presume?'

'Yes,' she acknowledged. 'Lady Bunty spoke of him as a ruthless man.'

'He is a most dangerous man, Gracie, and many believe he was responsible for whatever happened to Sir Hugh. I've met him,' he added.

'You have?' she said surprised. 'You never told me that.'

'It was a few months ago. There was a disputed insurance claim, and he came to the meeting. The first thing he did was place a gun on the table.'

'A gun? Whatever for?'

'It was a warning. A gun, in the middle of the City of London, as if it had been the Wild West, and he got what he wanted. We paid up, even though we shouldn't have,' he said indignantly. 'The head of the syndicate insisted.'

'Is this really relevant to me, though, Arthur?' she asked.

'The Cliftons were well connected and wealthy, and they were destroyed by their association with Sir Ernest. I don't want you to get hurt, Grace. I'm worried about you.'

She could see the sincerity in his eyes. 'I won't get hurt, Arthur. I promise to be careful, but I need to find out what happened. I can't believe that Elizabeth is the dreadful woman she is painted to be. You knew her. Did she ever seem the kind of woman to betray her husband? Or to kill in cold blood?'

Arthur was forced to shake his head. 'No, she struck me as quite reserved. Intelligent, I would say, most of all intelligent. But Grace, Lady Bunty has confirmed it is Lizzy Burdett-Smith in the photograph. She didn't deny the things her husband said about her.'

'I know,' Grace said reluctantly, 'but she was a very loyal friend to me, especially after Robert had gone. There were times when she was the only person who seemed to understand how I felt.' She hesitated a moment and then decided to ask a question that had started to haunt her. 'Robert was very close to her. They often talked together for hours on end when he came to the house. I felt almost jealous of her; I know that sounds ridiculous.'

He looked at her very carefully. 'Elizabeth and Robert didn't have a romantic association if that's what you're afraid of.'

'Are you sure? It's just that with all these revelations . . .' Grace's voice was rising, and she was aware of people starting to stare at her. She lowered her voice to a whisper. 'Are you sure?'

'Positive, absolutely positive. Robert found Elizabeth easy to talk to but there was never anything romantic there. You had nothing to fear from her.'

Relieved, she leaned back in the stall seat. An unspoken peace was declared between them and they merged into the generality of the other couples talking about the show and friends and what had happened that day. The play was a light-hearted musical and it passed quickly enough.

Parked around the corner on the Strand was Arthur's Crossley 20/30, his pride and joy. They walked from the theatre in the September breeze. The threatened rain had held off. Arthur was uncharacteristically quiet as he opened the door for Grace, and they set off to drive north towards Tufnell Park.

Arthur had just turned onto High Holborn when a black Rolls-Royce appeared from nowhere and almost forced them off the road as it overtook them.

'I say, talk about bad driving!' he exclaimed and hammered at the horn. The black car continued its speedy escape from the centre of London.

They talked briefly about how many motor cars there were on the roads nowadays, with Arthur declaring there really ought to be some kind of a proficiency test before people were allowed to drive.

'Tom was a pretty good driver, I seem to remember. Although once he crashed the CO's staff car into a ditch and then didn't hear the end of it for weeks.'

'He told me about the amputation of his fingers at the hospital in Étaples. And his fiancée.'

'That was a bad show. A very bad show. I didn't see him after that – not until I bumped into him in King William Street a few months ago, but you can see how it's changed him.'

'It's very sad that it ended his career as a musician,' she said.

'Well, it was partly his choice. He told me that the Royal College of Music offered him a scholarship on their composing course, but he refused to take it.'

'Why would he do that?' she wondered.

'I'm not sure. Tom can be quite secretive at times.'

They then fell into a silence that stretched out over

several minutes, until he suddenly said, 'I meant what I said back in the theatre. I don't want you to get hurt.'

'I know, Arthur. I really appreciate your concern but—'

'I care very much about you, Grace,' he said. 'I feel closer to you than pretty much anyone else in the world.'

'I know,' she replied, 'we share the same memories, like the holidays in Whitby and Robert's last night at home, when we climbed up to Parliament Hill Fields.'

'Not just Robert and not just the past,' he said.

She felt the night air cool against her skin and stared into the inky darkness, holding her breath and hardly daring to look at Arthur, unsure of what he was going to say next. Tom's words floated back to her. 'I only had to spend ten minutes with you and Arthur to see that he's in love.' She had denied what Tom had said at the time, but perhaps she hadn't wanted to admit it.

'Grace, I'm sorry if this makes everything awkward but I have to tell you how I feel. Have felt, in fact, for a long time.' He turned towards her briefly. 'I think that you really are the most marvellous woman I've ever met, and I admire you tremendously. I know that I can never be as glamorous or as interesting as Robert and I respect how you felt about him. But I would do everything I possibly could to make you happy.'

'Arthur, I don't know what to say. It's very kind of you, but—'

'No, no, I don't expect you to reply. It all sort of came out in a rush. I was just thinking in the theatre that was pretty much the first time we'd argued, and I couldn't bear it if we were to fall out.'

'Arthur, I'm sorry,' she replied.

'No, no, it's my fault, Grace. Please forget what I've said. I fear I've made rather a fool of myself. I don't want there to be any awkwardness between us.'

'Arthur, you haven't made a fool of yourself. And I'm very flattered. You are such a decent man and make me happy when no one else seems able to. It's just—'

'Just what?' She could hear a note of anxiety in his voice as they sped towards home. They had reached Camden Town and the roads were nearly empty. The only people out were those returning from the public houses, the red tips of their cigarettes glowing against the darkness.

It was impossible not to say something now.

'I've seen Robert again. He's alive.'

'No, absolutely not, Grace. Robert is dead. You can't have seen him.'

'I swear to you I have. Tonight, he was walking down the Strand. I thought it was him on the Underground train and when we went to Rectors, but those were just fleeting glimpses. This time I saw him clearly.'

Arthur gripped the steering wheel more tightly. 'Grace, he's dead. You can't have seen him tonight.'

'But it was definitely Robert,' she insisted. Grace turned to him, but he was looking straight ahead at the road.

'Did you speak to him? Did he acknowledge you?' His voice was strained.

'No, he disappeared. He was gone too quickly. He had changed. He looked wretched but I knew it was him.'

'He's dead, Gracie, you have to accept it.'

'How can you be so sure that he's dead? No body was

found, even though the men in his company searched that night. The newspapers have stories of men who've returned after being reported missing believed dead. Only the other day there was—'

He stopped her. 'I know that he's dead. You must believe me.'

'How can you be so certain? Tell me why I should believe you.'

He stared at the road ahead.

'See, you can't. And how would Robert feel if he were to return home and find that I had forgotten him? That I was with someone else?'

'I was right behind him coming out of the trenches, Grace. He walked into the smoke and hell of battle. He couldn't have survived.'

'You survived,' she pointed out.

'That was different,' he said.

'How was it different?' she asked, but he was silent.

They had reached Lady Eleanor Road now and Arthur pulled up outside the tall thin house. All the lights were off, except for the hallway. She felt for the house key in her handbag. 'Thank you so much for bringing me home, Arthur,' she said, 'and for the lovely show.'

'Please don't let us ever fall out,' he replied. There was a note of desperation in his voice.

'No, of course we never will,' she said. 'Goodnight, Arthur.'

CHAPTER TWENTY-ONE

Eighty-nine Sloane Street was slightly shabbier than its neighbours but wore its air of neglect with a certain defiance, as if their freshly painted facades were somehow rather vulgar in comparison. It was one of those mid-September evenings when there was a chill in the air that hinted at the winter to come. Bunty was half hidden behind the iron railings, wrapped up in layers of brightly coloured chiffon and furs. She pointed to a large yellow motor car which was randomly parked in the middle of the road. 'Rodolpho has left me. He was seduced by a vastly inflated remuneration from a widow in Buckinghamshire and now I've been forced to drive myself.'

They both watched as a horse-drawn cart took an elaborate detour around the car. Bunty shook her head. 'Anyway, honey, let's get our story straight. I've made a few notes.' She reached into a beaded handbag and produced several sheets of paper covered in her exuberant handwriting. She glanced at it for a moment. 'You can keep the name Grace. Augustus and his wife have so many daughters, there's bound to be at least one Grace among them.' She shuddered.

'Your surname is Jaggers, of course, and you've been edu-
cated at some dreadful girls' boarding school – I'm sure you
can come up with a suitable name.'

Grace nodded, still feeling a little guilty at their
dishonesty.

Bunty referred back to her notes and continued. 'You've
got a job as a journalistic reporter at the *Hampstead & Highgate Express* – *Nursing World* really wouldn't work for our
subterfuge.' There was a note of glee as she pronounced the
word 'subterfuge'. 'They want you to find out about the
whole Sir Hugh Clifton thing. And finally, you've recently
come down from Middleton-in-Teesdale. It's in the north,
so she won't bother to ask you anything about it.'

Bunty rang the large brass bell with a determined air, and
they heard its harsh clang echoing through the empty house.
After several moments she rang it again, but more vigorously. As she often explained to Grace, fresh air was a known
danger to the complexion, and she didn't wish to spend a
moment longer than necessary exposing herself to its haz-
ards. Nervously, Grace memorized her story, making sure
she was confident of the role she was about to play in front
of Lady Constance.

At last, the grand door was opened, and an unsmiling
woman blinked at them in the failing light.

'You have come to see Lady Constance.' A flat statement.
The speaker was elderly with white hair, dressed sombrely
in black, her only adornment a small golden crucifix around
her neck.

Lady Bunty produced an elaborate visiting card, embellished with hearts and an entwined R and B, chosen to

represent the supposedly happy union between herself and Lord Jaggers. 'I'm Lady Bunty Jaggers.'

The maid dismissed the card. 'Yes, Lady Jaggers, I know.'

Bunty returned the card to her purse. 'I don't imagine Lady Constance gets many visitors, so they'll have been expecting me,' she hissed in a stage whisper. Grace was sure the maid must have heard.

'Madam will receive you in the drawing room. It's on the first floor.'

They obediently followed her up the stairs.

'Lady Constance is not in the best of health. Thirty minutes of company should be sufficient.'

They nodded in response and entered a large room facing out onto the main street. The room was in semi-darkness and the long damask curtains were partially closed, with candles burning dimly in place of electric lights. Lady Constance was sitting in a straight-backed armchair by the window. She was wearing a burgundy satin day gown. Even from a distance, she had the look of a woman who had artfully arranged herself, the soft darkness creating the illusion of a beauty, unravaged by age. The room was filled with strange perfumes; Grace picked up notes of lily and something spicy. And yet under their scent was something darker: an odour of unaired rooms, doctors' visits and illness.

Even Bunty hesitated at the door, before exclaiming, 'Constance, honey, you look absolutely divine. I swear you have the secret of eternal youth.'

Constance raised her hand in acknowledgement. 'Thank you, Bunty. It is good to see you after so many years.'

'Yes, time flies, doesn't it? Thank you for agreeing to

meet me. This is Grace. A journalistic reporter, who's come to London from the north of England. One of my nieces. As I told you, she is interested in the events of 1900 and 1901. She wants to write an exposé. You know, tell the truth about what happened.'

Grace greeted Constance, who gestured that they should join her by the window. Walking into the room felt like entering another era. Her parents might cling to dated Edwardian furniture, but this room seemed frozen in the reign of Queen Victoria. Photographic portraits of severe men and women lined the walls, unsmiling in black and white, the men with fulsome beards and the women with severely corseted waists.

'Sit there,' Lady Constance commanded and pointed to a sofa, positioned so that the limited daylight in the room fell upon it, while she floated in flattering shade. 'I will ask Maria to bring us something to drink.'

Bunty visibly brightened. 'I've developed quite a taste for cocktails, Constance. Particularly the Manhattan. If you had some whisky, sweet vermouth and bitters, I'm sure it would be possible to rustle one up.' Her request hung hopefully in the air.

'In my home, I never serve alcohol, Lady Bunty. I have long been a member of the Temperance Society.' Her face was set with disapproval.

'Oh Constance, I never thought you'd come over all American on me. You'll be demanding Prohibition next.'

Constance tutted. 'When I think of the suffering I have seen as a result of drink in the homes of the working classes,

I am forced to conclude that Prohibition is altogether a good thing.'

Bunty slumped resignedly back into her chair. 'I'll have tea with lemon, then.'

Now that Grace was closer, she could see that the right side of Constance's face was rigid with the effects of a stroke, her eye half closed. The left side of her face still retained a formidable beauty, although lined with age, while her auburn hair, which she wore pulled back severely, was streaked with white.

Tea was served in fragile china cups decorated with blue roses. Lady Constance sipped carefully from the side of her mouth that was fully mobile. She turned to Grace. 'Your people are the northern Jaggers, aren't they? Bunty said you come from a village near Barnard Castle.'

'Yes, Middleton-in-Teesdale, Lady Constance. It's near to the family estate at Romaldkirk.'

'And you wish to investigate the death of my husband. The terrible lies that were told about him in court and the fact that those responsible for his murder went unpunished?'

Grace nodded.

'Bunty said you write for the *Hampstead & Highgate Express*.'

'Yes, Lady Constance. I've just started there.'

'I didn't think anyone was interested now. Eighteen years ago, there were journalists and writers from the *Pall Mall Gazette*, the *Evening Standard*, *The Times*,' she said, waving her hand dismissively, 'they all wanted to speak to me. They didn't care that I was beaten down with grief at the loss of my husband. They wished to believe the falsehoods about his illicit relationship with that girl, because it made a sensational newspaper story.'

The door opened quietly and Maria said, 'Madam, please don't upset yourself. I have told them they can only be here for thirty minutes.'

Constance shook her head and spoke about the maid as if she were absent: 'Maria has been with me since my girl-hood. She knows the truth. How can I not be upset when I speak of the past? My husband was vilified so that the guilty could walk free.'

'I am so sorry, Lady Constance.' Grace felt increasingly unhappy that she was here under false pretences. If it hadn't been for her desire to understand Elizabeth's role in the case, she would have left.

The older woman struggled for breath. 'Mrs Burdett-Smith, who was on the verge of bankruptcy, somehow hired Sir Benedict Huguenot, the greatest and most expensive barrister of the day, to defend her.'

'He refused to allow Lizzy Burdett-Smith to testify,' Lady Bunty added. She had put her teacup down with an expression of disgust and joined the conversation. 'From what I remember, Huguenot said any evidence against her was purely circumstantial and it was insulting to ask a lady to respond to such questioning.'

'She was not a lady,' Lady Constance said emphatically.

'What was the circumstantial evidence?' Grace asked. Lady Bunty's scrapbook had run out before the crucial information had been revealed.

While Lady Bunty could remember little of the ins and

outs of the case, each detail was burned into Lady Constance's mind.

'The Burdett-Smiths were a notorious couple. They lived on their wits and their marriage was a sham. She was beautiful, that I will grant you, but she used her beauty as a trap. There would be extended flirtations with married men, feverishly planned assignations, and then photographs of them entering boarding houses together. Taken by Captain Burdett-Smith, who would demand a substantial payment for his supposedly injured feelings and his discretion.'

'Blackmail! That was the scandal involving Lizzy!' Bunty exclaimed. 'I knew there was something particularly scurrilous but couldn't quite recall what.' She sat back satisfied, but then the implications struck her. 'Sir Hugh didn't, I mean, there weren't—'

'No, my husband would have repelled any such advances,' she declared. 'He refused to allow her family to visit him at Sloane Street.' She sniffed. 'Very low-class people, much like Lizzy herself.'

'My grandfather was low class, as you call it,' Lady Bunty declared. 'From the slums of Duisburg in the Rhineland. He arrived in America with nothing, but he made his fortune. I find that admirable, not reprehensible.'

'Things are different in America,' Lady Constance said dismissively. 'In any case, Lizzy Burdett-Smith was a slut and an adventuress. In the spring of 1901, a close friend had warned us that there were rumours Captain Burdett-Smith intended to divorce his wife and name my husband as the co-respondent. She would confirm details of the supposed adultery.'

'Why would she do that unless she had had a relationship

with him?' Grace said. 'I apologize but I have to ask,' she added hastily, 'as a reporter.'

Lady Constance composed herself. 'Mrs Burdett-Smith was in the pay of a powerful enemy of my husband, someone who wished to be revenged on him. Perhaps murder was not the original intention, for any allegations of an adulterous affair would undoubtedly have destroyed Hugh's political career.'

'Honey, who do you think that was?' Bunty wanted to know.

'My husband was a noble man and that is a dangerous thing to be in politics. It made him the sworn enemy of Sir Ernest Whitehouse.' She stopped for a moment as she remembered the past. 'He had threatened Sir Hugh, unafraid of any consequences. Yet no one dared to accuse Whitehouse openly. He held many in the Metropolitan Police in his pay and they would not investigate him.'

'Sir Ernest Whitehouse.' Bunty feigned astonishment, although she had already told Grace about him. 'I know there was some talk at the time.'

'But would the Burdett-Smiths really tell such a terrible lie to benefit Sir Ernest Whitehouse?' Grace asked.

'By the winter of 1901, they were living hand to mouth in rented accommodation in Redhill. Their reputation preceeded them. No society hostess would entertain them, and no gentleman would allow himself to be ensnared by Lizzy's beauty.' Lady Constance shuddered. 'They were without morals.'

Grace glanced across at Bunty. None of this was what she had expected to hear.

Lady Constance wrung her hands and continued to speak, 'Yet I am to blame because I sent Hugh to that sordid place. The rumours had caused me such distress that when he showed me the note signed 'L', I insisted he go to Norwood to warn her off. I believe that he then refused to submit to their blackmail demands and was killed as a result.'

A terrible silence descended on the room. Finally, Grace asked, 'What was the evidence against Mrs Burdett-Smith?'

The older woman spoke slowly. 'A train ticket. The police found a return railway ticket to Redhill in the bedroom, dated 17 April, the night of the murder. Redhill is the exact place where the Burdett-Smiths had lodgings. My husband had taken a hansom cab from Westminster, so it could not have been his.'

'The final missing piece in the jigsaw, I believe it was called,' Lady Bunty added helpfully.

'It was not only the ticket that placed her at the scene,' said Lady Constance. 'There was the evidence of the land-lady, Hannah Ryman. She identified Mrs Burdett-Smith as the woman who had hired the room in the name of Mr A. Clarke and had also spoken to her as she entered the back stairs of the Golden Hind on the night of the murder. However, she was veiled, and Huguenot disputed this piece of evidence.'

'It didn't sound good for Lizzy,' Lady Bunty acknowledged.

'Nor did her refusal to say anything during police questioning or in the court. On the instruction of her barrister, she must merely sit in the dock and look beautiful. Too young and angelic to have her delicate neck snapped by the hangman's noose. But when the prosecution called her husband as a witness,' her frail hands were trembling now, and she wiped her eyes with a lace handkerchief, 'he made the most terrible and salacious allegations about my husband.'

'They were quite some allegations, as I seem to remember,' Bunty muttered. Grace pretended not to hear. Perhaps Bunty was feeling bitter at being forced to drink tea and unprepared to behave wholly charitably towards Lady Constance.

'Captain Burdett-Smith saved himself by claiming that Lizzy had acted alone. He invented details of a sordid affair, painting her as a fallen woman who had been ruined by her love for Sir Hugh and driven insane with jealousy when the relationship ended.' Lady Constance's voice shook with anger.

Grace said, 'I believe that you hold documents relating to the murder.'

'Yes, I hold many pieces of evidence. Eighteen years devoted to proving what really happened. Only the determination to redeem my husband's reputation has sustained me through the shame. All the ambitions for good he held, all forgotten. You are very young, Miss Jaggers, and perhaps will not understand how much I want his name to be cleared, to hold my head high in society, without the whispers that have followed me for so many years.'

Grace nodded in sympathy. 'How did you seek to find out the truth?' she asked.

Lady Constance took a sip from the delicate teacup. 'You will know, of course, of the "disputed dates" – the days in the summer of 1900 on which Captain Burdett-Smith claimed his wife was with my husband? He had supposedly discovered the information recorded in her secret diary.'

'I don't know the full details of the case,' Grace was forced to admit.

Lady Constance looked at her more closely. 'You must understand what was alleged. Maria, please bring Miss Jaggers the bundle of documents in the top drawer of Sir Hugh's writing bureau.' When the maid had left the room, she continued, 'I paid thousands of pounds to private detective agencies. I had her – that girl – followed, until she just disappeared from view. Over the years, I sought out all the witnesses and paid them to tell the truth. And for what? Although I could refute almost all of the claims that were laid against him, with sworn evidence of dates and times, bills and receipts, there were some dates I could not. And, of course, there were those who were glad to see my husband brought low.'

Lady Constance's voice was threaded through with bitterness. Grace felt sorry for her, of the years she must have spent alone in the decaying grandeur of a Chelsea town house when society had turned its back on her.

Lady Constance turned to face Grace. 'And you are truly interested in these stories from the past? It's all so long ago for a young woman like you.'

'Yes, I am,' Grace said, hoping she sounded convincing.

'Good.' She tried to smile.

Maria had returned to the room. 'Madam, this is what you requested.'

Constance took the sheaf of papers. 'These are the dates

when Lizzy Burdett-Smith had supposedly been intimate with Sir Hugh. I have found as much evidence as I could for each, and where it is clearly a lie I have noted that too.'

Bunty asked, 'Couldn't you just use Sir Hugh's journal to prove where he was on each of those days?'

'He did not record his appointments in a journal. Something that would have been well known in his circle. It meant we were forced to recreate his movements from the memories of others.'

Grace looked at her in surprise. 'Why wouldn't he do that?'

'He was a man blessed with the finest intellectual powers and could commit to memory any arrangements he had made. It was misrepresented by those who would do him harm as a deliberate attempt to obscure his actions.'

Grace could see how, for a man in his position, not keeping a journal might seem suspicious.

'It was a detail that counted against him in the newspapers, I seem to remember,' Bunty added somewhat indiscreetly. 'Made him look devious.'

In response, Constance gave Grace the papers. She looked at them and asked whether she might write down some of the details. Lady Constance murmured her assent.

Disputed Dates: Summer 1900

24 July 1900: Lizzy B-S claimed she was at London residence. First act of physical intimacy took place in bedroom.

Mrs Keppel, housekeeper, able to swear that LB-S was never there.

26 July 1900: Alleged encounter with Lizzy B-S after visit to the British Museum.

Hugh had a Board of Trade meeting. Both Charles Brewster and Augustus Johnston can vouch for this.

28 July 1900: Lizzy B-S claimed two acts of intimacy took place in a hotel in Brighton.

Unable to retrace Sir Hugh's movements on this day?

After a while, the list of allegations and evidence against them merged into one and she turned to the next document. It was a newspaper clipping and, with a start, Grace realized she was looking at a picture of a much younger Elizabeth. Her hair appeared to be golden, and she was dazzlingly beautiful. She began to read the article.

Testimony Challenged in Dramatic Exchange
Mrs Burdett-Smith booed outside the Old Bailey.
Allegations of 'damnable lies' and a 'Machiavellian plot'
against Sir Hugh Clifton. A dramatic intervention
by Justice Trevelyan

Yesterday morning, Mrs Burdett-Smith was booed and jostled by members of a large crowd gathered outside the Old Bailey. As the closed prison carriage arrived from Holloway, there were shouts of 'Shame on you!' and police constables had to intervene when a man tried to throw a missile in her direction.

Despite this, she looked composed and acknowledged the waiting photographers as she entered the building in the murder case that has scandalized the country.

Mrs Burdett-Smith was accompanied by her counsel, Sir Benedict Huguenot, and was dressed in a frilled white blouse and black fluted skirt. She was wearing a hat embellished with flowers in the palest of pastel pinks and blues.

This was the second day of her husband's evidence as to the alleged relationship between his wife and the victim. When he entered the stand, Captain Burdett-Smith spoke confidently as he swore under oath to tell the truth and nothing but the truth. He drew audible gasps from the public gallery when giving further details of an encounter he had discovered in her diary. She said that on 3 August, Sir Hugh Clifton had taken her to his house at 89 Sloane Street and introduced Clara Bilesdale, a servant, into their shared bed.

Justice Trevelyan then made a most unexpected intervention at the request of Lady Constance Clifton, who could furnish incontrovertible evidence that Sir Hugh was at the Austrian Embassy that night and afterwards went for a late supper at Oscar's. There was an array of distinguished witnesses who could vouch for his presence at both of these venues. Captain Burdett-Smith then said that he might have been mistaken as to that particular date. Lizzy Burdett-Smith was seen to visibly pale in the dock and whispered to one of her wardresses that she felt faint. As a result, the proceedings were adjourned early and will recommence at nine o'clock tomorrow morning.

A source close to the investigation has sensationally claimed that Sir Hugh's murder was the unintended result of a 'Machiavellian plot designed to destroy his political career and advance the interests of his enemies.' Those involved in this supposed plot are known to the *Pall Mall Gazette* but we are unable to publish their names on the instructions of our legal advisors.

'What strange reading!' Grace exclaimed. 'Who was behind the Machiavellian plot?'

'Sir Ernest Whitehouse,' Lady Constance said bitterly. 'Look at the final document.'

It was an invoice from Sir Benedict Huguenot's chambers for the sum of one thousand pounds for the defence of Mrs Burdett-Smith. It was addressed to Sir Ernest Whitehouse. How horrible to realize that Elizabeth had a confirmed association with Sir Hugh's sworn enemy.

Constance now looked at her tearfully. 'I was able to prove her a liar many times over on most of the dates she gave her husband, but that wasn't enough for the sordid world of the newspapers and penny dreadfuls. When you come again, I will find other documents and testimonies.'

'Thank you, that is very kind.'

'Maria will bring me my appointments diary.'

Lady Constance spent several moments perusing its contents, maintaining the pretence of having a full social calendar, although Grace was close enough to see that the pages were blank. 'The earliest date I will be able to see you is Wednesday 8 October. At six o'clock. Is that agreeable? Bunty, it will be delightful to see you again.'

'Yes, of course, Lady Constance,' Grace said.

Lady Bunty muttered her own reluctant agreement.

As they were shown out of the house and into the fresh

air, Grace felt a sense of relief at being free of the oppressive house and its artificial smells and lights.

It was a feeling echoed by Bunty, who said, 'I always found Constance Clifton to be a cold creature. Why have I agreed to return to that mausoleum and drink more tea? Are you really sure you want to see her again?'

'I want to understand what happened. Perhaps the truth is buried somewhere in those boxes of documents.' She paused. 'It's so hard to believe that the Elizabeth I knew was a murderess and part of a conspiracy with Sir Ernest White-house. Do you think it possible?'

Bunty looked directly at Grace. 'I don't know. Lizzy was ambitious and there was a ruthlessness about her. She was close to Sir Ernest Whitehouse and he was an immoral man.' She shivered and opened the door of her motor car. 'Now, I must get out of the dreadful open air before my skin positively shrivels. If I wasn't so angry with Rodolpho, I'd double his salary rather than have to drive this thing. Would you like me to take you any place?'

Grace looked at the car's precarious position, right in the middle of the road.

'Bunty, that's very kind, but no thank you.'

CHAPTER TWENTY-TWO

As they had agreed, Grace and Tom met at Norwood Junction station and then found a small tea room nearby, just off Portland Road. She noticed that he looked tired, but when she tried to ask if everything was all right, he brushed aside her question, saying, 'It's nothing you'd understand.' He ordered tea and iced buns for them, then fell silent.

'I'm still hoping to find Elizabeth's family before the funeral,' she began.

He looked up. 'Do you think that's possible?'

'I don't know. The inquest has been delayed, so we have more time.'

'But I don't see how coming to South Norwood is going to help.' He was clearly in a low mood today. 'Grace, it was a long time ago. What new facts could you discover?'

'I'm not sure but surely it's too much of a coincidence. Elizabeth died in mysterious circumstances and was involved with an infamous murder in the past.' She looked at him directly. 'I'm sure there must be a link.'

The waitress had brought over their order. He took a

mouthful of iced bun and chewed before replying. 'Perhaps you're right, Grace. Does the Golden Hind still exist?'

'It's in the London telephone directory, so yes. Although, I'm actually not quite sure what we should do. Do you think we should tell them we're interested in the murder?'

'Maybe not,' he laughed, putting down his cup of tea. 'So, what do you know already?'

She took out the notebook from her bag and told him what she had discovered from the newspaper articles, conversations and Lady Constance's documents. The Lizzy Burdett-Smith they had revealed seemed hard and brittle, defiant as she entered the Old Bailey despite being accused of murder, nothing like the real Elizabeth.

After listening carefully he said, 'So, there are Mr and Mrs Ryman who might be witnesses?'

'Yes. Mrs Ryman would probably be the more important. She testified that Elizabeth had booked the room several days before and returned on the night of the murder.'

'Which would be eighteen years ago. Well, we can try to see if they are still at the Golden Hind. I think we should visit the room where the murder took place.'

Grace shivered. It seemed rather gruesome but perhaps it would help her to understand what had happened.

The public house was a short walk from the station. Grace was surprised at how large it was. A substantial Victorian building, although a little dilapidated, it was set back from the busy road, meaning that it was a shaded and private place. They tried to imagine how it might have changed and what it must have been like on the night of the murder.

At the side was a narrow alleyway and they walked down it to find a plain locked door.

'Do you think this leads to the back stairs?' Grace asked. 'It's very hidden away.'

Tom went to open the door and a stout middle-aged woman suddenly appeared, coming round the corner from the front of the building.

'What the 'ell d'you think you're doing? Breaking and entering?' She was carrying a heavy shopping basket, which she put down indignantly.

'We're looking to see whether you've any rooms to let. We thought they might be round the back,' Tom improvized, in his cut-glass accent.

She was still looking at them suspiciously. 'You're not from round 'ere, are you?'

'No, north London,' Tom replied.

'I see, you want a bit of privacy, do you, away from your usual haunts?' She had now relented a little. 'I'm Mrs Alder, the landlady. Will you be renting the room by the hour or by the day? We've got three rooms upstairs and they're all available at the moment.'

So Mrs Ryman had gone, Grace thought. They had lost their most important connection to the past.

'Could we see them first?' she asked. 'Before we make up our minds. We'd like the largest room, if we may.' That was the room, according to the newspapers, where Sir Hugh had been killed.

'Yes, 'course you can. I'll just put this basket down in the kitchen and get the key. It's very private here. We don't ask no questions.' She picked up her shopping before disappearing around to the front of the building.

'She thinks we're here for some kind of assignation!' Grace exclaimed.

'And they rent rooms out by the hour. What kind of a place have you brought me to, Grace?'

'I can only apologize, Mr Monaghan.'

They both began to laugh, stopping abruptly when the landlady reappeared with a heavy key.

The room she showed them was starkly ordinary. It was at the front and had a bay window overlooking the grey street. A large bed dominated the room and there was very little furniture apart from this, just a washstand with an empty basin and jug and a single armchair. The only distinguishing feature was the elaborate fireplace, which was surrounded by tiles decorated with a small bird in a cage, repeated over and over again.

Grace felt the blood drain from her face. She knew this room, the room where Sir Hugh had been shot and left to die in a pool of his own blood. It was the place drawn so feverishly by Elizabeth in the dull greys and blacks of charcoal on a summer day long ago. The pictures she had snatched from Grace and been so determined to hide. The nightmarish images of fear and entrapment. She knew with certainty that Elizabeth had been in this room before.

Mrs Alders carried on oblivious to the horror on Grace's face. She pulled back the threadbare curtains. 'A nice room this. Good and spacious. We can talk terms if it's what you're looking for.'

'Does Stephen Ryman still work here?' Tom asked.

'Stephen, he's long dead. Over eight years now. Did you know him?' the woman asked, without any obvious interest. She rubbed dust off the washstand with the side of her sleeve.

'Not directly, but wasn't he in the newspapers? When there was a murder here at the Golden Hind,' Tom said.

'Now that really was a long time ago,' the landlady replied, slightly more alert now. 'It's Sir Hugh you mean, isn't it?'

'Mr Monaghan fancies himself as a bit of a Sherlock Holmes,' Grace said, forcing herself to join in the conversation. 'He's very interested in the case. No one was ever convicted, I believe. You're hoping to solve it, aren't you, Tom?'

Tom agreed and the landlady seemed to relax a little. She confided in them: 'It doesn't need solving. Clear as day that Lizzy Burdett-Smith was guilty. She lured him here and it's shocking that she didn't hang. I did my bit, mind.'

'What do you mean?' Grace asked.

'Well, it was me that took the booking for the room. I had to testify at the Old Bailey, in front of everyone.'

'You're Mrs Ryman?' Grace was astonished.

'Well, I was – before Stephen, my first husband, died. They let me keep on the tenancy. When I remarried, Mr Alder became publican.'

'And you're certain it was Lizzy Burdett-Smith who booked the room?' Tom asked.

'I never forget a face or a voice,' she said, 'and I certainly didn't forget hers. She come here all hoity-toity and calling herself Mrs A. Clarke and claiming it was for her husband. I knew exactly what she was booking that room for, and she didn't have the right to look down her nose at me. Not that there's anything wrong with having a bit of private time with loved ones,' she added pointedly, realizing that this might be their situation.

'You saw someone like her on the night of the murder, but heavily veiled?' Grace couldn't bear to think of her friend as guilty.

'It was her all right, her and the others too. She was heavily veiled, but I knew it was her as soon as she opened her mouth.'

'The others?' Grace interrupted. 'Lizzy – I mean, Mrs Burdett-Smith – wasn't alone?' There had been no mention of anyone else being present on the night of the murder.

Mrs Alder paused, as if suspecting she had said too much. 'The superintendent said they knew for definite it was her what was the murderess. It would just muddy the waters if I suddenly started talking about the two men as well.'

'Did you know the men?' Tom asked, astonished at her revelation.

She shook her head. 'No, and I really need to be getting on. Now do you and your lady friend want this room or not, because I don't have all day.'

Tom took Grace's arm. 'We'd just like a few minutes to discuss whether it meets our requirements.'

The woman looked slightly put out but said, 'Well, let me know when you've decided.' She walked out of the room ahead of them. They followed her down the back stairs.

'Why don't we go into the public bar and see whether anyone can remember the night of the murder or those two men? We can pretend to be discussing whether the room is suitable,' Tom suggested.

They opened the door and were engulfed in a cloud of tobacco smoke and sour hops. Even though it was not yet four o'clock in the afternoon, the bar was crowded with men huddled over their pints of beer and stout. Grace was the only woman there and she could feel the hostile stares of the drinkers. Her confidence evaporated a little, and she stood closer to Tom.

At the bar, the publican was wiping a glass on his grubby white apron. Without even looking up, he said, 'It's the lounge only for ladies. She shouldn't be here.'

'We don't want a drink,' Tom said. 'We're trying to find information about the murder that took place here in 1901. Sir Hugh Clifton.'

The publican selected another glass and held it up for inspection. 'If you don't want nothing to drink, then a public house ain't the right place for you.'

'We wondered if you were here at the time of the death.' Grace replied.

'I've lived in South Norwood for the last thirty years,' he said. 'I won't talk about Sir Hugh, and you'll find that nobody else here will.'

'Mrs Alder said—' Grace began.

'Sometimes my dear wife don't know when to be quiet.' He turned away and a threatening silence fell across the room.

In the corner of Grace's vision she saw someone walking towards them. A large man with a shaved head. 'These two causing you a problem?' he asked the publican.

'I'd just like to know who sent 'em,' he replied. 'They're asking about the murder.'

'Nobody's sent us,' Grace told him. 'We just want to—'

'I don't care what you want. I don't need nobody agitating my customers or my wife, so get yourselves off of the premises.'

'But—' she started to say.

'You heard him,' the second man added. 'You're not wanted here. No one needs to stir up things that are finished with. You might find that you bring a lot of trouble on yourselves.' There was a cold edge to the man's words, and she was aware that the drinkers in the pub were waiting to see how she and Tom responded. The air was thick with menace, and she felt her breathing become shallow in the silence that surrounded them.

'Grace, I think we should go.'

The publican followed them with his eyes as they walked towards the door and out into the daylight.

Once they were outside, Grace exclaimed, 'What did we just walk into there? It was like a chamber of horrors!'

Tom nodded grimly. 'There must be secrets about the murder of Sir Hugh that are still dangerous all these years later.'

'The two men,' Grace said. 'We need to know who they were. And Elizabeth had definitely been in that room before, Tom, I know that for certain. Years ago, she drew it exactly as it is, but there was nobody in it.'

'Really,' he said interested, 'although we don't know whether she was there on the night of the shooting.'

'No,' she had to concede.

CHAPTER TWENTY-THREE

As they walked back to the railway station, they were both lost in thought until Grace suddenly glimpsed a man on the other side of the street. He was young, probably in his twenties and, at first glance, there was nothing remarkable about him. It was only when your eyes lingered for a moment longer that it became apparent how different he was. The centre of his face was frozen. Not living, moving flesh, but a rigid veneer made of galvanized metal, with his nose and cheeks painted on in unnatural shades of pink. His terrified eyes peered from the top of the mask.

The familiar horror of recognition overcame Grace. She slumped against the wall, breathing hard, pale and shaking. 'Tom, I'd like to stop for a moment. Do you mind?'

'What's the matter, Grace?' he asked and followed her gaze. 'God help him. His face must have been destroyed in the war.'

The man had learned to make himself deliberately oblivious to all stares as he walked through the Saturday crowd, but perhaps he realized their eyes were on him. He turned sharply into a shop and out of view.

'I didn't mean to make him feel ashamed,' she said, feeling distraught. 'It's just . . . I can't bear to see it because of Edward.'

'What do you mean?' he asked.

'It makes me remember what happened.' She didn't want to look at him. Her anguish would have been too clear.

'Edward?' He came and stood next to her. 'What's the matter? Tell me, Grace, please.'

At first she found it hard to speak; she had that familiar sick feeling in her stomach. 'Let me take a minute to calm myself.' She paused, trying to control her shaking, and looked up at him, hesitating. 'You were there when he was hit by shrapnel at Ypres, weren't you?'

He nodded. 'Not when it actually happened, but I knew about it afterwards.'

'It was his face that took the brunt of it. His nose, his mouth, half of it was blown away. I suppose something similar had happened to that poor man we've just seen. Edward was so handsome. I used to tease him about being vain.' She paused. 'He was sent to the Queen's Hospital, out in Sidcup. It specializes in facial surgery. He was desperate to look like himself again and had several operations. But his face was too damaged.' She put her head in her hands. 'The doctors wanted to fit him with a tin face, but he demanded one more operation.'

She could see that Tom was looking at her intently. 'There wasn't really anything they could do, and he died under anaesthetic. I don't think he wanted to live in the end. Not enough to fight against his own body anyway.'

'Poor Edward,' Tom said quietly. 'He lost touch with all of us once he was back in England.'

She nodded. 'He cut himself off from the world. I have awful memories of travelling out to Queen's Hospital. He would sit silent in his chair, his face hidden in bandages. It was worse for Mother. She was there more frequently, and I think it destroyed her mind to see her son quite broken.'

'You don't often talk about your mother,' he prompted.

'I find it hard to speak about that time. It was too dreadful.' How much should she tell him? 'Mother was so terribly unhappy and so furious at the same time. I think she became quite mad. Edward had just died – wasted away before her eyes.' She remembered the bleak desolation of last December. 'After the Armistice, just before Christmas, there was a memorial service at his old school for the alumni who had died. With hindsight, it was too soon. Mother's grief was too raw. She started crying in the middle of the eulogy and walked out of the church. Father and I followed. She screamed at us that Edward's life and those of all the other boys had been pointlessly wasted.'

'That must have been very hard for you, Grace. And for your father,' he had the tact to add after a moment's thought.

'Yes, it's very important for Father to believe that Edward's death had a value.'

'But I agree with your mother,' Tom said, quietly. 'It was a waste.'

'Perhaps.' Grace took a deep breath and forced herself to speak more calmly. 'All I know is that my loving mother disappeared overnight. She stopped talking, she stopped caring very much about anything. All she could do was cry all day and hold Edward's pillow from the hospital.'

'Where is she now?'

'At a private nursing home in Worthing that specializes in nervous disorders. Lady Bunty, my mother's friend, is worried she's being sedated too heavily. She just doesn't seem to be getting any better.'

'Maybe she needs to be with her family and not locked away in a nursing home.' He let the words trail away. Perhaps realizing how insensitive he was being, he then asked, 'How do you feel?'

'That I miss Mother very much,' she said. 'She has refused to see me. I'm hoping she comes home to us soon. The house is so empty.'

He shook his head. 'You've had a bad time of it, Grace.'

'Is there really anyone of our age who hasn't?' She smiled weakly and stood up straight.

They walked back to the station, not speaking but with a new understanding established between them.

Tom broke the silence. 'Do you believe what the landlady said about Elizabeth being there that night? And the two men?'

'She had no reason to lie, but the woman didn't have to be Elizabeth. It could have been someone who looked like her, especially if she was veiled on the night of the murder.'

Tom looked a little sceptical. 'She recognized her voice, though. I wonder whether it was Sir Ernest or Captain Burdett-Smith who were also there. We could show Mrs Alder a picture and see if she recognizes them.'

'Assuming she wants to speak to us again. I think she might regret being so open,' she said. 'Her husband certainly wasn't forthcoming.'

'No,' he agreed. 'Look, I'm going to be out of London for a while. There's no more painting work at the moment which means I can't afford to pay for my lodgings. So it seems a good excuse to go home to Yarm to see my mam. I'll try to telephone to see if you find out anything further.'

Grace suddenly felt even more despondent. She wondered if the lack of work explained his pallor and the way he had wolfed down his bun at the café. Suddenly, she had an idea. 'Tom, Arthur said you were a pretty good driver in the war. Well, my mother's friend Lady Bunty is looking for a chauffeur. It would be a well-paid position and secure. Would you like me to ask her?'

'I'm not a charity case, Grace. Don't patronize me.'

'I'm not patronizing you,' she protested. 'And why do you always reject help when someone offers it to you?'

'What do you mean?'

'Arthur told me that the Royal College of Music offered you a place on the composing course, with a full scholarship, and you turned it down.'

'He did, did he?' Now it was Tom's turn to sound angry. 'I suppose he told you why.'

She shook her head.

'Having lived through the horror and destruction of the trenches, I didn't feel that this is a world where music, or love, or anything good belongs. There's nothing left to say that could take away the horror of that war. Certainly, there's no music that could drown out what happened.' He turned to go.

She felt sorry for him and didn't know what to say. He was too proud to accept sympathy. Instead, she fished in her handbag and took out her address book.

'Look, here's Bunty's telephone number. You can contact her if you want. It's a job if you change your mind.'

He nodded reluctantly and took the piece of paper. 'Goodbye, Grace. I'll be in touch.'

'Goodbye,' she replied, distressed that they were parting on such a bad note.

Her dreams were haunted again that night. She returned once more to the desolate scene of the battlefield, a place she had come to think of as the staging post between the living and the dead. It had the feeling of a sepia photograph, but rather than being washed through with brown, it was overlaid with the red of blood. It was a blasted and devastated place. Dead stumps of trees, shorn of any green leaves, held their skeletal branches up to the bleak sky. In this dreadful landscape she saw three figures. Black silhouettes against the crimson. When they turned to face her, each wore a face of tin. Robert, Elizabeth and now Edward. As in a dumb show, Elizabeth mimed the actions of weeping and the two men moved to console her.

Grace tried to call out to them, but no matter how loud she shouted, no sound came. She could only watch from a distance. The woman began to shake her head vehemently and then she turned again towards Grace, although not acknowledging her. She began to rip at the metallic mask that covered her face, desperately trying to remove it. When the men saw what she was doing, they stopped and began to remonstrate with her, turning her roughly from Grace and leading Elizabeth away, into the horizon between the land and sky until they had all disappeared.

CHAPTER TWENTY-FOUR

That Monday, Grace spoke to Miss Boddy to request a week's leave so that she could visit her mother. The office manager was unsympathetic. Roger Dale was still on his Paris jaunt, as she called it, and the periodical was hopelessly understaffed. However, when her father received an unexpected telegram from the proprietor of Seaview Nursing Home stating that Isobel Armstrong would like to see her daughter, Grace telephoned Uncle Neville and arranged to go at the end of the week. She ignored Vera Boddy's mutterings about flighty young things who felt they could come and go as they pleased and prayed that her mother was now on the road to recovery.

As the train pulled into Worthing, Grace reflected that there is nothing more melancholy than a seaside resort once the summer crowds have gone. The platform was deserted, except for a solitary seagull, and a grey sea mist blotted the horizon. She hadn't visited her mother since the end of July, two months ago. The silent telephone calls and letters that went unanswered were no substitute for seeing her mother in the flesh. Guiltily, she wondered whether she should have ignored the proprietor and her mother's insistence that there were to be no visitors and fought harder to see her. Perhaps Grace had been too fast to accept the excuse it offered, a defence against the hopelessness of watching the brilliant, vibrant Isobel reduced to a husk of herself. But her mother wanted to see her, she reminded herself; surely that was an optimistic sign. Perhaps Mother was ready to return to the living.

Seaview Nursing Home was a former hotel which had an air of decaying grandeur and a saltwater swimming pool in the grounds. They had been lucky to get Isobel Armstrong a place there, the brisk proprietor, Mrs Pickford, had informed them last December. Very few nursing homes were able to offer their range of therapeutic and medical facilities, with a dedicated doctor on the site. Since the war, they had been swamped by families desperate to secure the home's services for those whose peace of mind was destroyed. Some were much worse off than Mrs Armstrong, she continued. Mrs Wilkinson, the lady in the room adjacent to hers, had lost all three sons in the war and had been totally mute when she arrived at Seaview. With gentle exercise and a regime of sedation, she was slowly learning to speak again. It was to be hoped that Isobel Armstrong would make a similar recovery.

The place had filled Grace with dismay from the start, but it had come highly recommended and claimed impressive rates of success. Father told her that he had been shown a folder of letters of gratitude from families whose broken relatives had been put back together by its services. He just wanted his wife to be well again.

The home's motor car was waiting outside the railway station and rattled along the narrow roads to their destination. As soon as Grace arrived, she was greeted by Mrs Pickford, a tall blonde woman who was impeccably dressed in different shades of mauve. 'I must speak to you urgently, Miss Armstrong, before you see your mother. Please could you come into my office?'

As they sat down, Grace felt her heart sink. 'Is Mother very unwell? I had hoped the fact she wanted to see me meant that she was starting to recover.'

'I'm afraid, Miss Armstrong, there has been a most marked deterioration. I believe you were a VAD during the war?' Mrs Pickford tapped immaculately manicured nails on her desk.

'Yes, I nursed at the First Camberwell,' Grace confirmed. 'A marked deterioration—'

Mrs Pickford interrupted her sharply. 'Then you will know the absolute importance of patients taking their medication and following doctors' orders. Your mother has been prescribed a high dosage of Veronal to help her sleep and sedate her nervous disorder. Since the unexpected visit of some American lady—'

'Lady Bunty Jaggers,' Grace supplied.

'Yes, that's right. Well, after the visit of that woman, Mrs Armstrong began refusing to take her doses of Veronal and has been trying to hide her medication, despite our most robust vigilance. Such behaviour is against the regulations at Seaview and can only be likened to a form of mutiny.' Mrs Pickford fixed Grace with a steely look. 'You must persuade your mother to restart her regime of medication.'

Grace nodded bleakly. 'I will speak to her.'

'Or else she will have to vacate her room for someone else on the waiting list. I don't need to remind you that there are many who are desperate to reside here. Your mother's actions are causing unrest among the other patients, and I fear her hysteria is returning,' she added, as a parting shot.

It was with trepidation that Grace climbed the sweeping central staircase to the second floor and knocked quietly on the door to her mother's room. To her surprise, her mother said, 'Come in, Grace. It isn't locked.'

Directly opposite the door was the large window facing the sea, which was opened wide, despite the brisk wind. Her mother was sitting on the bed in her hat, gloves and coat, a packed trunk and Gladstone bag in front of her. She stood up and greeted her daughter affectionately and then said, 'She got you, didn't she? That old witch kidnapped you before you even set foot on the stairs. I'd been waiting for you at the window and could see the motor car come up the driveway.'

Grace looked at her mother, her voice filled with concern. 'Mrs Pickford's very worried about you. She said you've stopped taking your sedatives, and you know how important medication is to your recovery.'

Isobel Armstrong's eyes blazed. 'My recovery!' she exclaimed. 'All those wretched pills were doing was numbing me until I couldn't feel anything at all.'

'But you were so unwell.'

She snapped back, 'I certainly won't become well if I stay here, sleeping my life away. It took Bunty's visit to wake me up to that fact.'

For the first time in months, she looked alive, Grace

acknowledged. She had also forgotten how argumentative Isobel Armstrong could be.

'Anyway, I started to flush the pills down the lavatory and tried to wean myself off them.'

Grace went to remonstrate, but her mother stopped her.

'Gradually, I was forced to face the facts of my life. Edward's death was dreadful and a waste. It was the most terrible thing that has ever happened to me, and I'll never fully recover, but I have to go on living. That's why I asked to see you.'

'What do you want me to do?' Grace felt anxious about whatever might follow, but keen to please her mother.

She looked at her directly now and took her daughter's hands. 'This may be too big a request, but I'd like you to come with me to Whitby. I'm still too frail to go there by myself.' Grace hesitated, so her mother continued. 'Brambles Cottage is such a special place and holds so many happy family memories. I think I could begin to heal there – to become myself again.'

Grace couldn't speak for a moment. Finally, she said, 'What about Father? How will he feel about your being up in Yorkshire? And the cottage will be in such a state, none of us has been there since . . .' She was forced to remember. 'The last time we were there was in June 1916.'

When Robert had proposed. When the world was perfect. When the skies were endlessly blue and filled with the cries of curlews. Grace had been unable to return since.

Her mother grasped her hands more tightly. 'Perhaps this is too much for you, Gracie. I can stay at Brambles Cottage alone. It's been cleaned. The Crawfords – you know, the publicans at the Hope and Anchor – they've made it habitable for me. I wrote to them two weeks ago.'

'You seem to have planned it all,' Grace said, still shocked.

'I've been thinking a lot about things, ever since Bunty's visit. It's just that I feel strangely nervous about travelling on the railways alone – ridiculous, I know, when I sailed halfway across the world before I was twenty. Bunty will drive me up there in that new motor car of hers.'

'No!' Grace exclaimed. 'That really wouldn't be a good idea.' The thought of her vulnerable mother being driven by Bunty was simply impossible. 'We can travel together and spend the week by the sea. What could be better than the bracing Yorkshire coast in late September?'

They smiled at each other.

'We can celebrate your birthday there too,' her mother said.

She was twenty-three in a few days' time. With everything that was happening, Grace had almost forgotten about it.

'Now, the next thing we need to do is escape from this place. You'll have to be my accomplice.'

'I must tell Father our plans,' Grace insisted. Despite agreeing to the plan, she felt a nagging anxiety that this was too soon for her mother to leave the nursing home.

Isobel made a small gesture with her hands. For the first time, Grace noticed that her wedding finger was bare. 'Yes, of course. He has a right to know,' she said.

It would be hard to describe the look of horror on Mrs Pickford's face as Grace and her mother asked that the Seaview Nursing Home motor car should be used to deliver them to Worthing railway station so they could catch the train to London and then on to Whitby.

'It's irregular, very irregular,' she muttered, 'but probably for the best given your wilful refusal to follow the Seaview regime of medication.'

As they drove along the country roads of Worthing, they laughed together and sang songs from holidays long ago. Grace had a feeling of liberation. However, during the journey to the north, she became less sure that they were doing the right thing. Her mother was still pale and weak. She slept for much of the time, lying awkwardly against the railway carriage seat, and cried out fitfully in her sleep. At King's Cross station, Grace had telephoned her father, who was furious and accused her of endangering her mother's health. She felt miserably caught between them. At Isobel's insistence, she had also telephoned the Hope and Anchor to arrange transport from the train station.

They had broken the journey by staying overnight at Doncaster and arrived late the next morning. Brambles Cottage was cold and damp, despite the best efforts of the Crawfords. In an act of recklessness, her mother threw open the windows to rid the place of its musty smell and fill it with sea air. They went for a long walk along the deserted beach, walking with their heads bowed and arms linked together in the strong north-easterly breeze.

Firewood and a basket of food had been left for them in the kitchen. Grace lit a blazing fire in the small sitting room when they returned from their walk. The cottage had no electricity, so they sat before the fire, propped up on cushions and wrapped in blankets, having decided to sleep in this room on the first night, until they had managed to warm the cottage through. They toasted bread, which they ate with salted butter and raspberry jam, and boiled a kettle to make endless cups of tea. The fire's warm orange flames illuminated their faces, casting them partly into shadow as they talked for hours.

It felt easier to speak in this half-light and it reminded Grace of childhood and the security of her life before. The last few years had been terrible. There had been so much death, so much loss. The way that they had all lived had been thrown into chaos. It was a relief to steal a few moments of contentment, all the more precious because she knew how quickly happiness and security could disappear.

At first, it was too painful and too early to talk about Edward and Robert, whose past selves still haunted the cottage. The memories of Elizabeth were also raw. As were all the dreams and hopes that had died alongside them. Instead, Grace told her mother about Arthur and his declaration of love.

Isobel stared into the fire for a few minutes before saying, 'I always knew Arthur had feelings for you. Edward thought so too.' Then she turned to face Grace. 'If you want me to be honest, I think that you're much more suited to Arthur than you ever were to Robert.'

'Why do you say that?'

Her mother shrugged her shoulders. 'I don't know. A mother's instinct. There was always something rather aloof about Robert. Oh, he was very charming and charismatic,' she added hastily, 'but I never felt I knew him. I think Arthur loves you and would make you happy,' she concluded.

'That's what Tom said,' Grace replied.

'Who's Tom?'

'He was an officer alongside Edward and was with him at Ypres. He's been helping me find out about Elizabeth. I do so hope that her family will come to the funeral.'

Isobel grasped her daughter's hand. 'I'm very sorry about Elizabeth. I know you were close to her. Have you found out anything more about the Lizzy Burdett-Smith connection?'

'A little,' Grace responded. 'Bunty has been helping me. Did Elizabeth ever tell you anything about her past?'

'No,' her mother said thoughtfully, 'but I did always get the sense that her life before Tufnell Park had been very different.'

'In what way?' Grace asked.

Her mother shrugged. 'Little things, I suppose. Places she'd been or things that she'd done. I suspected that she must have been wealthy when she was younger.'

'Did she really say nothing else?'

'No, Gracie, and I didn't like to probe. She was quite guarded about her past and always seemed so sad. Poor Elizabeth, to have to hide her identity and live with such a secret. I can't believe she was capable of murder.'

The flames were starting to die down. Outside the magic glow of the fire, the rest of the room was now deep in darkness and becoming cold. They were both tired.

'Mother, I trusted Elizabeth completely and yet everything she told me was a lie.'

Her mother turned to look at her. 'She must have had her reasons. Don't judge her too harshly.'

'It's myself I'm judging harshly! What if I'm a bad judge of character?' she asked. 'I was so close to her but the Lizzy in the newspapers and the one spoken of by Lady Constance, and even Bunty, is a thousand miles away from the Elizabeth I knew.'

'You're not a bad judge of character.' Her mother smiled. 'You see the good in everyone and that makes you the best kind of judge of character. Now I think it's time we tried to sleep.'

There were no nightmares that night as she slept curled up in a favourite armchair. Her old life hadn't been restored; it never would be. Edward was gone forever and Elizabeth too. Robert was still missing. Even her mother, although determinedly cheerful most of the time, could sometimes become suddenly silent. Grace had heard her sobbing in the early hours of the morning and knew that no words could console her. But slowly a sense of the future was returning.

The week was spent together, going for long walks across the beach and cleaning the cottage from top to bottom. Grace couldn't help feeling that they were trying to wash away the pain of the past, but it was good to lose herself in physical labour. Gradually and haltingly, they found themselves able to talk about past holidays in Whitby, about Edward and Robert too. On Grace's birthday, her mother took her to Botham's Tea Rooms, a longstanding family tradition, where they celebrated with lemon buns and Earl Grey tea.

Their surroundings, the bleak beauty of the Yorkshire coast in autumn, started to restore them too. The long, bracing walks brought a kind of healing to both women. But Grace still couldn't bring herself to retrace Robert's footsteps, the long walk towards Loftus, before he returned red-faced and declared his love for her. In the same way, her mother still insisted that Edward's bedroom remain just as it was before he left for the last time.

All too quickly, the week came to an end. However, her mother still refused to go back to London. 'I'm not ready to face the world yet, Grace,' she said sadly.

CHAPTER TWENTY-FIVE

That October, the weather turned dull and overcast and London appeared to close in on itself. Grace felt rootless and dissatisfied with her life. Her mother remained in Brambles Cottage. Sian was busy at the hospital and the limited time she had away from the wards was spent with her beau Maurice. Arthur was up in Durham for a couple of weeks. No invitation had been extended to Grace. And Tom still hadn't returned from his visit home. He telephoned once, to see if anything new had been uncovered and to tell her he was trying to find a photograph of Sir Ernest Whitehouse, which was proving to be surprisingly difficult.

On 8 October, as arranged, in the space between the last dregs of summer and the full arrival of autumn, Grace returned to the gloomy house on Sloane Street.

Lady Bunty accompanied her reluctantly. Grace noticed that the yellow car had been replaced by a shining silver model. Seeing the direction of her glance, Bunty commented, 'The steering was faulty on the other car. Took me straight into a tree. The faster that young man Tom returns from Yarm, the sooner I'll have a chauffeur again.'

'Tom got in touch?' Grace was amazed.

'Why yes, Gracie, a week or so ago. Didn't he tell you? We agreed he could try out for the position from this Friday onwards.'

'That's nice,' she replied weakly, annoyed that he hadn't let her know.

Bunty then asked in great detail about her mother and said how relieved she was that Isobel had escaped from Seaview Nursing Home. 'Although I am worried about the amount of time she's spending in the fresh air of Whitby. She tells me she goes walking every day, and it will destroy her skin!'

'I wish she would return to Tufnell Park,' Grace said in response.

Bunty didn't reply to this, but instead said, 'Honey, I cannot believe I am being forced to endure two visits. Yes, two visits,' – she shook a gloved hand at Grace – 'to sit and make frigid small talk with Lady Constance. You owe me for this, Grace.'

The procedure was the same as the first time. Maria showed them into the shaded sitting room, where Lady Constance had composed herself by the window.

She nodded regally. 'I have instructed Maria to bring us tea before you begin your research, Grace.' She turned to Bunty. 'And while your niece is thus engaged, I have brought out some pamphlets on universal suffrage that may be of interest to you. We may review them together.'

It would be impossible to think of a pursuit more ill-suited to Bunty, and Grace speculated that Lady Constance might be demonstrating a highly developed sense of irony.

The room itself was warm and soporific, and Grace felt clumsy as she drank tea from the delicate cup, all the time aware of Lady Constance's eyes upon her.

'I have tried to put the documents into a kind of order. I want you to see that the plot hatched by Lizzy and her accomplices was to blackmail my husband. It was always monetary and never a failed love affair.' Her desire for vindication was palpable.

'Hugh and I had waited over twenty years to be together. So much of our lives wasted, until we were finally both free to marry.' She clasped her hands, before looking directly at Grace. 'We enjoyed such a short period of happiness. I knew finally what it was to be loved as a woman. We were at the centre of society in London. Our world was politics, most especially the battle to obtain suffrage for women. Sometimes I think that we would have gained the vote before 1918 if Hugh had not been so brutally killed. He was so persuasive and articulate. If you had known him . . .' She paused and took a breath. 'If only you had known him.'

'It must have been very difficult for you, Lady Constance,' Grace sympathized.

'Did you ever wonder whether he might have been involved with her? Lizzy was a beautiful girl,' Bunty commented, somewhat tactlessly, Grace thought. 'And men stray all the time. Lord Jaggers has had what he believes is a secret liaison with a dressmaker in Darlington for the last ten years.'

'I know that Lizzy Burdett-Smith was a liar. Maria will show you to Sir Hugh's study, Miss Jaggers.' She turned away, seemingly wearied.

Maria led her down the hall and unlocked an oak door. It was an immaculate shrine to the dead husband. On the bookshelves stood political tomes and copies of Hansard. The writing bureau was neatly set out, as if awaiting his return from the House of Commons, with the blotter and ink pot ready to sign off on some ministerial dispatch. A formal photograph of Hugh and Constance taken on their wedding day was the only evidence of a personal life.

Maria pointed to the bureau. 'The documents are all there.'

'Thank you,' Grace said.

'Please let me know if you require anything.' Maria left, closing the door firmly behind her.

Grace began to look through the papers. They were arranged chronologically and included bundles of letters, court documents and newspaper cuttings tied in a black silk ribbon, with the earliest documents dating to 1900. In some places, Lady Constance had simply noted what the item was and its date; in others she had added a furious commentary in black ink.

At first, there was little of interest. A series of sworn statements obtained over several years, which seemed to confirm that a relationship between Sir Hugh and Lizzy could not be possible, certainly not for many of the key dates. The evidence was from a range of sources: his parliamentary undersecretary; housekeepers and waiters at Claridge's; a stable boy whose job was to prepare Sir Hugh's horse for a ride in Hyde Park.

Grace was surprised to see Hannah Ryman's original police statement, taken soon after the murder. It was covered in corrections and crossings out, which made it difficult to understand, but it supported her claim that the room was booked by a woman, who she later identified as Lizzy Burdett-Smith. Furthermore, she said that the same woman had returned heavily veiled on the night of the murder but that she had recognized her voice.

At the very end of the document, in the faintest of pencil, was a note. 'Exclude extraneous details from court case. Males unknown and not relevant to the murder.' She must tell Tom this. The statement confirmed what the landlady had said, but it also raised a number of questions. Why had the police dismissed the two men from their investigation? And, most significantly, if Lizzy had been there with two other people, why hadn't she revealed their identities?

Grace replaced the documents neatly in order. For much of the summer, it seemed Sir Hugh's whereabouts could be proved, but there were still a number of missing days. Separate from the main bundles of papers was a single envelope. Inside was a sheet of paper, which was marked 'Strictly Private and Confidential.'

She held it for a moment, hardly daring to read.

Police Intelligence Report on Captain and Mrs Burdett-Smith : Highly Confidential
Date 15 May 1901
Informant (Central)

Reliable police sources indicate that <u>at least four men</u> of social standing were most likely blackmailed by Captain and Mrs

Burdett-Smith between September 1899 and December 1900. Unverified gossip puts the figure closer to six.

Probable – Sir Peregrine Mottram, Rev. Charles Wentworth, Albert Chalcott, George Spencer.

Possible – Sir William Hardy, Edward Stevenson-White.

In each case, a similar modus operandi was used by the perpetrators. Mrs Burdett-Smith ('Lizzy') would form a flirtatious attachment to an older married man and engineer a series of seemingly spontaneous meetings, where she would flatter him. These would progress until the victim was persuaded to travel away for a weekend (Brighton was the usual choice), with the enticement being the prospect of a sexual liaison with Mrs Burdett-Smith.

Captain Burdett-Smith would then apprehend the victim and 'Lizzy', before any such activity could take place, claiming to be shocked by his wife's infidelity. He would obtain photographic evidence of the meeting, often in a hotel bedroom, and threaten to make public the indiscretion.

It has proved <u>very</u> difficult to obtain any concrete evidence of these blackmails. Both husband and wife seem to have been skilled in their joint enterprise and selected victims who had much to lose by disclosure of their intended adultery. In all cases, it is believed that the victims paid up in order to avoid disgrace.

It is possible to identify cash transactions which most likely relate to the blackmail, but in each case, the married male victim has given a valid reason for the payment, for example, Sir Peregrine Mottram is prepared to swear under oath that the transfer of two thousand pounds to Captain

Burdett-Smith was related to the sale of thoroughbred horses. We believe that the destruction of photographs was a condition of payment made by the victims. Certainly, we have been unable to locate any such photographs.

None of the named men is prepared to testify in court and all deny that they were blackmailed. Although the inclusion of this evidence in Sir Hugh's murder trial would give a more accurate representation of the coarseness of Mrs Burdett-Smith's moral character (and that of her husband), we have been advised that it would be impossible to compel such reluctant witnesses.

Grace sat for several minutes, thinking about Elizabeth. How could she reconcile her loving, kind friend with the dark double, who leered out at her from the police documents?

As she was about to replace the piece of paper, a sheet that had been caught behind it fluttered to the floor. A solicitor's letter and another sworn statement, that of a Mr Archibald Pratchett. Scrawled across it were the words, 'Even her own family knew her for a liar!'

The letter itself was couched in the dry language of the courtroom:

I am related to Lizzy Burdett-Smith through marriage. My wife is her sister, Adele Pratchett, née Howard. I can vouch that on the date of 17 April 1901, Lizzy Burdett-Smith did not stay in our home at 75 Admiral Avenue, Penge, South London, despite her claiming to have done so in an interview with the Metropolitan Police. Therefore, I am unable to support the alibi she has given in relation to the murder of Sir Hugh Clifton. Signed and witnessed, 5 May 1901.

She looked at the letter. Lizzy had a sister and there was a potential address for her. It was dated more than eighteen years ago, but even if she no longer lived in Penge, neighbours might know something of the family. She scribbled down the details and went to rejoin Lady Constance and Bunty.

In the stuffy heat of that darkened room, Bunty was asleep. Her mouth was partly open and gentle snores broke the silence of the house. Lady Constance was gazing out of the window but as soon as Grace entered the sitting room, she turned around and demanded of her, 'Do you believe now that my husband was cruelly maligned in court? Will the proof be sufficient for your editor?' Propped up on her silken cushions, it was clear that she had been tensely awaiting Grace's return.

'There were many who testified against her. Even her brother-in-law.'

'Ah, yes, Archibald Pratchett. He was a solicitor and a man of stern principle. He would not allow her false alibi to stand.' Passion briefly animated her pale face and she raised her voice.

Bunty started in her sleep and opened her eyes for a moment. Constance looked across at her with contempt.

'Thank you, Lady Constance, for showing me the

evidence. There is much to think about.' Grace had seen too many documents and been confronted with too many truths. She wanted to be away from this oppressive room so that she could think freely. She needed to decide who Elizabeth really was.

'It must be obvious to you, Miss Jaggers, that the Burdett-Smiths and Sir Ernest colluded against my dear husband to destroy him. Whitehouse had long been jealous of the way that Hugh's star burned so much more brightly than his own. He would have gladly used this lying girl to bring him down.'

Maria was suddenly there. 'You have made madam speak for too long. I think now is the time to leave.'

'But you will return,' said Lady Constance, a note of desperation in her voice. 'A heavy burden lies on my heart until Hugh is publicly vindicated.'

As soon as Lady Bunty had been woken, she and Grace left. The second they were out on Sloane Street, she exclaimed, 'I will never go back to that mausoleum again, Grace, never. She made me listen to her interminable political tracts. Constance has become more obsessed as time has gone on. No, I've done my duty by you.'

'I am grateful, Bunty. Really. I won't make you go there again.'

Placated, she hugged Grace and set off in the motor car, having passed on her love to Grace's mother and made her promise to stay in touch. 'You must come over. What about Sunday the 19th,' she suggested. 'Maybe about lunchtime. Your Tom should have arrived by then.'

Before she had a chance to reply, Bunty had disappeared, accompanied by bangs and crashing gears.

When she arrived home, there was a scribbled message in her father's hand. 'PC Alston. Contact about release of ES body. Signature will be needed. Cloak Lane.' The coroner must finally be about to rule on Elizabeth's death.

CHAPTER TWENTY-SIX

As she had arranged with Lady Bunty, Grace arrived at Cheyne Walk the following Sunday, where she found Tom washing the silver car on the road at the front of the house.

'Lovely car, this,' he said, smiling up at her. 'Good to see you, Grace. Did you enjoy yourself with your mother?'

'You could have told me you'd taken the position,' she said. 'I felt foolish, not knowing.'

He looked a bit taken aback and then said sheepishly, 'I'm sorry. You're right, I should have telephoned you. Thanks for the tip about the job. I like Lady Bunty. She's not at all stuck up.'

'No,' Grace agreed, deciding to forgive him. 'And I did have a good time, thank you. Mother decided to escape the nursing home and we stayed the week at Brambles Cottage in Whitby. It's where we spent our childhood holidays.'

'I'm glad to hear it. Your mother sounds as if she's quite a character. Bunty often talks about her.'

'Oh, she is,' Grace laughed, surprised at how easy it was

to speak to Tom, even though they hadn't seen each other for several weeks.

'And you look happier,' he said.

She nodded. 'Yes, I think I am, although I wish Mother would decide to come home. What about you? How was Yarm?'

'I caught up with friends and it was good to see Mam, although she won't stop nagging me about giving up on music.'

'I'm not surprised,' Grace ventured to say.

'Don't you start too,' he said, wringing out the wet cloth. 'Anyway, when you've finished luncheon or whatever it is that her ladyship's got planned, come and see me. I've got something to tell you.'

Mystified, she rang the doorbell and was taken through to Bunty, who was in a particularly exuberant mood. She had managed to find a waiter from the Ritz in Paris, who made even better cocktails than Rodolpho and whom she had employed as a sort of butler. 'Quite frankly, I'm glad to see the back of Rodolpho now. He had terribly bad breath,' she confided, 'and one of my bridge partners told me there were rumours he wasn't Italian at all. His name is actually Rodney and he's from Skegness.'

Over smoked salmon, brown bread and butter and cucumber salad, she chatted away about her round of social events, before suddenly dropping her voice. 'I spoke to your mother on the telephone yesterday. She's starting to sound a little more like her old self.'

'Yes,' Grace agreed, 'and I'm so grateful you warned us about that medication. Mother believes the heavy doses of

Veronal trapped her in grief, rather than letting her come to terms with what's happened.'

'Your mother is a strong woman. She was devastated by Edward's death but she will learn to face it.'

Grace nodded, reassured, before asking, 'Do you think she'll come home?'

Bunty wouldn't quite meet Grace's eye. 'Things will be resolved as they should be, and you must trust in that.' She changed the subject quickly to describe a concert she had attended the previous evening and they began to talk of other things.

When the meal was finished, Grace explained that she was going to speak to Tom.

'I like him,' Bunty declared. 'An intelligent young man and handsome, but a bit too deep for me. Isn't he some kind of musician?'

Grace shook her head. 'In the past, but I don't think he's interested in music any more. I presume he's found out something to do with Elizabeth.'

'I do hope you can exonerate her. It's horrible to think of Lizzy's life ending in such a sad way. But, new information or no, I'm never going back to Lady Constance's. I hope that's understood, Grace.'

'Of course. I think I've found out as much as I can from her, anyway.'

Tom had finished cleaning the car and was sitting at the vast kitchen table when she went to find him. A mug of tea and a newspaper clipping were set in front of him. He asked whether Grace would like something to drink.

'No thanks.' She was impatient to know what he had

discovered but first she told him about Hannah Ryman's police statement and how it confirmed what she said about the presence of two unknown men that night.

'That's exactly what I've been thinking about,' he said. 'I wanted to find photographs of Sir Ernest and Captain Burdett-Smith, to show them to Mrs Alder and see if she could identify them.'

'On the telephone you said it was difficult to find any pictures of Sir Ernest.'

'Almost impossible!' he exclaimed. 'Luckily, it's not the most onerous job in the world being Bunty's chauffeur and I've had quite a bit of time on my hands in the last week, so I've been going to the Reading Room at the British Library. They keep past copies of *The Times* and I looked through them to see whether there was anything relevant.'

'And?' she asked, eagerly.

'Well, I found the death notice and accompanying photograph for Reginald Burdett-Smith. Just as Bunty told you, he died about two years after the murder trial. What was interesting was that he left an estate of twenty thousand pounds.'

'But he was bankrupt in 1901,' Grace said.

'Well, he'd obtained money from somewhere but didn't leave any of it to his wife. It all went to his sister.'

'They definitely weren't reconciled, then,' she responded.

'No, not at all. Then I had to go back to December 1900 to find a photograph of Sir Ernest.'

'You found time to review nearly twenty years' worth of newspapers,' she gasped in astonishment.

He laughed. 'I told you it isn't a very onerous job. Interestingly enough, he was on trial for extortion and making threats to a rival property company. He was defended by Sir Benedict Huguenot . . .'

'Who also defended Lizzy,' Grace continued. 'What happened?'

'The chief witness for the prosecution mysteriously disappeared before he could give evidence. Reading between the lines, foul play was suspected, but there was no body so the police could do very little about it.'

She gasped at this piece of information.

'The case seems to have fallen apart after that. Sir Ernest was found not guilty, but not before Sir Hugh testified against him.'

'Which would explain the animosity between them.'

He nodded. 'I cut out the article when the librarian wasn't looking.'

Grace picked up the newspaper and stared at the photograph. The man in it glared at the camera, his face exuding menace. His mouth was partially open in a forced smile that was more of a grimace. His teeth were chipped and crooked.

'This is just as Bridget described the man who came to see Elizabeth,' she said quietly. 'The man in the Rolls-Royce.'

'She must have been linked with Sir Ernest right up until her death,' he concluded.

'Yes,' she agreed reluctantly.

'It gets worse, I'm afraid,' he said. 'On one of my days without a lot to do I travelled out to South Norwood to see Mrs Alder. I took the photographs with me.'

She looked at him with keen interest now. 'Did she say that they were the men from the murder night?'

He paused. 'Grace, the poor woman was terrified. She

showed me a fading bruise which covered half her face and told me that was what she'd got for being helpful. She swore that she had nothing further to say and didn't want me to come back.'

Grace thought of the brash landlady who'd seemed scared of no one. 'Who could have done that?' she said.

'I tried to ask her, but she began shaking and became tearful. Her husband came over and said you'd brought all this trouble on them.'

'What? Me in particular?' Grace asked.

He nodded. 'He thinks you're being watched. He said they just wanted to live a quiet life and they had no interest in the past.'

'The poor woman,' Grace said, aghast. 'But does he mean I'm being spied on?'

Tom shook his head. 'I don't know. Is it possible someone is following you?'

The thought made her shudder. Perhaps there had been times in the last few months when she'd felt as if she were being observed but had dismissed it. 'If someone is following me, then there must still be secrets about Sir Hugh's murder.' She replied. 'I've got to go back to Cloak Lane police station, to sign the papers to release Elizabeth's body. I can let Constable Alston know what you've found.'

'I'll come with you if you want,' he said. 'It's a difficult thing for you to do alone.'

'Tom, I would really appreciate that.' She had been secretly dreading returning to the police station and had been putting it off. 'I was planning to go after work on Tuesday. Shall I meet you there? At about six o'clock.'

CHAPTER TWENTY-SEVEN

As agreed, they met at the front counter of Cloak Lane police station. The duty officer went to fetch Constable Alston, who ushered them into Sergeant Williams's empty office. Grace introduced the two men and Alston disappeared to get the necessary documents to authorize the release of the body and Elizabeth's personal effects.

He returned with the papers, which Grace reviewed and signed.

'I have found out some information about the deceased,' he said awkwardly, 'now that we know her real name was Lizzy Burdett-Smith. I'm not sure whether you'll like it.'

Grace dreaded what was coming. 'You'd better tell me, Constable.'

'Well, it seems Mr and Mrs Burdett-Smith made their money from luring married men into compromising positions and then blackmailing them.'

'Yes, I've seen a police document that suggested as much.' She glanced across at Tom. If only he could have met Elizabeth. Then he would understand that she was nothing like the woman everyone else seemed to know.

Tom asked, 'If that was the case, why wasn't it mentioned in the trial and why were they never prosecuted for blackmail?'

'That's the thing.' Alston coughed. 'They were very devious about it and chose their victims carefully. To be honest, what married man wants his indiscretions held up for all the world and its wife – especially his wife – to see. The Metropolitan Police have a file of the men they targeted but none would testify in an open court.'

Grace felt herself bristling. 'All of this was so long ago. Elizabeth must only have been twenty or twenty-one. Her husband was much older and may well have coerced her.'

'That's the other thing.' Alston went on, resolutely not looking at Grace. 'Once I had the deceased's true name, I made a number of standard checks. I did promise you I'd carry on looking,' he added, almost apologetically.

'You found something else?' Her heart sank.

'Yes, there was a bank account registered to her at Coutts & Co. Ten thousand pounds was paid into it a few days before she disappeared.'

'Oh,' was all Grace could manage, while Tom just whistled and said, 'Ten thousand pounds.'

'That's right. A small fortune. Supposedly remuneration from a brandy company based in France. Coutts aren't giving much away. Did Miss Smith have any links with Paris? Or trade in cognac?'

Grace shook her head, feeling totally deflated. Everything seemed to confirm her friend's guilt. Tom flashed her a sympathetic smile.

Constable Alston folded the documents neatly and asked, 'Do you still want to take Elizabeth's personal effects?'

'Yes, of course,' she said defiantly.

'And you know that you'll need to arrange the collection of the body?'

'I've spoken to J.H. Kenyon in Hampstead. They were the undertakers for my brother's funeral,' she said quietly. Since Constable Alston's telephone call, she had set in motion all the arrangements for the burial, even buying fresh clothing for Elizabeth. She only needed to trace Adele Pratchett, her sister.

He left the room and Tom looked across at her. 'Are you all right, Grace? You've gone very pale.'

'Yes,' she said, 'but I don't understand the ten thousand pounds at all.'

The police constable returned. He was carrying a bundle wrapped in brown paper and tied with string. 'It doesn't seem very much to leave behind,' he said sadly as he handed it to Grace. 'Would you just like to check everything's there?'

She agreed, then picked up the parcel and looked at the label. 'These aren't Elizabeth's belongings.'

'What do you mean?'

'They belong to another woman.' She turned the parcel to show the label. 'Miss Charlotte Harcourt of 80 Thurloe Square, SW7; 18 July 1919.'

Alston went crimson. 'I'm terribly sorry, Miss Armstrong. They must have got mixed up. They'll both have been marked "London Bridge drowning". I'll go and get Miss Smith's personal effects right away.'

'There was another death at London Bridge?' Grace asked, amazed. 'And so near in time to Elizabeth's. What happened?'

'I wasn't involved in the investigation into Miss Harcourt's death. That was Sergeant Williams, but I believe the coroner has found that it was suicide, that's why the personal effects are available for release. The family didn't question the verdict at all,' he added, as if that somehow explained everything.

Tom had picked up the parcel and scrutinized it more closely. 'These were released over a month ago. Didn't anyone come to collect them?'

The police constable looked more and more agitated. 'Sir, I must take them off you and return the parcel to the stockroom. I know very little about the case.'

He left the room hastily and returned with a second parcel. 'I'm very sorry about that, miss. Do you want to check everything is as it should be?'

This time, the label clearly stated 'Elizabeth Smith'. However, Grace couldn't help observing, 'Constable Alston, it does seem very strange that there were two drownings so close to each other and both found to be suicides. Are you sure there was no one else involved in the deaths?'

He was silent for a moment. 'Coincidences can happen,' he said, somewhat defensively.

'Is London Bridge a common spot for suicides?' asked Tom.

'I don't rightly know. The strangest thing is that the rate of suicide plummeted during the war. Terrible though it was, it was like everyone suddenly had a purpose and was united.' He thought for a moment. 'Maybe it is unusual to have two drownings that close together. I'll ask around if you want. Just on the quiet, to see if there could be any link between them. If I find out anything more, I'll let you know.'

As they went to say their goodbyes, Sergeant Williams appeared. He smirked when he saw Grace. 'Very interesting what we found out about your Lizzy Burdett-Smith, isn't it? Maybe a guilty conscience made her top herself.'

'You mind what you say,' Tom snapped back at him. 'Elizabeth Smith was a good woman.'

'Really?' he sneered. 'And what's your name, sir?' He glared at him, unused to being challenged.

'Tom – Tom Monaghan, and don't forget it.' He stood to his full height and seemed about to square up to the police sergeant.

'Don't worry, sir, I don't forget a name. Or a face.' He sauntered past the counter, whistling 'It's a Long Way to Tipperary'.

Tom was white-faced with anger.

When they were outside, Grace said, 'I told you Sergeant Williams was vile.' She looked at him. 'Thank you for defending Elizabeth, when you've heard so many terrible things about her.'

'You said what a moral person she was, and that's enough for me.'

They walked along Cloak Lane. He was meeting some friends at the George on Borough High Street. Gallantly, he asked if she wished to come, but looked relieved when she said no. She knew she wouldn't be good company at the moment and the walk to Bank station might help to clear her head. She couldn't escape the fact that Lizzy Burdett-Smith had made her living from blackmail and that a very substantial amount of money had been deposited into her bank account days before she died. And almost immediately after the visit from Sir Ernest Whitehouse. But why? If she had wealthy, influential friends, why had she chosen to live such a modest life. Nothing made sense.

It was in this confused state that she glanced upwards and saw the number 11 omnibus parked on the other side of the road. A pale man was sitting by the window on the top deck and looking straight at her. He was dressed in a brown, ill-fitting suit. Robert. His face was haggard, and he turned away, not recognizing her.

The bus began to drive off and she ran across the busy road, darting between motor vehicles and horse-drawn carts, determined to speak to him. She would not lose Robert again. Not now. Up along Queen Victoria Street, immune to the bemused stares of passers-by, she raced to catch up with the bus. The traffic was slower here and finally the vehicle shuddered to a halt. She jumped on and ran up the stairs. Looking around the top deck, she was stunned to find it almost empty. There was nobody apart from a mother with two children. Out of breath, she pointed to the seat at the front and asked, 'Where is the gentleman who was sitting there a few minutes ago? A tall man, with fair hair.'

The woman looked confused. 'There were a few chaps at the front, but they got off. Near Ludgate Hill, I think.'

'Are you sure? Did you see where they went?' She knew that her voice sounded too desperate.

The woman looked at Grace with alarm and pulled the two children closer to her. She shook her head. 'Perhaps you should ask someone else about it.'

The bus conductor had followed Grace up the stairs, but when she questioned him, he merely repeated what the woman had said. ·

In a daze, she got off the bus and tried to retrace her steps, but Robert was long gone.

CHAPTER TWENTY-EIGHT

The next day, Grace caught the 5.50 p.m. train on the London, Brighton & South Coast Line, determined to find information about Elizabeth's sister. The train gathered speed as it left behind London Bridge and the grime of the city, burrowing its way through Brockley, Honor Oak Park, Forest Hill, Sydenham and Penge. A litany of suburbia. Dusk had fallen, and the lit windows of houses formed spots of safety in the half-darkness. Each with its own carefully fenced garden, creating a small rural idyll within thirty minutes of the city.

In her bag was the address of Mr Archibald Pratchett, Elizabeth's brother-in-law, taken from Lady Constance's documents about the murder case. It was where he had lived in 1901. The whole world had changed since then, and he and his wife might be living anywhere. It was a gamble coming out to Penge, but if she was still there it seemed better to speak to Adele Pratchett face to face, rather than convey the sad news of her sister's death in a letter.

She dreaded having to reveal that Lizzy had drowned. Now that the body was to be released, the funeral could go ahead and her family would want their say in what should happen.

Number 15 Admiral Avenue, West Penge was only four or five minutes from the station and easy to find. An oversized Victorian villa set back from the dusty road, with an uncared-for front garden and a bicycle propped precariously against the side wall. It was the tail end of a damp autumn day and the street was empty. The house felt abandoned, its front door standing solid and uninviting. She rang the doorbell and heard distant voices from somewhere at the back. After several more minutes of waiting, she rang the bell again and heard one of the voices moving closer, clearly raised in complaint.

Then came the sound of bolts being pulled back and the door was opened. A thin, upright man stood before her. He was undoing the cuff buttons of a white work shirt and had a sour expression on his face. Grace suspected he was aggrieved that he had been forced to come to the door.

'We're not donating,' he said. 'We've done our bit.' He pointed to a pinned notice on the porch, which stated, 'No Hawkers, Beggars or Charitable Collections'.

'I'm not looking for any donations,' she replied.

'I've answered the door as no one else would,' he shouted down the hall and then turned suspiciously to her. 'Then how can I help you?'

'I'm looking for a Mrs Adele Pratchett. I know that she lived at this address in 1901.'

'She still does. She's my wife. What d'you want her for?'

Feeling uncomfortable at standing on the doorstep, she said, 'Do you mind if I come inside? I've got some news for her, and it would be better not to tell it in the street.'

He looked at her hard and opened his mouth to say something, but at that moment a woman in a light-blue dress appeared. Even though it was early evening, she was immaculately made up, with red lips and elaborately styled blonde hair. She looked to be in her mid to late thirties, Grace thought.

'What is it, Archie?' she asked her husband while looking at Grace.

'She wants to speak to you.'

Deciding it was best to introduce herself, she said, 'My name is Grace Armstrong. I believe that your sister was—'

The woman cut across her with a stifled cry, 'She's dead, isn't she? You've come to tell me she's dead.'

'I'm terribly sorry, Mrs Pratchett. I thought you would want to know.'

Adele slumped against the door frame and put her hands briefly to her face. 'It was inevitable, I suppose,' she said in a weak voice, then shook her head and began to cry – a choking, dry sob.

Mr Pratchett looked at his wife with contempt, before saying to Grace, 'You can see the effect you've had. How dare you come to our home bringing poison with you? I wouldn't allow that woman to pollute our lives when she was living; we don't need to be reminded of her now she's gone.'

'You spoke against her in the murder case,' Grace said, remembering his sworn statement. 'You said her alibi was false.'

'Well, it was. She was a liar who didn't care who she harmed, so long as she could save her neck from the noose.'

Taken aback by the savageness of his response, she glanced across at Adele, who stood pale beside the door. Grace ignored him and continued talking to his wife. 'It's Elizabeth's funeral next week. I thought you would want to be there and perhaps choose the readings or hymns.'

Adele shook her head and looked away. She had stopped crying now.

'She won't be going. None of us will be going. Don't try to drag us back into that hell again.' Archibald glowered at Grace and, for one moment, she thought that he might hit her, so great was the pent-up aggression of his response.

Their mother's distress had brought the two children out into the passageway.

'Who is it, Pa? Who's at the door?' A boy of about fifteen loomed behind his father, all gangly legs and a voice that seemed artificially low alongside the youth and pimples of his face.

'You and Margaret, stay inside the dining room. Let me and your mother deal with this,' he snapped at him.

His son exclaimed, 'I was only asking, Pa.'

'Don't answer back. This is nothing to do with you.' Their father stormed towards the two children, who backed away. The two of them were swallowed up in the gloom of the passageway.

Finally, Adele spoke, 'He's right, you know. None of us will go to the funeral.'

'She was your sister,' Grace pleaded. 'Surely she deserves to be remembered by her family.'

She shook her head bleakly. 'Lizzy died to us a long time ago. As soon as she was arrested for murder and all those terrible things came out about her life. She wanted me to lie and say she'd been here the night Sir Hugh was killed, but I refused. Archie wouldn't let me perjure myself. He's a solicitor, you see. You'd best go. There's no point in staying.'

'But she was so close to her family,' Grace pleaded. 'Every Sunday, she left her lodgings to visit home.'

The woman laughed bitterly. 'Our home doesn't exist. Father was forced to sell it to pay off the huge debts accumulated by his poor business sense and my mother's extravagance.'

'It was called Arcadia Farm?' Grace wanted to establish that at least one thing Elizabeth had told her was true.

'Yes, Father changed the name from the more prosaic Bank Farm to suggest that it was a place of rural bliss. When it held very little happiness for any of us, particularly Mother.'

'What do you mean?' Grace asked.

Adele looked directly at Grace. 'Father was a kind man and a wholesaler of root vegetables. We once had a comfortable life but our lack of social standing was a source of grave disappointment to Mother. To compensate, she would amuse herself with "distractions".' She shook her head. 'Lizzy and I were not allowed to enter the sitting room when Father was away on business and she was entertaining visitors. One time, when I was a very young girl, I had fallen over and cut myself, so I ran to my mother, daring to open the forbidden oak door. I can't remember quite what I saw – but it was a scene of disorder and dishevelled clothing. I stood on the threshold, bewildered, before Mother's smart slap across my face brought me to my senses. I never again dared to disobey her rule that we must not disturb her when she had important guests.'

'How awful for you.' Grace was truly shocked.

'It was what I became used to.' She stopped. 'Like mother, like daughter. That's what Archie used to say about Lizzy.'

There was an awkward silence.

Grace turned to leave, and then on an impulse said, 'I'll give you my telephone number, in case you change your mind about the funeral.'

'I don't have a telephone.'

'My address, then. Take my address.' She produced a pen and blank envelope from her bag and scribbled the details down. She thrust it at Adele.

'I won't change my mind,' she responded, but she took the envelope anyway.

Grace was convinced that she was going to screw it up and throw it away, but she stared at the envelope for a few moments. They both heard her husband returning and Adele put the piece of paper into her pocket.

'Hasn't she gone yet?' he demanded of his wife, ignoring Grace completely.

'She's going,' his wife replied.

Grace walked slowly back to the railway station, dazed at the violence of Archibald Pratchett's response and Adele's certainty – even before Grace had spoken – that her sister was dead. A sense of failure seeped through her whole body. She had vowed she would find the family so they could be at the funeral, but Elizabeth would now be buried unmourned by those who should be closest to her.

The rain had begun to fall steadily. It was cold and dark. Admiral Avenue was deserted, even the latest commuters safely home. Through the darkness, the headlights of a large black car illuminated her briefly before speeding away.

CHAPTER TWENTY-NINE

The day of the funeral dawned equally gloomy. At breakfast, Grace wasn't hungry and couldn't touch the egg or toast in front of her.

Her father looked at her over his copy of *The Times*. 'It's not even November and we might as well be in the depths of winter.'

'It's Elizabeth's funeral today. At four o'clock,' she reminded him.

He put the newspaper down reluctantly and made a noncommittal noise.

'I wondered if you could leave work early and be there.' This was greeted with silence, so she added, 'She lived in this house for eight years.'

'I won't be able to come, Grace. Things are very busy at the ministry right now.'

'Mother would have come but the journey from Whitby is too difficult for her.' She paused. 'I will be the only member of the Armstrong family there.'

'What about her own family? I thought you said her sister was going.'

'I hoped she would, but when I went out to Penge, her husband refused to allow anyone to come.' She didn't want to admit that Adele had shown no desire to attend.

He shook his head. 'I never knew Elizabeth very well. In fact, given how things have turned out, none of us knew her very well at all. I've got a meeting with the minister that would be impossible to cancel.'

'Father, please, it will look so strange if the church is empty.'

'Grace, I wish you'd stop badgering me at the breakfast table and let me eat in peace for once. I seem to suffer from permanent indigestion these days.'

'But—'

'Right, I shall get myself off to work. At least there I'll have an uninterrupted half an hour or so.' He rose from the table and left.

Once Grace heard the front door close and knew her father was safely on his way, she got up and went to her room. She would have to find something to wear for the funeral and the thought filled her with horror. In her wardrobe, pushed away at the back, was the black dress and coat she had worn to the memorial service at Edward and Robert's school. She hesitated before them, running her hands over the fabric that seemed to be soaked through with grief. She couldn't bear the thought of putting on mourning clothes again so soon. Better to wait until the very last moment, just before they had to leave for the funeral.

On her dressing table sat the sad brown paper parcel of Elizabeth's personal effects. She hadn't had the heart to look at its contents yet. The package seemed such a meagre summary of a life. However, it couldn't be left unopened. Slowly unwrapping it, she shuddered at the smell of damp and death that seemed to permeate everything. There was nothing here that Elizabeth would want, she thought. She had deliberately chosen to destroy all evidence of her existence and Grace resolved that she would burn her personal effects after the funeral.

Mechanically, she checked through the pockets of Elizabeth's blue coat and was surprised to find a piece of card, which seemed to be a ticket of some kind. There was a splash of red at the centre and some writing around it, but it was badly water-damaged and most of the writing was too blurred to read. She thought she could possibly make out 'June 1919' – just before Elizabeth had disappeared. It might be significant in some way, and she put it into her handbag.

She had sent notices of the funeral to anyone who had even the most tenuous of links with Elizabeth. Even then, there were few people she could invite. Sian had agreed to come to the house, so that she had some moral support walking to the church. Bridget would be there, she reflected gratefully, and the women from the Roman Catholic bookshop too. Bunty, perhaps. She counted the meagre numbers on the fingers of her hand.

Mrs Watson had refused to attend. When asked, she had pursed her lips and shaken her head. 'I've got a busy day ahead of me. Someone has to stay and make sure the household is running properly.' Ever since she had known Elizabeth's true identity, her opinion had grown more critical, as if angry at herself for being fooled into liking her. After a sherry or two, Grace had heard her say to

Bridget that, 'Lizzy Burdett-Smith was a little trollop at best and it wouldn't surprise me if she murdered that poor dear man!'

When Grace came downstairs shortly after three, dressed in mourning clothes, she was surprised to see that Bridget had disappeared. She asked the cook where she had gone. 'Off again! She's up to something that one, mark my words, and I intend to find out what.'

Grace was surprised at her vehemence but remembered there was often bad blood between the two servants. She was relieved when Sian arrived, and she was able to close the door of Ryedale Villa behind her and step out into the dull October afternoon. The two women had agreed to walk the short distance to the Roman Catholic church in Kentish Town, where Elizabeth had worshipped.

Lady Eleanor Road was bathed in suburban normality. Ahead of them, a nanny walked briskly along the road, two small children tugging at either hand, while a boy delivering groceries was navigating his bicycle between the parked motor cars. But for Grace, the pleasant scene had been transformed and lay heavy with the thought of death.

'Thank you for coming,' she said to Sian. 'I'd hate to have to walk there alone, but you do look dreadfully pale. Are you sure you're well enough to be here?'

'I was at a jazz club in Soho last night. A little bit too much champagne. Nothing serious.'

'With Maurice?'

'Yes, I'm worried I'm becoming too attached to him, Gracie. Anyway, it was three in the morning before I got home. I had to take my shoes off and sneak across the hallway of the nurses' quarters. If Matron got wind of it, I'd be out.'

'What about Aunt Regina?'

'I've used her too many times – Matron has become awfully suspicious and wants to meet her. In fact, she insists Aunt Regina come to high tea the next time she visits London.'

'That could be difficult,' Grace commented, as they arrived at the door of the church. She had never been inside Our Lady Church before and it was smaller than she had expected, with whitewashed walls, and stained-glass windows reflecting the dull light through prisms of royal blue and rich red. There was something unbearably sad about the darkness of the day and the almost deserted church. A swell of organ music announced the pall bearers, who carried the simple oak coffin into the church. As they walked solemnly down the aisle, she was forced to look away. Elizabeth had been beautiful, kind and intelligent, and yet her life had ended in tragedy and obscurity.

Father Daley began to utter the solemn words of the funeral mass, the air heavy with incense. She looked around. Two women, with their faces shrouded in black lace mantillas, were kneeling deep in prayer in a pew on the other side of the church. Grace decided one of them must be Mrs Hewitt, Elizabeth's friend from the church bookshop. She was surprised and grateful to see that Arthur was there. As soon as he had spotted her, he came over and squeezed her arm slightly awkwardly. A little apart from them were Bunty and Tom. She nodded across at them. Here was the sum total of Elizabeth Smith's thirty-nine years of life.

Suddenly, the door at the back of the church opened and Grace turned around, hoping that Adele had changed her mind and come to pay respects to her dead sister. Instead, she was surprised to find herself staring at Constable Alston. He nodded, embarrassed, and she saw him go slightly red. The two bookshop ladies turned and tutted, presumably at his lateness. He glanced at the almost empty pews before seating himself close to the back. Grace looked away and lost herself in the age-old words of the requiem.

CHAPTER THIRTY

They left the church and came out into the north London dusk, busy with traffic and people hurrying homewards. They stood silent for a few moments.

Arthur was the first to speak. 'That must have been difficult for you, Gracie. I'm really so terribly sorry about Elizabeth's death. Perhaps her funeral has brought some kind of peace to you.'

She heard the heartfelt concern in his voice and nodded, frightened that if she spoke, she would start to sob.

'I wanted to pay my respects by being here, but I'm afraid I have another engagement. It's a meeting with some of the brokers and I can't get out of it,' he continued. 'Please accept my apologies that I won't be at the burial.'

'I'm very thankful that you came, Arthur,' she smiled up at him through tear-stained lashes.

He smiled back and then said, 'There is one more thing, Gracie. Robert's parents have been in touch. They've returned from France and would like to see you – us.'

'Oh,' she said. It was impossible to tell Arthur that she

was increasingly sure Robert was still alive. Should she reveal the truth to Mr and Mrs Hammond?

He seemed to sense how anxious she was. 'I'm sorry. I shouldn't have brought it up when you have so many things on your mind. I'll telephone you later.'

'Yes, of course,' she agreed.

At that moment, Lady Bunty came over, resplendent in an oversized hat of black feathers and gauze, which seemed perched at an impossible angle. She offered the use of her car to ferry the mourners to Highgate Cemetery. 'Tom's gone straight to the motor car.' She looked around sadly. 'D'you know, I believe we could do it in one journey and fit the entire congregation in.'

Constable Alston had drifted over to the group, looking uncomfortable in a formal suit. As if in response to a question, he said, 'It's my day off. I thought that I should pay my respects, not that I knew her in life, but I feel some kind of link to her in death. I pulled her out of the river. Too late by then, of course.'

'Thank you for coming,' Grace replied.

'Not many here, are there?' he commented bluntly.

'Nine, counting the priest,' said Sian, who had reached into her bag and found a packet of Woodbines. 'Anyone want one?' she asked. 'That was the most miserable hour of my life. It's as if Elizabeth never existed.'

'Didn't you ask her sister to come?' Alston wanted to know.

'She refused. Elizabeth was already dead to her, apparently.' She felt weighed down by a sense of unhappiness that she couldn't shift.

'That's not family-like,' he exclaimed.

'No,' Grace agreed sadly. 'Would you like to come to the cemetery? Bunty said we can use her motor car to drive there.'

'Well, there's some things I've found out that might be interesting to you, so perhaps we could speak after the burial, if that's convenient.'

'We'll go to a café later and get tea and cake. Gin even,' Sian declared. 'We'll have our own wake for Elizabeth.'

Lady Bunty nodded approvingly at Sian. 'Or perhaps a cocktail or two.'

The priest and the two ladies from the cathedral went separately. It was fully dark by the time they reached the cemetery. The air was damp with a cold that was peculiarly British and chilled to the bone. The forlorn group stood around the grave, their faces pale against the early evening shadows, while the priest intoned the prayers for the committal of the dead. Grace glanced around and was surprised to see a tall, thin man standing in a knot of trees opposite them. He watched intently as the coffin was lowered into the ground. Who was he? Perhaps someone from Elizabeth's past, come to pay his final respects. She nudged Sian discreetly and looked in his direction.

She was determined to speak to him. However, once the mourners had thrown their handfuls of earth into the narrow grave, he walked away.

'Another mystery about Elizabeth,' Sian commented.

After some muted discussion, the small group set off for the Flask public house and found themselves sitting around a large pine table in the back room. Lady Bunty insisted on ordering doubles for everyone – even the constable – and raised a toast to Elizabeth. 'May God rest her soul, and I hope that Lizzy finds the happiness in the afterlife that eluded her here. Amen.'

Once the toast was complete, Constable Alston leaned forward, 'Would this be a convenient time to give you some information about Charlotte Harcourt?'

He turned to Tom. 'This is probably for you as well, Mr Monaghan.'

Hearing his name, Tom came over and squeezed into the place next to her.

'What you said at the station about it being a big coincidence to have two drownings so close together, well that got me thinking. Anyway, a few days ago, I bumped into Bernard Jones.'

Grace looked at him questioningly. 'Did he know Charlotte?'

'Not exactly. He was a constable who started at Cloak Lane but got transferred to Mile End. It turns out that Sergeant Williams thought he was a bit wet behind the ears and needed toughening up. So he took Bernard along when he informed Charlotte Harcourt's parents that her body had been found.'

'Really?' said Grace, all attention now. 'I remember you said that they accepted it was suicide without question.'

'How were the police able to trace them?' Tom asked. 'You couldn't trace Elizabeth.'

'She had no form of identification on her. Miss Harcourt was wearing a gold bracelet engraved with her full name. The Harcourts are what I'd call high society. It meant they were easy to track down.'

'Was the bracelet valuable?'

'Yes, very. That's one of the reasons the coroner decided it wasn't a deliberate act of violence. There were no signs of injury on her body and the bracelet hadn't been taken, ruling out robbery as a motive.'

'But it doesn't rule out other motives, does it?' Tom said.

The constable agreed. 'Perhaps not.'

'Poor Charlotte's parents, learning of her death,' said Grace. 'They must have been distraught.'

Alston paused and screwed up his eyes. 'Well, that's the strange thing. Bernard said that they took it very calmly, coldly even. Sergeant Williams announced that a body had been found in the river and the girl was wearing this bracelet, which indicated the body was that of their daughter. He showed them the bracelet and the father said that yes, that was Charlotte's. Then the mother said that they'd not seen her for the last two days.'

'Had she been reported missing?' Grace asked.

He shook his head. 'No. Mr Harcourt said that Charlotte had a mind of her own and often disappeared for several days at a time. They had become reconciled to it.'

'Reconciled to it,' Grace repeated. 'Whatever does that mean?'

'I don't know. Those were his exact words, apparently. It was such an odd response that it stuck in Bernard's mind. He got the impression that Mr and Mrs Harcourt just wanted the police out of there as soon as possible.' He hesitated. 'They even sent their butler to represent them at the inquest As you know, they haven't collected her personal effects.'

'There were no obvious signs of violence on either of the bodies?' Grace asked.

'No,' Alston replied. 'Bruising, but only consistent with being in the water. Mind, neither of them left a note.' He flushed slightly. 'Now, I shouldn't really have told you about Miss Harcourt, but there are similarities to your Elizabeth.'

'I found something too,' Grace said. 'I'm not sure if it's significant or not, but it was in Elizabeth's coat pocket when I went through her personal effects.' She took the crumpled piece of card out of her handbag and put it on the table in front of them.

He picked it up. 'I can't make anything out, I'm afraid. It's too damaged.'

'There's a partial date there,' Grace said, pointing to the writing at the edge.

Sian looked up from her second whisky. 'Let me see.' She put on her spectacles and spent a moment or two looking at it before exclaiming, 'I think I know what this is!'

'What?' Grace asked.

'An entrance ticket to the Red Lantern. See, in the middle is a picture of what's supposed to be a lantern. Goodness, it's not the kind of place I'd have expected Elizabeth to go.'

Constable Alston picked up the piece of card and held it at arm's length. 'I believe you're right, miss. The Red Lantern on Tooley Street. Not the most salubrious of places.'

'It's not so terrible,' Sian protested. 'Maurice and I go there sometimes. It's always open, even when the rest of London is closed.'

'What's it like?' Grace asked.

She pulled a face. 'They've got good music – lots of jazz – and there's an edge of danger that's quite exciting. A real mix too. The rich Mayfair crowd alongside barrow boys from south of the river. But there's something not quite right about it. Maybe we should all go and find out if anyone there remembers Elizabeth?'

Grace agreed. 'It's a link to her.'

'What about Friday night?' Tom asked.

Grace shook her head. 'Father has friends coming for supper. I said I'd be there to keep Arthur company.'

'I'm working Friday and Saturday nights for the next few weeks,' Sian said grimly. 'What about the 15th?'

Grace and Tom agreed.

'I love a night out and it will let me forget the misery of today. Sometimes London can feel a soulless place,' Sian said.

'I know what you mean,' replied Constable Alston. 'I've put in to work at the Cambridge Constabulary. Jane, my wife, and me are planning to start a family, so we'd like to get out of the city.' He blushed slightly at mentioning something personal.

Grace couldn't help contrasting herself with him. Constable Alston knew what he wanted to do with his life and was making a future. What was she doing? Still stuck in the past.

'Penny for them.'

She glanced up in surprise at Tom, who was looking directly at her.

'Penny for your thoughts. You seemed miles away.'

She laughed, 'I suppose I was. There is something about funerals that makes you reflect on your own life – at the final reckoning, how much have you achieved?' She sighed.

'Poor Elizabeth, she seems to me to have had a life half lived. Even her death has been ignored by the world. She needs some kind of justice.'

'I have a belief that bad deeds always come to light.' Alston put down his empty glass. 'Try as the criminal might to hide their tracks, they'll be tripped up in the end. They'll betray themselves through something they say or do. Or be betrayed by someone they're close to – an aggrieved friend or angry wife will turn up at the station and reveal everything.'

'I think you may have an optimistic view of policing,' Tom suggested.

'Mark my words, you'll see it's true. Now I must be going, or mine will be the angry wife.' He smiled at them and made his goodbyes.

Soon after, they all left the pub. Sian hooked her arm into Grace's. 'D'you know, if it wasn't for Maurice, I could quite go for that Tom of yours. He's very good-looking and tortured, in an interesting way.'

'He's not *my* Tom!' she declared.

'Oh no, I know that. He's not your sort at all. Arthur is the right man for you.'

But Robert, what about Robert, Grace thought to herself.

When she got back to the house, Bridget was there, looking a bit sheepish.

'I'm ever so sorry, Miss Armstrong, that I couldn't be at Elizabeth's funeral. Something came up, something urgent that I couldn't get out of.'

There was a tone of such genuine regret in her voice that Grace asked if she were quite well.

'Yes, miss. There's just things going on at the moment.'

Grace remembered Mary's assertion that Bridget was up to something.

Bridget continued, 'I'm supposed to go to a séance tomorrow evening and promised I'd bring Betty, one of my friends from the munitions, but now she can't make it and I know Doris will be furious.' She sighed and went to turn away. 'You can't really have a séance with only three there and that's a true fact.'

On impulse, Grace said, 'I could go. I could take Betty's place.'

'Really, miss. Whatever for?'

'Robert.' She wanted to know whether he was alive or dead. Maybe in a séance, she could find the answer.

CHAPTER THIRTY-ONE

The darkness came too quickly that day and there was a biting chill to the air that was in keeping with the bleakness of what they planned to do. The séance was being held just off the Holloway Road. Both Bridget and Grace talked nervously throughout the tram ride but became quieter as they got nearer to the house.

'I never thought I'd do something such as this,' Bridget said eventually. 'Let's hope Father Daley never hears a whisper of it. Only last Sunday, he said in the homily that dabbling with the dead opened a doorway to the devil. I might be putting myself at danger of mortal sin.' She dropped her voice dramatically.

'I'm sure that can't be the case,' said Grace.

'Well, I need to know that my Patrick is happy now. I loved him so very much.'

They had reached the narrow terraced house and Bridget's hesitant tap on the door was answered almost immediately. Doris had clearly been waiting for them. She was a thin, fair-haired woman who had a washed-out prettiness about her. On the tram, Bridget had explained that her husband had been killed in the 1918 spring offensive and she had two children both under the age of four. Without a greeting, Doris said. 'She's here, Bridget. In the kitchen, we've been drinking cups of tea for over an hour. What took you?'

'The tram was late, I'm sorry.'

Doris looked at Grace in surprise.

'Who's this?'

'Grace Armstrong. I've brought her to make up the circle. Betty had to work an evening shift at the biscuit factory.'

Doris smiled at her but looked anxious. 'Maisie and Samuel are at my mum's. So it's a bit quieter. You'd best come into the kitchen.'

The medium was seated at the scrubbed table. Doris introduced her as Mrs Kelly. She was a tiny, elderly woman, with sharp dark eyes and she stared at Grace for a moment. 'You're not Betty,' she said.

'Betty couldn't come at the last minute,' Doris told her.

The woman nodded. She was dressed in black, with arms that were covered in copper bangles and her hair was hennaed bright red. Her face was deeply wrinkled under a layer of powder and rouge. The effect should have been ludicrous and yet, in these circumstances, in this silent house, there was something otherworldly and powerful about her.

'Is this to be the full circle, then?' the medium asked.

'It's all I could get at such short notice, Mrs Kelly, I'm sorry. Would you like us to begin?'

'We need to go into another room. There is no presence here. The spirits won't come.'

She stood up from the kitchen table and went out into the

narrow hall, where she started walking back and forth, waving her arms above her head.

'What's she doing?' Grace whispered.

'She has to find exactly the right spot where she can tune into the spirit world,' said Doris.

'How will she know that?' Bridget asked.

'I think it's to do with the temperature,' Doris said nervously. 'When I was at my friend Alana's, she walked right through the house – every single room, even the bedrooms, until she found somewhere that made her heart freeze – she said it was like being in a bath of cold water.'

However, in this case Mrs Kelly didn't feel the need to climb the stairs. She stopped at the closed parlour door at the front of the house. 'This is the room,' she said.

Doris gasped and raised a frightened hand to her face. 'Mrs Kelly, I'd rather not go in there. I keep it locked and, like I told you, we've not really used it since Bert passed away. It will be very musty.'

'The spirits are telling me that this is the portal they must pass through.' She looked at Doris, who hastily went into the kitchen to get the key. With trembling fingers, she unlocked the door.

'I'd best pull up the blinds and let some air in.' She walked towards the small bay window at the front of the room.

'No. This is what the spirits demand.'

The room was in half-darkness and Mrs Kelly produced a tiny lamp from her bag which she placed upon the small circular table in the middle of the room. It shone blood red when it was lit, creating an unearthly glow. In the light, Grace could see that the room had become a shrine to the dead soldier. Framed pictures of Bert in uniform lined the room, and pride of place on the mantlepiece was given to the black-edged telegram.

'I don't let visitors in here,' Doris tried to explain. 'I come in to think about Bert and . . .to speak to him.'

Mrs Kelly laid a comforting hand on her arm. 'That's why the spirits will have chosen this place. He is very strong in this room.'

Doris nodded, placated.

'Now, we will sit around the table.' She brought a black oblong tray from her bag and placed this alongside the lamp.

Reluctantly, Grace took her place between Bridget and Doris. She was aware that Doris was crying quietly, but she didn't want to look at her too obviously.

'Did you bring your tokens?' Mrs Kelly asked.

The three women nodded. Reluctantly, Grace produced a letter from Robert. She saw Bridget take out an opal ring, while Doris added a gold, heart-shaped locket. Mrs Kelly looked at the contents of the tray and then asked the women to join hands to create a circle and allow the spirits to enter into the living world.

'None of you must speak,' she commanded.

There was a thick silence in the room and nothing seemed to exist apart from the circle of their lightly touching hands.

'They've never left us. Those who have passed are just on the other side of the thinnest of boundaries. I could put my hand through and touch them, if I chose.' Mrs Kelly raised a bony finger and Grace was worried that she might seek to illustrate her point. 'They're just waiting for us to call them.'

Doris suppressed a sob. 'Is Bert there, Mrs Kelly? I miss him so much. It's hard not having him here, what with the kids and no one to hold me and tell me everything is going to be all right.'

'Don't be impatient, Doris. The spirits will come when they are ready.'

Doris nodded bleakly in response.

'Now clear your minds of everything except your token. Focus all your energy on that link with the dead. You will find the room becoming colder as the curtain between the living and the dead is pierced, and the spirits start to enter our world.'

Even as she was speaking, Grace felt a chill begin to seep into the room and the temperature drop. Her heart slowed down.

Suddenly there was a rustling of fabric and some kind of movement in the corner of the room. Grace held her breath and heard a low moaning noise coming from Mrs Kelly, whose face had become contorted and taken on a blank, glazed look.

'He is coming. The spirit guide,' she said, in a voice that was like her own but higher pitched.

'Her spirit guide is a soldier who died at the Battle of Waterloo. Lance Corporal Oscar Appleton,' Doris whispered. Grace found herself caught between belief and cynicism while Mrs Kelly remained in a trance-like state. Then her voice changed and became lower. It was a man's voice, with a harsh, arrogant tone. 'I see you've got all the ladies there, Mrs Kelly.'

'Yes, Oscar. There are three of them here and they want to know if you have messages from their loved ones who've passed.' There was some strange scratching and Mrs Kelly moaned softly. Suddenly she sat bolt upright.

'Is there a Doris there?' the man's voice asked.

In a trembling voice, Doris replied, 'Yes, have you got a message from Bert?'

The voice softened slightly. 'He wants you to know that he loves you and wishes he could be with you.'

'I miss him so much. I love him.' Doris began to weep, and it was a few moments before she added, 'Tell him I visited his nan just as he asked me to.'

'He's pleased about that. He knows how much she likes to see the kids, but he's worried about something.'

Mrs Kelly stopped speaking and the room felt on tenterhooks.

'What is it? What's he worried about?' Doris's voice caught with anxiety. 'Is there something wrong?'

The medium looked carefully at Doris. 'He wants you to bring me something belonging to the children.'

Doris jumped up and left the room. When she returned, she was carrying a framed studio photograph of a baby and a toddler. They were both dressed in the black of mourning. 'I got this taken just after Bert died.'

Mrs Kelly took it and ran her hand over the surface. 'The boy, I'm getting a . . .'

'Samuel, it'll be Sam. He never got to see his dad in this world. Bert was killed just after he was born. It breaks my heart that he doesn't know his dad.'

'Don't worry. His dad is walking right beside him,' Mrs Kelly said. 'He'll look after him, but he's worried about that cough he's got.'

'I know he's got a bit of a cough at the moment, but he's usually such a healthy little boy,' Doris said defensively.

'Well, the spirit world is telling me that he needs to have a doctor look at him. We want to look after young Samuel, that's what your husband is telling me through the lance corporal.'

Doris nodded fiercely. 'Tomorrow, I'll take him to the doctor. Will you tell Bert that I'd give anything to have him with me right now?'

'He already knows, love.'

'Thank you, thank you.'

Grace noticed the strained look dissolving from her face and some of its colour and prettiness return.

Mrs Kelly then reached into the tray and took out Bridget's narrow opal ring. She held it in both hands for a moment, as if squeezing some essence from it. She turned to Bridget, 'This is very precious to you, isn't it, dear?'

Bridget nodded.

'It was given to you by your sweetheart, wasn't it?'

'Yes. We'd been talking about marrying for a terribly long time. And then he surprised me by producing this ring.' She drew a breath. 'But I fell into a terrible rage, for opals are unlucky. He wasn't to know.'

'You loved him, although you didn't always show it.'

Bridget put her head in her hands and started weeping.

'Don't break the circle,' Mrs Kelly said sharply.

Tears coursing down her face, Bridget held out her hands to the spiritualist and Grace. 'We had a tiff, you know, just before he left for the Front. I, I want him to know that I'm sorry and would have married him, opal ring or not.'

Mrs Kelly nodded. 'Let me see what I can do. What was his name, love?'

'Patrick. Patrick Hannon. He was in the Royal Artillery.'

Mrs Kelly looked up to the ceiling. Still clutching the hands of the other women, she lifted her arms, so they were all forced to follow. Her body began to convulse and then stiffen. Again, the low, gravelly voice took over and seemed to speak from somewhere outside the body of the diminutive woman.

'Bridget, there is someone here to speak with you.'

'Is it Patrick, Mrs Kelly?'

The medium spoke again in her normal voice. 'I'm hearing a woman's voice, dear.'

'Who might that be?' Bridget asked, frightened. 'His mother?'

'I must ask the lance corporal.'

After a moment, Mrs Kelly began shaking her head vigorously and spoke in an agitated voice. Suddenly, she lowered her hands to the table.

'Indeed that was Mrs Hannon.'

'Oh,' Bridget said, in a small voice. 'We never did see eye to eye, if truth be told. For I always feared Patrick favoured her over me.'

'She's with her son now, Bridget, and is happy.'

'She passed away, not three months after his death. Of a broken heart, they said. Could you tell her that I'm sorry?'

'She's returned to the other side now, but she knows that, Bridget. She wanted me to tell you that any bitterness is gone. You'd have been a fine wife for her Patrick.'

'Thank you. That takes a weight from my shoulders,' Bridget said quietly. 'Is Patrick there?'

'We can't command the spirit world,' Mrs Kelly said sharply.

'It's just I'd just like to know about how he . . . how he died. I cannot sleep at night for thinking of him suffering. They told me it was quick and painless but that's what's written in every letter from a commanding officer.'

There was a long pause before a response came. 'It's difficult for Patrick to talk about. He was alone, in a place of mud and death.'

At this, Bridget began to sob loudly. 'In no man's land. They told me he was shot down as the company tried to make it across to the German trenches.'

'He was sad to die alone, but it was very quick. He had only time to say an Our Father and he was gone.'

'He always was a pious man, was Patrick,' Bridget said, relieved. 'And is he happy? In the place that he is now.'

'It took him a while. He didn't want to die. But he had spirit guides to help him pass over and he's been reunited with family long lost to him.'

'Thank you, Mrs Kelly. I feel much better for knowing.'

'That's why we speak to the spirit world, dear.' Finally, she turned to Grace. 'Now, what is this?'

'It's a letter from my fiancé. I wondered whether there might be a message for me.' She didn't want to admit that her true intention was to find out whether he was alive.

The medium held the envelope in her hands and looked at it carefully. She muttered something and threw her head back as if to go into a trance. They held their breath as she sat rigid for several minutes. Suddenly, she slumped forward, hitting her forehead on the table. When she looked up at them, she said blankly. 'I'm not getting anything from the spirit world. There's nothing for you there, love.'

'What do you mean?'

'Nothing for you. No, nothing. I'm sorry. The spirits have gone now. They've been drained of their energy and must go back to their own place.' Mrs Kelly gave Grace the letter. 'You must seek your answers among the living.'

She stood up and they all followed her. Doris lit the gasolier at the centre of the room, throwing the shabby parlour into sharp relief. 'You've been a great comfort to me,' she said. 'I just needed to know that Bert was there for Samuel. It's not so bad for Maisie. She don't need her dad, not like Samuel does. That's what worries me day and night.'

'Well, now you mustn't worry,' Mrs Kelly replied, 'although remember about seeing the doctor.' She looked at her significantly and laid a comforting hand on her arm.

'Oh, I nearly forgot,' said Doris. 'You need five shillings.' She took the coins out of her purse, which were quickly taken by Mrs Kelly, who stuffed them into an elaborately beaded bag. 'Thank you, dear. Will you be coming to the meeting at Mrs Gladstone's next Thursday?'

'If my mum will take the kids again, I'll be there. Thank you, Mrs Kelly.'

The medium left and the three remaining women looked at each other awkwardly, as if they had exposed themselves too much during the séance.

'She's ever so good,' said Doris, almost defensively. 'She can see things.'

Bridget nodded bleakly. 'It affected me more than I thought it would.'

'It was so cold,' Grace responded. She had put on her coat, but it failed to warm her.

Doris agreed. 'It's always cold when the spirits come. I suppose they bring that from the other side. It's a shame, mind, that Mrs Kelly couldn't contact your Robert in the spirit world. Maybe you need to bring a different token next time.'

Although she murmured politely in agreement, she knew there would be no next time. Robert wasn't dead. Mrs Kelly couldn't speak to him because his spirit wasn't in that other world. The ghost who haunted her on the streets of London and in her nightmares was living.

Her feelings of deep unease only increased when Doris sent Bridget a note the next day to say that she had taken her son to the doctor and he had been diagnosed with pneumonia, which had been caught in the nick of time. 'Mrs Kelly has saved little Samuel's life,' her letter finished.

CHAPTER THIRTY-TWO

As Arthur had told her at the funeral, Robert's parents had now returned from their extended trip to northern France and wished to meet with them. They had spent several months touring the battlefields, in what was understood to be an act of pilgrimage for their son. Mr and Mrs Hammond had always struck Grace as being very different from each other, and yet they had contrived to be happily married for almost thirty years. Eric Hammond was a little abrupt, a hard-headed businessman who held tyrannical sway over a successful empire of theatres. She was always slightly awkward in his company.

His wife, on the other hand, was altogether much gentler. Sylvia was graceful, softly spoken and determined to blunt the harsher edges of her husband's character. She loved music and literature and the family numbered many successful writers, musicians and actors among their acquaintance. Their stuccoed home in Maida Vale was discreetly bohemian, tucked away on one of the wealthiest, tree-lined avenues. Grace remembered when Edward had first gone there and returned with stories of its large picture windows, sheets of silk hung like sails across the walls and the acres of books that lined each room.

Robert was their only child. She supposed he must have been a combination of their characters. His good looks and love of poetry and the arts was inherited from his mother, while his fiercely competitive spirit on the fields of sport and combat came from his father.

They were to come for afternoon tea on the first of November, at a time when the approach of Armistice Day was on everyone's mind. They called her the daughter they had never had, and Sylvia Hammond wrote long and affectionate letters to Grace during their time away. Inevitably, they would speak of Robert, and she didn't know whether she would be able to bear hearing his name spoken aloud. Not when she was convinced that he was alive. If she'd had any doubts, the séance had removed them. Grace was relieved that Arthur would also be there. He could be relied upon to fill any gaps in a conversation.

Bridget and Mary had spent most of the previous two days cleaning and polishing the sitting room and now the glass and brasses glistened in the late afternoon sun. Grace, Arthur and her father sat waiting for the Hammonds, all of them strangely subdued. When they heard the sound of the large front door knocker, Arthur started from his chair and then sat down again.

Bridget ushered them into the room. Mr Hammond spoke loudly and shook the men's hands a little too firmly, but Mrs Hammond lovingly embraced Grace. 'How are you, my dear? It's been so long since we last met.'

'I'm very well, Mrs Hammond, thank you,' she replied.

'It is good to see you. I hope you're fully recovered after
your trip to France.'

'We are, thank you. We returned last Tuesday and have
been able to rest.' She carefully removed her gloves. 'How is
your mother? You must send her our regards.'

'Of course. She's convalescing by the sea. In the cottage at
Whitby.' Grace changed the topic of conversation quickly.
'Was the sea very choppy?' she asked. 'It can be quite unset-
tled in October.'

'No, we had a smooth passage. We befriended another
couple who were also visiting the area where their son was
lost.'

'It's good to be with people who can understand your
sorrow,' Grace said.

Mrs Hammond nodded and sat down next to her husband.
He had been carrying a large briefcase, the kind that City
gentlemen took on their morning commute. He placed this
carefully by his side. Grace wondered about its contents.

After the initial greetings, she noticed that Arthur had
placed himself in the furthest corner of the room and looked
pale.

Grace asked, 'Are conditions still dreadful in France? One
of my friends from nursing is still over there and said—'

Mr Hammond cut across her. 'Dreadful. Absolutely
dreadful. I've never seen anything like it.'

His wife agreed and looked down at her hands before saying, 'We stayed in Amiens. It was quite some distance from
the battlefields, but it was impossible to find lodgings closer.
Nothing remains of the town of Albert. Even the cathedral
has been destroyed.'

'The place we were staying was pretty basic,' Mr Hammond added. 'No luxuries, not even hot running water. We'd hired a former officer from the Welsh Guards, Lieutenant Braithwaite, as our guide and driver. Thank goodness we did. He knew his way around and how to avoid the unexploded munitions. The roads themselves were a nightmare and almost impassable at points because they were so rutted with holes and debris.'

'I was glad,' Mrs Hammond said quietly, 'to witness the destruction.'

They looked at her in surprise.

'I wished to share some of Robert's suffering. To understand the terrible conditions and the blasted landscape in which he lived. I did not mind the deprivations at all.' She put her lace handkerchief to her mouth to suppress a sob. 'I have always envied your wife,' she said, turning to Grace's father. 'She at least has a grave where she may mourn Edward. She knows where her son is lying.'

Grace thought of her mother's own unhappiness and found it hard to believe that there might be anything desirable about her situation.

'I'm sorry, that sounds insensitive to Isobel's plight. I remember her in my prayers every night.' She paused for a moment. 'It is small things that sustain me. I know your engagement to Robert was so brief, Grace, but it gives me great consolation to know that he found love and happiness with you before he died. Although I know it has caused you pain.'

'Thank you, Mrs Hammond. I have never stopped loving Robert.' She shook her head, finding it difficult to continue.

At this point, Bridget came in with a tray of sandwiches and cakes; they busied themselves with eating and the conversation moved to the weather and mutual friends.

Once they had finished, Mr Hammond turned to Mr Armstrong, 'Which brings me to this,' he said and pointed to the bulging briefcase. 'May I use the table, James? I need somewhere to spread out the research documents.'

Grace and Arthur caught each other's eye. She saw him shake his head slightly.

For the last three years, Robert's parents had been obsessed with finding their son. Initially, Sylvia Hammond was adamant that he was alive, but now she accepted he was dead. Her husband had always believed Robert had been killed. They hoped that they might find a body to bury. It had become an all-consuming goal for both of them.

Mr Hammond placed a large hand-drawn map at the centre of the table. It showed the battlefields of the Somme and was covered with a grid and coordinates. At various points, red and black crosses had been added. 'Whenever I obtain new information, I mark it up on here. He pointed at the document. 'I know that if I can only keep going, I'll find the exact spot.'

'The exact spot?' Grace's father asked.

'Yes, where Robert fell. We have to eliminate all the possibilities. A red cross indicates a sighting that suggests he survived. A black cross that any wound was fatal.'

Mrs Hammond reached across and took his hand. 'It's very difficult for us both. We want a grave to tend. Somewhere to go each year and place flowers.'

'Yes, that would be the ticket. Now if we look at this area

here.' He jabbed his finger at a central point of the map. 'There have been a lot of sightings.'

Reluctantly, Grace, Arthur and her father gathered around the table. What did each of them think, she wondered. For her, there was the certainty that the Hammonds were looking for something that didn't exist. Their son wasn't lying in the heavy clay of the Somme plain. He was still alive. Her father felt obliged to nod and add words of encouragement. And Arthur? He seemed reluctant to even look at the map.

'Over the years, we've had a lot of contact with the W&MED, of course,' Mr Hammond said.

When Grace looked at him enquiringly, he supplied, 'The Wounded & Missing Enquiry Department. Run by the Red Cross. They had reports from a Sergeant Drummond that he saw someone who looked like Robert next to the German trenches. Anyway, the chap he spotted was shot in the leg.'

'I hoped, for a long time, that the Germans had carried him off and taken him prisoner,' Mrs Hammond said sadly.

'Sergeant Drummond was pretty certain of his facts. That would place Robert on the map here.' He pointed at a red cross. 'It's right by the German front line, don't you see? This sergeant said Robert should have been awarded a VC for the courage he showed leading his men over the top.'

For the first time in several minutes, Arthur spoke, 'There are always lots of stories. The men want you to believe the best. If he were a prisoner of war, he would have been returned by now.'

Mr Hammond continued without acknowledging him.

'We had another report that wasn't so reassuring, I'll admit. I've been tracing survivors from his battalion, visited them in hospital and the like. There was a Private Marshall, who thought he'd seen Robert lying in no man's land, just here.' Again, he indicated the place on the map. A large black cross had been drawn there. 'He'd seen Robert shot down and not moving.'

Mrs Hammond had her handkerchief in front of her eyes and turned away from them all slightly. 'He said Robert was dead, of that there could be no doubt.'

'If he saw a body, why didn't he bring it in?' Mr Armstrong wanted to know.

'He'd been wounded himself. There had been heavy shelling from the Germans' big guns. Marshall said it was impossible to retrieve the dead bodies; even the wounded were left out because no one dared to leave the trenches. He said it was piteous to hear the pleas for water.'

Mrs Hammond put her hand on her husband's arm. 'No more, please, Eric.'

'I'm sorry, my dear, but we must report the truth,' he said. 'When we toured the battlefields, we saw an officer who was still lying where he was shot. They hadn't got round to exhuming that section and the body was surrounded by the detritus of war – respirators and rifles, even fragments of letters and photographs.'

'How dreadful,' Mr Armstrong said. He hesitated for a moment. 'How could you continue with your tour after seeing such sights? Wasn't it rather morbid?'

Mrs Hammond reproached him mildly. 'I wanted to walk on the ground where Robert fell.'

'What was the Somme like?' Grace asked, curious.

'When one stood close to the battlefield, it was impossible to ignore the devastation of the fighting. It was etched into the landscape. However, if one stepped back, there was a terrible beauty about the place. It is a vast area, yet there was not one tree or hedgerow standing for miles. Instead, there was a sea of scarlet poppies and among the blooms were makeshift crosses to mark the dead.' She turned again to Mr Armstrong and smiled at him faintly. 'So you see, for me it was not at all morbid. The battlefields of the Somme are sacred ground, for that is where Robert died and where I feel closest to my only child.'

Grace could contain herself no more. It was impossible to see her suffer in this way. 'Mrs Hammond, Robert isn't dead.'

They turned to look at her in astonishment.

'Robert isn't dead,' his mother repeated. 'But he must be. Why do you say that?'

'I've seen him,' Grace replied.

Mrs Hammond was on her feet now, crossing towards her. 'Where have you seen Robert? Where? Are you sure it's him? Oh, my dear Robert!'

Arthur too was standing up. 'No, Grace, no. You haven't seen him. He is dead. Please don't do this to yourself. To his family.'

Mrs Hammond was desperate, pleading, 'Where is my boy? Where have you seen him?'

'Everywhere,' Grace said, her voice shaking. 'On Underground trains, the omnibus, at Rectors. In my dreams. I see Robert everywhere.'

'No,' said Mr Hammond. 'No. Don't give her false

optimism. It's taken so long to accept he is gone.' He took his weeping wife in his arms. 'I can't bear to hope again.'

It was all confusion now. Grace was crying too. The Hammonds left quickly.

She heard her father apologizing. 'She's been through a very difficult time, what with her mother and now the tragic death of our lodger, Elizabeth, who'd been a good friend to Grace.'

Arthur and Grace were left alone in the sitting room. He said, 'Robert is dead. I know that without a shadow of a doubt.'

CHAPTER THIRTY-THREE

Ever since Edward's schooldays, Arthur had been a fixture at Ryedale Villa, as familiar and comfortable as a favourite armchair or childhood memory. Following his declaration of love, Grace was aware of an awkwardness between them that had not existed before. Her father was oblivious to this, as he was to most matters of the heart, and often invited Arthur to their home.

A few days after the visit from the Hammonds, Arthur was expected for dinner at seven-thirty. At the last minute, her father telephoned to say he was likely to be delayed at the office, but they should begin eating and he would join them as soon as he was able. Grace was slightly alarmed at the thought of an evening spent with just the two of them but felt she couldn't cancel at the last minute. They sat in the dining room, making conversation about work and the miserable weather.

Bridget bustled in and out bringing dishes of food, her face red from the heat of the kitchen. When she had left the room, Grace said. 'I did appreciate your coming to Elizabeth's funeral.' She paused for a moment. 'I know you weren't as close to her as me.' Arthur rarely talked about the former lodger now that he knew of her other life as Lizzy Burdett-Smith.

'Gracie, I wouldn't allow you to be alone. I know you'd hoped her sister would be there. Obviously, blood wasn't thicker than water.'

'They seemed a very broken family.' She remembered Adele's bitterness when she spoke of her mother.

'It does rather raise the question of where Elizabeth went every Sunday,' Arthur said.

'I don't know,' Grace replied. 'So many mysteries have sprung up around her, Arthur, but I just want to remember her as the true friend she was.'

They had eaten by candlelight. Once the final course was served, Bridget asked whether they would like the electric light turned on.

'No thank you, Bridget. It's really quite nice in the softer light.'

'Very well, miss. Would you mind if I took myself off now? There's a WEA evening lecture at Muswell Hill I've taken a mind to attend.' She had already started to untie her apron.

'Well, yes of course, Bridget. What lecture is it?'

'Oh, it's about classical civilization or some such thing. Anyway, I must be gone. Let Mrs Watson know if you need anything else.'

'Goodness,' Grace said, when she had left. 'Bridget has never shown an interest in the ancient world before.'

Arthur laughed. 'I don't think it's a lecture at all. Several times when I've come over, there's been a young man waiting at the end of the road, not that I wanted to say anything.'

'Bridget has a young man?' she asked, surprised. 'I'm sure you must be wrong. She seems so devoted to the memory of Patrick, her fiancé who died.'

'Life has to move on,' Arthur replied. 'It's only right.'

A silence fell.

Finally Arthur said, 'Look, dear Grace, please would you forget what I said that evening, after the show? Let's just pretend it never happened and go back to how we were.'

'Arthur, what you said was kind, but it would be impossible to have a romantic relationship.' She had to be honest and tell him about the medium's words. 'I know unequivocally that Robert is alive, just as I said to the Hammonds.'

'Grace, I swear he's—'

'No,' she cut him off. 'I've seen him. I keep seeing him. In the end, I became so desperate to know the truth that I went to a séance with Bridget.'

'You went to a séance?' He sounded shocked. 'Should you really be dabbling in something so dark?'

'I had to know if there was a message for me.' Her voice trailed away. 'The medium said there was nothing for me in the spirit world. My answer lay with the living. I know you don't believe in such things, but . . .' She glanced at Arthur.

His face was white and his eyes were downcast, but with an effort of will, he looked up at her. 'I know without a shadow of a doubt that Robert is dead.'

Grace felt herself becoming angry. 'How can you be so certain? Why do I keep seeing him if he's not alive?'

'Because you haven't got over his death,' Arthur said

simply. 'Because you're still grieving for him. Just like your mother is mourning Edward. People have to find ways to come to terms with the whole mess that was the war. But please accept my word, I know Robert died at the Somme. You must stop loving a ghost.'

'Don't patronize me, Arthur. If you know something, then tell me.'

Arthur took a deep breath. 'Do you really want me to tell you the truth? I intended taking this knowledge to the grave because it will hurt you and I wouldn't do that for the world.'

As he said those words, a cold sense of dread grew within her. 'I would like to know,' she said slowly. How could she not ask now? She was suddenly aware of the loud tick of the grandfather clock out in the hallway.

'When we went back to France after our leave in June 1916 . . .' he began.

'Just after Robert and I became engaged?'

'Yes. There was a sense of tension running through the trenches. We all knew a big push was coming and that we should prepare for something significant at the start of July.'

'The Battle of the Somme?'

He nodded. 'The night before, we couldn't sleep. We drank whisky and talked until two or three in the morning. We both believed it might be our last night alive. Robert was in a very maudlin mood. He said he wanted to be truthful with me. That we'd been friends for a very long time, but he had never been honest with me. The thing is, Grace, the thing is . . . he did admire you tremendously.'

She looked at him, fearing what was coming.

'There really is no easy way to put this. Robert was in love with someone else. Not with you.'

As he said those words, Grace felt the blood drain from her face. 'Who? Elizabeth?'

'No. It wasn't Elizabeth.' He seemed to brace himself. 'Robert told me that he knew from the age of about fifteen that he had feelings for other chaps, sort of romantic feelings. I tried to tell him that it was quite normal to have crushes on other boys – one of the realities of boarding school life – but he said, no, it was more than that. For him it was part of who he was and not just something that would fade away with time.'

'I don't understand. We were engaged.' But she remembered the look of anguish on his face as he had returned from his long solitary run along the cliffs. When he had declared his love for her. He had been panting and out of breath and had begged her to marry him. Robert, who was so dazzling and handsome that she always felt mundane in comparison. There was his insistence that they walk a mile to the nearest hotel to telephone his parents and announce their engagement and plans for a wedding on his next leave home.

'It was a lie, then. He never loved me.'

'Robert tried to love you.' Arthur replied.

'No,' she said, putting her head in her hands as the certainties of the last three years unravelled.

'He felt guilty about using you, Grace, but didn't know what else to do.'

'What do you mean by that?'

'Robert had had several relationships with men, nothing serious, but then he fell in love with John Harris, a private under his command. The strength of their feelings made them reckless. He wanted to be honest with his parents and tell them how happy John made him.' He stopped. 'I'm sorry. None of this is making it any easier for you.'

'No, I asked to know the truth,' she said flatly. 'What happened?'

'He had decided that he would speak to them before returning to France. He thought they would understand. But they . . . Just before he left for the holiday in Whitby, the family was discussing the trial of Sir Roger Casement for treason.'

'And they spoke of the rumours about his sexual relationships with men?' Even in her shocked state, Grace was determined to know everything.

Arthur nodded. 'His father described Casement as an immoral degenerate, who should be shot for his sexual deviancy, never mind his dealings with the Germans. His mother said it would break her heart if Robert were to be afflicted with such unnatural desires.'

'Robert must have known then that he could never tell them the truth.'

'Yes. He loved his parents very much and perhaps he thought his mother suspected his real feelings so—'

'So then he asked me to marry him.' She finished the sentence for him. 'My love for him must have been transparent. Had the long run along the cliffs been to steel himself to propose?'

'Please don't hate Robert. He despised himself enough for involving you in the whole mess. He would have tried to be a good husband.'

She was quiet.

Arthur took a deep breath. 'There had been rumours about Robert's relationship and the CO had transferred John Harris to another unit. They wrote to each other and were perhaps too unguarded in what they said. In any case, on his return from leave, Robert got word that the letters had been picked up by the military police and they intended interviewing him.'

'Why would they do that?'

'Oh Grace, their relationship was illegal. He would have faced a court martial.' Arthur looked away from her. 'I don't think he could have borne the seedy awfulness of it. The shame of his most private letters being read aloud. The condemnation of his fellow officers. The paragraph in the newspaper about his imprisonment for unnatural practices and weakening the morale of the troops at the Front. He, who was the bravest of us all.'

'Would those things really have happened?'

'Of course. He was worried about the effect on his parents, and on you too, Grace. The shame of being the fiancée of a man who was publicly denounced as being morally depraved.'

Grace thought of how infrequently she and Robert had actually been alone together. How the etiquette of the pre-war world dictated that they should always be chaperoned. 'I never really knew him,' she acknowledged quietly.

Arthur shook his head. 'I had been friends with Robert since we were both seven. He was charming and charismatic, someone that people were drawn to. He was also arrogant and self-centred, but this was the ultimate selfless act. Robert thought that if he were dead, the whole mess would disappear. The British Army wouldn't pursue a case against John. They could overlook it as the foolish indiscretions of a young man who had been seduced by his senior officer.'

'You believe he chose to die?'

'To save John, yes. It was the most heroic thing he ever did.'

They sat for a moment in silence. The chimes of the clock in the hallway broke the quiet. Her whole world had changed.

Arthur continued, 'The Somme was madness. We all had to wait until we heard the whistle at seven o'clock that morning. Then lead our men out of the trenches to almost certain death. Some of the keener officers kicked footballs because that was supposed to encourage the men to follow them over the top, as if it were all a game.' He shook his head, 'It was reckless madness. Walking with our eyes open into hell. I was behind Robert. I saw him rush ahead into the smoke and gunfire and I think he embraced death. He was ahead of everyone else. He was running. I didn't witness him go down, but it was impossible to see more than two feet in front of you with all the smoke, the mud being flung up by mortars and artillery fire, but I heard the hail of gunfire burst around him. He couldn't have survived. He didn't want to survive.'

'What a waste of a life.' She was glad of the dimness of the candlelight because it hid her face. 'Robert was always so unknowable,' she said. 'I think that was part of the attraction – the sense of mystery that existed around him.

I made him into the lover I wanted him to be, never who he really was.'

'No, Grace, no. He felt dreadfully alone.' He paused. 'You were worried about his relationship with Elizabeth. He told me that she was the only person he could talk to about his feelings. Robert said what seemed the strangest thing at the time, but now it makes sense.'

'What did he say?'

'That Elizabeth too had learned to live with shame.'

'The war, all of it was such a terrible waste of life, but this most of all.'

'I haven't told you this to hurt you.'

'No,' she said into the darkness. She wanted to reassure him. 'You were right to let me know. Before I mourned his death. Now I need to mourn the passing of a relationship that never existed. I must learn to live with that.'

She began to cry, and he instinctively took her hand, 'Grace, I'm sorry – very, very sorry.'

'Oh, Arthur, I seem to have got everything wrong. I just feel so foolish and so heartbroken.'

'Please don't cry. I can't bear to see you sad.' He hesitated. 'I would do anything in the world to make you happy.'

She looked up at him; her mother's words came into her head. 'Arthur loves you. He would make you happy.' With Arthur there would be peace. She would know security and what it was to be cherished. He held no darkness, no secrets. He moved imperceptibly closer and took her in his arms to comfort her. At the séance, she had been told to find her answers in the world of the living, not the dead.

'Gracie, darling, there is probably no worse time to say

this, but you mean everything to me. If you would marry me, it would make me the happiest man in the world. I hope that in time you would grow to love me as I love you.' There was a catch in his voice.

Here was safety and calm, after storm and tempest. Finally, she would not be alone.

She had made so many mistakes. With Arthur there would be none. She knew him, had always known him. She should choose love with her head and not her heart. Quietly, she said, 'Yes.'

'Gracie, we'll move on from the past – all its suffering – I promise you,' he said, smiling at her. His lips brushed against hers and he took both of her hands.

At that moment, they heard the front door open and her father's voice booming down the corridor. 'Hello Grace? Arthur? Are you still in the dining room?' He came into the room and switched on the electric light. They both stood up.

'Mr Armstrong, I have the most wonderful news.' Arthur moved towards her father, beaming. 'I can only apologize that I didn't ask your permission first but, if I may retro-spectively, would you allow me to marry Grace?'

Her father held out his hand and Arthur took it. 'Arthur,' he said, 'nothing would make me more delighted. I've long hoped that you two young people might find happiness together and now, well now . . .' He stopped and Grace realized that he was overcome with emotion. He started again. 'There has been so much sorrow visited on this house-hold, so perhaps we can look to a kinder future. I know that Isobel will be as happy as I am. Now let me see if I can find some champagne. It's not every day that a chap's daughter becomes engaged.'

The champagne was found and James Armstrong jubilantly poured three glasses. 'A toast to the future and to your marriage. I couldn't have hoped for a better son-in-law, Arthur; you're practically part of the family and now – well, this will make the ties all the stronger.'

They raised their glasses.

'We must place an announcement in *The Times*,' her father continued.

'No . . .' she began.

They both turned to her in surprise.

'We have to tell Mother before it is made public. She would be terribly hurt if I didn't tell her in person. I'll travel to Whitby at the weekend.'

'Grace is absolutely right, Mr Armstrong. My parents would also never forgive me if the world knew before they did.' He put his arm protectively around her. 'I'd be very happy to drive you up to the Yorkshire coast.'

She nodded dumbly.

'Absolutely, absolutely,' said her father. 'But I'm getting ahead of myself. Perhaps Isobel wouldn't mind if I accompanied you both.' There was a shyness and uncertainty in his voice that surprised Grace.

'I'm sure Mother would like to see you,' she said. Maybe her marriage to Arthur would bring their fractured family back together again.

The rest of the evening passed in a blur. Bridget returned from her supposed lecture and she and Mrs Watson were told the news and invited to join them for a glass of champagne, although they were sworn to absolute secrecy. Mrs Watson began to cry with delight. Perhaps she was imagining children in the house again. Bridget glanced across at her and Grace thought she saw something questioning in her look.

It was a relief to escape to her own room at the end of the evening. There was so much to think about. Arthur's revelation about Robert. The proposal and her acceptance. Everything had happened so quickly. She knew that she had felt no explosion of fireworks when Arthur kissed her, but he was a good man. This was what mature love should be – something to be worked at, to grow over time. This was more real than the illusory feelings she had had for Robert. She would learn to be happy again.

In bed, she thought of Robert's sealed lips. Of the secrets he wanted to tell but couldn't. And Elizabeth too. Her lips had also been sealed. Did she have more secrets to tell?

CHAPTER THIRTY-FOUR

There was a sense of adventure that Saturday morning, as Grace, Arthur and Mr Armstrong set off at six in the morning to drive up to Whitby in Arthur's Crossley 20/30. It was a freezing cold day, and they were all well wrapped up against the wind. Grace regaled them with stories about Miss Boddy's battle with Roger Dale. Arthur joked about finally giving up his tiny bachelor flat in Fulham. Her father was a little quieter. He hadn't seen his wife for several months. His hair was freshly cut and he had invested in a new tweed jacket.

When they finally arrived, Brambles Cottage had been transformed. Her mother was waiting at the door and proudly showed them around. All the rooms were immaculately clean and decorated with collections of shells and driftwood. Isobel had overseen the painting of the sitting room in a calming sage green and had plans for the other rooms too. The occasional tables were dotted with potted plants and a photograph of the whole family was prominently displayed, as was one of Edward in his uniform. The black ribbon had been removed.

Grace and Arthur broke the happy news to her, and she took the young couple into her arms. 'How lovely that at last there is something to celebrate,' she said, her eyes wet with tears.

Her father stood awkwardly in the background, smiling. 'Splendid,' he said, 'something splendid has happened.'

The four of them went for a long walk across the beach at Sandsend. Her mother was arm in arm with Grace, while the two men walked ahead. She was smiling and animated. The wind blew in off the sea, stinging and cold, and the November daylight was eked out from the sun that battled from behind the clouds. 'It's such good news, Gracie. Arthur is like family already, and he will cherish you in a way that Robert never would have.'

'Yes, Arthur is a good man,' Grace replied. It was a simple statement of fact. He was a good man. 'The last few days have been so hectic,' she continued, moving her hair from where it had blown in front of her face. 'I almost feel as if I'm in a dream. Arthur would like us to have a spring wedding.'

Her mother stood still. 'Your father and I had a spring wedding. I think there's something very wonderful about that time of year, with all its associations of fresh starts and new life. But make sure you don't marry in May. That's unlucky. Bunty married in May,' she confided.

'Bunty seems to be quite fine, unlucky wedding or not.'

Her mother laughed. 'She's certainly resilient.'

They were silent for several moments, before her mother said, 'Grace, you are in love with Arthur, aren't you?'

She looked out at the grey sea and took a deep breath. 'Yes, of course I love Arthur. It's just Robert, perhaps.' She hadn't told her mother the truth about Robert and probably never would. 'It's all happened quickly.'

Her mother looked at her carefully. 'Do you mean too quickly?'

Grace turned away from her gaze and started to walk towards the two men. She said, 'No. It has been very fast – the engagement, I mean – but I know Arthur well and we've always been close.' She looked at her mother now. 'I'd become quite frozen in grief. Stuck in the past. It's important to rejoin the living. I want to enjoy life again.'

'Sweetheart, I think it's devastating that your generation has had to suffer through so much loss. It's against the natural order to experience death when young.' Her mother shivered slightly, whether with the cold or with the sorrow that still haunted her, Grace didn't know. 'Mrs Wilkinson, a poor dear lady at that awful nursing home, lost all her sons in the war.'

'How sad!' Grace exclaimed.

'She was quite broken for a time, as I suppose I was – still am in some ways. Well, she wrote to me the other day and told me that she and her husband had travelled across to Ypres, where two of her boys had fallen. As they travelled along the Menin Road, she said that they were aware of the souls of the tens of thousands of young men who had died there, hovering just above them.'

'Robert's parents travelled out to the Somme. It's hard to face the finality of death,' Grace replied. 'Perhaps it's easier to believe the dead are still among us. I went to a séance, you know.'

Her mother looked at her in astonishment. 'Grace, you

didn't! I'm not sure how I feel about such things. But I must admit I'm intrigued. Tell me, what happened?'

They had just about caught up with her father and Arthur. Grace was relieved to be rescued from describing that evening by her father insisting that they hurry because both the chaps were starving, and the Hope and Anchor would stop serving food soon.

Her mother laughed, the sea air bringing a warm glow to her face. 'Your father has always been governed by his stomach. I hope for your sake Arthur doesn't turn out to be the same!'

They walked more briskly now. Grace had one final question for her mother. 'I worry that my determination to find out the truth about Elizabeth and her death is another way of avoiding the present.'

'And perhaps you should forget it?' her mother prompted, questioningly.

'That's what Arthur said. He's more practical than me, I suppose. He wants us to live in the present – to think about the future and a family.'

'Goodness, Grace,' Isobel laughed. 'Imagine grandchildren running around Ryedale Villa, just like you and Edward did!'

The future. It was good to think of the future. And perhaps her mother might return to London.

The rest of the evening passed pleasantly enough. They stayed up until midnight, playing cards, talking and drinking hot chocolate in front of the fire. Arthur slept in the attic bedroom, while Grace and her mother shared the main bedroom, and her father was on the sofa in the sitting room.

The next morning, they were all up early to prepare for the journey back to London. Grace cooked a huge breakfast of bacon and eggs, while her parents went for a long walk along the beach. When they returned, her father shook his head slightly and mumbled to her, 'Isobel needs some more time by herself.'

CHAPTER THIRTY-FIVE

Arthur would have come to the Red Lantern with Grace, even though she suspected he found the whole business of Elizabeth and her past rather sordid. However, at the last minute, he had been called away to a meeting in Paris. It was linked to the reparations treaty and very high profile. He was flying from Croydon and would be away for several days. The night before he left, he told Grace that he was frightfully sorry to be going but would try to telephone while he was away. 'If it leads to an advancement at Lloyd's, so much the better. Perhaps we can start to look at houses when I return.'

'Arthur, you must go,' she agreed. 'It's really quite splendid being involved in building a new Europe. How exciting as well, to think about buying our own house.'

She didn't feel the devastation at his absence that she had felt when Robert had gone to the Front. It was a totally different situation, of course. No longer one of life and death. This less dramatic type of love was better. One built on friendship and shared plans for the future. A love that didn't threaten to destroy her.

Before Grace left for the Red Lantern, she carefully cut out the image of Elizabeth from a spare copy of the large household photograph. She put it into her handbag, ready to show people at the club, and hurried to meet Sian and Maurice at London Bridge station. Tom would already be at the Red Lantern.

Maurice, as always, was impeccably dressed in a well-cut suit. He and Sian walked hand in hand and looked for all the world as if they were the perfect couple. Her friend had always claimed that she was too busy for romance. Grace wondered whether her feelings had changed. Meanwhile, Sian was delighted about the engagement to Arthur and chatted excitedly about the arrangements for the wedding, which they had tentatively planned to take place in April.

'I'll be chief bridesmaid, Gracie,' she said. 'Although you must promise me that I won't have to wear a dress in some pallid pink or pastel blue.'

'Of course,' Grace agreed. 'We need to visit Selfridges to pick out dress patterns and look at material. I was thinking of quite a simple wedding dress, in an ivory silk.' It was good to be caught up in the excitement of the preparations. Finally, life was fun, she told herself.

The Red Lantern was hidden away at the back of a wholesale warehouse on Tooley Street. Customers had to walk down a narrow flight of stairs to reach the dark smoky club.

'A bit different from Rectors, isn't it?' Sian said.

'Absolutely,' Grace agreed. 'It's probably a good thing Arthur didn't come. I don't really think it's his kind of place.'

Before they could enter the club proper, they had to pay their entrance fee to a woman who was sitting at a small table at the foot of the stairs. She was beautiful and immaculately made up, with red lips and blonde hair, but as she handed over the ticket and Grace went to thank her, she could see that her eyes were dead and her face blank of expression.

Where Rectors had been spacious, with tables spread out around the dance floor, soft lanterns and green palm plants, the dance floor here was tiny and dotted with a few plain deal tables and hardback chairs. It was dark, hazy with cigarette smoke and the murmur of voices. The jazz band had just finished their number and were swigging drinks before playing again. The trio looked round the room for Tom.

'Oh, there he is,' declared Sian. 'He's brought someone with him.' She wasn't wearing her spectacles and had to peer rather obviously across the dance floor.

Sitting close to him at the table was an attractive woman with dark hair, who looked as if she was engrossed in whatever it was that he was saying. He spotted them and waved. Grace's heart sank. She wasn't sure why it should bother her that Tom was there with someone else – perhaps it was the thought of playing gooseberry alongside two couples.

As they approached the table, the woman got up. She was dressed in a long, closely fitting black dress.

'This is Angela,' Tom introduced her. 'She's the singer tonight.'

They all greeted each other and said their hellos. 'I'd better get back, I suppose. Jim will be getting anxious to start.'

'I didn't expect to see you here,' Tom said to her.

'I didn't expect to be here either, but the band begged me to help.' She nodded at them. 'The usual singer has come down with tonsillitis.'

'Angela and I were both at the Royal College of Music,' he explained.

'It seems so long ago now,' she said. 'It's such a waste that you haven't gone back, Tom. Composing is—'

He cut her off. 'I know, I know, but they're tuning up now. Let me ruin my own life.'

She shot a glance at him and left.

The group agreed upon a bottle of champagne and settled down to listen to the music.

'Congratulations,' Tom said, turning to Grace. 'I hear you and Arthur are engaged. Bunty was delighted and has invented a celebratory cocktail in your honour.'

'That's nice,' she said weakly. 'We're planning a small wedding in the spring.'

'Arthur's a good man. He'll make you happy.'

All she could do was nod. The whole world was certain that Arthur was the right man for her.

The music started and their conversation died away. Angela had a low husky voice that seemed to fill the club with a sense of yearning and lost love. In her present state of mind, Grace wasn't sure whether she could bear to listen. To distract herself, she started to look around. Elizabeth had come here several weeks before she died. Had she come alone or with someone else, Grace wondered.

There was a strange, electric atmosphere about the place, which Grace couldn't quite define. People kept disappearing to corners of the room and then drifting back to their tables. And, just as Sian had said, the crowd was very mixed. At the table next to them a large group in evening wear were drinking whisky and talking loudly in upper-class accents.

They were arguing about whether they should stay at the Red Lantern or drive out to the country, where one of them had a large house. At another table, a dishevelled old man sat drinking alone, a whisky bottle placed in front of him.

She returned her attention to the table to find Tom looking at her. 'Angela said she could introduce us to the club owner if we like,' he said. 'Although she warned me to be careful. Said he'll be pretty jumpy. Death is bad for business, apparently. He's called Frank Jameson.'

When the sound of the saxophone had died away, Angela came over, hand in hand with the trumpet player. Grace found herself oddly relieved that she wasn't with Tom. It was strange to see the change from the sad yearning of her songs to her practical everyday self.

'Frank will see you now. His office is over there. I've said that Elizabeth Smith was your aunt, Tom. That's why you want to find out what happened in the weeks before her death.'

He smiled at her. 'Thanks, Angela, I appreciate this.'

The club owner's office was tiny and smelled of strong spirits and stale cigarette smoke. There were three men present, all seated at a small table on which stood several half-empty glasses and an overflowing ashtray. One man's face was disfigured with a number of livid scars. Grace was surprised when Tom put his arm protectively around her, but in this unfamiliar place she felt comforted by his presence. It struck her that Tom seemed more confident here. Before they entered the room, he'd suggested she leave him to do the talking.

Frank Jameson was younger than she'd expected and very thin, although he was expensively dressed. His eyes were artificially bright and he was constantly jerking his head this way and that, as if checking exactly what was going on. A silver pistol lay on the table in front of him. Grace sensed that he was a man whose mood could change in a second.

He ignored Tom's outstretched hand but nodded his head slightly at the two men, who got up, creating a space for them to sit down at the table.

'Angela said you wanted some information about your aunt, Elizabeth Smith. Reckoned she used to come here.'

He wasn't a man who indulged in small talk, Grace reflected as she perched awkwardly on the narrow chair.

'Yes,' said Tom. 'My mam is devastated about her death. She drowned in the Thames. The police reckon it's suicide, so Mam wants to know what drove her to it. I said I'd ask around and we know she came here a few weeks before she died.'

Frank lit a cigarette. 'Terrible thing that, especially a suicide. But I don't rightly know what help I can give you.'

'She sometimes used the name Lizzy. We wondered if she might have friends here. Who might know anything about the night she died?' Grace said.

Ignoring her, Frank addressed his comments solely to Tom. 'The Red Lantern is a popular place. A lot of people come here, and the name Elizabeth Smith don't mean nothing to me, if I'm honest. Maybe if you tell me what she looked like I could help.'

'We've got a photograph. From about five years ago,' Tom offered.

Grace produced it from her handbag and handed it to

Frank. He held the image up to the light and scrutinized it for a few moments. She was sure he recognized the face, but he shrugged and claimed he'd never seen her before. His attention span was clearly short and it felt as if the meeting was coming to an end but, at that moment, a burly middle-aged man burst through the door. 'There's trouble at the doors, Frankie. A geezer we banned last week is demanding to come in.'

'Some people never learn. Right, let's make sure he don't forget this time.' Frank sprang up and took the gun from the table. 'Just in case.' He nodded at them and left the room, followed by the two silent men.

Grace also stood up. Tom looked at her, surprised. 'What are you doing?'

'The photograph, on the wall,' she said. 'It's a picture of Elizabeth. Quick, look.'

She pointed to an image of three women. All beautiful and all exquisitely dressed in evening gowns. 'The one on the left. That's her when she was young.'

Tom was now on his feet too. He peered at the image. 'It can't be. The picture is recent. Look at their clothes – they're too modern.'

'Are you sure? It's the absolute image of her.' She examined it again and realized he was right. The young woman in the photograph wore a hem that fell just below her knee, not like the formal skirts and petticoats at the turn of the century.

Tom interrupted her thoughts, saying, 'Quickly, one of them's on their way back, we'd better sit down.'

Hastily, they returned to their seats.

The thinner of the two men came into the room and

looked at them suspiciously. 'What you been looking for? I seen you.'

'We were just admiring the photograph,' Grace said, and pointed across to it.

'Yeah, it's a nice one. Sad about what happened to Charlotte, mind,' he replied.

'Charlotte Harcourt?' Grace asked, amazed.

'You knew her? Yeah, lovely girl, but Frank had to ask her to leave. Charlotte had got herself into drugs – addicted. There were customers asking questions about her behaviour and this is a business. You know how it is.' He settled himself down at the table.

'Did you know that she'd died?' Tom asked.

'Frankie sent a wreath to the funeral. He's caring like that.' The man lit a cigarette.

Grace was absolutely shocked. She believed there was the closest of all links between Charlotte Harcourt and Elizabeth Smith.

Frank returned. He was panting slightly and his face was red. 'We got that sorted,' he said to the thin man as he sat down behind the table. 'He won't be back.' Then he turned to them. 'As you can tell, we're busy right now. I saw you as a favour to Angela but there's nothing more I can do to help. We don't know nothing about Elizabeth Smith or her death.'

They stood up. Grace wanted to ask about Charlotte Harcourt, but the meeting was clearly at an end. They went to leave the room and Grace looked across the dim dance floor. To her horror, she saw the bulky figure of Sergeant Williams. He was dressed in a grey, greasy suit and a young woman was huddled against him, smoking a cigarette.

Suddenly, he glanced over and stared at them in astonishment. He shoved the woman roughly aside and pushed his way through the dance floor. What on earth was he doing here?

Behind her, Grace heard Frank Jameson ask, 'What's the matter, Jack?'

'Them. What are they up to?' He jerked his head towards Grace and Tom.

'They've come about an Elizabeth Smith. A lady what was found in the Thames. His aunt,' Frank said, pointing to Tom.

'She's not his auntie – they're lying. See, I don't forget a face, Mr Monaghan.' He stared at Tom for a moment before moving over to the table and speaking quietly in Frank Jameson's ear. The tension was palpable. Grace thought that just one wrong word or gesture and everything could snap.

'You've played me.' Frank said. 'I don't like to be crossed,' he continued, almost conversationally. 'People who cross me have a habit of ending up with problems.' As he said this, Grace remembered the gun lying on the table. Frank was watching her intently. She felt her heart race.

In that instant, he shoved against the table and stood up. The glasses and ashtray fell to the hard floor and shattered into a hundred pieces.

He turned to the men who had been sitting with him. 'Get them out before I lose my temper!'

Tom put out his hands in a gesture to show that they meant no harm, 'We're going, we're going. No offence meant.'

The two men jumped up and moved towards them. Tom almost pushed her from the office. 'Grace, we need to get out of here quickly.'

'What about Sian and Maurice?' she whispered.

He paused for a moment, uncertain. 'Sergeant Williams has never met them, so they should be safe. I'll let them know we're leaving when I get our coats.'

Terrified, she ran up the stairs.

Minutes later, Tom emerged from the club. He was out of breath. 'Just keep walking,' he said. 'There's someone following us. Quick.'

They could hear the sound of footsteps getting closer and closer. Tom suddenly grabbed her arm and dragged her into a shop doorway.

'What are you doing?' she hissed.

He laughed, 'Don't get all ladylike on me. You're the one who antagonized a man who'd kill you as easily as he'd change his suit. If we're in here, we shouldn't be spotted and we can get away.'

They stood together hidden in the darkness, sheltered from the street by the shop porch. 'We'd best pretend we're a couple, stopping for a few minutes of privacy together.'

The footsteps came closer. They heard shouts.

He seized her and pulled her tightly towards him. She was aware of the closeness of his body, melting into hers. Their breathing had slowed down and was now in unison. Neither of them spoke. Someone stopped a few feet away from them and then started walking away. Finally, he said, 'They've gone. It's safe.' He let go of her.

Looking around carefully, they left the shop doorway and came out onto the empty street. They moved apart, as if suddenly too conscious of each other.

She felt shaken but didn't know whether it was from the averted danger or their brief moment of intimacy.

'Apologize to Arthur for me and let him know it was that or be beaten up by a gang of thugs.' His voice was unsteady.

She nodded. 'I'm sure Arthur would understand. He would know it didn't mean anything.' She had to be very clear about that.

'We might as well go straight to London Bridge station,' Tom said, still looking round to make sure they weren't being followed.

They walked quickly, talking about what they'd discovered. 'Charlotte Harcourt and Elizabeth must be related,' Grace said. 'They're almost identical in appearance. Mother and daughter?'

'It would perhaps explain why she came to the Red Lantern,' he agreed. 'If her daughter was working there – particularly if she knew she'd become addicted to drugs. Had she ever talked about having a child?'

'No, she rarely talked about her past. How terrible to see Charlotte being destroyed in that way! And Frank Jameson was such a frightening man – could he have been involved in what happened to them?' She had to hasten her step to keep up with him.

'Perhaps. I don't know.'

'Surely, it's not a coincidence that Sergeant Williams was the investigating officer for both deaths,' she offered.

'Maybe.' Tom was non-committal. 'Certainly, neither of them was investigated properly. They were both put down as suicide.'

She shivered. 'I suppose we definitely know he's not to be trusted now.'

Tom agreed.

On the journey home, she kept her mind resolutely on what they had found out that night, but once she reached Ryedale Villa, she slumped against the front door. Try as she might, it was impossible to wipe away the memory of her closeness to Tom and the way it had made her feel.

CHAPTER THIRTY-SIX

Constable Alston believed that the truth would always find a way of being revealed. Grace had thought him naïve, but the next evening she received a frantic telephone call from Lady Bunty.

'Grace, dreadful news. The worst!' she exclaimed. 'For you at least.'

'Whatever has happened?'

'Lady Constance has been in contact. It turns out that she's been buying the *Hampstead & Highgate Express* religiously, expecting to see an article exonerating Sir Hugh.'

'And, of course, there's been nothing,' Grace replied mechanically.

'It gets worse, Grace. She's convinced there's no article because you didn't believe her.'

'I didn't say that, Bunty,' she responded.

'Well, it doesn't matter whether you said it or not, because she wants to see you again. Alone, mercifully. Constance has something to tell you that she has never revealed to anyone. Something that proves Hugh could never have been with Lizzy that summer.'

'I wonder what it could be?'

'Honey, I have no idea. When she said it, I was too busy celebrating her insistence on it being for your ears only. Sorry, Gracie, but I've done my bit.'

'I don't mind going back there. When does she want to see me?'

'Wednesday, six thirty on the dot. Send her my best regards and let her know that I'm drinking a Manhattan in her honour.' There was a definite note of triumph in Bunty's voice.

Mr Wagstaff kept Grace working later than expected that Wednesday afternoon. The memory of Armistice Day hung heavy over them all. Having spent much of his time walking aimlessly around his office, he had suddenly been seized by a surge of energy and insisted on dictating his extensive views on Sir Edgar Watson's speech on the general nursing examinations. Grace suspected the piece would never be published; he just didn't want to be alone.

He finally finished speaking a little after 6 p.m. As she reached for her coat from the peg, he said, 'Thank you, Miss Armstrong. I hope I haven't inconvenienced you.'

'No, no. Not at all, Mr Wagstaff.'

Once she had turned the corner of Tavistock Square and was out of sight of the offices of *Nursing World*, she began to run. Lady Constance struck her as someone who did not approve of lateness. On Regent Street she saw a long queue for the number 17 bus.

'Shocking, the buses,' one of her fellow queue members muttered. 'There hasn't been one for the last twenty minutes.'

'They only travel in packs,' another one commented.

When the bus finally arrived, it crawled its way through the busy streets of the West End and Knightsbridge. She looked out at the colourful shop windows, lit up with Christmas displays of dresses and dolls and overflowing hampers of food. The world was starting to return to some kind of normality.

At last she reached her stop and ran to Lady Constance's house. She was greeted at the door by Maria, who said glumly, 'Madam thought you were not coming. She is indisposed now.'

Grace was about to turn away when an imperious voice floated down the stairs. 'I will see Miss Jaggers. You may bring her to the sitting room.'

Lady Constance was seated by the fire, which provided the only light in the room, and was dressed in her night-clothes. When Grace had seen her previously, she had worn discreet rouge and powder, which had brought warmth to her face. Stripped of these, she looked pale and old. The darkness of the room and the lateness of the hour lent a new intimacy between the two women. After the briefest of preliminaries, Constance began to speak in a way that felt prepared. 'I wish to be completely honest with you, Miss Jaggers. The end of my life is approaching, and I want the truth to be known.'

Grace looked at her expectantly as the older woman gathered her thoughts.

'Hugh was my second husband. My first marriage had not been a happy one. The Reverend Lincoln was much older than me, an academic and scholar at Oxford. I was dazzled by the chance to be among great minds – the men who promoted the leading ideas of our day.' She sniffed. 'Frankly, I was disillusioned. My husband proved to be most mediocre intellectually and had only attained prominence through the annoying habit of flattering whoever was the most important man in the room.'

'How disappointed you must have been.'

'I accepted it as my lot. My second husband, however, was a great man. A flawed man, perhaps, but a man with the potential to do much good. Hugh had loved me from the first time he saw me at Richmond Park.'

'But you were married then, I believe?'

'Yes, and Hugh married several years later, although his wife died in childbirth. Very sad, of course. We both knew we couldn't be together until I was free from my obligations to my husband, but we were unable to deny the strength of our feelings. We met at the houses of mutual friends. And I counted the days until I could be his wife.'

'When your first husband died?'

In the flickering firelight, Grace saw that she nodded. 'He was in poor health. I nursed him as a faithful wife should, but I knew his death would bring my release.'

Grace wondered whether her first husband had known that she was only with him through a sense of duty and longed for her younger suitor.

'When, finally, we married, Hugh was relieved to leave behind the ungodly world in which he had moved.

'Ungodly!' It seemed to Grace a strong phrase to describe his life before their marriage.

'The world of politics and high society has always been linked to late nights, weekend house parties and an endless round of infidelities. It's a world with which your Aunt Bunty will no doubt be familiar,' she sniffed.

Grace started to defend Bunty, but Lady Constance continued, 'She once asked me if I doubted him. Of course, I doubted him. Lizzy was a beautiful woman and much younger than me.' Constance took a deep breath. 'I was afraid he thought he had made a bad bargain, to wait half a lifetime to marry and then . . .' Her words died away. She put her hands to the ruined beauty of her face.

The room was dark and the window an oblong of navy illuminated by the street lights all along Sloane Street. She did not look directly at Grace. Maria came into the room to attend to the fire and asked whether the candles should be lit. Constance shook her head and dismissed the maid from the room with a gesture of her hand.

'There are things I have not told you, because I was ashamed,' she spoke into the darkness.

'What things?' Grace prompted, gently.

Finally, she whispered, as if she might be overheard in the deserted house, 'I knew that previously he had led a dissolute life. When his first wife died in childbirth, he blamed himself for that. He went through what he called his dark period. He had relationships and encounters that he said meant nothing. He had been intimately involved with Anna Howard, the mother of Lizzy Burdett-Smith.'

'What?' Grace gasped. Adele had spoken of her mother's liaisons, but she had not said that one of her lovers had been Sir Hugh Clifton.

'It was not the daughter,' Constance went on. 'Never the daughter but the mother. In his time of grief he slept with that woman, and she conceived for him what she thought was a grand passion. She lived with her husband in the dull comfort of Essex and Hugh, my Hugh, represented an escape from all the boredom of her life.'

Lady Constance turned away. She didn't speak for several minutes. The silence was broken only by the soft crackling of the fire. Finally, she took a breath. 'I knew the Burdett-Smiths lied. Lizzy claimed to have been with Sir Hugh on the night of 28 July. That was not possible.'

'Why wasn't it possible?' Grace asked.

'On 28 July 1900, Hugh accompanied me to a discreet doctor in one of the less salubrious suburbs of our city. I was carrying his child – our child. I was forty-four years of age and never thought that I would be blessed in that way.'

Grace went to speak, to console her, but Lady Constance shook her head fiercely. 'No, I must tell the whole of my story. I have hidden it for too many years. The Reverend Lincoln was still clinging on to life and would have known it could not be his. My reputation would have been ruined, and so I was forced to destroy the thing I most desired.' She stared at the fire, as if seeing that time so long ago. 'It was to be my only chance of motherhood, but Miss Armstrong, I can prove beyond doubt that he was not with Lizzy Burdett-Smith on that Saturday, or the days immediately following. He held me while I wept endlessly.'

The flames in the fire were dying down. A dull red glowed at the heart of the black coals. Grace was suddenly aware that the room was cold. There could be no doubt now that Lady Constance was telling the truth. This was a secret she had never spoken out loud.

'You will help me,' Constance pleaded. 'It is a stain that has seeped through every layer of my life. I want to die knowing that my husband's name is free from taint. He did not commit adultery with Lizzy Burdett-Smith.'

The proud woman was begging her for the one thing that would allow her to die in peace. Yet Grace knew that her very presence in this room was dishonest. In the face of such sincerity and desperation, she couldn't lie any more. 'Lady Constance, I have something to tell you. I must . . .'

'Go on. What is it?'

The room was in shadow. She needn't look Lady Constance in the eye but still the words wouldn't form. A vulnerable woman, living in the past and haunted by the ghosts of shame and scandal. What could she say? When it was light, in daytime, she would tell the truth.

'Nothing. It's nothing. It's late now and you must be tired. We'll speak of it when I return.'

Impulsively Lady Constance seized her hands, 'You are a good girl. You have shone a light into my home.' She gestured at the darkened room. 'You care about the truth of what happened.'

Grace burned with shame. She hoped Constance couldn't sense her guilt. She could only vow to herself that she would reveal her identity when she was next there.

As Grace left the house, Maria murmured, 'You will come back, yes? She looks forward to your visits. You have brought her back to life.'

'Yes, of course. I will return.' And she promised herself that she would tell the truth.

CHAPTER THIRTY-SEVEN

The next day, a single letter lay upon the doormat. Grace recognized her own handwriting on the envelope. It was the one she had given to Adele. She picked it up quickly and stuffed it in her dress pocket.

Her father was already sitting at the breakfast table. 'You look pale, Grace,' he observed. 'Late again last night. You always seem to be off gallivanting somewhere these days. It'll all change when you're married, you know.'

'Yes, Father, I was later than I intended,' she said and took her place at the table. In her pocket, the letter burned a hole. She was desperate to know its contents and wished her father was gone – disappeared off to work – so that she could read it alone.

'Any plans for today?' he asked, glancing up from the morning newspaper.

'If Sian's not working, we might go to Selfridges and look at dressmaking patterns for the wedding.'

'Good idea.' He smiled and heaved himself from the table. 'The ministry calls. Can you let Mrs Watson know I'll be home a little later this evening?'

'Yes of course, Father. What time should I say?'

'Oh, about seven or so. I've got a meeting with one of the junior ministers, Jonathan Doddington. A dreadful stutter – a touch of shellshock, poor chap. I suspect the meeting will run on for quite some time.' He sighed. 'Anyway, goodbye, Grace dear.'

He left her contemplating a breakfast she had no appetite for. Soon Bridget came in and began to clatter the plates as she cleared them. 'It's all right, Bridget. I'll put everything away. I'm sure you have many other things to do.'

'I'm glad someone recognizes that because Mrs Watson will not be told.' She disappeared from the room.

At last, Grace was alone and opened the letter. It was written in a neat, precise hand. She leaned back in her chair and began to read:

Dear Miss Armstrong,

It is perhaps right that the <u>truth</u> is finally told about Lizzy, and my family's ghosts laid to rest. I have information that may surprise you. Presumably, my sister never told you that she had a daughter. It was one of her many secrets.

A month or so after that dreadful trial at the Old Bailey, she revealed that she was expecting Captain Burdett-Smith's child. It was a shock to us all, particularly as we believed relations of that kind had long ceased. However, one night, when heavy in drink, he had demanded his rights as a husband. Thankfully, the corsets so fashionable at the time had hidden her condition from the scrutiny of the courtroom and the world.

However, poor Lizzy was destitute – those whom she had hoped would support her quickly disappeared. Through friends from the Suffrage movement, she found a place at a home for unmarried mothers. It was here that she met a priest, Father Daley, who seems to have taken an especial interest in her. Perhaps he relished the ecclesiastical challenge of redeeming an alleged murderess and known adulteress.

Indeed, my sister underwent quite a road to Damascus conversion and became a practising Roman Catholic. I have never dared to ask whether she was responsible for Sir Hugh's murder, but she seemed to have been much afflicted with guilt afterwards. I must admit, the religion seemed to me a little alarming, what with all the candles, bells and the like, but it gave her a kind of peace.

She had believed she would hate her husband's child, but instead she fell in love with Charlotte and nursed her for the first six months, before the inevitable happened and she was forced to relinquish her daughter. Captain Burdett-Smith's sister, Victoria Harcourt, agreed to take Charlotte and bring her up as part of the family.

Grace put the letter down. The photograph at the Red Lantern had told the truth. It was with trembling fingers that she carried on reading.

Frankly, Victoria Harcourt was the coldest and least maternal of women, and she despised Lizzy. However, there was no choice in the matter. Penniless, and branded the most immoral woman in England, no court in the land would have allowed Lizzy to keep the child. It was agreed that each year she would be sent photographs and details about her daughter's life – through the family's solicitors Payne & Partners, who are known for their discretion and lack of scruples.

When Charlotte was eighteen, a meeting would be brokered between mother and daughter where Charlotte might be told the truth about her parentage. As Captain Burdett-Smith pointed out several times, it was most generous of him in the circumstances.

Lizzy told me that she lived for the day she would be reunited with Charlotte, and the thought of it sustained her through the many long, barren years she endured. She had planned to leave England, but instead stayed to watch over her daughter.

My poor, dear sister! First, she discovered that Charlotte was addicted to drugs and working as a nightclub hostess. Then she received the letter telling her of Charlotte's death, which destroyed any hope of happiness. It is my belief that this drove her to kill herself, in the exact spot where Charlotte's body had been found.

I hold some documents which may be of interest to you, but I would rather disclose their contents in person. There is a small restaurant, the Peloponnese, which is on Ensign Street, near to Tower Bridge. I propose that we meet there on Sunday 30th at 7 p.m. If this is convenient, please could you reply by return of mail? My husband is away on business now and will not be able to intercept any correspondence. As must have been clear to you, he has such an antipathy to Lizzy that I am forbidden to say her name in his company.

Kindest regards,
Mrs A. Pratchett

Grace sat a long time at the breakfast table, thinking of the dreadful, dreadful waste that had been Elizabeth's life. Almost eighteen years waiting to be reunited with a daughter who was ignorant of her existence, and who had died before they could meet. Was there any point in finding out more? The truth seemed to be a dangerous thing. Robert's declaration of love to her had been a lie, no more than a disguise to protect him from the rest of the world. And perhaps there was another damaging truth too. A fact that hovered just beyond her consciousness, no matter how she tried to push it away. The sensations she had felt when Tom pulled her close as they hid from the thugs outside the nightclub. The reality that there were no such feelings with Arthur. Safe, decent, reliable Arthur. The man she should have loved but could not. She let Adele's note fall to the table.

Bridget came bustling into the breakfast room and jumped with surprise. 'Well, the Virgin Mary and all the holy saints, whatever is it that you're doing here? It's almost eleven o'clock and you've not moved an inch.'

'I've had a letter, Bridget, from Elizabeth's sister. She had a daughter, who also drowned at London Bridge. Here, you might as well read it for yourself.' She passed over the letter.

Bridget read through its contents and slowly sank into her chair. 'Well, was there ever such a blighted life? Poor Elizabeth. That final letter from Payne & Partners must have told her of her daughter's death.'

When Grace looked up at Bridget, her eyes were filled with tears. 'All I can think of is how alone she must have felt. I wish she had been able to confide in me, allowed me to help her in some way.'

'Shame is a terrible thing, Miss Armstrong. It can silence even the strongest of characters.'

'It was a life full of shame.' Grace took a deep breath. 'Elizabeth who was so beautiful and intelligent, and to die—'

''Tis sad, very sad,' Bridget agreed.

'Do you think I should meet with Mrs Pratchett? Perhaps it's better to leave things unknown.'

Bridget looked at her directly. 'Miss Armstrong, I'm surprised at you even asking the question. It seems to me that you've come so far in the story that you might as well find out its ending, good or bad.'

CHAPTER THIRTY-EIGHT

Grace had just stood up to fetch writing paper from the bureau when Mrs Watson flew into the room, her arms filled with an assortment of half-opened boxes and parcels. Her face was red with rage. 'You dirty thief, you. I knew I'd catch you out in the end! You and your deceitful ways!'

The two women turned and looked at her in amazement. 'Mrs Watson, whatever do you mean?' Grace demanded.

The older woman stopped short. 'Miss Armstrong, I didn't think you were still here but it's better that you find out what she's been up to. The viper in the bosom!'

'What have you got there?' Bridget demanded. Her voice was loud with indignation. 'Have you been sneaking around in my bedroom?' She looked as if she were about to fling herself at her fellow servant.

Grace hastily interposed herself between the two women. 'Mrs Watson, you must explain yourself. Have you been into Bridget's bedroom?'

'Oh yes, and with good cause too. I've been waiting for my moment, and look at this. All of this!' She placed the boxes on the table and Grace went to peer inside, to find a collection of silverware, crockery and ornaments. 'Look what she's taken from this house!'

'Bridget?' Grace looked at her questioningly.

Before she could answer, the cook jumped in. 'Oh, I've had my suspicions for a while. Whenever her bedroom door was half opened, I could see it was a veritable Aladdin's cave in there. But I could never get more than a peek because she always kept it locked, so I bided my time until she was careless and left the key on the kitchen table. What do I find? A magpie's hoard all set to be sold on.'

It was now Bridget's turn to be scarlet with anger. 'How dare you! You are an interfering old woman. There's not an item there that's not been slaved and saved for. Bought bit by bit over the last few months from department stores like the Army & Navy and Woolworths.'

As the two women squared up to each other, Grace looked carefully at the collection of items the cook had placed on the table. 'I really don't think these are from the house, Mrs Watson. They look similar but they're not the same. I don't think they are silver, in fact. But a very good replica,' she added hastily, seeing the offended look on Bridget's face. 'See, this ornamental clock is very like the one on the mantlepiece in the sitting room, but that's still there.'

Mrs Watson suddenly stopped and, after a moment's thought, said, 'Whatever would you want all these bits and pieces for? It's not as if you have a place of your own.'

Bridget retorted, 'Do you really think I've the slightest intention of staying in service for the rest of my life? If so, Mrs Watson, then you're more of a fool than I took you for.

I shall be getting a proper home. And then there'll be a place for everything.'

'How can you afford to pay for all of these things on the wage of a general maid?' Mary Watson demanded suspiciously.

''Twas not my wage alone that paid for everything. Michael has paid half or more.'

'Michael?' Grace asked wonderingly. 'Who's he?'

'Why my fiancé, of course. We'll be putting down a deposit on a house in the next few months. Now that we've got our ornaments and furnishings.'

'Mrs Watson, I think you probably owe Bridget an apology. I'm sure the items are not stolen. But your fiancé. Bridget? This is news to everyone.' Arthur had been right, after all, about the young man and the true reason for Bridget's sudden interest in evening classes.

'Well, she might not be a thief, though she's certainly the sly one,' Mrs Watson muttered, 'but if I've called you something you're not, Bridget, I'm sorry,' she finished. 'I shall go back to my duties in the kitchen. Fiancé, indeed!'

Grace sank down weakly at the table, which was still covered with the breakfast dishes and now, in addition, the boxes of gleaming silver and pretty crockery. 'Bridget, perhaps you'd like to join me for a cup of tea.'

The maid sat down, and Grace poured them both a cup of cold tea.

'I suppose I should congratulate you on your engagement, Bridget, but who on earth is Michael and when did you meet him?'

'Why, he's Michael O'Shea, the son in Michael O'Shea &

Sons. The butcher's in Kentish Town,' she added for Grace's benefit. Suddenly she exclaimed, 'Mind, but this tea is disgusting. I'll just go fetch a new pot for it's impossible to tell a story without a hot beverage to hand.'

When she had returned and poured them both a fresh cup, Grace took a sip and asked, 'How long have you known each other?'

'Well, 'tis less than a year now. Ever since he came back from the war. I began to notice I was always given the choicest cuts of meat – even that old sour-face Mrs Watson commented on the quality of the lamb chops. It seemed to me that Michael must have taken a shine to me.' Bridget leaned back in her chair, enjoying telling her tale. 'Over time, we got talking about more than sweetbreads and sausages. Then we started walking out and, next thing you know, we're planning a future together. Getting our own home and furnishing it with all the nice kinds of things you have here, Miss Armstrong.'

'Do you love him, Bridget?' Why was it so important to Grace to know the answer to this question?

'He's a good man and I'll learn to love him,' was the practical response. 'It's a foolish thing to hold on to heartache. If you don't mind me saying, Miss Armstrong.'

Grace digested this silently before saying, 'But why were you so secretive about your relationship?'

'As to why I told no one, well, with Patrick, I told the world and then he died,' she sighed. 'It made my sorrow all the worse, for the world kept asking me how I was, and it meant I could think of nothing but his death. I'm sure you'll appreciate how that feels.'

Grace nodded gravely.

'And so, I kept it to myself. Maybe it was superstition too. I didn't want to curse my hope of happiness until I was sure it was right.'

'When we went to the séance, you were desperate to speak to Patrick. Why?'

'I did love Patrick dearly and I've never forgiven myself for the argument we had before he left for the Front. Michael had asked me to be his wife a month or so before the séance, but I thought I had to set things right with the past before I was free to marry someone else. Now I know that was just foolishness on my part.'

'But you had messages from Patrick and his mother?'

Bridget looked at Grace sharply. 'Now, don't be telling me that you believe all that nonsense about speaking to the dead? I'd have thought better of you.'

Grace replied indignantly, 'But it was you who took me there. You said you needed to speak to Patrick.'

She shook her head. 'That's as maybe, but I just needed to reassure myself. The mind has a funny way of working and it was my way of drawing a line between the past and present. D'you know that Doris leaves the back door unlocked every night just in case Bert should return. With her head, she knows that he never will, but there's a part of her that can't help hoping.'

'Mrs Kelly knew things about you and Doris.' Grace protested. 'She had the message from the spirit world that Samuel should see the doctor and that saved his life. I felt the intense cold, something otherworldly when she was speaking to the spirits.'

Bridget cackled with laughter, 'Well, I've had time

enough to think of that. Before we got there, Mrs Kelly had spoken with Doris for an hour or more. There's nothing she won't have found out and she'll have known that the front parlour was dedicated to Bert's memory and never used. So, which room in the house would have been colder and more likely to feel deathly? And as for little Samuel! You've never met him, but surely there never was a more sickly-looking child. He was crying out to be sent to the doctor!'

'She told me that there was nothing for me in the spirit world,' Grace said defensively, 'and it's true.'

'Doris thought Betty was coming,' Bridget said simply. 'So she didn't tell Mrs Kelly anything about you. She'll have been worried about getting her facts wrong if she claimed to have a message for you.'

'Oh,' Grace replied quietly. 'At first I thought it showed that Robert wasn't dead, which was why she couldn't communicate with him, but then I believed it was because he never loved me.'

Bridget looked at her, astonished. 'What do you mean by that, Miss Armstrong?'

Grace drew a deep breath, tears stinging her eyes. 'Arthur told me that Robert deliberately walked to his death.'

Bridget gasped, 'And why ever would that be?'

Another deep breath. 'I hope this won't shock you too much, but he was in love with a man. One of the men from his company. It wasn't me he loved at all. The engagement was just a pretence. He used me,' she finished sadly.

Bridget leaned across the table and took Grace's hand.

Falteringly, on the verge of tears, she continued. 'Some

letters were found. From him to his lover. He died to avoid bringing shame on us all and to save the man he loved from imprisonment.'

'Oh, poor man!' Bridget said. 'And him who seemed to live a charmed life. Grace, I think he never meant to use you.'

'That's what Arthur said.'

'And surely you must feel pity for him. To be forced to kill himself, just for being in love. And you're alive and can still find happiness.'

Grace nodded slowly at this simple truth.

'Speaking of which, Miss Armstrong, I'll be putting in my notice with immediate effect. A servant's life is not for me and I'll be a married woman soon. I must think to the future.'

'You're leaving? Oh Bridget, I shall miss you dreadfully.' Then acknowledging she should be more generous, she wiped her eyes and continued, 'But I'm happy for you too.'

'Thank you, miss. But marriage or no, after this morning, I've no intention of breathing the same air as Mrs Watson, never mind working alongside her. I shall pack up my belongings and move in with my sister in Kilburn until the wedding.'

CHAPTER THIRTY-NINE

Bridget might insist on the importance of the future, but the recent past was too raw to be forgotten so easily. Too many people had been wounded by the war, and the remembrance of the dead was well suited to bleak November. Across the villages, cities, hamlets and suburbs of Great Britain, subscriptions had been raised to erect memorials to those killed. The long lists of names chiselled into stone hinting at the stories of lives and love destroyed. In London, the Cenotaph was covered in a sea of lilies and chrysanthemums. Now, in the weeks leading up to Christmas, many churches began to hold commemorative concerts.

On that Saturday, Sian and Grace met for a performance of Mozart's Requiem at the church of St Martin-in-the-Fields. They hadn't seen each other since the Red Lantern, although Grace had telephoned to apologize for her departure. Sian had sounded distracted during their conversation, finally excusing herself by saying that she was very busy at the hospital. Grace suspected her friend was preoccupied with Maurice and he was eating up all her time away from the wards.

They were to meet first in the Lyons' tea room on the corner of the Strand and Trafalgar Square. The café was filled with the bustle of the early evening crowds, shop assistants and office boys, still in the uniform of the working day, sharing tea and buns before catching suburban trains back to Kent. The wealthy of London were out too, dressed in silks and furs and drinking cocktails at the Ritz or Savoy, filling in the hour or so before the theatres opened.

Grace found a window seat and looked out at the people hurrying towards the commuter stations of Charing Cross and Embankment, before being swallowed up in the Underground. She was lost in her thoughts and didn't see Sian arrive until she sat herself down at the table. As always, Sian was immaculately dressed, in a black coat and fur-trimmed hat, with a slash of bright red lipstick across her mouth, but her eyes were tired.

After the obligatory greeting and ordering, Grace asked, 'Sian, is something wrong? You don't seem yourself.'

She shrugged, 'Is it so obvious?'

'What's happened? Is it Maurice? Is he going back to New York?' Grace was shocked to see that Sian's eyes had filled with tears.

'In a week's time.' She took out her handkerchief. 'The worst thing is, he didn't ask me to go with him, Gracie. I was absolutely convinced he would.'

'Would you have gone?' Grace asked.

'I don't know,' Sian answered honestly, 'but it would have been nice to have been asked. Perhaps he didn't love me as much as I thought he did.'

'Well, he's a fool then!' she replied indignantly.

Sian tried to laugh. 'It's probably only my pride that's hurt, but I had grown to care for him.'

'Are you sure you still want to go to the concert?' Grace asked, concerned.

'Yes, I absolutely wouldn't miss it. I think there might be something rather comforting in listening to Mozart's Requiem.'

The two women linked arms as they walked into the beautiful, spacious church. It was lit by golden chandeliers of candles, hanging in bunches from the ceiling. All along the window ledges were huge vases of white lilies, which made the air heavy with their scent. At the front of the church stood the choir of young boys, their pure voices ringing out the soulful words of hymns performed across time and continents to mourn the dead. Grace realized that the last time she had heard the Requiem had been at Edward's memorial service, held nearly a year ago.

Listening to the innocence of their voices was heartbreaking. Grace thought of other choirs, ones that had sung the exact same words a decade ago and who had ended up in the mud of Flanders. For those other choirboys, their own Requiem had been the sound of machine guns heard in the stinking trenches. It was pure chance, an accident of birth, that they had been slaughtered, yet this new generation sang with an absolute belief in continuity and safety. She found herself praying, 'Please don't let there be another war. Don't let another generation be destroyed as mine has been.' She turned to look at Sian and saw that she too was weeping.

In truth, Grace sensed a terrible sadness swell among the congregation. There was nobody here who was untouched by the war. The sublimity of the music reached a nerve deep within her and stirred up feelings and emotions she had thought long buried, for the music brought a sense of hope. Perhaps it was an idealistic, naïve view of what the future might be – yet surely hope was part of what makes us human, she reflected. The future can't be forever blighted.

Grace and Sian left the church in silence, thinking about the message of resurrection contained in the music. She heard a shout of, 'Grace, Sian, hello!'

Surprised, they turned around and there was Tom, standing right in front of them. He looked oddly ill at ease, his coat too thin for the chill evening air, his smile lopsided as he ran his fingers through his dark hair. Yet there was something about him that made her heart leap.

'The music was beautiful,' he said, nodding towards the church.

'Yes, it was incredibly moving,' Grace agreed. 'The choir at Edward's school sang the Requiem at his memorial service.' She stopped, unable to continue.

He looked at her closely and she almost thought to challenge him. He had claimed that there was no longer a place for music in a world that had shown itself so bloodthirsty, where young men had died as if they had been machines, not humans with beating hearts and dreams. She stopped herself. There was something so glorious about the music that she didn't want to argue or be petty.

Perhaps they all wanted to avoid serious topics of conversation. They talked instead about the weather, about Christmas hurrying towards them, and Lady Bunty's new thirst for scavenger hunts, driving across the streets of

London with a group of her society friends in search of clues that were scattered at prominent locations. Then celebrating their finds with copious cocktails.

It was getting colder as the three of them stood outside the church, moving from foot to foot to keep warm. The crowd who had attended the service had dispersed and disappeared into the evening.

Eventually Sian said, 'I'm going to have to leave. I've got an early shift tomorrow and need to get back. Do you mind awfully if I go?'

'No, it was good to see you,' Grace replied. 'I'm sorry about Maurice.'

Sian nodded and the two women embraced.

Grace and Tom were left standing in the middle of the pavement, the street around them strangely deserted.

He half smiled at her.

'Wasn't Arthur able to come tonight?' he asked.

'No,' she replied. 'I don't think he enjoys church music very much. That is, I only ever intended to come with Sian.' It was ridiculous that she could think of nothing coherent to say.

There was another silence before he asked, 'Have you discovered anything more about Elizabeth? Bunty told me that you were going to see Lady Constance.'

'I meant to telephone you,' she paused. 'I'm sorry. I've been busy.'

She should have told him earlier, but the reason she hadn't contacted Tom was because of how she'd felt when he held her as they hid outside the Red Lantern. Which was absurd, of course, because he'd done it simply as a way to avoid being seen by Frank Jameson and his thugs.

'Let's walk towards Goodge Street, and you can tell me what's happened,' he suggested.

So they set off, walking amid the bruised fruit and vegetables of Covent Garden market, the stalls forming a ghostly backdrop to their conversation. In a few hours' time, the market would be loud and vibrant, filled with the calls of the costermongers and their customers, but for now it was shrouded in silence. They walked up Tavistock Street, weaving past the occasional drunk falling out of a public house, all the time keeping a determined distance from each other as they walked north.

She told him everything – Lady Constance's revelation and Adele's letter.

'I think her sister is right,' he said when she had finished. 'Elizabeth killed herself once she knew Charlotte was dead, but I don't understand why she lied about a relationship with Sir Hugh.'

'No, I don't understand either, but Lady Constance was definitely telling the truth. Lizzy couldn't have been with Sir Hugh on that date.' She shook her head. 'Perhaps Adele has some more information.'

They had reached Goodge Street Underground station, where Tom stopped.

'I'll catch the bus from here. Will you be safe getting home on your own?' he asked.

'Tom, I often catch the Tube.'

They looked at each other and were both silent. The streets around Tottenham Court Road were quiet now, except when the doors of public houses opened to let out the sound of talking and music. Finally, Tom said, 'I've moved out from Lady Bunty's and stopped working as her chauffeur. I'm going to look for something else to do.'

'You have. Why?'

He chose his words carefully. 'I'm not ungrateful that you found me a job, Grace, but I can't be someone's servant. I tried to fool myself for a time, but when I wear a uniform . . .' He shook his head. 'I want more than that. Bunty is a good woman, but it wasn't a life I could live.'

'I understand,' said Grace quietly. She wanted to ask when they would see each other again, but somehow their relationship seemed too fragile for those words. 'I wish you good luck with finding a new job. There must be so many things you could do—'

He interrupted her with a wry smile. 'Thank you for your faith in me. I only wish I felt the same.'

'How will I let you know if I discover anything more about Elizabeth?'

'Is there anything more to find out?' he asked and then stopped. 'Look, I'll telephone you. I promise I'll telephone. Pass on my best wishes to Arthur. I'm sorry I didn't get to see him again before leaving.'

She nodded her head. 'Yes, of course. I'll tell him.'

The red outline of a London omnibus loomed out of the darkness of Tottenham Court Road. 'I think this is mine.' He took her hand. 'Goodbye, Grace. I wish you every happiness for the future.'

It seemed as though he was saying goodbye forever. She looked at him and felt as if her heart would break. The moment stretched as they gazed at each other. And then they were in each other's arms, holding each other close, with a desperate, unspoken yearning. His lips found hers, as if it were the most natural thing in the world. Everything was focused on that moment, on that kiss.

Until cold reality flooded in. Arthur. Her fiancé, the man she was supposed to love. She pulled away. Tom, too, started guiltily, 'Grace, I'm sorry, I didn't mean—'

'No, no, I didn't either.' She replied, putting her fingers to her lips in horror.

'Grace, I'm sorry. Arthur is . . .' he started to say. 'It's best we don't see each other again.'

She nodded numbly. 'I know. Goodbye, Tom.'

'Goodbye, Grace.' With those words he climbed on board the omnibus and turned to give her a final, brief wave. The bus moved off and Grace was left standing on Tottenham Court Road feeling utterly bereft. Try as she might, it was impossible to wipe away the memory of his kiss, or the way it had made her feel. It was as though she were waking up after a long sleep. The part of her that she had buried, the part of her that was tied up with dreams of the life she wanted, had somehow been awoken. How odd that it appeared to be Tom Monaghan of all people who was the cause.

CHAPTER FORTY

The next day, Grace opened her eyes with a sense that something was terribly wrong, but couldn't identify what it was. As she struggled to turn on her bedside lamp in the winter gloom, cold reality hit her. She would never see Tom again. The knowledge was like some terrible load, weighing upon her and forcing every breath out of her body. She turned back over and shut her eyes, as if she could shut out the truth. Why had she lied to herself? It was Tom who made her feel alive again and now he was gone forever.

It was a normal Sunday morning. Her father in the breakfast room, his newspaper in front of him; Mrs Watson in the kitchen, even more disgruntled now that Bridget had escaped from domestic service. Outside in the road were the cheery sounds of children racing to the park; the clink of milk bottles being collected from a neighbouring doorstep. But for Grace, everything had changed; the light had been sucked out of the day. It was Tom, whom she had never considered loving but whom she had learned to love. Now he had gone. This was not a romanticized, false love, nor a practical compromise, but something that had crept up on her unawares.

As she quietly took her place opposite her father at the table and mechanically poured herself a cup of tea, he looked up. 'Are you quite well, Grace? You look dreadfully tired.'

'Yes, I'm well, Father,' she replied, wondering what explosion it would occasion if she were to reveal the source of her unhappiness.

Mrs Watson came into the breakfast room, looking slightly flustered. 'There's a telephone call for you, Miss Armstrong. I said I'd come and fetch you.' The cook was suspicious of the telephone and always tried to avoid answering it if she could.

'Who is it, Mary?' she asked.

'It was a man. He didn't say who he was.' She wiped her hands on her apron, as if cleaning away some kind of contamination.

She hoped her father didn't see her tremble as she left the table. Perhaps Tom had changed his mind and wasn't leaving her after all. 'Can I use your study, Daddy?' she asked.

'Yes, of course, my dear.' He looked at her with concern.

She settled herself at the desk and spoke falteringly into the receiver. The voice that answered was unexpected and unknown. A male voice with a harsh West Riding accent. 'Hello, Miss Armstrong, or may I call you Grace?'

'Hello,' she responded, confused. 'Who is speaking? Do I know you?'

'I am Sir Ernest Whitehouse and I know you very well indeed, Grace.'

'What do you mean?' Her heart was racing.

His next words were simple and blunt. 'How might Mr Arthur Broadbent feel if he were to know that you, his fiancée, had been consorting with another man?'

She gasped. She had been spied upon as she parted from Tom the previous evening. She remembered how the publican of the Golden Hind believed that she was being watched. It was true.

'Betrayal will always be discovered, Miss Armstrong. I would advise you to be more prudent,' Sir Ernest continued.

'Are you threatening me?' She was determined not to be intimidated.

'As I've said, merely advising you, Miss Armstrong. The past is best left behind. I am sure you don't want your indiscretions to be shared, any more than I do.' The telephone line went dead.

She sat in stunned silence for several minutes. Whatever mysteries surrounded Elizabeth, they must still be dangerous to Sir Ernest.

Frightening though the conversation had been, it at least gave her a strange clarity. She couldn't lie any more. Arthur deserved better. He had been her truest friend and she had not been honest with him. He was kind, he was honourable, he was gentle, but he was not the man she wanted to marry. She owed him the truth, no matter how hard that might be. She picked up the receiver again and asked to speak to the operator.

When Arthur answered the telephone, it was impossible not to hear the delight in his voice when she suggested they meet later that day for tea in Fuller's. Impossible not to wish that she loved him in the right way or not to imagine the voices of her family and friends telling her that she was insane to refuse the love of a man as true as Arthur. And for what? She had nothing in common with Tom. On several occasions, he had made clear that he disapproved of almost everything about her and her social class. Worse still, she could only hold on to a vague promise of a telephone call that might never come.

The meeting with Arthur was as brief and brutal as she had dreaded. Her ashen face must have told him that something had changed. She couldn't maintain the pretence of pleasant conversation when she knew that what she had to say would destroy in an instant their close friendship. It was hard to explain to Arthur that he was someone whom she loved and admired but could not marry. That he deserved someone who would make him happy in a way that she could not. She slowly handed back the ring he had given her. It had been his grandmother's.

'Is there someone else?' he asked desperately.

She hesitated for a second too long.

'There is,' he said. 'A man you love more than you love me. Have you been seeing him while . . . ?' His voice broke.

She shook her head. 'There is no one,' she said, because in truth, there was not. Tom could have no idea of her feelings for him. He might be horrified if he knew that she was making life decisions on the basis of one kiss. Yet he was responsible too. If it hadn't been for the feelings that he had awakened in her, the vision of a new and glowing world where anything might happen, then she would have accepted Arthur's love and never known – or known too late – that there was an alternative.

'Arthur, you will always be my dearest friend. I would hate to think that we couldn't be close again.'

Their teas lay cold and undrunk. She went to reach across the table to take his hand. He moved it slightly away and looked down.

'Grace,' he started to say, and then took a deep breath. 'Grace, I've loved you for five years. Your mannerisms, the way you screw up your eyes when you have something difficult to do, or how you throw yourself into every task. All these things I have loved – still love. I'd hoped – foolishly, it seems – that one day you might feel the same way.' He faltered. 'The prospect of friendship is a poor one after I had believed that you finally reciprocated my feelings and we were to be married and spend the rest of our lives together.'

'I'm sorry.' Her words were inadequate, but there was nothing else that could be said. They both knew that.

He stood up suddenly, pushing the chair back and stumbling slightly in his haste. 'Grace, I will always love you. It is part of who I am now and perhaps I will learn to love you in time as a friend. But until then, I think it better that we don't see each other.' He half smiled. 'I think that I need time to recover and that it would be best spent away from you.'

She went to stop him, the grim reality of no Arthur in her life hitting her.

'Please thank your parents for their many kindnesses to me and tell them I regret I will not be visiting Ryedale Villa for the time being.'

With those words he left, and Grace sat for a few moments feeling empty and hollow. The logical part of her said she was a fool to lose Arthur in this way – and for nothing. But her heart told her she could have done nothing else.

As she always did when she wanted to escape her feelings, Grace walked the long way back to Tufnell Park, embracing the biting cold wind as if it were right to be punished for destroying Arthur's happiness. She was supposed to see Adele that evening and would have gladly called it off but had no way of contacting her. She slipped into the house and quickly changed into an evening dress, indifferent to how she looked. It was well past six o'clock and she was already late. She raced downstairs. As she opened the front door, Mrs Watson appeared from the kitchen. 'I didn't realize you'd come in, Miss Armstrong. You must have been as quiet as a mouse.'

'I'm dreadfully sorry, but I must dash. I have an appointment.'

'There was a telephone message for you.'

Her heart stopped for a second. Perhaps it was Tom. 'Who was it?'

'Police Constable Alston,' the cook replied. 'He said—'

'Can you leave a note for me, Mary? I shall telephone him in the morning.' With that she was gone, shutting the door firmly behind her.

'He said to warn you that he'd found out something and you must telephone him urgently,' Mrs Watson concluded to the closed door.

CHAPTER FORTY-ONE

Just as Adele had promised, the restaurant was tucked away, and Grace had to retrace her steps on Ensign Street to find it. The Peloponnese was filled with couples, who looked as if they hoped to go on to somewhere more exciting later in the night. A sad orchestra played in a corner of the room, and an air of Edwardian gloom hung about the place. A brisk woman in black appeared and directed her to Adele, who was already seated at a table. She was impeccably dressed, in a tailored suit of powder blue and a matching cloche hat. Nervously fidgeting with her gloves, she was smoothing out a non-existent crease. A look of relief crossed her face when she saw Grace.

'I almost didn't come,' she said, not even bothering with a greeting. 'Are you alone?'

'Yes, of course,' Grace responded, as she sat down opposite her. 'I'm very glad you did come, though.'

'I don't often get up to town now. When I was younger and before Father lost his money, we were always going to the theatre or suppers or dancing. Our lives were really quite gay.' She looked around sadly at the faded décor of the

Peloponnese. 'We used to come here but it's much changed. One should resist revisiting the past.' She lowered her voice, even though the nearest guests were some distance away. 'Archibald would be horrified if he knew I was here. He's in Colchester at the moment. At a trial for fraud, a very complex case,' she sniffed. 'The head clerk is accused of forging invoices valued at over five hundred pounds.'

'In your letter you said that Charlotte Harcourt was Lizzy's daughter,' Grace prompted, 'and that you believe she killed herself when she found out Charlotte had died.'

'I have no doubt that is the case. It's very sad, but there are other matters too.'

'About Lizzy's past and the murder case?'

Adele nodded, then said, 'I've ordered cocktails for us. We might need a stiff drink, but you will need to pay, Miss Armstrong, Archibald asks me to account for any money I spend.'

Grace agreed and the waiter brought them two coupe glasses filled with an artificial-looking orange liquid. A perfectly red cherry was skewered through with a cocktail stick and balanced at the top of each drink.

Once he had gone, Adele continued. 'I couldn't believe the things Captain Burdett-Smith said about Lizzy under oath and then her counsel agreed they were true.' Her pink mouth formed an 'O' of horror. 'Of course, Mother was terrified her dalliance with Sir Hugh would be revealed in court. Did you know of their relationship?' she asked.

Grace nodded. 'Lady Constance told me.'

'We had journalists outside our house for weeks on end, asking questions.'

'It must have been a terrible time.'

'Oh, it was. I was only recently married to Archibald, and I could see his horror as the newspapers carried yet more revelations about the murder. I think he regretted linking himself to my family.' She stopped and took a sip of the drink. Her painted lips left a stain on the rim of the glass, which she carefully wiped away with a lace handkerchief. 'I had to agree never to see my sister again.'

'You agreed to that?'

'What choice do you think I had? Lizzy had sullied our name beyond all redemption. My husband made it clear that I was lucky he stayed with me. Half the world thought she was a murderess and the other half believed she was the most immoral woman in Great Britain.'

'But she was your sister and she needed you,' Grace said, aghast.

'I knew Lizzy had lied. She begged me to provide an alibi for her on the night of the murder. I probably would have done so.' She shrugged. 'However, Archie wouldn't allow it. She never told me where she really was.'

Grace digested this fact slowly and then asked, 'What about your parents? Are they still living?'

'No,' she stated flatly. 'Father died soon after the murder. Mother said it was the shame that had killed him, but the doctor put cancer of the bowel on the death certificate. Mother gained a kind of fame of her own. She was one of the civilians killed in the 1916 Zeppelin air raid on London.'

'I'm very sorry for your loss.' The same words that had been repeated so many times.

Adele shrugged. 'We were not close. I was at Father's deathbed, but when Mother died, I hadn't been in touch with her for several years. It was the family solicitor who informed me that she had passed away.'

'Why was your family so broken?'

'Because there was a deceit lying at the heart of the family that tainted every relationship.' Adele twisted her wedding ring.

'Did Lizzy have a relationship with Sir Hugh?' Grace asked.

'Look, I need to tell the story in order, otherwise it won't make sense,' she said, slightly pettishly. She took a breath. 'Lizzy was foolish to involve herself with Sir Ernest Whitehouse. Archie had some legal dealings with him and believed he was a frightening man.'

'Yes, I know,' Grace said simply.

Adele looked at her in surprise and then continued, 'He used her and cast her aside once the case was over.' She bit into her cherry with sharp white teeth. 'Lizzy still had power over him, though. They both knew that they shared secrets, or so she told me. That's why he visited her at Ryedale Villa.'

'You were aware of that?'

Adele nodded. 'Just before she died, she came to my home in Penge and told me.'

That would explain part of the lost time before her death. 'Why did she see you after so many years?'

'Lizzy had nowhere else to go,' Adele replied. 'I was in the breakfast room with the children and there was a commotion at the front door. I could hear Archibald's raised voice and a woman's that was familiar, but when I went outside, I almost didn't recognize her. She had this ridiculous brown hair.' She touched her own immaculate blonde head. 'And dowdy clothes. Lizzy, who was always so fashionable and took such a pride in her appearance.' Adele checked herself. 'Not that it matters now.'

'What happened next?'

'Archibald wouldn't have her in the house. He was frightened of what she might say in front of the children. We'd never spoken of her, of course,' Adele added defensively, 'and Stuart and Margaret wanted to know who this strange woman was, with her tear-stained face. We could hardly tell them it was their aunt.'

Until then, Adele's eyes had been trained on the table, but now she looked up. 'My husband was adamant. He said her presence would contaminate our home. So we walked together in the municipal park.'

'Poor Lizzy.' Grace was appalled how men like Archibald Pratchett could dictate the destiny of the women around them.

'I was the only person to whom she could speak of Charlotte's death. It had broken her totally. The menaces of Sir Ernest Whitehouse were nothing compared with that. Charlotte was all that she'd lived for.'

Adele took a photograph from her handbag and presented it to Grace. It was of a radiant Elizabeth smiling up at the camera, a baby girl who was the image of herself in her arms. She continued, 'When she placed Charlotte with her sister-in-law, she had forced herself to believe that Victoria Harcourt was capable of being anything other than a cold-hearted and vindictive woman.'

'Would Mrs Harcourt really have been cruel to Charlotte?'

'She hated Lizzy for the disgrace brought on the family.' Adele smoothed an imaginary crease from her gloves again.

'There was a small park opposite the Harcourts' house. Lizzy told me that every Sunday afternoon, she would go and stand there, hoping that she might catch a glimpse of her daughter. When she saw Charlotte, it was as if a light went on and she could bear any hardship, knowing that they would be reunited eventually.'

'Every Sunday afternoon, Arcadia Farm,' Grace responded.

'She could hardly have told you the truth,' Adele said. 'In the last few years, there had been fewer and fewer sightings of Charlotte. Then she was forced to track her down to some dreadful nightclub.'

'The Red Lantern,' Grace supplied. She then asked, 'Did she learn of her death from Payne & Partners?'

'They forwarded a letter from Mrs Harcourt, which destroyed what peace of mind she had left.'

'What had she written?'

'She informed her that Charlotte had killed herself by jumping from London Bridge and described her as a deeply troubled and difficult girl, who had failed to fit into the family. Charlotte had sold her body to buy drugs. She concluded the letter by saying that the daughter was like the mother.'

'What a cruel woman!'

'Yes, she was. Perhaps she felt the letter was some small piece of revenge for the shame the murder had brought on the family.' She looked pensive for a moment and then said, 'Lizzy wanted to give me some keepsakes of our childhood. She had intended to destroy all evidence of her existence – she wanted to be obliterated from the earth – but in the end she changed her mind. Perhaps we all want to leave a small trace behind.'

'What keepsakes did she give you?'

'The photograph of her and Charlotte, and these.' Adele rummaged in her handbag and produced a brown paper bag, which she placed on the table in front of them.

The waiter reappeared, depositing two more cocktails, and they were silent for a moment.

'Lizzy said the contents would prove the truth of what she said. I didn't want to look at first, but in the week of her funeral, curiosity got the better of me.'

Adele removed two photographs and passed them to Grace. The first was of Elizabeth, standing hand in hand with her younger sister. They were by the sea. There was something arresting about her – her face upturned, her hair a shock of gold and her eyes wide and frank, looking defiantly at the camera.

'How old were you when the photograph was taken?'

'I must have been eleven. Lizzy was thirteen. We stayed in Sidmouth for the summer.'

'She looks invincible,' said Grace.

'I thought she was. But that was the year everything changed. When she changed.'

'How?'

'She became secretive and moody. Mother and Lizzy argued constantly. Father retreated to Woodford and pretended he had some gainful employment there. This is a photograph of Mother and Father.'

The second image was taken in a Victorian photographic studio against a marbled backdrop and with a ludicrous stuffed parrot on a pillar. The father was looking at the camera, but whereas his daughter's stare dared the world to contradict her, he had the appearance of a man who might be struck at any moment by a capricious fate. His wife, however, was different, with the same startling beauty as her eldest daughter.

Taking in Grace's scrutiny, Adele replied to an unasked question, 'Yes, Lizzy and Mother were alike. In appearance, at least.'

'What happened that summer?' Grace asked.

'At the time Lizzy wouldn't tell me. She said I was too young to understand.' Adele put the two photographs side by side – the portrait of an unhappy family. 'Mother was prone to terrible outbursts of temper. I think that both Lizzy and I married early to escape her. That and financial necessity, once Father was made bankrupt. Neither of our marriages was altogether happy, but I've done my duty and Lizzy . . . well, Lizzy was Lizzy.' Adele shrugged her shoulders. 'She didn't believe that one needed to play by the rules. But one does, you know.'

Suddenly Grace felt desperately sad. 'Poor, poor Lizzy.'

Adele twisted her wedding ring again. Her fingernails were long and smooth and painted with the exact pink of her lips. Then, for the first time, her brittle self-control faltered. 'Was anyone there?' she asked. 'At her funeral.'

'There were some ladies from the Catholic bookshop and Father Daley. Lady Bunty.' She halted. 'A few people.'

'I wish I could have come,' Adele said in a small voice, 'but it really wouldn't have been possible.'

'But what happened that summer?' Grace asked.

'Sir Hugh was the most significant of Mother's lovers. He

opened up a world she dreamed of – one of high society and power – far from the flat lands of Essex. Once Father had returned home, Sir Hugh arrived at Sidmouth. He was to take a kindly interest in our family – a protective, uncle-type figure.'

'But that was not his true intention?' Grace asked.

'No,' said Adele bitterly. 'Mother was a silly, vain woman who needed to be reassured constantly about her attractiveness. She was never what you would describe as *loving*. You may think me unfeeling towards my sister, but in all my dealings my main concern has been the welfare of my own children.'

'I didn't say you were unfeeling.' Grace felt the need to defend herself.

'No, but I know you think it. That was the summer when Sir Hugh began to take an interest in Lizzy. He would talk to her for hours about art and literature. She was desperate for knowledge and an insight into the world. We both were, and I was jealous that she had his special attention. It was only when I read her diary that I fully understood what had happened.'

'What do you mean?' Grace had a sense of foreboding.

'Lizzy always seemed incredibly sophisticated to me. But now, as a mother, I realize that she was only thirteen – younger than my Margaret is now. This is the journal she kept that summer. I believe it can tell her story more effectively than I can.' She pushed a book, bound in dark-blue silk, across the table.

With trembling fingers, Grace opened the journal and

started to read, feeling the other woman's eyes upon her. The early pages were filled with an excited record of trips to music concerts, suppers and dances. Increasingly, the initial 'H' started to appear. 'H was so amusing today. He is so unlike anyone else I know.' 'H told me today about all the treasures of the Egyptian Room at the British Museum. How I long to see them for myself!'

'"H" is Hugh Clifton, of course?' Grace looked up at Adele for confirmation.

'Yes. Our childhood was really quite neglected, Miss Armstrong. It didn't take much to make Lizzy feel special. As we walked through the park in Penge, she told me about how the process had been so gradual that it felt normal. A hand that rested on hers a moment too long as they spoke of the Impressionists. His fingers lingering on her waist as if by accident.'

'Did your mother notice what was happening?'

Adele pondered this for a moment. 'I don't think so. She was a very self-centred woman.' She took a sip of her drink. 'After much persuasion, Lizzy was allowed to stay with Sir Hugh in London for several days and attend the Royal Academy of Art Summer Exhibition. His mother was supposed to be there as a chaperone, but she was not. They were alone together in his house, apart from the servants.'

Grace began to read: '24 July. When I arrived at the house, I was sent straight upstairs and he was there waiting for me. It was a bedroom. There was a large bed standing against the wall on the same side as the door.' She stopped. 'But this passage, why this passage suggests that . . .' Her voice trailed away as the implications of what was written there hit her. 'What happened between them was not when she was an adult but when she was thirteen. Sir Hugh was what age?'

'He was forty-seven.'

'She was just a child!' Grace gasped.

'We were very innocent, Miss Armstrong. What young, well-brought up lady isn't before her marriage? We could have no knowledge of sexual intimacy – we thought only of the swooning delight of romantic novels. I fear during that time in London Hugh Clifton introduced my sister to the full range of his desires. And she was totally trapped in the house in Sloane Street. When she tried to protest, he told her that she was no innocent party. Her actions in kissing him and agreeing to stay in London meant she had consented to an intimate relationship between them.'

'She was a child! Did she tell anyone?'

Adele nodded. 'When we returned home to Essex, she requested a meeting with Father and Mother. She tried to tell them what had happened, although it was difficult to find the words to describe her experience.'

'Did your parents act upon what she said?'

Adele laughed bitterly. 'Apparently, Mother told her that she was not to make such dreadful accusations about a very dear friend of the family. Father was simply silent.'

Horrified, Grace asked, 'Did your parents continue to have contact with Sir Hugh?'

'For a period, yes. Although the relationship weakened over time. It was Sir Hugh who ended the connection in the end. Once he was sure my family would not make any accusations against him.'

'Lizzy must have felt betrayed.'

'She hated our mother with a passion from that point. When she met Captain Burdett-Smith at a party in Chelmsford, she saw him as a way to escape the poisonous atmosphere at home and our precarious financial situation. Sadly, he had misrepresented himself and was quite as penniless as Lizzy.'

'The police believed that they made money from entrapping and blackmailing married men,' Grace said.

'It was all true – absolutely true.' Adele looked down.

'So, it wasn't lies told by the Cliftons and their allies?' Grace asked.

'No,' Adele shook her head and looked thoughtful. 'I did speak to Lizzy about her . . . her behaviour. She was much changed after Sidmouth – so distant and heartless – not the loving sister she had once been. She said she felt contempt for the married men who could be so easily seduced.'

'I don't understand. Why on earth would she pursue such relationships? Did she gain some satisfaction from them?'

'No, that was the tragedy. There was a degree of financial security in the money she and Reginald received, but for her the encounters were soulless and empty. That final time I saw her, she told me that Hugh Clifton had taken something fundamental from her – the right to choose what she did with her own body. The relentless round of dreary flirtations was nothing more than an attempt to rub out the memory of what he had done by making such intimacies meaningless.'

'So, the events Lizzy described were true, although they were much darker than was revealed in court and happened when she was a child?' Grace said soberly.

'Exactly. Sir Hugh Clifton was a corrupt man, Miss

Armstrong, for all his abstract ideas about equality and fairness. The world that mattered was people like Lady Constance, with her wealth and status, who must be treated as equals. That was his daytime life. But his life away from the public gaze was dark indeed. My family were people of no importance. He had no respect for Mother because she had indulged in an affair with him – and therefore, we were all lessened in his eyes. Father was treated as a fool and mocked. Lizzy he used and discarded once she had no value to him. And I . . . I realize now that I was the observer, although I didn't understand the significance of what I saw.'

'Why didn't she tell the truth about what he had done to her as a child, rather than allowing it to appear that she had entered into an affair willingly?'

'She was too ashamed to admit what had happened, even to Captain Burdett-Smith when he found her hidden diary. It was something she found almost impossible to speak of.'

Grace looked at her in surprise. 'Why?'

Adele made an almost imperceptible shrug. 'Hugh Clifton had so convinced her that she had somehow colluded in the relationship that she didn't want to admit how young she had been at the time. And she could not bear to hold Father up to contempt as a man who had failed to protect his daughter.'

'So, Captain Burdett-Smith truly believed she had been unfaithful to him?' Grace asked.

'Yes,' Adele replied. 'That was the irony. She had not written the year in her diary, so Reginald believed the events depicted there related to the summer of 1900. He didn't tell Lizzy that he had found her diary, instead he copied down the details and worked out who the 'H' in it must be.'

Surprised, Grace asked, 'Why should he care? I thought theirs wasn't a romantic relationship. Surely, he wouldn't care about his wife's presumed infidelity?'

'They had formed a partnership of a kind. The two of them against the world, was how Lizzy put it.' Adele considered for a moment. 'Reginald genuinely believed she had betrayed him by going behind his back.'

'Why did her husband speak of the relationship at the murder trial? Was it relevant to what happened?'

Adele shook her head. 'I don't know. I think Reginald wanted to hurt her and protect himself, but I don't understand why she allowed her barrister to agree to the details. It meant that her reputation was destroyed, even if she didn't hang.'

'Perhaps she wanted the world to know something of the man Sir Hugh truly was,' Grace suggested.

'My sister was very reckless at times.' Adele smiled sadly. 'She thought – wrongly – that Sir Ernest's protection would shield her from society's disapproval. As I told you in my letter, Lizzy intended to leave England and begin a new life, in a place where she was not known. Sir Ernest had claimed that he would finance this. It was only Charlotte's birth that tied Lizzy to London. Otherwise, she would have gone.'

'What will you do with the truth?' Grace asked.

'Nothing, Miss Armstrong. It's in the distant past now. You may keep everything.' She gestured towards the pile of documents. 'You can choose what you do with this knowledge. Lizzy would have wanted you to know the truth. In the end, you've been the only person who cared about her.' She took a pink lipstick from her handbag and applied it carefully. 'Now I really must go. My son Stuart is meeting me at Penge Lane.'

She called the maître d' over so that he could call her a taxicab and Grace paid the substantial bill for their cock-tails. 'Do you want a cab too?'

'No, thank you, Mrs Pratchett. I think I would like to walk to clear my head a little.' She had only drunk half of the second glass, but she felt light-headed. Her purse was almost empty.

'Very well. Obviously, we will have no further contact, but thank you for what you did for my sister. Sadly, in the end we were not close. I wasn't prepared to sacrifice the life I had made for myself and my children.' Adele pinned her fox fur tighter around her neck and fiddled with the gold wedding band on her finger. 'I may not have had Lizzy's beauty or talents, but I have the more mundane and import-ant skill of learning to live with the hand life has dealt me.'

CHAPTER FORTY-TWO

As Grace walked to London Bridge station, the damp winter chill whispered of the year coming to an end. A heavy, cold rain fell and soaked through the flimsy coat she was wearing. Her mind was not on the journey home. Instead, it was filled with the horrors of what she had learned. In her handbag were the photographs and journal, the last remnants of Elizabeth's life, other than seedy headlines in newspapers and the fading pages of a private detective's notebooks.

Darkness surrounded her on the deserted street when suddenly the silence was broken by the insistent throb of an engine. Instinctively, she moved further away from the road, but a black Rolls-Royce shuddered to a halt a few feet ahead, partly blocking the pavement. She went to step aside when a bulky figure emerged from the passenger seat. He had opened the door and now stood in front of her so that the path was blocked. A moment ago, she had been lost in plans of how she would tell Elizabeth's story to the world. Now all her senses were alert. She swung round, planning to run back the way she'd come, back to the sanctuary of the Peloponnese, but the man reached out to take hold of her and the back door of the car opened. She started to struggle and scream, trying to get some purchase on her attacker, but he was much stronger than she was. With his hand firmly gripping the top of her head, he forced Grace into the back of the car. In its shadowy interior, she made out the figure of a much older man on the seat beside her. He looked expensively dressed in a black cashmere coat with a cravat at his throat. She could see him only in profile, but even in the half-light he exuded a sense of menace.

'Miss Armstrong, no one can hear you. Screaming is a little melodramatic and, in the circumstances, would serve no purpose.' The flat West Riding accent was at odds with the wealth of his outfit. The voice was familiar. It was the man who had spoken to her on the telephone.

'Sir Ernest Whitehouse,' she said, a cold sense of fear seeping through her.

He tapped the glass screen that was positioned between the back of the car and the two men in the front. The car set off.

In the darkness, she grappled with the handle of the door.

'The door can't be opened from the inside,' he said conversationally.

'I insist you let me out immediately. You can't just snatch me off a London street.' She was so terrified that she could hear her own heart thudding.

'Snatch you off the street? My motor car was passing you, a woman alone at night, and I thought to myself, how vulnerable you might appear to someone with foul intentions. It's a lucky coincidence that I am able to help you.'

'You have been following me,' she said.

He turned to her and smiled. A cold, unpleasant smile. 'A conversation between us is long overdue. It seems we have something in common. Payne & Partners alerted me to your interest in Lizzy Burdett-Smith several months ago. I believe you've just met with Mrs Adele Pratchett, her sister.'

A car approached on the other side of the road and in the blaze of its lights she noticed his broken teeth. She stared at him in horror.

Aware of her gaze, he said, 'You must wonder, Miss Armstrong, why I have never chosen to have my teeth replaced. Well, they are a reminder of where I come from.'

Keep him talking, keep him talking, make him believe that he might be your friend. Suddenly words from a long-forgotten advice column in *Nursing World* insinuated their way into her head. *Try to make the situation appear as normal as possible.* And if she did not? She couldn't remember whether the column had disclosed the terrible things that might happen to her if she failed to befriend him.

'What was the life you were born into?' she asked desperately.

'I come from Bradford, Miss Armstrong, the illegitimate son of a mill worker. Every year, I return there and walk a sobering three miles. I start at the great City Hall, where men of money hold influence. But as I continue my journey, the streets become narrower and dirtier. There are furtive alleys where men stand idly, smoking cigarettes and talking of a future that they will never inherit. I go to stand outside the two-up two-down house where my mother lived until I was able to buy her something grander. Very different, I imagine, from the suburban warmth of Ryedale Villa. Or from my own home in Park Lane.'

'Then why do you return there?'

'Not from a sense of nostalgia, you understand. No, I stand outside that house and swear that I will do everything necessary to ensure I'm not dragged back down to that life again.'

'How did you escape poverty?' Despite herself, Grace was interested in what he had to say.

'Oh, I started small. Skimming business off street book-makers, threatening shopkeepers and publicans, providing protection – whether it was wanted or not. It seems I had a talent for such things and I invested wisely, buying up prop-erties and land. Whitehouse Ltd is one of the largest companies in Great Britain and one of the most successful. However, I wanted the power that only a political position can bring.'

Her mind was jumping around frantically. Finally, she asked him, 'Why did you visit Elizabeth after so many years?'

He was silent for a moment. It was still raining and the windscreen wipers beat steadily as the car made its way through the now deserted streets.

'She had become desperate and that made her behave foolishly. It seems Lizzy Burdett-Smith had discovered maternal feelings.'

'Charlotte Harcourt?'

'Yes. She wrote to tell me she needed money to take her daughter to America. Apparently, your mother had spoken of it as a place where it was possible to start a new life.'

'Why should that concern you?'

'Lizzy's secrets were the only thing she had left to sell.'

She took a deep breath, before daring to say, 'You were frightened that she would reveal the part you played in the death of Sir Hugh. You threatened her to be silent.'

Sir Ernest looked pensive. 'That ugly word again, Miss Armstrong. It is best to avoid melodrama. No, it was she who threatened me. It seems that Lizzy Burdett-Smith had never lost her fondness for blackmail. She wrote to me, demanding payment for her silence. However, she was shocked when I appeared at Ryedale Villa. She needed to be reminded that she was playing a dangerous game.'

'You paid the ten thousand pounds into her bank account!' Grace realized.

He leaned back in his seat and seemed to weigh up the situation, before saying, 'It was to keep her silent in the short term, but I fully intended to retrieve my money. Lizzy's suicide meant that I could take no further action. I even sent Mortimer to the graveyard.' He jerked his head in the direction of the driver. 'I wanted to make sure she really was dead and buried.'

'I saw him there,' she gasped, remembering the man who had lurked by the trees and watched intently until the coffin was lowered into the earth. Grace felt a cold shiver run through her. She realized how vulnerable she was – trapped in a car with this cold, violent man. She edged away from him and moved closer to the locked door.

'As you have risked so much, you have a right to know the story.' He turned to face her. 'Captain Burdett-Smith came to see me one day in the spring of 1901, I forget quite when, but I remember exactly his words and the proposition he put to me. He had the means to destroy the reputation of Sir Hugh Clifton and believed that I would be prepared to be a co-conspirator.'

'You plotted to murder him?' she said in horror.

'If you repeat what I tell you, I will deny it, but no, the original intention was never murder. That was an unfortunate consequence. I ask you to remember, Miss Armstrong, that the idea was his. I was not the originator, merely a supporting player in the action. Reginald knew I hated Sir Hugh and wished to ingratiate himself with me. He had found evidence of his wife's infidelity in a diary that she had kept hidden from him. He intended to use it in their divorce case. It was a gift to me – a gift, my dear.'

'How did you become involved with Lizzy?' Grace was intrigued, despite her repulsion at being in the company of such a man.

'They both needed money.' He looked pensive again. 'By that point, Lizzy also wanted a divorce and a fresh start. She had agreed to swear to adultery with Sir Hugh if I would make a generous financial settlement to allow her to leave the country. As we both know, her pregnancy put an end to her plans to escape.'

'Lady Constance knows that Lizzy lied about the disputed dates.'

He shrugged. 'Truth is a relative thing. In any case, it didn't matter. The moment Mrs Burdett-Smith stepped into the witness stand and swore to an adulterous relationship with Sir Hugh, he would be finished. People would always believe it was true, otherwise why would she claim it?'

'Why did you meet Sir Hugh in South Norwood? Surely, that wasn't needed as part of your plot.'

'Ah, that meeting at the Golden Hind. In hindsight, it is something I regret.' He flashed one of his grotesque smiles. 'A salacious divorce case was all I needed, but I desired to see Sir Hugh's face when Lizzy recited the sordid infidelities she would swear to in court. His reputation shattered forever. Although I didn't know it then, Lizzy wanted him to acknowledge what he had done to her. She was fool enough to think that a man like Sir Hugh would feel any guilt,' he said cynically. 'He laughed in her face, of course, and said that it was she who had seduced him, and Captain Burdett-Smith had married nothing but what he had cast away.'

'No! Poor, poor Lizzy.'

'I was not to know in advance, but Captain Burdett-Smith had brought a gun. Whatever sense of honour he had was offended at Sir Hugh's words. He fired it ineffectually and wounded the man in the arm.'

'Sir Hugh was shot several times,' she said, remembering the details of the court case.

He nodded in response. 'Hugh taunted us that he would go to the police unless we agreed to his terms. Captain Burdett-Smith began to grapple with him. It was confusion and noise, which needed to be ended. Lizzy took the gun and fired repeatedly through the cushion. She was not stupid enough to aim at his arm.'

'Lizzy killed Sir Hugh?'

'Yes. I'm sure that was not the answer you expected, Miss Armstrong. She was shocked afterwards and wept as we travelled back to London in my carriage. However, when she pulled the trigger, she was very calm. She said, "You will never have power over me again." '

Grace thought of the guilt Elizabeth must have suffered. The years of repentance and denial. She understood now why she could not take the stand at the Old Bailey.

Sir Ernest continued his story. 'Reginald was covered in blood and stayed behind to clean himself up and, as it transpired, to help himself to the contents of Sir Hugh's wallet. He was fool enough to leave behind the railway ticket. It tied at least one of them to the scene, but, of course, he was not the killer.'

'If either of them dared to tell the police the truth about that night, you too could be tied to the murder,' she pointed out.

'I had already paid Horatio Wright handsomely to ensure that my presence there would not be investigated. He altered Mrs Ryman's police statement at my request.'

'He was corrupt!' she exclaimed.

'Money is a powerful force. I paid for Lizzy's defence, on the understanding my name must never be mentioned. Captain Burdett-Smith rather relished destroying his wife's reputation in the witness box, knowing that she could not defend herself when she was already guilty of murder.'

'I have proof that Sir Hugh had violated Lizzy when she was just thirteen,' Grace told him. 'He tricked her into going to his London house and then attacked her. He made Lizzy believe that he loved her and then abused that trust in the worst possible way.'

His sinister smile again. 'So, that was the acknowledgement she demanded. How can you know what happened so long ago?'

'Adele Pratchett. She gave me Lizzy's journal from the summer the assault happened.'

'You hold the journal; why not Adele? She is her sister.' His eyes flickered with interest.

'She didn't want it.'

'She's wise. What is the point in holding onto old documents? I find you a very interesting character, Miss Armstrong, but fail to understand your fascination with Mrs Burdett-Smith and her rather sordid life. She is dead and life moves on.'

'She deserves to be remembered as the good woman she truly was, not as the world forced her to be.' Grace forgot her fear in her indignation at his words.

'We rarely get what we deserve, Miss Armstrong.' He moved nearer to her so that she could feel the heat of his breath on her cheek.

'Why should you fear blackmail if it was Lizzy who killed Sir Hugh?' Grace asked.

'One of the quirks of the English legal system.'

She looked at him questioningly.

'Lizzy had been tried at the Old Bailey and found innocent of Sir Hugh's murder. On the advice of her highly remunerated counsel, she had not taken the witness stand and so had not lied under oath. As she pointed out in her letter, even if she were to reveal exactly what happened that night, she could not be tried twice for the same crime. She would remain free, while I could be charged as a party to murder. That's why she threatened me with exposure and blackmail.'

She tried to lean away in the enclosed space, repulsed and terrified. She had no doubt that Sir Ernest was totally ruthless and he had revealed his involvement in Sir Hugh's death. His secrets were now hers to tell.

'I would like to get out of this car, please,' she said, trying to keep her voice from trembling.

'I'm afraid that is not possible, Miss Armstrong. We have not concluded our conversation.'

An ominous silence fell upon them. The driver lit a cigarette and its smell seeped through the glass partition.

After a moment, Grace said, 'Elizabeth was terribly wronged. She lost everything.'

'Lizzy was always impetuous. She made a bargain and didn't think of the consequences. A little like you, perhaps.' He turned to her. 'I will need the journal, of course. There is no point in reopening the wounds of the past.'

'It's not your story to have,' she replied.

'And nor is it yours,' he responded. 'The principal characters, Hugh, Reginald and Lizzy, are dead. What it reveals would only hurt Lady Constance, and she has been hurt enough by your betrayal.'

'What do you mean?' Grace stammered.

'I paid Lady Constance a visit for old times' sake. At first she refused to see me, but she listened when I told her that you were passing yourself off as Grace Jaggers, a journalist, to obtain confidential documents and her most intimate secrets.'

Grace was horrified. Lady Constance had learned to trust her. 'I was going to tell her the truth when I next visited.'

'I don't think there will be a next visit. Betrayal is a terrible thing. Now I will need to have the journal.'

With a sudden jerking movement, he snatched her bag and threw it out onto the indifferent streets of London. Grace went to protest but he ignored her and tapped hard on the glass panel. The motor car accelerated away. It would be impossible to find the journal in daytime, Grace reflected. It was gone forever.

'Please, just let me go home.'

He ignored her while the car drove swiftly through the night-time murk. The houses became smaller and meaner and the street lighting more sparse.

'Why are you doing this to me?'

'I need you to understand that I'm not a man to be trifled with.'

'What do you mean?' Would he be prepared to kill to protect his secrets? Suddenly, she remembered the newspaper report from long ago, the one Tom had shown her, where the chief witness against Sir Hugh had mysteriously disappeared.

'Your adventure is over, Miss Armstrong.' He spoke in the tone of a man who knew he would not be contradicted.

'I will report you to the police. You snatched me off the street and stole from me.' She was aware of how ineffectual her words sounded.

He laughed outright at this. 'Report what? I have kindly provided you with transport. You were a little careless with property that was not yours in the first place. I hardly think you're in a position to threaten.'

Grace was filled with a terrible sense of guilt. She had let Elizabeth down. The diary was the proof of the horrors inflicted by Sir Hugh. It would finally have allowed the frightened thirteen-year-old girl to find her voice. Despairingly, she covered her face with her hands and so did not see the drunk stumble across the road. The driver honked his horn and swerved violently, skidding on the wet road so that the car hurtled into a lamp post, crushing one side completely. Grace was thrown forcefully against the door and blacked out briefly.

When she came to, there was total silence.

Shaking violently and too frightened to feel any pain, she crawled out of the car and looked around. There was an overpowering smell of petroleum and parts of the car were strewn across the road. A crowd of onlookers had started to gather and were staring at a large figure lying on the ground – Sir Ernest Whitehouse. The chauffeur and front passenger were bent over him. Blood poured from the side of his head and his face was contorted with fury. Suddenly, he sat up and roared dreadfully. Then he slumped back down and was motionless.

She stared at him, expecting that at any moment he would leap up and attack her. It was only when the chauffeur shouted out that he wasn't breathing that she knew he was dead. Then she began to run frantically along the narrow street and away from the prison of the black car. When she could run no more, when she could hardly breathe, she stopped. The cold bit through her fashionable coat, which was drenched in the heavy rain. She was alone, penniless and lost in night-time London. What little money she had was in the handbag Sir Ernest had tossed from the car window.

She had to get back to Tufnell Park and the safety of Ryedale Villa. Home felt a million miles away. Looking around for some kind of clue to her location, she saw the giant gas holders of King's Cross, which dominated the landscape and pumped flames into the night-time sky. Using them as a guide she began the long, slow journey home. When at last she arrived on the doorstep, her father opened the door immediately. 'Grace, I've been worried sick about you. Where have you been?' But seeing her exhausted face and dishevelled appearance, he took her in his arms. 'Come in, Gracie, you look as though you could do with a stiff brandy.'

CHAPTER FORTY-THREE

When Grace awoke the next morning she discovered a giant bruise all along one side of her body. Fear and adrenaline had protected her from pain at the time, but now she ached all over, particularly when she tried to move her arm. The realization of how close she had been to death haunted her – if not in the wreckage of the car, then perhaps at the hands of Sir Ernest. She tried to climb out of bed but was surprised to find that her legs were shaking too much to support her.

When she didn't appear at the breakfast table, her father came upstairs, and she haltingly told him everything that had happened the previous evening.

'Sir Ernest Whitehouse is a monster! How dare he trap and threaten you. We must go to the police, Gracie. For years, rumours have swirled around Whitehall of his brutality and violence. He must be stopped.' He bristled with indignation at the thought of his daughter in danger.

'I think he's dead, Father. It was awful to see him lying there on the ground.' She hesitated. 'I would really rather that no one knew I was in the car. I want to forget the horror of what happened. It might also stir up all the old stories around Elizabeth.'

'Grace,' he began to remonstrate. 'It's our duty . . .' He looked at her pale face and paused. 'If he's living, then you must reveal the whole story – his abduction of you and his role in the murder of Sir Hugh. That much is your duty, to protect others from him.'

She was forced to agree with the logic of what he said. 'But if he isn't . . . ?' she suggested.

'Very well, then we'll say nothing,' he agreed reluctantly. 'Now, I've already telephoned Uncle Neville and agreed you won't be in *Nursing World* for the next few days. You must take time to recuperate.'

'Miss Boddy will be furious,' Grace said weakly.

'No, no, apparently not. Neville spoke to her. Some chap called Roger Dale has just returned from Paris and she said he would be delighted to pick up your workload as well as his own.'

At that moment, Mrs Watson came into the room, carrying a heavy breakfast tray and complaining about the lack of a general maid at Ryedale Villa. 'It's not a cook's job to leave the kitchen and go climbing stairs.' However, when she spotted Grace, she exclaimed. 'Oh, Miss Armstrong, you do look dreadful! Whatever has happened?'

Grace shook her head. 'It's a long story.'

She was surprised at how ravenously she ate her boiled eggs and toast. Her brush with death had clearly increased her appetite. She spent most of the day sleeping and allowing her body to heal itself. It was also a chance to think about what she had learned and the whole tragic story of

Lizzy Burdett-Smith. She had not intended to kill Sir Hugh in cold blood but had been driven to it in a moment of anguish, when she witnessed the mocking laughter of the man who had abused and destroyed her. Her life afterwards had been one of regret and penance, as if she sought to make amends for one moment of madness. Perhaps the story didn't need to be told now, it was enough that Grace knew the truth about her friend. Everyone who had been present at the killing was dead and the ghosts of the past could only bring harm to the living.

James Armstrong returned home from work earlier than usual that day. He was carrying a late edition of the *Evening Standard*. Splashed across the front page was a headline on the death of Sir Ernest Whitehouse in a motor car accident. In the days that followed, the papers were filled with his obituaries. They spoke of his meteoric rise from humble beginnings, his philanthropic work, and his powerful manoeuvres behind the scenes. He was described as a most wonderful example to the young of Great Britain. No one dared to print the truth about him. Even in death, he remained feared.

Grace felt desperately guilty about lying to Lady Constance and wrote to apologize. She tried to explain why she had deceived her, but the letter was returned unopened. The older woman could not forgive what she saw as the ultimate betrayal.

Ever practical, Bunty told Grace that she should count herself lucky that there would be no more enforced expeditions to Sloane Street.

'I'm just hoping that she refuses to see me too, honey. I was part of the subterfuge, after all, and I shall insist on it.'

Bunty then smiled serenely. 'In any case, I'm far too busy for any social visits. I have my motoring lessons to think about.' Disappointed at the frequent departures of her chauffeurs, she had hired Hamish Winston-Scott, a dashing former captain from the Royal Horse Artillery, who was supposedly teaching her to drive on extended excursions out to the Surrey countryside.

Feeling the need to tie up loose ends, Grace returned to Cloak Lane police station to see Constable Alston. He was someone whom she instinctively trusted. She learned that the missed telephone call had been to warn her about Sir Ernest Whitehouse. There had been whispers from the criminal fraternity that he was having her followed. They were hardened men who knew the violent truth beneath the peer's veneer of respectability. In turn, she told the constable everything that she had discovered about the murder and what happened subsequently. Alston could only nod in astonishment, before confiding that his request to move to Cambridge Constabulary had been accepted. Both he and his wife were delighted to be moving back to Huntingdon. Their first child was due in May and would be born in the fresh air of the countryside. As she left the station, she saw Sergeant Williams coming out of his office. She returned his cold, hard stare.

CHAPTER FORTY-FOUR

After a week's convalescence, Grace returned to *Nursing World* to find Vera Boddy jubilant. Roger Dale had left, and she had achieved her long-term aim. Unable to bear a return to writing about bedpans and hospital committees, he had absconded to France. Rumour had it that he had met a wealthy widow at the Paris Peace Conference and was moving into her chateau in Brittany. His position on the periodical was offered to Fergus, but he was poached by *Matron Today*, much to the horror of Miss Boddy, who described him as a traitor. Almost by default, the role of chief reporter had fallen to Grace, and she relished the thought of seeing her name printed next to the articles she had written. Finally, she could call herself a real reporter.

Christmas was fast approaching, and Grace threw herself into the bustle and excitement of festive preparations. At Sian's insistence, there were several visits to Rector's, Christmas shopping in Oxford Street and also a candle-lit carol concert at St Martin-in-the Fields. The Christmas goose had been ordered from Michael O'Shea & Sons, the butcher's in Kentish Town, where Bridget now held sway as the fiancée of the proprietor. In the midst of her frantic activity, there were things she was trying to avoid thinking about. She hadn't seen or heard from Arthur since the end of their engagement. In time, she hoped they might be friends again, but knew the intimacy that had once existed between them could never be restored.

There had been no contact from Tom.

It would only be herself and her father in Ryedale Villa on Christmas Day. The intention was that she would travel up to Whitby and see in the New Year with her mother. She couldn't quite rid herself of the aching void created by her mother's absence and the thought of another quiet Christmas. Just her and Father. Still, there was a new closeness between them. They had begun to talk more and enjoy each other's company.

On the Saturday before Christmas they had agreed to decorate the Christmas tree together. Grace and her father worked hard all day, fetching the boxes of decorations from the attic and transforming the sitting room. The finished tree now stood at the heart of their home, glittering with ornaments that had been in the family since she was a child. She remembered how she and Edward would fight over who should be the one to place the angel on top of the tree, until their mother was forced to intervene. As she positioned this final decoration, it was done on behalf of her lost brother too.

Her father was suddenly quiet, and she looked across at him and wondered what he was thinking. It was difficult not to reminisce about Christmases past and wonder whether it would ever be possible to be as happy again. For so many families that year, there would be absences at the festive table which were still raw. Long-held traditions and family rituals that could not be observed because those who should have been there were not. Perhaps it was better not to reflect on it too deeply.

Exhausted, they both sat down and celebrated their exertions with a pot of tea.

'I think we've done rather well with the tree, don't you, Grace?' her father declared. 'Not quite as spectacular as when your mother does it but . . .'

'I think we've made a good job of it,' she replied.

It was just then that they heard the front door open and the sound of someone in the hallway. Grace and James looked at each other in astonishment, before hurrying out to see what was happening. Her mother stood in front of them both, looking very pale.

'Isobel, you're not in Whitby.' In his astonishment, her father stated the obvious.

'I decided to return to Tufnell Park for Christmas.' She smiled.

After the initial surprise, Grace gladly threw herself into her mother's arms. Her parents shyly acknowledged each other.

Bunty came bustling into the hallway, carrying a small suitcase. 'Merry Christmas, James and Grace,' she declared. 'Let me just fetch your presents from the motor car.'

'Bunty drove me here. It's been quite an experience,' her mother confided. 'I don't know what she was doing during her driving lessons, but it doesn't seem to have included steering.'

Bunty was horrified that they had been drinking tea on a Saturday evening and immediately disappeared to the kitchen to establish whether there were any spirits to be had in the Armstrong household. She returned triumphantly clutching bottles of gin and champagne, and produced a lemon and packet of sugar from her pockets. 'Success! We'll be able to make French 75s. It really is quite a marvellous cocktail and comes highly recommended by dear Hamish, my driving instructor.'

As they all sipped hastily made cocktails, her father said, 'Grace and I made an attempt at the decorations.'

'It looks splendid, James,' her mother replied. She glanced around the room. 'It is nice to be home. I've missed it more than I realized.'

Grace didn't dare to ask whether her mother had returned permanently. The last few years had taught her to enjoy happiness where she could and worry about the future later. Isobel now had her wedding ring on her finger and Grace hoped that meant there might be the chance of a reconciliation.

Later that night, as the four of them sat around the crackling fire, James Armstrong said, 'I'd like to propose a toast to future happiness. We've already lost dear Edward and Robert and then Elizabeth also. Too much heartbreak, too many deaths.' He glanced at his wife. 'It's good to celebrate Christmas together. Might this mean . . . ?' It was unlike him to be so open.

Isobel half smiled as she replied, 'Perhaps. We've mourned our loss in different ways. I found Edward's death almost impossible to live with for a time and I still think the war was a dreadful waste—'

James went to speak again, and she raised her hand. 'James, you believe that Edward made a noble sacrifice and we must accept that we have a different view but we—'

'But we all have wonderful memories of Edward,' Bunty finished. 'Now Grace, this is an appropriate time for a cup of tea. As Mrs Watson has retired for the night, perhaps you'd come to the kitchen to help me make it.'

As she lay in bed that night, Grace mused that the Christmas of 1919 was a time to mark a change. Perhaps it was because there was a new decade ahead. Or maybe it was just impossible to live unhappily forever.

But first, Grace had to face her past. On Sunday morning, she decided to walk up to Parliament Hill Fields on Hampstead Heath. She hadn't been there since the warm night in June 1916 when she, Robert, Edward and Arthur had all made their toasts in warm red wine to the engagement. She wanted to pay her respects to the dead. To say a silent prayer for them, and for Elizabeth too. They were part of the fabric of who she was. There were still times when she thought she caught a glimpse of Robert, walking swiftly ahead of her. But she knew it wasn't him and that she must begin to embrace a new life that she would carve for herself. It was frightening to let go of the past and its certainties but the future, no matter how intimidating, was what beckoned her on. Her parents offered to come with her, but it was a pilgrimage she needed to make alone.

It was a beautiful winter's day. The skies were bright blue and the whole landscape was covered with fresh snow. During the war, trenches had been dug along the Heath so that battalions of soldiers could play-act trench warfare, as if this practice would ever prepare them for the horrors that lay ahead in France. It was this broken landscape that had haunted her dreams. A thick covering of white now hid the scarred earth and it was possible to remember again nature's enduring beauty. Grace thought it pointed to a time when she too might heal. Walking briskly, and breathing in the clear, sharp air, she felt invigorated and alive. Twenty-three. She was still young. She had a lifetime ahead of her. Perhaps she would find love, but if she didn't, there were other things too. Her career as a writer for one. She could make her own living. She had friends and family who loved her. Finally, she reached the top of Parliament Hill and there was London, spread out before her.

She heard a familiar voice behind and turned.

Tom was standing there. He had that half-smile, but his green eyes were anxious and fixed upon her. 'Grace, your parents said you'd be here.'

'You've been to Ryedale Villa?' She was amazed.

He nodded. 'I've met your mother. I like her a lot. She's very forthright, just as I imagined her to be, and even your father seems to have softened a bit.'

'Why are you looking for me? You haven't been in touch since . . .' She had tried to pretend to herself that it didn't matter that Tom hadn't contacted her, but it did. It mattered very much. 'You were never going to see me again.'

'It was the right thing to do.' He moved towards her. 'You were engaged to Arthur.'

'I broke off the engagement,' she said simply.

'I know. I saw Arthur. There was a reunion of our regiment. He told me and I thought that perhaps—'

'What did you think?' she asked, looking at him intently. 'I dared to hope.'

When he said this, she too dared to hope. He continued, 'If we are to be together, and I want us to be together,' he said with certainty, 'It has to be as equals.'

He pulled a sheet of paper from his coat pocket.

'I went back to the Royal College of Music and asked if they would take me onto the composers' course. They were reluctant at first, because I had turned it down before. They wanted proof that I was serious. They wanted to see a piece of music I had written.'

'You said that after the horror of the trenches, this wasn't a world where music, or love, or anything good belonged.'

'I was wrong,' he said simply. 'When I met you, I realized it was possible to love and to find happiness again. I wanted to write music. This is for you, Grace.'

She looked at the notes on the page and was surprised to find that they were blurred by her tears. 'I can't read music . . .' she started to say.

And then he took her in his arms and kissed her. This time neither of them pulled away or worried whether it was right. They knew it was.

ACKNOWLEDGEMENTS

I would like to thank all the team at Quercus for their support with *The Lodger*, including Katya Ellis, Ellie Nightingale and, most particularly, Jane Wood and Florence Hare, who have been the perfect editors – wise, kind, and generous with their advice and encouragement. Thank you also to everyone at the Madeleine Milburn Literary Agency, most especially Giles Milburn and Valentina Paulmichl – everything you do is appreciated.

I am hugely grateful to Sue Gardner, Catrin Huws, Tamara Evans, Althea Draper, Tony Widdrington, and Kathryn Donnelly for all their help, guidance, and friendship. Thank you as well to the booksellers, who have been really supportive of me as a new writer. I am full of gratitude to everyone at Waterstones in Yarm, Durham, and Darlington, Paul Jones-King at Chapter One and Fiona Sharp and Dan Bassett. You are all the heroes of the book world! Thank you so very much for your kindness.

Finally, my love as always to Izzy, Maddie, Mark, and Mary.